PALM BEACH

PALM BEACH

a Novel by

PAT BOOTH

Crown Publishers, Inc.
New York

Published by Crown Publishers, Inc., One Park Avenue, New York, New York 10016 and simultaneously in Canada by General Publishing Company Limited

CROWN is a trademark of Crown Publishers, Inc.

Manufactured in the United States of America

Library of Congress Cataloging in Publication Data

Booth, Pat.
  Palm Beach.

  I. Title.
PS3552.0646P3 1985   813'.54   85-10957
ISBN 0-517-55844-0

10 9 8 7 6 5 4 3 2
First Edition

To my friend Roxanne Pulitzer, with love

PALM
BEACH

Prologue

Everyone agreed it was the grandest and most beautiful wedding in Palm Beach history, but nearly everybody also felt that something was terribly, dreadfully wrong. Whatever that was, it was nowhere near the surface. Rather, it bubbled around in the collective unconscious, mysterious and threatening, shadowy but undeniable. The alien feeling seemed to lurk in the cool, formidably air-conditioned atmosphere of the old Mizner mansion, scurrying about in the dark corners of the carved wood ceilings, insinuating its presence along the somber Spanish-tiled corridors and the bougainvillaea-bedecked cloisters. Nobody who felt it could ignore it, and yet it was too intangible to describe—an uninvited guest at the wedding feast.

Lisa Blass and Bobby Stansfield were unaware of the disturbing undercurrents. It was their wedding day. They were two people who in short minutes would become one, and the aura of their mutual happiness insulated them effortlessly from the mists of dread that swirled round about. They stood close together, like the intertwined figures on the top of a child's music box, preparing cheerfully to dance their way through an eternity of togetherness. Occasionally, as if in mutual reassurance that this was not the unreality of a dream, their hands would reach out for the comfort of touch. "To hold is to have," their gestures seemed to say.

Lisa Blass squeezed hard on her fiancé's hand and leaned in toward the strong shoulders.

"Not long now," she whispered.

But it had been so very, very long. Almost as long as memory itself. All her life it seemed she had been traveling toward this point, and it had been the hardest and most dangerous road imaginable. Only Maggie could begin to understand the sorrow and the tragedy, the despair and the hurt, the struggle and the strife she

1

had suffered on the journey. Everyone else saw only the beautiful Lisa Blass, the girl of uncertain origins who had carved an empire and was now about to merge it with a dynasty. That was the *People* magazine version, and it would be the *Social Register*'s verdict, too. But Lisa alone knew that in the emotional roller-coaster ride that had been her life the dominant motive had been . . . not love, as this ceremony seemed to suggest . . . but another one altogether. Only Lisa could know that the years of her meteoric rise to fame and fortune had been clouded all the while by the mind-numbing fog of revenge.

Now, however, the metamorphosis was complete, and from the chrysalis of hate the butterfly of love had flown free. Love for the man she had wanted so much to destroy.

Bobby turned to look at her, straightening himself up and flexing his shoulders beneath the immaculately cut Anderson and Sheppard Savile Row-tailored morning coat. He took a deep breath. "It can't be soon enough," he whispered back.

He had never spoken a truer word. There had been so much wasted time. So many regrets since the decision he had made with such difficulty all those years ago. His prayers had been answered and he had been given a second chance, and now he wanted the deed done before once again capricious Fate could snatch it from him. It was not only a second chance to have the Lisa he had always loved, but a second chance for everything. Bobby's heart filled with happiness as he contemplated his future. With Lisa Blass at his side, her vast fortune allied to his political wealth, her calming, steadying influence available night and day, the shining vision was possible again. The presidency would still be his. The excited murmur of the crowd was the backdrop to Bobby's re-awakened dream, and he turned to look at his wedding guests.

The town of Palm Beach itself seemed to be present in the mighty room. It stood there in all its awesome self-satisfied glory —proud and defiant, parading its ancient wealth and social power. They were all there—the Old Guard—Phippses, Munns, Wideners, Pulitzers, Kimberlys, and those who would one day become Old Guard—Loy Andersons, Leidys, Cushings, Hanleys. The Polo crowd had made it over from Wellington: meaty Argentinians with hungry eyes and bulging quadriceps; smooth-tongued silver-haired socialites with beautiful wives and speedy daughters; and dispossessed Englishmen with high handicaps and low morals. There were political allies, the occasional political enemy, a liberal sprinkling of Euro-trash. Descendants of German armaments tycoons, a smattering of pseudoroyalty from the Balkans, the inevitable gaggle of suave White Russians.

Yes, they were all there to see the marriage of the town's two most influential fortunes. To them it was not so much a wedding—it was a coronation. Palm Beach was about to have a new king and a new queen, and the courtiers had come to pay homage.

Scott Blass, however, was existing on his own private cloud of horror. Slumped in a tall-backed chair, his eyes darted nervously, away from the soon-to-be-married couple who stood together by the side of the orchid-covered rostrum, toward the white telephone inches below his hand. Despite the electric field of anxiety that hovered around him, he found time to think that he had never seen his mother look more beautiful. The pale ivory of the seventeenth-century Milanese lace Pat Kerr dress, its almost virginal halter neck studded with pearls, gave to her a spiritual grace that he had never seen before. The exquisite features had not changed, but the tension had gone from her face and had been replaced by a quiet peace. His mother, cleansed by the fire, had been reborn, and the light of love that shone from her eyes—the light that Scott had prayed in vain would one day shine on him—was focused adoringly on her husband-to-be. The wheel had turned its circle. Wrong was about to be made right, cold to be made warm. From the fields in which evil had been sown the harvest of happiness was about to be reaped. Or was it? Again Scott stared at the telephone. Daring it to ring. Defying it to do so. He pulled unhappily at his stiff collar to let the air at the damp sweat that discomforted him, knowing as he did so that it would bring no relief from the torment.

From either side of the room two women watched him suffer. Caroline Stansfield had never met Lisa Blass's son before, but he had been pointed out to her, and she liked what she saw. As the matriarch of the Stansfield political dynasty, and abiding pillar of Palm Beach high society, she knew a thing or two when it came to sizing up voter appeal. Really he was a remarkably fine specimen. Tall, clean-limbed, and with the vote-catching deep blue eyes of her own son, Bobby. Obviously the boy would have inherited intelligence from the mother. The son of a woman like Lisa who had come from nowhere to rule the only world that mattered would have the right political instincts. He could be trained. Maybe she would take him under her wing and teach him the art of winning, as she had taught her own children. But what on earth was he doing fidgeting around like that? A man should learn how to sit still and exude dignity. As it was, he looked as if he were about to appear before a firing squad rather than witness his mother's marriage to possibly the most eligible man in the world. With the ease born of eighty-five years of practice, Caroline Stansfield banished the jarring thought from her mind and smiled regally around the room.

Everything was really quite perfect. How very clever of Lisa to have learned the rules. Bobby would have helped of course, but his heart wasn't really in things like the organization of weddings. In her mind's eye she made a checklist of the details that top-notch Palm Beachers like herself loved to contemplate: morning clothes for the groom, a single white carnation worn in the English style—plain and unadorned with greenery or fussy sprigs of this and that—the reassuring Andover tie, pinstriped trousers beautifully pressed, the highly polished shoes that had seen at least thirty years of comfortable service. And Lisa? Really a superb compromise between virginal white and hypocrisy. The lace was more ivory than white, and yet it was a hymn to purity. Very well chosen. No color in the bouquet. That was a nice touch. Just plain white daisies hinting at the simplicity and the hatred of affectation that the very best people affected. Caroline's knowing, snobbish old eyes continued their appreciative tour of the arrangements. More than enough ushers, each in identical charcoal-gray cutaways, striped pants, stiff collars, ascots and pearl-gray gloves. Not a single dinner jacket in the room. She checked her watch. Nearly time. High noon, the only time to wed, in her opinion.

A few latecomers were still taking their seats, spirited smoothly from their Rolls-Royces by the well-drilled boys from John Kavekos's Palm Beach Valet Parking, ushered down the long, petal-strewn corridors of the fabulous old house to the body of the room where their fellow guests were already craning their necks like ostriches on amphetamine to check out who else was there, and, more important, who wasn't. Caroline could have put them at rest.

4

All the "somebodies" were there. There were no "nobodies" in sight. Fords, du Ponts, Meeks, Dudleys. And what looked like a whole cabbage patch of Kennedys. The entire membership of the Coconuts, the elite club that met but once a year on New Year's Eve, and whose invitations were more treasured than telephone calls from the president; the complete board of Poinciana Club Governors, the ever vigilant watchdogs of the Palm Beach social scene; most of the Everglades Club, a judicious selection from the Bath and Tennis Club. A handful from the Beach Club, and none at all, thank the Lord, from the Palm Beach Country Club. Then there was the Hobe Sound contingent, with Permelia Pryor Reed, the autocratic ruler of the Jupiter Island Club, shepherding a small flock of Doubledays, Dillons, and Auchinclosses.

The Stansfield roving eye returned to Scott, and once again the harmony was replaced by discord. What on *earth* was he up to? He looked so incredibly—what was the silly word they used nowadays?—"uptight." And it was round about that time that Caroline Stansfield's finely tuned antennae, legacy of nearly a century of political and social intrigue, began to sense that there was something horribly wrong with her world.

Fifty feet away her granddaughter Christie stood, surrounded by flowers in what should have been paradise, but what felt like hell. On either side great banks of white orchids framed her delicate beauty, mocking the agony of her suspense with their majestic tranquillity. Her eyes, too, were on Scott Blass. But unlike her grandmother, she knew exactly what he was thinking. How much more time was there? What would they do when time ran out? In the absence of God's guidance there would be nothing for it but to steal His role. She tore her eyes away from the tormented figure by the telephone and glanced at the ignorantly blissful couple. Could she do it to her father at this late hour? Could Scott do it to his mother? She just didn't know, and she knew that he didn't know either. Across the sea of expectant faces she managed to catch his darting eyes. Perhaps telepathy would strengthen him. Christie concentrated hard and tried to send out the message of reassurance she wanted so desperately to receive herself. The blue eyes thanked her, and she managed a half smile. Scott. Poor Scott. He had been taken away from her only to be given back by Fate in the wild paradox that went by the name of Life. Scott who had abused her so dreadfully. Scott, who was now her partner, who had been her lover, who was now so much more than that.

Father Bradley, rector of Bethesda-by-the-Sea, that colonnaded sanctuary where Episcopalian Palm Beach was born and died, where it merged and worshiped, was gearing himself up for the time-honored ritual. He looked relaxed, suntanned, and at ease as he moved intimately among his phenomenally plutocratic congregation. He couldn't remember a wedding as important as this one, and everything seemed to be under control; but even as he stood there, making polite small talk with the more influential wedding guests, he could not suppress the frisson of anxiety that kept coursing through him. He could do this thing in his sleep. Why should he be worried? Of course it was easier in church, but home was quite the right place for a second wedding, and especially the Stansfield home. Father Bradley looked at his watch. Two minutes to twelve and all was well. But why in God's *heaven* did he want to add the words "so far"?

Maggie had escaped briefly to a private world of memory. She was Lisa's oldest friend, but nowadays their worlds were far apart. This house, the grandeur of this wedding, symbolized the gap that had opened between them. In the old days it had been the sweat and the tears of the West Palm gym, the hurried hamburgers in the downtown delis, the joy and heartache of building a business that they had both loved so much, that she still loved. But now the delis had given way to catering by John Sunkel, the sumptuous food laid out lovingly on the white organdy and moiré-taffeta-covered buffet tables that lined the wall of the huge dining room next door. Years ago, in Lisa's apartment, long since transformed into the underground parking lot of a South Flagler skyscraper, there had been potted areca palms and the occasional impatiens for color. Here there were deep purple and white orchids, and garlands of green vines snaking in breathtaking profusion over the buffet tables, running free over the spotless tablecloths, intertwining with the bowls of lush tropical fruits, kiwi, papaya, and muscat grapes. She had seen the small army of white-jacketed waiters as they prepared to receive the wedding throng; she had heard the ever green Peter Duchin, aristocratic spirit of Palm Beach parties, loosening his fingers on the Steinway piano; she had avoided the ubiquitous lens of Bob Davidoff, who had seen more society weddings than any other man alive, and she had noted the understated flowers on the four-tiered wedding cake, which replaced the tiny figures of bride and groom, which she, and the rest of America, would have unthinkingly preferred. They were perhaps little things in themselves, but they spoke volumes. They were all part of the silent language by which these people recognized each other. It was a secret society, full of signs and signals, of gestures and unspoken intimations. Things were "done." Things were "not done." Nobody taught you. Nobody could. You learned by osmosis. By being it. By living it. By the time you were a teenager you could pick an impostor from forty feet. It was as simple and as impossible as that. What rule dictated *eight* bridesmaids, all in identical pastel dresses? Who decided that the wedding presents should be laid out for all to see on white damask-covered tables in the library? Why Taittinger champagne? It was all a mystery, and Maggie couldn't help feeling totally shut out.

She turned to look at Lisa, and at once the familiar affection flooded back into her heart. Lisa, who had suffered so much and was, at last, poised on the brink of happiness. But why was Christie so white and Scott so deathly pale? And why was Caroline Stansfield watching them, her wise old face all wrinkled up with worry and alarm? And, as these unsettling thoughts came winging into her suddenly active mind, Maggie picked up on the subterranean vibrations. Dear God, something awful was about to happen. She felt her hand fly involuntarily to her mouth, the saliva dry on her tongue. No. Surely not. Not at this late stage. Could the sins of the fathers be the last of the wedding guests?

1

Bobby Stansfield caught the wave and for a brief moment it was his world. Beneath his feet the surfboard leaped and reared, and inside his chest his heart went with it. It was getting late, and the sun was weary behind the palm trees, the dancing shadows of gold rushing across the surface of the sea. This would be the last breaker of the afternoon, and it looked like it was the day's best.

Like an avenging bird of prey he swooped down on the waiting beach, his body crouched in the classic surfer's pose, and as he sailed toward the sand his soul flew too—thankful for the day and for its beauty. In this life there were few moments like this, and although he was only thirteen he knew how to recognize them.

The wave was nearly spent now. Bobby would see it out in style. He arched his back and tensed his legs as he felt the board's energy running out, and then, with a shout of what might have been farewell he lunged up toward the pale blue of the Florida sky. His eyes followed the mad kaleidoscope of textured colors as his body embraced the chaos. Sky, scudding clouds, the pink beach cabana, the champagne bubbles of the surf before the warm darkness beneath the North End rollers. For a few seconds he allowed the current to take him, safe in the confidence of his strong arms and legs, buffeted by the undertow of the waves. He felt the rough sand against his chest, the popping in his ears as the pressure built, and then he was going upward to reclaim the world he had so recently departed. Bobby broke the surface. He was cleansed of the fantasy.

He had made the journey a thousand times. A hundred yards across the still-warm sand, a hundred more along the bleached-out boardwalk to the bubbling tarmac of the road. Sometimes it was a laughing, joking journey as the other surfers, their boards dangling from wiry, sun-bronzed arms, their salt-stained hair pulled and plucked by the late summer Palm Beach breeze, traveled homeward with him. Today, however, Bobby was alone and grateful for it. Soon he would be back in the great big throbbing house, the engines of its constant activity roaring and grinding, impossible to ignore or to escape. He climbed onto his bicycle, slung his board casually beneath one arm, and set off down North Ocean Boulevard.

At the imposing gates of the big house, he decided on a whim to change the pattern of his journey. He'd take just one more look at the waves. Sometimes you could predict the next day's surf, from the sky, from the breeze, from the activity of the dive-bombing pelicans. So, leaving his board and his bike in their usual corner of the cavernous garage, he slipped along the side of the mighty house toward the breakwater that protected it from the unpredictable sea.

His father's den, a circular room, attached as a post-Mizner addition, was a feature on the journey. It was Bobby's habit to take a quick look through the window. The whole family was in awe of the imposing senator. Everyone, with the notable exception of his mother. Sometimes he would be dictating a speech at the big kneehole desk, his rich sonorous voice wrapping itself indulgently around the high-sounding platitudes, a smile of the purest pleasure on his face as he contemplated the reactions of some future audience. Or he might be catching a ball game, a thick cut-glass goblet in his right hand, sipping appreciatively at the dark amber bourbon he liked to drink in the evenings. Rarely, with his feet resting regally on a tapestry footstool, a crumpled copy of the *Wall Street Journal* across his still tight stomach, he would be snoring contentedly in the worn, chintz armchair. Today, however, he was doing none of those things. He was making love to someone on the sofa.

Bobby Stansfield froze, and his baby-blue eyes almost popped right out of his teenage head. The question of what to do did not for one moment arise. It wasn't every day that a son got to see his father on the job, and he wasn't going to miss a millisecond of it. Conflicting emotions coursed through him—fear, excitement, fascination, disgust—as intertwined as the unlikely lovers on the sofa of the den. Bobby was appalled, but the curiosity of youth held him rigidly in place.

10

Senator Stansfield was clearly no Rudolph Valentino. He was going at lovemaking with the same caution, sensitivity, and sophistication that had always characterized his immensely successful political career. It was a frontal assault, the position uncompromisingly missionary, the finer nuances of sensuality abandoned. The disturbing sounds of sexual activity drifted through the open window on the hot, liquid air to merge uneasily with the other sounds of the late Florida afternoon—the gentle hiss of the lawn sprinklers, the muted roar of the surf—and were to Bobby perhaps the most unsettling aspect of the whole remarkable business. Nobody had prepared him for this in the yard at school where "the facts of life" had been as available as booze and cigarettes.

Who on earth was the girl? The long suntanned legs provided a clue. The white shoes, still precariously in place, clinched it. It was Mary-Ellen. No question. His mother's maid. Christ! Bobby went hot and cold as his fevered mind considered the implications. First there was the matter of screwing the hired help. Second, and rather more pressing, was the question of jealousy. As far as he was concerned Mary-Ellen had all the qualities of a beautiful angel, and Bobby was not a little in love with her. She was funny, bright, and vivacious—all the attributes that his three bun-faced sisters so conspicuously lacked—and the very last place in the world that Bobby had ever expected to see her was beneath his father on the sofa.

Bobby watched transfixed. Both lovers were still fully clothed. His father's bright green poplin trousers hung loosely around his knees, and the navy-blue Brooks Brothers shirt still hid the powerful frame of his upper body. Mary-Ellen, too, had not taken time out to undress—and through the wide-open window Bobby could see the white cotton uniform rucked up to the waist, caught a glimpse of candy-pink-striped cotton briefs. Again the disgust rushed through him, but the Stansfield blood told him there were all sorts of points to be picked up from a close observation of this scene. The emotions could be sorted out later. For now, the trick was to catch the action.

And then, quite suddenly, the thought crashed into his mind like a breaking tidal wave. Mother! Did mother know? Would mother know? What on God's earth would she do if and when she knew?

But while Bobby struggled to deal with the thought of his

mother, the sofa's cargo was about to conclude its business. There was a frantic intensification of movement as the lovers danced in a maelstrom of flailing limbs. Suddenly Mary-Ellen's legs seemed to lose their coordination as they set off in a wild rhythm, thrashing the air, shaking, twitching, and vibrating as the shuddering feeling took her. For his father, too, the music had apparently stopped and he collapsed, exhausted, like a puppet on a suddenly severed string.

To Bobby—unwilling voyeur, witness to his father's infidelity, jilted by the Mary-Ellen of his fantasy—it seemed that in that brief moment his childhood had disappeared forever.

Bobby stared out moodily across the steam-ironed lawns to the glass-topped sea. It was only eleven o'clock but the sun was already imposing its will on Palm Beach, the beautiful town its slave and mistress. The early morning breeze had gone, and the lazy pelicans, content before to be passengers on the wind, now had to work for their prey. Theirs was the only sign of industry in the damp heat. Bobby himself lay propped up on the white-toweled sun bed, his thin, adolescent body baked honey brown by the southern sun. By his side the transistor radio played Connie Francis.

Caroline Stansfield's attitude toward direct sunlight was in contrast to her son's. Her skin a delicate, lily white, she sat shielded from the wrinkle-dispensing rays under a vast cream canvas umbrella. Her distaste for the sun was considered something of an eccentricity by the family and it was quite acceptable to make fun of it. Caroline would join in the somewhat stylized jokes at her expense and her small and precise features would light up with one of her rare, gracious smiles when the family made cautious fun of her. In many ways her preference for the shade was symbolic of her role within the Stansfield family. It was generally agreed that the limelight was the province of the gregarious, extrovert senator and, to a lesser extent, of the noisy children. But that did not diminish her undoubted authority. When Caroline Stansfield spoke, which was not often, everybody listened and nobody was quite sure why. Was it the pedigree stretching back to the eighteenth century? The extraordinarily substantial block holding in IBM? The quiet, unmistakable authority of her patrician voice? Nobody knew. One thing was certain; it was no longer her physical attraction. Perhaps she had once possessed a "fine" appearance—that euphemism among the rich and well-born for what the less fortunate might have described as "plain"—but the years had taken their toll. The generous childbearing hips had functioned well, but six children—two, like Macbeth, "untimely ripped" from her by Caesarean section—had not helped. Her bust, too, was large and formless, legacy of the religious breastfeeding her role of earth mother had demanded. In short, as a sexual object Caroline Stansfield left much to be desired, and, as a result, Senator Stansfield—who had always required a skinful of vodka before each dutiful procreative dance with his unalluring but phenomenally well connected wife—now avoided her bed completely. Most people didn't realize that Caroline herself preferred it that way.

Through the sultry night Bobby had been in an agony of indecision about what he should do, and the various elements of his personality were at war one with another. Part of him was sure that the thing to do was nothing. Hearts grieved only over what eyes saw and tongues repeated. Everyone knew that. By saying nothing he would save his mother pain and keep the faith with his adulterous father. On the other hand it could be argued that his duty was to tell his mother. Perhaps if she knew of her husband's extracurricular activities she would be able to nip them in the bud before unspeakable things like divorce or separation reared their ugly heads. But there was another element in the emotional equation, one that had been passed on in the blood, one that only a Stansfield could experience. For the very first time in his life Bobby found himself exposed to a commodity for which he had a genetically determined liking. Power. For a century the Stansfields had been addicted to it. They had fought for it, prayed for it, risked all for it, and they had never been able to get enough. The Senate, the Supreme Court, the great departments of government had all yielded up their fruits of office to generations of ambitious, cunning Stansfields. The presidency alone had escaped them, and, in their beds at night, all the family members worth their salt dreamed endlessly of this, the ultimate "fix" of power.

13

There was no escaping the fact that Bobby now possessed power. He had the drop on his mighty father at last. But here again there was a dilemma. On the one hand it was true that for thirteen years he had put up with the boisterous tyranny, the ceaseless exhortations to excel, the unthinking, almost casual cruelty, the scorn and humiliation when he, the eldest son, had failed to live up to the vaulting ambition of the Machiavellian senator. To that extent revenge would be welcome, and even intensely pleasurable. But at the same time, and despite the undeniable beauty of his predicament in that respect, Bobby didn't feel at all good about it. Okay, so his father had been an insensitive and demanding task-master, but he was a pretty impressive figure nonetheless and Bobby was enormously proud of him. Funnily enough this whole business hadn't really diminished his respect one iota. Quite the opposite. After all, making it with a gorgeous twenty-year-old two short weeks after one's sixtieth birthday just had to be pretty hot shit.

Then there was Mary-Ellen. Mary-Ellen, who'd been able to turn him on like an electric light when she sashayed across the room. Funny, kind Mary-Ellen who made him laugh, and who laughed at life. Suddenly her job security didn't look so good any-more. Part of him cared about that. With an effort he forced the thought from his mind. Stansfields had been programmed to con-trol their emotions. Toughness was the quality they were supposed to value. Their hearts were allowed to bleed for America, for the poor, for the weak, for the hungry, but the needing friend came way down on the list of priorities. Too bad people would get hurt. People always got hurt. *He* had been hurt. What mattered was that he possessed power, and he had been taught that the thing you did with power was to *use* it. The only real question was how.

And so as the tough side of Bobby Stansfield warred with the tender he shifted uncomfortably on the formidably comfortable sun bed as the horns of his dilemma dug into him. Then, quite suddenly, the decision was made. It made itself. Life was like that. Half an hour deciding when one would get out of bed, and then the surprised realization that you have thrown back the blankets. Con-nie Francis's insistent plea for greater consideration from her lover died in midphrase as Bobby flicked the transistor's switch.

"Mother, there's something I've been wanting to say to you."

Caroline Stansfield looked up, a resigned, unflappable expression on her face. Speeches that started out like this often contained discouraging news. A dent in the car, in the boat, in the pride? There wasn't a lot that could faze her, few things that couldn't be straightened out one way or another. That was one of the advantages of being a Stansfield. Perhaps the most important advantage.

"What is it, dear?"

Bobby made his voice as serious as he could, the sort of voice you used when the early voting returns were unfavorable.

"Mother. I've thought a lot about whether I should tell you this. I'm in a pretty terrible position, and I don't want to be disloyal to dad . . ." His voice trailed off uncertainly.

Caroline Stansfield winced inwardly. The field of possible disasters had been narrowed down drastically. It began to look as if she were going to be embarrassed, and of all the feelings in the world that was the one she experienced least and disliked most.

"You know there are some things that are often best left unsaid, Bobby."

Bobby had reached the point of no return. "I think you have the right to know that father and Mary-Ellen are having an affair."

Pain and distaste fought for control of Caroline Stansfield's facial expression. It was not, however, the content of the news that upset her. That was about as interesting as yesterday's cold potatoes. Her husband had been chasing the prettier female staff for years now. Some of them had even found it necessary to leave, without of course mentioning the reason for their departure to Caroline. By her silence on the subject she had in effect condoned it. Really, it suited her quite well. Emotionally, Fred Stansfield was still a child. His sexual adventures were the adult equivalent of childhood candy, the pat on the head, mommy's good-night kiss. Sex and votes were his method of keeping the score, his way of knowing that he was still loved—and in both he dealt in quantity rather than quality. Certainly she knew all about Mary-Ellen. She rather liked her. Full of spirit, ambitious for the good things in life. What more natural than that she should let the senator seduce her, the man who was the symbol of all the money and power she coveted but could never hope to have?

15

No, the maddening thing was that now things were out in the open, where they had no right to be; and that meant something would have to be done about them.

Wearily she forced herself to confront the immediate problem. Appearances had to be kept up. She managed a watery laugh, and accompanied it with an amused, patronizing expression.

"Oh, really, Bobby. What can you mean? Where on earth did you get that extraordinary idea?" Had he caught the smoldering glances? Seen Fred goose Mary-Ellen in the corridor?

Bobby took a deep breath as he plowed on. "I saw them screwing on the sofa in his den."

In many ways Caroline Stansfield's whole life had consisted of an endless training program in how best to survive unfortunate situations such as this. At the rarefied heights of the social pyramid on which she existed the emotions had to be mastered, suppressed, controlled. People like her would always keep their cool because they had been so effectively tutored in hiding their feelings.

So, Caroline just said, "Oh, dear."

"The caterpillars have eaten the citrus. Oh, dear."

"The town council has refused the variance on the beach cabana. Oh, dear."

Whatever response Bobby had expected, this had for sure not been it. With the wind metaphorically billowing his sails, he had run slap bang into the doldrums of his mother's magnificent indifference.

There wasn't anything to say.

"I just thought you ought to know," he added lamely, to cover his confusion. It seemed the world was a more complicated place than he had ever imagined.

Mary-Ellen was vaguely aware that trying on one's employer's clothes was a bit of a cliché, but she was enough of a dreamer to ignore that. Anyway, she saw it as one of the perks of the job. To Mary-Ellen, who loved the good things in life—and especially the expensive good things—Caroline Stansfield's closet, scrupulously air-conditioned to protect against the ubiquitous Palm Beach mildew, was indeed a magical place. Swathed from head to toe in a full-length ranch mink, she stood back to admire the effect in the long mirror.

She was not Caroline Stansfield's size, but with mink that didn't seem to matter. Ball gowns were a different story. With them it was vital to get the measurements right, and Mary-Ellen knew that Mrs. Stansfield never had less than three fittings at Martha's, the chic Worth Avenue store where she bought many of her evening clothes. Mink, however, was not so much clothes as a statement, and this mink was a very substantial statement indeed—far more explicit than anything you get from a bank. Mary-Ellen gathered it around herself tightly, hugging the soft, warm fur to her tiny waist as she pirouetted, flicking her long black hair from side to side, experimenting with the effect. Outside the thermometer was way into the middle eighties as the unforgiving sun poured down on the hot sand, but in Mrs. Stansfield's bedroom the temperature was rock solid at seventy degrees, the colder air from the separate closet air-conditioning system wafting past Mary-Ellen as she modeled the fur in front of the mirrored door.

God, she was happy. Everything was happening for her. She loved this job. The vast, rambling old house with its Mizner architecture, the jewels, the servants, the exotic food, constant parties, the cars and the cheerful chauffeurs, famous guests, the shimmering Olympic-size pool, the ogling sons, the gracious mistress, the senator . . . Senator Fred Stansfield. His semen inside her. This all-powerful man, who lunched at the White House, headed the Senate Foreign Relations Committee—whatever that meant—who appeared on the cover of *Time* and *Newsweek*. Who cared that he was three times her age? She'd always been drawn to older men, to their worldly wisdom, their sophistication, to the security they symbolized.

Mary-Ellen's body began to tingle at the delicious thought of her lover, and she wrapped the coat around her more closely. Really she should be naked, the fur caressing her warm skin. That would be nice. The senator making love to her while she wore his wife's mink coat. For a split second she paused. Had Fred Stansfield been telling the truth when he had said that his wife and he had an "understanding," that actually she didn't mind him making love to her maid? It seemed pretty odd, but then these people were different. Wonderfully, gorgeously different. They were so much richer than anyone else. With an effort Mary-Ellen banished her doubt. She didn't like to hurt people, and she believed the senator when he told her that it was all right. That made it so much better. She was safe. Safe in her beautiful job—able to stand in the middle of a life she had always dreamed of having, and as a participant not just a spectator. There was a sense in which *she* was the senator's wife, that this was indeed *her* fur coat.

Once again the flame of sensuality flickered. She would allow herself to turn it up . . . just a bit. Still watching herself in the mirror, she let the coat hang open. Her legs were good—very good. Slowly she lifted up the knee-length white skirt of her uniform to show the cotton briefs, a dramatic contrast to the black stockings and brown mink. With her left hand she hitched the skirt up high, and with her right she drew down the panties to midthigh, admiring the visual effect of the collage she had created.

"Do you like that coat, Mary-Ellen?"

The voice was Caroline Stansfield's, and she was standing in the doorway to the bedroom. Her question was simple, direct. There was no edge to it. None at all. It appeared that she really wanted to know whether Mary-Ellen liked her coat.

Mary-Ellen felt the shock wave hit her. The rosy red flush of acute embarrassment invaded her cheeks. "Oh, Mrs. Stansfield, I'm so dreadfully sorry. I really shouldn't have . . . but it was just so beautiful. All your things are so beautiful."

"I'd like you to have it, Mary-Ellen."

"What?"

"It's yours. I'd like you to keep it. As a present."

Mary-Ellen wondered if in some mad way her mind was playing tricks on her. Was Mrs. Stansfield in fact screaming abuse at her, yelling at her to take off the coat, while her fevered brain misinterpreted the words, desire the mother of invention? "You mean it's mine? You want me to have it, to take away with me?"

Caroline Stansfield smiled a kindly smile. Really this was a very nice girl. Quite unspoiled. Fresh, vivacious—and very, very pretty. It was easy to see why her husband found her so irresistible. She had never understood what he had seen in some of the others, but there was no doubt that Mary-Ellen was uniquely desirable. Life was really so cruel. At times, the cruelty was so unnecessary. Why couldn't Fred draw the drapes like any other respectable man cheating on his wife? Really, it was most inconsiderate of him—especially as she was the one who had to clean up the mess, pick up the pieces. Strangely enough, she felt sorry for the lovely little maid. She'd been a real gem. Her clothes beautifully kept, suitcases perfectly packed, everything always in its place. Now of course she'd have to go. It was a question of form.

But it would have to be done carefully. There was only one really important thing on this earth and that was the Stansfield name. It must be safeguarded at all costs. This girl lived in West Palm Beach and West Palm was only a bridge away across the lake. It would not do to have her bad-mouthing the Stansfields. Wouldn't do at all. Not that she thought for one second that Mary-Ellen was that type of person. Far too nice.

A great tear of relief and joy began to form in the corner of Mary-Ellen's eye. Far from being berated she had just been given a present of incomparable beauty, a thing that never in her wildest dreams had she thought of possessing. Great waves of innocent affection shot out from her toward the cause of her happiness. Her mind raced as her lips tried to find the suitable words of thanks.

But Caroline Stansfield's upraised hand halted her fumbling speech before she could begin it. "Now, Mary-Ellen, there was one other thing I wanted to discuss," she said.

"It looks like our fine neighbor is going to run Nixon close. Gallup's got 'em neck and neck." The senator sat at the end of the long, highly polished mahogany dining table, the *Wall Street Journal* propped open in front of him. At the Stansfield family breakfast he was the only one allowed to read the daily newspapers, and this gave him a considerable advantage over everyone else. As usual he was making the most of his privileged position.

The Stansfield children groaned openly.

The Kennedys' Mizner on North Ocean Boulevard had gone up a year or two after the Stansfield home, and from the lawn of their house the ugly bulwarks of the massive Kennedy seawall could be seen pushing out aggressively over the North End beach.

"I think Kennedy can win." Bobby, sitting on his father's right in the traditional position of the eldest son, was playing devil's advocate. On occasions like this, only Senator Stansfield's opinions were "correct."

"Rubbish, Bobby. Shows how little you know. Nixon'll bury him. Kennedy gets Massachusetts, Maine, New York—the eastern liberal states. Nixon sweeps the South, the West, and the Midwest. No contest."

"Well, I certainly hope so," said Caroline Stansfield from the other end of the table. "It would be so inconvenient from the traffic point of view to have a president just up the road. There are quite enough sightseers from the mainland anyway."

Her husband grunted his agreement. "And all those Secret Service people crawling all over the beach and snooping into everything," he added gloomily. For the briefest of moments he allowed himself to dream. Twenty years ago there had been a chance at the presidency for him, but the glittering prize had escaped him. God, how he had wanted it, the power and the glory, and all the trappings of high office that went with it—Secret Servicemen included. He snapped back into optimism.

"It won't happen. Can't happen."

Caroline's quietly determined voice disagreed with him. "I'm not sure you're right, dear. You know, I saw Jack Kennedy and his wife in Green's last Sunday. They go in there after church at St. Edward's. My word, she's pretty, and with lots of style. And he's really very attractive. I'm afraid they make poor Nixon look like he's hustling real estate, or something worse. I think looks are getting so important nowadays. Especially with all that television. You're always saying that, dear."

Fred Stansfield put his cup down on the shimmering table rather harder than was strictly necessary. Both his wife and his son were contending with him openly at the breakfast table in an area in which he was considered the acknowledged expert. Far worse, they were suggesting that a Kennedy was about to make it to the White House.

To an outsider the Stansfields and the Kennedys appeared to have much in common. Both families were rich, had been Palm Beach neighbors for a quarter of a century, and now each had representatives in the most exclusive club in America, the United States Senate.

There, however, the similarities ended. Fred Stansfield was the epitome of the difference. From his silver gray, Brylcreemed patrician hair to his immaculately polished brown slip-on tassel loafers, worn of course with no socks, the senator was pure, old Palm Beach. The tattered, green Everglades club blazer, the deep, rich tan, and the cream linen shirt merely confirmed his aristocratic status.

As far as he was concerned the Kennedys were pushy social climbers—about as grand as Ole Opry. What was worse, they were northern Democrats who dared to live, at least part of the time, in a staunchly southern Republican town. To the Stansfields the Kennedys were class enemies, liberal poseurs who had sold out to the dreaded ethnic minorities, adventurers who had turned their backs on their own kind in order to achieve power. Okay, so he himself had occasionally to woo the Negro and Jewish vote, but he would encourage neither group to enter his front door. Then there was the whole Catholic thing. Bells and smells. Popery. That alone was the kiss of death in real Palm Beach high society. In this town the WASPs had stings and the Kennedys were thoroughly ostracized. The only galling aspect of the whole business was that since old Joe Kennedy had been turned down by the Everglades Club, the Kennedys had withdrawn from the game, refusing to show the slightest inclination to participate in the society that was so eager to exclude them.

The three Stansfield daughters, scenting the beginnings of a promising family argument, sided as always with their charismatic father. That was usually, at least in political matters, the winning team. Bunny Stansfield, nineteen and a prelaw student, chipped in. "They'll never elect a Catholic in preference to Eisenhower's veep. Anyway, we don't think he's so good looking. *We* think he's a creep."

Bunny Stansfield always spoke for the other girls, and the three tended to vote as a bloc.

It was a way to survive in the male-dominated Stansfield environment.

Fred Stansfield beamed his approval on his three unremarkable daughters. The politician in him was trained to accept support from wherever it came.

"Of course you're right, Louise. Obviously they're teaching you something up there in Charlottesville." He refused to call his children by their nicknames.

Caroline Stansfield stared dreamily down the ancient table. In many ways, she thought, the gleaming wood looked more permanent, more substantial than the entire assembled Stansfield clan. So for that matter did Brown, the ancient but distinguished English butler, who hovered ineffectually at the vast sideboard. For some reason, long since forgotten, it was traditional practice for him to pour the hot Kenya coffee. This he did with a shaky, uncertain hand, lending an element of danger to the family breakfast. Otherwise one helped oneself—kedgeree, bacon and eggs in a silver salver, Kellogg's corn flakes. Caroline liked this meal best. It was the one time everyone was guaranteed to be present—a sort of informal meeting at which family business could be discussed.

"I'm sure you're right, dear. You usually are." Caroline conceded defeat; Fred would need that victory to survive the next little missile.

Fred Stansfield beamed down the table at his wife. He stuffed a large piece of toast into his mouth and leaned back in his chair contentedly. It was going to be another good day. Some letters with the secretary. A game of golf at the club, followed by a heavy lunch. And then, in the late afternoon, perhaps a delicious action replay with Mary-Ellen. Lazily he pushed away the Limoges china plate, its contents half eaten. Must look after the waistline. He owed that to the pretty maid.

"I'm afraid I've had to let Mary-Ellen go," said Caroline Stansfield pleasantly to nobody in particular. She glanced around the table for a reaction to her news.

Bobby's head was low, his eyes apparently fascinated by the heavy linen napkin he saw every day of his life. He felt the color begin to rise up his cheeks.

"Ah," said the senator. Words for the first time in many years entirely failed him.

The girls were united in their approval. The sensationally attractive Mary-Ellen had put noses out of joint all over the place.

Joe, the youngest son, was totally unmoved. Nine was a bit too young to see the point of Mary-Ellen. Tom at twelve was the only one who spoke. He was not too young. "Oh, mom, why? I thought she was really neat."

"Well, yes, she was rather 'neat'—I'm sure we all thought that, didn't we, Fred? The fact is that just lately she hasn't been concentrating on her job, so I let her go."

Her tone was conversational, but not one single person at the table, her husband included, dared to question Caroline Stansfield's authority. Mary-Ellen would not reenter their universe.

For Mary-Ellen, the last few days had been hell on earth, but now, as the wet heat of the humid summer gave way to the dry freshness of the Florida winter, there seemed to be new hope. The excitement of the election had helped. They had stayed up all night as the mighty electoral battle had raged. At seven fifteen in the evening with the CBS computer predicting a Nixon landslide, and with Tommy and her dad sunk in the depths of despair, Mary-Ellen had been rooting for a Republican victory, but strangely, when one hour later the forecast was revised to a Kennedy victory by 51 percent of the vote, she found herself joining in the cheers. Kennedy might live there but they had all hated him. The Stansfields in particular would be plunged into gloom at the thought of their neighbor in the White House, and paradoxically Mary-Ellen found herself wanting the thing they feared most. They had stayed up all night demolishing the six-packs, and cheering the Democrat victories until five forty-five in the morning when Michigan had put JFK over the top. It had been the dawn of a new day, and as West Palm had nursed its hangover and the Negroes had gone wild with hope at the promise of the New Frontier, Mary-Ellen's spirits had revived.

On the bottom of the bed, a living representation of Mary-Ellen's changed attitude, lay Caroline Stansfield's fur coat. No longer was it an ankle-length testimony to a bygone era. It had updated itself, and like the brand-new president, it was looking forward and not back. With the effrontery of the natural anarchist, Mary-Ellen had taken the scissors to it, and in a daring morning it had been transformed to the new fashionable length just above the knee. She had used the extra material provided by the radical surgery to make a fur pill box hat just like the one she had seen Jackie Kennedy wear on the news, and now it lay with an identical muff next to the shortened coat on the bed.

Mary-Ellen peered out of the window hopefully. Was the freshness in the air the first of the winter cold spells that could lower the temperature to the forties and below? She prayed that it was. Screw the citrus crop. What she wanted was to wear her coat. There were few enough days in Florida when she could get away with it.

Impatiently she swept it up and put it on over the T-shirt and jeans, fighting back the bittersweet memory of the Stansfield bedroom. It was hers now. A bribe for her silence? An anesthetic for the pain? A hand-me-down cast-off for a defeated rival? Whatever. It didn't matter anymore. There was a life to live. Here. Now. At the beginning of the sixties. And the doctored fur would be her talisman in the years ahead. When the blades of the scissors had cut into it they had severed more than the skins. They had cut the umbilical cord that had bound her to the past. She was free at last. Free to be herself.

Mary-Ellen threw back her head and looked at herself in the mirror. Screw them all. She could laugh at the world. She was young and very beautiful and if Palm Beach was not possible for her then West Palm was.

But even as she challenged fate with her beauty and her vitality she nursed her secret thought. One fine day, if God blessed her with a daughter, her child would be what she could never be. She would send her across the bridge to conquer the promised land that had so cruelly expelled her.

The mind-bending, ear-shattering rock 'n roll blasted all thought from the brain. Like a hurricane surge it blanketed everything around—people, machinery, the shimmering air in which it vibrated. There was no fighting it. You had to give in, to surrender completely.

Like a ballet dancer performing his own intricate pas de deux, Jack Kent weaved his magic on the railway roundabout. It was his best moment, repeated a couple of hundred times a day. The train started slowly on its undulating course, and its human cargo, all souped up and ready to go, were grooving on the excitement building within them. Shouting to friends in the audience on the parched grass, to others in neighboring box cars, they screamed to be heard above the wild, all-enveloping music as the train began to accelerate. Supposedly Jack's job was to collect the tickets and to make sure everyone was safely seated, but here he was the rodeo cowboy, the essence of the fairground, his every movement amplifying the tingling feelings of scarcely suppressed sexuality, of violent danger that were just below the surface in everyone. Holding on, and letting go. That was what it was all about. His ropelike muscles, smooth and shining with a thin film of axle grease, contracted and relaxed as, like Spiderman, he moved effortlessly among the howling passengers, launching himself bodily from the stationary boardwalk onto the speeding cars, only to return a second later, his short, powerful legs whacking solidly into the timbers of the platform. Pain and destruction hovered all around. One missed step, one tiny miscalculation and Jack Kent would have been the baloney he so often talked. To pile on the pressure he would make it more difficult for himself, light a cigarette, drink a can of beer, comb his black oiled hair—flicking it competently into the duck's-ass style as he diced with death.

All the time he kept up the dialogue with the paying customers. "Hey, honey. You's sure a cute little thing. You hang on tight now. Take care." That way they came back for more. Sometimes a great deal more. Jack Kent's darting, practiced eyes told him everything. He could see the love light start in the teeny-bopper eyes, the legs crushed close together, the tautness in the pubescent tits. He's gotten to need the tight little up-turned asses, the slinky soft teenage skin, the doelike eyes of the virgins as they took it from him on the grass or standing up in the generator shed. He'd rip the clinging jeans down like some spoiled child tearing open the last of too many Christmas presents, and sock it to them with no thought of their pleasure or pain. They merged into one. Warm quivering contraptions that existed only to make him feel terrific.

Mary-Ellen had lost count of the times she'd watched her father work, and she never tired of it. Throughout her childhood she had followed the fair. In the early days Jack Kent had done it all. Hustled the darts, flogged the cotton candy, even spieled on the "let me guess your weight" spot. But when he had hit the railway he had come home. He was a natural. In two short years he had tripled the roundabout's income, been taken into partnership, and then bought out his partner. The money wasn't that good, but he'd had the sense to buy the ramshackle old wooden house in West Palm that had always been the family's security. Constantly on the road himself, he had made a home for his wife and for Mary-Ellen. It wasn't much of a place with its faded, peeling paint, broken slats, and warped, uneven timbers, but it was full of love and life. At night when she would return home it would loom up out of the darkness like some tramp steamer out of a pea-soup fog, the kerosene lamp flickering its welcome on the porch. Her father, if he was in town at all, would be drinking at Roxy's bar with Willie Boy Willis and Tommy Starr, but her mother would be home— and there would be the smell of chili on the heavy night air, the soft sounds of the country music that she loved, and the shout of welcome as she trod the creaking floorboards of the veranda.

Breathing in deeply, Mary-Ellen gathered the strength to shout above the music. "Dad's sure in good form today," she yelled.

Tommy Starr smiled and made to reply. Then he gave up, splaying his big hands open in a gesture of defeat. He stuck two huge fingers in his ears to make the point.

He smiled fondly at her, his great big craggy face breaking up in a look of total adoration. He could hardly remember when he hadn't loved her, and every day when he woke and each evening when he fell asleep he had experienced the bitter pangs of her rejection. Now, he had almost come to terms with the reality. She was too good for him, and unfortunately she knew it. It wasn't that she was stuck up or snobbish, just that she had dared to dream the dream. The town across the water had gotten to her, and now Palm Beach and all it stood for pulsed in her blood. It had been like that from the moment the Stansfields had taken her on. She had seen paradise, and West Palm had been forgotten. A little while ago there had been a chance. The rich, pompous assholes had fired her. Why he would never know. Mary-Ellen had been devastated, plunged into the very depths of depression, and it had hurt like hell to see her so upset. He had tried to cheer her up, to take her mind off the rat pack across the bridge, but still she had refused to see herself as the West Palm girl she was.

Once, one drunken evening, he had persuaded her father to take him home after a hard session in Roxy's. As Jack had led the way across the creaking porch with its empty·rocking chair and its unraveling wicker furniture, there had been the sound of crying from the house's interior. They had gone to investigate and there by the light of the soundless, flickering TV Tommy had seen the vision that would remain engraved on his memory forever. Like some discarded, sad rag doll, Mary-Ellen lay across the brass bed, its rumpled, untidy sheets framing her perfect body. Inhabiting that no-man's-land between sleep and wakefulness she lay still, her white dress crumpled and dirty, only partially clothing her. One of the straps had fallen away from the shoulder, and from the upper border of her dress, a pink nipple protruded innocently, the crowning glory to a perfect conical breast.

Across her upper chest and above her lip, a thin film of sweat glistened. Her tousled, untidy hair lay on the pillow, framing the open face whose honest, uncomplicated beauty had so enslaved him. As he had stood there, peering into Mary-Ellen's innermost life, into her torment and her misery, he had experienced the shocking realization that he could never have her. Her anguish and sorrow were too strong for him. He could not compete with whatever had caused this emotion.

Mary-Ellen looked at him quizzically, watching the replacement of the smile with the puzzled expression of contemplation. Dear Tommy. So big, and safe. He was built like a mountain, and he would be as constant. For so many years she had listened to her father sing the praises of the hardworking construction worker he wanted her to marry, but although she had heard she had never believed. Always the siren voices had lured her to the land across the water where the titans lived, men who in their sophistication and worldly wisdom dwarfed Tommy Starr. But that was then, and this was now. She had been thrown out by the world she wanted, and she had gotten over the pain. Only a masochist would wish to prolong it. So at last she slipped her small hand into Tommy's massive one and laughed as she pulled him away to escape from the prison of sound which had held them.

It was high noon, and the crowd was braving the unforgiving heat. Mary-Ellen seemed to be thriving on it. Like the most delicate, most delicious hibiscus blossom she was all opened up. The simple white cotton dress told the world almost all it needed to know about her breasts—the perfect geometry, the pointed aggressive nipples, the faultless superstructure that neither needed nor received any artificial support. A big conch belt, brought back by her father from Albuquerque and her most prized possession, surrounded the small waist that in turn led down to long, lingering brown legs. She wore no stockings or tights, and the silhouette of white panties encasing the firm, boyish bottom was just visible through the thin material of her frock.

From time to time Tommy stole a glance at her, as if to reassure himself he wasn't dreaming. He hardly dared to entertain the idea but it seemed there had been a dramatic change in Mary-Ellen. He had noticed it a few days before, but now it was undeniable. There was a new cheerfulness about her, and it appeared that he was its main beneficiary. Her attitude toward him was different, and somehow he was no longer merely the dependable elder brother, the arm's length friend. Their relationship seemed to be hovering on the brink of something else entirely.

"So what d'ya think of the fair?" Mary-Ellen squeezed on the outsize hand.

Tommy wasn't thinking about the fair at all, but he was probably as happy as he had ever been. For him magic danced in the air, the cheap, tacky side stalls a magnificent background to the main event —the drama of his love for the girl by his side.

Mary-Ellen wanted him to like it. It was her childhood, its atmosphere filtered into her blood. Tommy's emotions were at her beck and call, desiring only to please.

"I like it real fine, Mary-Ellen."

"I guess you oughta see the headless corpse, or would you prefer the fattest man in the world?"

"I think we should take a ride on that ghost train."

"Okay, but now you be sure an' keep your hands to yourself. I've had to fight for my life in that darn thing before now."

The laughter bubbled from her throat, but the message was ambiguous. Tommy felt the blood begin to move within him. It rushed up like a fountain into his cheeks, coloring up the skin. At the same

28

time it roared south, and with that well-known feeling of helplessness he sensed the buildup in his distending penis.

Mary-Ellen saw his confusion, and laughed louder. Her arm
snaked out around his waist, building up the pressure. She, too,
felt the buzz begin. Flicking her tongue over suddenly dry lips she
allowed her gaze to wander downward. She could see its outline
clearly, and she watched fascinated as it grew and grew. With an
effort she tore her eyes away, but the vision remained in her mind
as she guided Tommy toward the ghost train's pay booth.

Now, as they boarded the open coach and braced themselves
for the voyage of surrogate suspense, she leaned in toward him,
pushed herself up, and whispered suggestively in his ear.

"I didn't mean that, Tommy. About keeping your hands to yourself."

With a clatter the coach shuddered off into the darkness, and to
Tommy's extraordinary delight the soft words and warm breath in
his ear were replaced by the exquisite wetness of a probing tongue.
His low-pitched moan of desire was in dramatic contrast to the
shrieks of nameless horror in the murky gloom, as skeletons and
demons flashed and glowed.

He half-turned toward Mary-Ellen, and cupping her warm
cheeks in his hands he moved her face toward his. As if taking the
sacrament at a first communion he bent his mouth toward hers, full
of reverence and awe at this their first kiss. Mary-Ellen's knowing
lips rose hungrily to meet his. At first she played with him, the
touch feathery light, occasionally withdrawing, to return once
more. Mouth half open she covered him with her warm, sweet
breath, letting him smell her scent, feel her passion.

Tommy shook with excitement. He had never dreamed it could
be like this. So slow, so intense. Already he was on some private
astral plane of ecstasy, and it was only a kiss. It must go on and
on. Nothing must stop it. He pushed in toward her, his penis rock
hard inside the tight jeans, thrusting his body against hers.

Mary-Ellen heard the messages of his body and responded with
her own. First she took his lower lip between her teeth, nuzzling it
gently, and then her tongue was there, the wet oasis in the parched
desert of dry lips. At first it was careful explorer, cautious, an
inquisitive traveler in a foreign country, but then as the orchestra
of passion struck up within her, it discovered courage. Now

29

Tommy could taste the saliva, feel the darting invader as it made free with his mouth—a conquistador now, relentless and unforgiving in its pursuit of pleasure.

His strong arms held her to him, and she clung to him desperately, her left hand at his neck, her right at his chest. And then her right hand was on the move. Suspended in his own world of joy Tommy both wanted and feared what he knew would happen.

Mary-Ellen's hand reached its destination, and for a second she held him tightly through the straining denim. Then, her tongue, intertwined in his, she began very gently to rub him, sometimes letting her fingers trace the outline of his erection, at others massaging firmly with the flat of her hand.

In Tommy's mind the crazy thoughts crashed against the messages that zoomed in from the mad environment. The rocking, roaring boxcar careered around ridiculous hairpin bends and collided endlessly with saloon bar doors on which skeletons and nameless demons danced. Screaming coyotes howled in the darkness and ghostly cobwebs plucked at his hair and face as the divine fingers of his lover encouraged his passion. Mary-Ellen was loving him. At last it was happening. After all the years of desperate wanting, and now, here, at last—in the chaotic darkness of a fairground ghost train—ecstasy had arrived. It seemed a cruel and wonderful trick of Fate, to be handed heaven in a place in which it was impossible to receive it.

Mary-Ellen too was half aware of the paradox. She hadn't known that desire would take over so effortlessly. For so long Tommy had been one thing. Now, for reasons she could not understand, he was another. It was as if a veil had lifted. She had been blinded by the vision of Palm Beach, and the real world—of warm flesh and rampant needs—had been beyond her touch. Somehow the events of the past few weeks had healed her. She was a prisoner no more, living no longer in the fairy castles of fantasy, a slave to her ambition and lust for betterment. In the heat of the early afternoon, the scent of corn dogs, kabobs and roasted peanuts in her nostrils, the wailing laments of the country music wafting into her ears, she had found herself once more and it was a wonderful feeling. Like a reprieved prisoner under sentence of death, she had been spared and the world was new. Now she wanted above all to live, and the best way to do that was to love.

To love this good man, who wanted her so badly. Whom now she so desperately wanted.

She looked into his face, revealed intermittently in the ghostly light, its kind features bathed in oranges, purples, and vivid greens as the train passed through grottoes of dread, and headless corpses dripped blood round about. There was so much there. The almost stricken look of the man suspended above the ultimate abyss, uncomprehending, wondering, powerless in the grip of Destiny. His mouth was open and his eyes were gleaming, the breath coming fast through distended nostrils. The gales of crackling laughter mocked the savage intensity of feeling, but they accentuated it too, emphasizing the peculiar beauty of the moment when hearts met and souls touched. She whispered to him, her voice firm in the storm of horror that surrounded them.

"I want you to make love to me, Tommy."

His voice was drowned in the adrenaline surge that had engulfed him. Yes. To make love to her. The sacrament. The beauty of wholeness. All his life he had wanted that.

"Yes."

"I want it here. Right now." Mary-Ellen's voice was insistent, urgent. Her hand pressed down hard on him, emphasizing her unmistakable meaning, invading his essence with the spears of pleasure.

"How?"

And then Mary-Ellen smiled at him. She hadn't known until now, but now she knew.

There would be a place for them. Somewhere a place. The moment demanded it, and its request was granted. In her laughing eyes Tommy saw she wanted to forget the humiliation of the past in the abandonment of the present. And he longed only to join her. As the coach slowed down he stood as she stood, jumped as she jumped, and in seconds they were together, hidden in the darkness as the empty boxcar trundled out of sight.

There was no time to wonder about it. No time to worry. Only time to hear the gurgling, abandoned laughter, to see the beautiful head thrown back, the passion glittering in the sparkling eyes, to feel the soft body crushed against him. For an age he held her, smelling the warm scent of her, his fingers running in wonderment over the soft skin of her neck. She was his, and here in the anonymous blackness, as the other seekers of thrills rushed past a few feet away from where they stood, he reveled in the joy of possession.

Electric screams knifed through the air, drawing from the human voyagers delighted yells of conspiracy as they milked the moment of its terror, but Tommy could only hear the pounding of his heart, could only feel the cool hands that were drawing him toward the union of bliss. He watched her closely, trying to etch her beauty into his mind. For him, the black, dirty wall against which she leaned was a frame of monumental loveliness, the dusty air they breathed fresh and sparkling as the first day of spring. She held him in both hands, her eyes locked on to his as, slowly, gently she pulled him toward her. Tommy felt the weakness in his legs, the throbbing rhythm in his stomach as he followed where she led.

Mary-Ellen leaned toward him, her warm breath painted onto his cheek, and the white dress raced up eagerly toward her waist, the white cotton panties plunging gratefully downward. She was the high priestess controlling and guiding the ancient ritual of love.

Tommy tried to slow each moment, unwilling to let go, but he was unable to hold back.

"I love you Mary-Ellen, oh my God I love you."

Mary-Ellen took him into her, her warmth comforting him, wrapping him in her love, making the home in which he would always live. She let out a long, shuddering sigh of contentment at the joyful peace that his presence brought. It was so right. It was how it should be, how it always should have been. This was the moment. The timeless moment of unity. Later there would be the sweet conclusion as their souls communed, but now there was the reality of the only true togetherness—awe-inspiring in its simplicity and its beauty.

Like sleepwalkers they moved as one, dancing to an ancient rhythm that had never been taught, never explained. They held each other close, swaying, inclining in the little motions that conjured up the exquisite sensations, bathing their minds in the potent potion of the purest pleasure. Sometimes they stopped, hovering on the abyss's brink, staring down in wonder at the lush valley that would be their destination. At others they swooped down, brave hawks with the wild wind beneath their wings, soaring above the cool streams and the green pastures of the paradise where they would live. They muttered soundlessly to each other, their lips moving as they sought in vain to express the inexpressible, oblivious to the mad hell that surrounded them on every side. The make-believe hell that had made possible their heaven.

Together they seemed to decide when the voyage must end, its mystic conclusion negotiated at some magic place where no thought lived, no words were spoken. For an eternity of time each lover was still, paying homage to the force of life that soon would move through them, bathing the fires with its balm, signifying an end, the new beginning. And then, at last, it was upon them. Creation's act, accompanied by two lovers' screams of ecstasy, harrowing, piercing in their reality among the clamorous counterfeits on every side.

2

*L*isa Starr slipped her mind into top gear and went for the burn. From the screaming, protesting muscles the messages flooded back to her racing mind—pain and ecstasy, ecstasy and pain. You had to feel it, to suffer it if you were to take the class along with you. That was the secret. The air waves of the small, stuffy gym reverberated with the insistent drum notes as thirty pairs of track shoes beat out the rhythm of the aerobics routine.

"Higher. Get 'em higher." Lisa's yell was lost in the raucous sound of the stereo, but everyone knew what she was saying. All round the room the piston action of the dancing legs intensified, as their owners searched for the reserves of strength.

Lisa saw the increased effort. Great. They were going with her. All the way. There was exhaustion in the dripping, glistening faces, but there was something else too. Admiration, and gratitude. Lisa was teaching them to do something difficult, to seek and find that little bit extra. They were being taken to the limit, and the feeling was good.

Time for a change of pace.

"Jumping jacks, and one and two and three and four . . ."

Lisa liked this one. There was something so satisfying about the regimented geometry of the movement, the hands clapping above the head as the ever-mobile legs sprang apart, and then together.

For her, and for many of the class, this was coasting. Relaxation in the midst of total activity. They had needed the rest after the frenetic exertion of the knee raising. But not everyone found it easy. Lisa's eyes sought out her friend. Poor Maggie. She came religiously to the classes, and tried harder than anyone, but somehow she always looked like a spastic. It wasn't that she was ugly, and piece by piece her body looked passable, but somehow the effect of the whole was aesthetic disaster.

Unbeknown to Lisa, Maggie's eyes told a very different story as she gazed in open admiration at her friend and teacher. Sometimes Maggie wondered just which bit of Lisa's superb body carried off the ultimate prize. Her bottom, turning up in the perfectly flowing line of one side of a heart before heading down to join the immaculately sculpted upper thigh? Her tits, pushing out self-confidently, impervious to the forces of gravity, crowned by the assertive, conical nipples as they pushed impatiently against the already soaked pink leotard? Her silky dark hair, with its dancing fringe, the pageboy bob rising and falling on her muscular shoulders? Or, perhaps, it was the face itself. Great big saucer eyes, blue as the Coral Sea. Lisa could make them so much wider, when she wanted to look surprised or interested, and they seemed to work on men like twin magnets. The small pert nose, which could wrinkle up in distaste. The generous, welcoming lips, which, when she was feeling good, would part to show the perfect teeth. Whichever way you looked at it you had to admit there had been cheating in the lottery of life. Lisa Starr just had too much.

In front of the class, Lisa forced herself to concentrate. These people were giving their all, and they wanted to see the color of yours. A moment's loss of attention and she would lose them, blow their confidence in her total commitment to the physical experience. Other teachers made that mistake, and their students would begin inexorably to dwindle. Lisa for sure didn't have that problem, nor did she intend to. This evening class was bursting at the seams, the prancing bodies all but touching as they fought to make every inch of the small floor count.

"Okay now, knee raising one last time. Go for it now. Feel the pain . . ." Lisa screamed the last word at the top of her voice, and with the furtive joy of group masochism the class pushed into overdrive. Once again the staccato beat rocked the wooden floor of the West Palm gym. Before her eyes Lisa could see the calories burning. Smell them, too. Through the open door the humid air of the early Florida evening wafted into the small room where it hung immobile, saturated with the sea's moisture, resisting scornfully the feeble attempts of the ancient ceiling fan to circulate it. Sweat soaked the skin-tight leotards, revealing the contours of the firm, muscular bodies beneath.

"And twenty, now twenty more, and one and two . . ."

35

"Lisa, you're *cruel.*" Maggie's joking wail was lost in the force field of violent concentration as muscles were once again asked to do the impossible, to incur the mighty oxygen debt.

Now Lisa herself was almost there, at the magical moment of transcendence when body and soul merged, when delicious agony melted into the total experience—the exercise high. Her body suddenly light, she had reached the cloud on which, it seemed, she could float forever. But she was the teacher. She couldn't leave the class behind, a straggling convoy, leaderless and abandoned, their engines seizing as they fought to keep up.

"Now we ease," she shouted. "Don't stop. Keep jogging, but relax now."

Groans of relief greeted her words, but the atmosphere of mutual congratulation was almost palpable.

"Hey, Lisa, where did they train you, Dachau?" shouted a big, muscular girl from the back.

Lisa joined in the general laughter. "It'd take more than whips and jackboots to make you shift ass, Paulene." She felt good. This was what she was paid for, but it was more than that, much more. In the faces of these girls was a respect she had not seen before she had taken this job. And it wasn't just an ego trip. She was doing them good, helping them to do themselves good. The results were actually visible. In looking better they were actually feeling better, and it showed in a thousand little ways. In six short weeks she had seen body postures improving, walks becoming more confident, the formerly shy girls cracking jokes, becoming more extroverted as they learned to like themselves more. It was incredibly rewarding, and Lisa wanted it to go on and on.

"Okay, you guys, now for some leg work."

Leopardlike, Lisa stretched herself out on the rubber mat.

Knees together, the weight of her torso balancing on splayed fingertips, she looked up at the sea of expectant eyes. What was their average age? Thirty? Twenty-five? Something like that. It was a good feeling for a seventeen-year-old to have them literally dancing to her command, performing to the crack of her ringmaster's whip. What would they do for her? What could she make them do? The little thrill of power shot through her as she watched them love her, saw them admiring her splendid body, jealous of it, wanting to possess it—and in the eyes of some of the girls just the faintest hint of something scarcely admitted, barely available to conscious thought. Yes, it was unmistakable. Like a fine Scots mist, hovering ethereally in the damp atmosphere was the heady scent of physical desire. Nothing was said, no action taken, but it was there in the shining eyes, in the sometimes lingering glances, in the torrents of intermixed hormones that coursed vigorously in the pumping blood. Lisa smelled it, knew it, but like the others she rejected it, forcing it down into her subconscious by an effort of will. There it lived on, giving a delicious subterranean meaning to the agony and the ecstasy of the physical exertion.

"Now I want you to work those buns. Turn those asses into beautiful things. Right leg raising thirty times. Go for it, and one and two . . ."

The music was softer now—the mind-blowing heavy rock of the exercise routine replaced by a more subtle sound—urging, caressing, creamy. Each phase of the hour-and-a-quarter advanced routine had a different character, and Lisa's thought processes slipped into the appropriate gear to complement them. Somehow this was always the sensual bit. Here the pain was absent. The class could probably cope with fifty or sixty leg movements on each limb but Lisa could happily keep going for half an hour. So for her the stretching movements were like scratching an itch, the delicious feeling of squeezing muscles that were already in the peak of physical condition. Now as she lifted her right leg out high to the side she felt the tautness in the gluteals, the warm glow in her groin as her vagina opened up, its lips levered apart and then forced together by the piston action of her lower limb. At moments like this Lisa wondered what it must be like to be made love to by a man.

Usually she was far too busy for such thoughts, but there was something about the glorious physical abandonment of the workout that summoned them up from some vasty deep. Here, buried in the blood, the sweat, and the tears, the flame flickered. Lisa wanted to be held in warm, strong arms, by someone who belonged to her, to whom she belonged. She wanted to feel the hard body against the hardness of hers. A man who would love her and please her all at once. Tender, strong, sensitive, powerful. It was a fantasy that she was determined time would turn into reality. Not now, but later. Soon.

Careful Lisa. Stay with their minds. *Be* with them.

"Okay, you girls. Go for it. Left leg, and one, and two, and three . . ."

Ten minutes more and it was nearly over. First the vital relaxation movements. The gentle stretching, the slow measured breathing.

"Okay, guys. That's it. Thank you and see you tomorrow."

"Oh, Lisa, you killed me today. I think I'm actually dead. No, really!" Maggie's affection beamed out in waves as she rested her hand on Lisa's damp shoulder.

"Nonsense, Maggie. You were moving like a dream. I noticed you several times. You're getting there, for sure."

"Listen, Lisa, I love you anyway, but thanks for the encouragement." Maggie was under few illusions about her performance. Sacks of potatoes had a way of looking more graceful. It was just like Lisa to spare her feelings. As far as Maggie was concerned Lisa could do no wrong, and she was content to bask in the warm glow of her aura.

"Come on, Maggs, let's get some coffee and something to eat. I get so hungry around this time."

Neither girl bothered to shower. That could wait. If they cleaned up and cooled down now the Florida humidity would have melted them again before they got home. Somehow the sweaty Lisa looked infinitely more alluring than the perspiring Maggie.

In the diner on Clematis they ordered decaffeinated coffee and doughnuts.

Maggie made her face all serious. "You know, Lisa, really you are so *good* at teaching that exercise thing. I think you should seriously think of doing it full time."

Lisa laughed. "You just think I'm soft. They might replace me with somebody who calls for a little effort in there."

"No, Lisa, I mean it. You're a natural. None of the other teachers can touch you. And it's not just me. Everybody in the class says it. Ronnie is getting pissed off that his other girls haven't got anyone in their classes anymore."

Lisa's laugh was rather more thoughtful. It was true, and it was becoming a bit of a problem. She was miles better than the others, and the consumers, not unnaturally, had noticed it. Ronnie was the guy who owned the gym, and it was true that over the last few weeks he had begun to cool toward her. If the other instructors were into a whispering campaign, she might just end up a victim of her own success. "Yeah, those cats are just longing for me to burn myself out, screw a ligament or something. Well, for sure they've got a long wait. This body intends to hold together all the way."

Maggie saw the determination in her friend's eyes. Sometimes it seemed to her that Lisa was composed of the finest tempered steel. Nothing seemed to throw her. She was only a year away from the worst tragedy that could have befallen anyone, and yet she had bounced back, stronger than before, tested and not found wanting by the dreadful experience. It was not that she hadn't suffered the grief. She had felt the pain all right, because she was tough, not hard. There was a difference.

Maggie sowed the seed. "Me and a couple of the girls were saying you ought to branch out on your own. Start your own place. You'd strip Ronnie of all his customers if you did. We'd all go with you, to a man."

They both smiled at the reference to the opposite sex. Some habits didn't give up without a fight.

Lisa looked thoughtful as she spoke.

"But Maggie, love, starting a gym takes things like money. You remember the stuff. And you have to know about accounts, property, leases, and things. I can take class but those other things are for the birds. Jumping jacks and muscle burn are my field, not business."

"You could learn all that—and I could help. And perhaps some of the others would put up some money. I've got five hundred dollars. That might pay for some professional advice."

"I suppose there is the insurance money," said Lisa uncertainly. "But I was kinda relying on that to get me through college and possibly into a career in teaching."

Maggie saw that she was making progress. "Listen, honey. This world is full of teachers and they know shit-all, except what others have told them. What was it that artist Braque said when they asked him whether he had any talent as an art student? 'If I did, my teacher would have been the last to know.' "

Lisa could sympathize with that. In the teaching profession original thinking tended to go down like soul food at a Klan rally. But a career in teaching was security. Unexciting, perhaps, but a meal ticket for life. She would have a profession, a husband, 2.5 children, and she would help with the mortgage payments. It was the American dream. Lisa shuddered instinctively. She tried to put her dilemma into words.

"The teaching thing would be so easy, Maggie, so safe. It'd be tough to turn down all that steady money. The trouble is I know it'd be a cop-out. It'd be so much more fun to take life by the balls and give it a swing, like with the exercise trip. I guess I could always go back to teaching later . . ."

Lisa's voice faltered. Life wasn't quite like that and she knew it. Once you got off the conventional ladder, somebody else moved in to take your place. There would be new A students, teacher's pets with no suspicious gaps in their curricula vitae. And when Lisa tried to get her foot back on the lower rungs, their shoe leather, or worse, would be in her face. It was the way the system exacted obedience from the slaves who serviced it. Move out and the door slams in your face. Stay put and obey the rules and the addictive drug of security is dripped in increasing quantities into your veins, each additional fix carefully metered and spread out tantalizingly through time. The more you got the more you wanted —the higher the ladder the steeper the jump to get off. It was a trap into which Mr. and Mrs. Average were all too pleased to fall, willing junkies to the habit of conformity. The thought filled Lisa with horror. At the tender age of seventeen she had no idea of what she wanted to be, but she knew that whatever it was it would represent phenomenal success in one sense or another. For now she was ambitious in a vacuum, a rebel against mediocrity waiting for a cause; but it would not always be like that, and in her guts Lisa knew that the thing to do was to fly by the seat of your pants, letting instinct be the pilot.

Maggie licked the last of the doughnut's sugar off her stubby fingers. No way should she have eaten that, let alone be about to order another. Furtively, she caught the waitress's eye.

"Oh, no you don't, Maggie—it's not all muscle yet." Lisa laughed as she played the policeman. Maggie's fat cells were very far from transformation into muscular protein.

Maggie didn't put up a struggle. Not many did against Lisa. She had the sort of charm that magicians had in children's comic books, a kind of velvet-gloved force that you couldn't resist, and didn't want to. Maggie had often tried to analyze it, and on the

40

whole she had failed. It had something, she had concluded, to do with motive. Lisa wanted the best for people.

"Hey, Lisa—you know I'm really high on this gym idea. You really ought to go for it. Make it happen." Visions of wizard's wands were conjured up. If Lisa wanted it she would have it.

For a second or two Lisa was silent. Both hands cupped around her chin, she stared thoughtfully at her friend.

At last she spoke. "You know, Maggs, I think I'm going to give it a try. I just want to say one thing. I really appreciate what you offered—you know, the five hundred bucks. It was really sweet of you, but when I do it I'm going to do it alone. Perhaps I can borrow from the bank, and use the insurance money. It'll be dangerous as hell, but it should be *real* fun."

Maggie couldn't contain a little yelp of enthusiasm. Great! Lisa was going to do it, and as always she would sweep her friend along in her wake. A thoughtful look swam into Maggie's big brown eyes and hovered there between the bright patches on the excited cheeks. What a friendship it had been. A cliché, of course. The wild-looking girl and her plain sidekick, but in these difficult days when fortune favored the beautiful rather than the brave it was a fact that the Maggies of this world tended to be wallflowers at life's party, watchers and waiters, while the Lisas twirled and pirouetted to the abandoned music. And she genuinely didn't mind. She was more than content to live vicariously, to experience Lisa's triumphs as her own and to be thrust down into the depths by Lisa's misfortunes. It had been like that for as long as Maggie could remember. Since those far-off days in the schoolyard when she never had to be told to share her candy and her cuddly toys with the little girl who was prettier by far than any Alexander doll; since the times when she had not minded that Lisa was the teacher's pet; since the steamy West Palm afternoons when she had been so proud to walk the streets with her, responding haughtily to the "come-ons" of the boys that "they" were not interested.

"Oh, Lisa, that's just *wonderful*. I just know you can make it work. You make everything work. Everyone'll come with you, and I just can't bear to think of you wasted in some dreary classroom." Maggie clapped her hands together in excitement. Then her expression of pure joy clouded over. "But you'll let me help, won't you? I don't mean with the money if you don't want that, but like with all the organization. I won't need wages. Well, not much anyway.''

"Come *on*, Maggs. It's your idea. I couldn't possibly do it without you. I couldn't possibly do *anything* without you. Anyway, we've got to put the finishing touches on your new body.''

They both laughed.

Maggie was under few illusions about where she stood in the beauty stakes. Her face wasn't so bad, and for sure she wasn't exactly *ugly*, although the bone structure lacked definition and the pasty color of the skin tended to merge without trace against the beige coloring of the gymnasium's walls. No, it was the body that let her down, and it needed far more than the "finishing touches" of which Lisa had spoken. But there had been a dramatic improvement, and although things still didn't hang together, at least they no longer *"hung."* At the beginning she had been unenthusiastic about Lisa's love affair with exercise, and she had wandered into the gym in a cynical frame of mind, with lots of jokes about body fascism and a cheerful irreverence about the almost religious faith in things physical that had surrounded her. As always, Lisa had won her over. Never once had she made fun of her, as so many "friends" would not have hesitated to do. Instead she had led her gently through the agonizing introduction classes, and Maggie's natural self-confidence, which had survived despite the handicap of her personal appearance, had received a massive transfusion as her body had begun the painful process of reorganizing itself before her eyes.

Now there was even a boyfriend, and there hadn't been one of those before.

"I promise you, Lisa. You won't believe this, but one of these days it'll be me up there in front of the class. You remember that.''

"Listen, Maggs. I'm *counting* on it.''

Maggie smiled. By saying things out loud like that it helped to make them come true. To have Lisa agree made it almost certain that they would.

"Okay, Lisa. Let's go right to work on it. The first thing we need is a space. There's a great one for rent on Clematis. I was just thinking the other day how perfect it would be for a gym. God knows how much they want for it. What are you doing right now, Lisa? Can I come home with you, and we can start making plans?''

Lisa cut into the bubbling enthusiasm. "I'm afraid it's no good tonight, Maggie. Willie Boy Willis said he'd drop by at around five thirty to talk about old times. You know what he's like when he starts on the beer."

Maggie saw the veil of melancholy descend on Lisa as she spoke. Her shoulders sagged, her voice was heavy, eyes suddenly misty. Maggie knew what it was all about, and her hand sneaked out across the table to comfort her friend. "Oh, Lisa, baby. If only I could help. You're so brave. Keep fighting."

And Maggie watched the great big tear roll down the beautiful but now strangely haunted face.

The bags under Willie Boy's eyes were practically big enough to have contained bar trash, and there were times when, late at night, as he passed out among the Roxy's garbage containers, they were not far off doing just that. The beer belly hung down over his belt like some obscene apron, and between the sweat-stained T-shirt and the top of his equally unclean jeans a couple of inches of unhealthy skin protruded. His ginger beard looked as if it contained things, and the occasional foraging expedition of his blunt and blackened nails tended to confirm this disturbing possibility.

Lisa, however, didn't see or smell the Willie Boy Willis that others saw and smelled. For her he was faded dreams, bittersweet walks through her memories, a passport to the past where things had been so blissfully different.

"Yup, Lisa babe, I remember the time when your ol' man and your granpappy set to arm wrestling on the bar. Remember it like yesterday. Nobody in there that night wanted money on who'd win. Never seen nothing like it. You know they'd cuss and yell at each other like they was worst enemies, yet sure as I stand here now I've never seen two men more fond of each other."

Lisa knew. Her mother had always pretended to be infuriated by the alliance between her father and her husband, but secretly she was pleased by it.

"So what happened, Willie Boy?" Lisa tucked up her long legs beneath her on the threadbare sofa and fixed her eyes on her guest's face in studious attention.

Willie Boy burped theatrically. A lifetime tending bar at Roxy's had taught him a thing or two about storytelling. The trick was to tell it as slowly as the audience's attention span would permit. He drew hard and long on the can of beer as if to appease the complaining stomach gods with some valuable sacrificial offering.

"Well, there was money riding on it, fer sure. Big money as I recall. Fifty bucks at least—real money. An' your dad says to me, 'Now you hold this money, Willie Boy, 'cause ol' Jack's meaner'n mouse shit an' never done pay his debts.' "

In her mind's eye Lisa saw the scene, heard the beloved voices.

"Then they set to it. Well, I'll tell you this an' no mistake, in my time I seen arm wrestling—big uns, small uns, tall uns, short uns —but I never seen nothing like that match on the Roxy bar that night between old Jack Kent and young Tommy. You could have heard a roach fart in that room—sure as I'm alive."

Lisa could feel the tension in the steamy bar, as the hushed drinkers witnessed the battle of giants.

Willie Boy could see he was carrying his audience. No sweat. His memory wasn't too good anymore. The drink had seen to that, but he knew the value of exaggeration. "An' strike me down if I tell a lie, but I swear that match went on for fifteen minutes by the clock, an' in all that time I didn't see a drop of beer pass anybody's lips, they was so intent on that contest—and fer sure that ain't happened before or since in Roxy's during opening time."

Lisa was in there, too. Rooting for both sides. For the father who had loved her, protected her, given her the happiest home in the world, for the grandfather who had excited, amused, and frightened her, who had been the color, and the danger, and the adventure.

"You know, when old Jack's hand finally hit that bar there was a cheer went up like the ones you hear at the dogs. That cheer was for both of them, an' no mistake."

Willie Boy sat down heavily and reached for the Bud that was his reward for the story. Singing for a liquid supper was no new thing to him. The leathery hand transferred surplus beer and spit from his mouth to the leg of his once-blue jeans.

"How did Jack take being beaten?"

44

Willie Boy laughed. "Oh, Lisa. That was *Tommy* done beat him. Tell you something for nothing. Old Jack was a mean one. Real ornery. Seen him beat guys to pulp in that bar 'cause he didn't like their faces. Slapped me around more'n once. But that Tommy Starr could've cut off his balls an' he'd still have loved him. That's how close those two guys were."

For a second or two Willie Boy said nothing, as he appeared to weigh the advisability of his next remark.

"Then that Jack wanted to get drunk as a skunk, but Tommy all he wanted to do was get back to your momma. I never seen a man love a girl so much as young Tom loved Mary-Ellen. Never, an' that's the truth."

He looked across the small room to see its effect on Lisa, but he could see that she had gone, vanished to some private world of memory.

The old rocking chair's creak was to Lisa the safest sound in the world, but it came as part of a package deal. It was attached firmly to other sensations—her mother's warm, hard thighs beneath Lisa's squirming legs, the opulent scent of the night flowering jasmine, the bittersweet complaints of the singer on the country station, the tricky light of the kerosene lamp. Sitting on her mother's lap on the porch of the old house, Lisa came closest to heaven—and it was always of paradise that Mary-Ellen spoke. Lisa Starr's five hectic years had not prepared her for the nuances of her mother's message, but there was no mistaking the gentle passion with which it was delivered—and Lisa could remember the words as if it were yesterday. Night after night they had tumbled out, seeping deep into Lisa's consciousness until they were a living part of her, sometimes, she felt, the most important part. The intense pleasure of the circumstances surrounding these conversations formed powerful associations for the young girl, and firmly but delicately, her mind had been washed clean of all heresy that might dilute the force of the gospel truth.

Never for one moment had the content of the message deviated. Across the bridge, a few hundred yards away, was a magical world peopled by gods and demigods, beautiful, kindly people who could do no wrong. Charming, urbane, witty, sophisticated, and thoroughly good, the citizens and part-time residents of Palm Beach inhabited a different planet, behaved and thought in a way alien to the mere mortals of West Palm. Theirs was a glittering life of music and dance, of genteel conversation, of culture and excellence far removed from the game of financial and moral survival that was played with such intensity on the other side of the coastal railroad. Her eyes glistening with the faith of the convert, Mary-Ellen had told and retold of the sumptuous banquets, the intricate arrangements of flowers, of the comings and goings of the rich and famous; and all the time Lisa had sat in wonderment, soothed and stimulated by her mother's lilting voice. Other children, her friends and adversaries of a hundred make-believe street battles, had other champions—Batman, Superman, and Captain Marvel—but to Lisa these were paper heroes, insubstantial specters who would melt away when confronted by the transcendent reality of a Stansfield, a Duke, or a Pulitzer. To Lisa's childlike questions the responses were patient, self-assured.

"Why don't we live in Palm Beach, mommy?"

"Folks like us just don't live there, honey."

"But *why* not?"

"It has to do with birth, Lisa. Some people are born to live like that."

"You lived there once, at the Stansfield house."

"Yes, but I *worked* there. I wasn't *really* there." Then her mother's eyes would film over as she dared to dream, and her voice would say cautiously, "But one day, Lisa, if you grow up to be very beautiful and very good, like a fairy princess, who knows but some prince might take you there. Across the bridge."

Far from wise in the ways of the world, Lisa had nonetheless picked up on the inconsistencies of her mother's logic, but it had not been enough to cause her to doubt the truth of her mother's words—nor did she want to. This was the realm of fantasy, of dreaming, of white knights and dashing ponies, of superhuman powers and ultimate wisdom—and Palm Beach was the mysterious universe in which mythical beings cavorted, in which deeds of derring-do were endlessly performed. And there was one shining belief that Lisa kept always to herself. In her dreams Lisa would one day be a part of it. She would be drawn across the bridge in a golden carriage, serenaded by a marching band, welcomed into heaven by a choir of angels, taking her mother and her family with her as she crossed in glory to the other side. And then her family's mighty gratitude would break all over her. She, Lisa, would have been the instrument for the attainment of the impossible dream, and could bask forever in the loving respect that such an achievement must bring.

Willie Boy's gritty voice sawed itself into Lisa's consciousness, interrupting the sad, sweet memories.

"Seems like I lost you there, Lisa."

"Yeah, I was thinking of mom." Lisa smiled a wan smile.

"Sure was one hell of a lady. Best-looking lady in the county I ever saw. Yup, she had style—real style—your mom did, Lisa. Tommy was one lucky man."

They looked at each other warily. Both knew what would happen now. Both willed it. Each in a way dreaded it.

With fascination, a serpent in the grip of the charmer's spell, Lisa watched it start, having no power to stop the doomed attempt at exorcism, the futile longing to lay the ghosts to sleep.

"I'll never know how it happened. Never forgive myself for that night."

Willie Boy often started like that.

But Lisa knew. Knew every single detail—would carry it with her through her nights and her days forever.

Tommy and Jack. The drunken march home. Thoughts flying high, alcohol the wind beneath the wings of imagination. Arm in arm, the masculine smells, the comradeship of tried and trusting drinking partners. The old house, quiet but well lit. The giggled lip service to the necessity of silence. Creaking boards, unsteady feet, uncertain eyes. Whose unknowing elbow had dislodged the kerosene lamp, what extraneous sound had camouflaged its fall—a car? the wail of the train whistle? some needless joke?

The fire had started before each man had crawled beneath the hot sheets; it was gathering force as they slipped into drink's stu-

47

por. Racing hungrily through the willing timbers baked and cracked by the sun's heat, driven on by the capricious nocturnal breeze, it had enjoyed its wicked orgy of destruction. Lisa, sleeping fitfully, had heard and smelled it first. Throwing open her door, she was hit by the wall of heat, the snapping, hissing roar of the flames in her ears. Instinct alone had saved her. She had closed the door against the fire, and in the few seconds that the inspired action had bought her she had climbed out of her bedroom window into the dark safety of the backyard.

Standing alone, her senses in turmoil, scarcely aware of what was happening, Lisa had watched her world consumed. The time between sleep, wakefulness, and action had amounted to a few brief seconds. Now, the awful dread had welled up within her. Beyond the fence the neighbors were shouting, their urgent cries of alarm seeping into Lisa's half-awake mind.

Her father, her mother, her grandfather were in the roaring tinderbox. Had they, like her, escaped? Or had they already left her —gone forever, with no possibility of even a sad farewell? She had walked toward the pitiless flames, felt once again the merciless heat on her face, the suffocating fumes of the smoke. She had recoiled from it, from the singeing pain on her exposed and naked nipples, from the dreadful, nameless horror it represented. And then she had seen the specter.

From the midst of the conflagration, moving jerkily like a sleepwalker, the figure emerged.

Numb with horror, Lisa took a second or two to realize who it was. It was her mother, and she was burning. Mary-Ellen had emerged from the inferno, but she had not escaped it.

Lisa leaped forward, her stricken eyes on the dancing, darting flames that jumped and pranced from her mother's bare flesh. In her nostrils was the stench of burning skin, as the body which had borne her was consumed in front of her. In her heart was sick dread.

Already blinded by the fire, Mary-Ellen stumbled toward her, a dry, parched shout of pain and alarm seeping out between burned lips. Her arms made strange beseeching gestures, the movements of the blindfolded child playing blindman's buff, as she sought the comfort she would never find.

Oblivious to the flames, Lisa rushed into her arms, giving her

48

naked body to her mother, as balm for the unhealable wounds, as an alternative source of fuel for the deadly fire. Roughly, she pushed Mary-Ellen to the ground and, straddling her, she offered her body as a blanket in her wild attempt to starve her mother's flesh of the oxygen without which the flames could not burn. She felt no pain as the fire sought to transfer its attentions, had no thought of the scars she might incur by her selfless action. She was an animal driven only by the power of instinct, by the power of love.

Together mother and daughter rolled on the parched, sparse grass of the backyard, their brains and bodies screaming. And then there were other hands, other voices, the rude shock of the cold water, muted exclamations of horror.

With Mary-Ellen cradled in Lisa's arms, their time-honored positions were reversed; mother and child clung together resisting the hands that sought to separate them. Tenderly Lisa looked down at the ravaged face, its beauty liquidized by the unforgiving fire, the well-remembered features twisted and tormented by the flames' force. Murmuring words of reassurance and desperate hope, she smoothed the stricken hair, but Lisa could feel the presence of death's angel hovering, swooping, backing away again— and she knew that her mother was dying.

And then the tears had found their strength as the emotion of sorrow burst through the raging torrent of fear and anger, the adrenaline surge of action.

"Oh, momma," she sobbed, as the big salty tears welled up in Lisa's eyes, cascading down dry cheeks, dripping steadily onto the swollen, discolored, and weeping skin.

"Oh, mom, stay with me. Don't go away. Please stay."

She hugged her dying mother, crushing her to her body, trying to merge with her—to force life into death, to stave off the inevitable moment of eternal emptiness. Mary-Ellen was unrecognizable, reduced to the wickedest caricature of her former beauty, but inside her ruined body the heart still beat, the lungs still breathed. For Lisa that was enough, and she prayed to her God not to take away the gift of existence without which nothing was possible, no future could be.

Through hurting lips Mary-Ellen had tried to speak, and Lisa had leaned down to listen to the pained words. They would never be forgotten, always respected, would be carried through life like a talisman—the magic charm that would show the way forward.

"Darling Lisa. I love you so much . . . so much."

"Oh, mom, I love you too. I love you. Stay with me. Stay with me."

"I went . . . to your room. But you're safe. I'm so happy." Her voice weaker now, she spoke again. "Lisa. Darling girl. All those evenings, on the porch. You remember those things I said. Don't throw it away like I did. You can do it. I know you can. Do you know what I'm saying. Oh. Lisa . . . hold me tight."

"Don't talk, mom. The doctors will be here soon. Don't try to talk." Now the waves of grief began to break all over Lisa, and she began to sob as in her arms she felt the shudder course through the broken body, as her mother fought to hold on to elusive life.

"I remember, mommy. I remember everything. Don't die. Mommy, please don't die."

Then in open defiance of her most fervent prayer, Mary-Ellen's back arched and her body contracted. Like a leaf carried on the wind, the message was borne on the sweet, dying air.

"Palm Beach . . . Lisa . . . it's only a bridge away . . ."

It was twelve noon and the sun sliced down like a javelin, boring into the baked sidewalk, shimmering and quivering in still air. Lisa and Maggie, however, seemed to be in some way immune to it as, heads together, they talked intensely outside the bank.

"But what are you going to *say*, Lisa? These guys are real smart, you know. Pop always says they only lend money to the folks who don't need it."

"It'll be okay, Maggs. I can make the gym work. I know that, and I'll make him know that, too. We'll get a good deal. You'll see."

Maggie looked doubtful, but as always, Lisa's self-confidence was infectious. "You got all the paperwork."

Lisa waved the manila folder in her friend's face and laughed.

"It's just props, Maggie. Bankers lend to people, not to scraps of paper. Do I look okay?"

It was Maggie's turn to laugh. As far as she was concerned Lisa always looked great. Loose, sky-blue linen jacket over white T-shirt. Long brown legs exploding out of the short, white, pleated cotton skirt, ankle socks, canvas lace-up shoes. But the clothes were really an irrelevance, a distraction from the main event—the superb body that they so ineffectively concealed. "Let's just hope the guy's happily married and a pillar of the church—otherwise you'll get molested in there."

"Don'tcha think of anything else, Maggs? Hey, it's late. I'd better get on in. Wish me luck."

In the elevator Lisa's self-confidence sank as she rose. It was a week or two since she had made her decision, and every day since her desire had grown geometrically. She was going to open the most successful gym the world had ever known—a center of bodily excellence whose reputation would spread far and wide. She would create it, shape it, be it, and in turn it would give her what she wanted. It would be her passport across the bridge, her posthumous gift to her dead mother. Soon the gods and goddesses would hear of her on the celestial grapevine, and, as the word filtered across the gleaming surface of the lake, the younger inhabitants of paradise would seek her out, give their bodies to her to shape, to sculpt, to condition. In their gratitude they would reward her by allowing her to move among them. Only one thing stood in Lisa's way. A banker by the name of Weiss. Without finance she would be nowhere, a nobody condemned forever to mediocrity.

Lisa allowed the gloomy thought to swirl around her mind. It was a trick she had learned. To get things in this life you had to want them like hell. That was the secret. If the desire wasn't there you were lost. And the way to tank up desire was to dwell on the consequences of failure, as she was doing now. By the time the elevator was ready to decant her Lisa Starr was gripped by a steely resolve. She would have her way no matter what. Weiss would give her the loan, and she would do whatever it took to get it. By fair means or foul she would win.

The hatchet-faced receptionist had not been encouraging when she had made the appointment, and she didn't seem to have changed her tune. Luckily there wasn't any waiting time. Throwing open the door to the office, she said briefly, "Ms. Lisa Starr, Mr. Weiss—your twelve o'clock appointment," as she ushered Lisa inside.

Weiss, small and owllike, leaped to his feet as Lisa entered, his face lighting up, the wizened features illuminated by the spark of instant lust. Lisa could almost hear what he was thinking as he beamed his welcome, and she could feel his eyes as they roamed over the pleasing contours of her body, lingering lasciviously on the erogenous zones, the full lips, the unrestrained nipples, darting down hungrily to speculate on the hidden Mecca barely covered by the short skirt.

"Ah, Ms. Starr." The pudgy hands spread in welcome. "Do please sit down." Weiss hovered at Lisa's shoulder. He didn't actually pull out the chair for her, as if unwilling to undertake so subservient an action despite the phenomenal physical charms of his young customer. Instead he angled his body from the waist, leaning over Lisa and making little darting movements with his arms as if orchestrating the complicated physical process of sitting down, a puppeteer attached to Lisa's limbs by unseen strings. Lizardlike, a small tongue darted out to wet dry lips as the restless eyes flickered over the highest point of the crossed thighs where the incompetent skirt did its best to cover Lisa Starr's candy-striped cotton briefs.

Reluctantly Weiss retreated behind the imposing desk and took up his position in the tall, dark green leather chair. The libidinous smile lost some of its intensity, as the fantasy visions faded and cold reality reasserted itself. Damn. Joseph Weiss—Casanova, Don Juan, lady's man—merged relentlessly into old Joe Weiss, sixty-two, with halitosis and fallen arches.

He peered down at his desk, staring intently at the almost blank sheet of paper. "Well, Ms. Starr. How can I help you?"

"What I really need, Mr. Weiss, is a loan of twenty thousand dollars to open an exercise studio here in West Palm." That was the bottom line. Lisa had considered all sorts of other possible beginnings, but had been congenitally drawn to the most straightforward one. "I have twenty thousand dollars of my own from an insurance policy, and I would be putting that into the venture,

too,'' she added. Presumably bankers liked you to join them in the
risk.

"Aaaaaaaah," said Weiss approvingly. That was better. She
wanted something from him. People usually did, and it tended to
make him feel good. Sometimes they were prepared to do things
in return. It was far from unknown in his experience, and this girl
was so young, so very pretty.

For a second Lisa waited, but Weiss added nothing to his enig-
matic expression. Was this the moment to start the long speech—
her credentials, her profit predictions, the already discovered
premises on Clematis Street? Instinct told her no. She sat up as
straight as she could in the high-backed chair and watched the
banker evenly, noting the dramatic return of prurient interest in
the restless eyes.

"That seems a lot of money, Ms. Starr," he said at last.

"It'd be a good investment for your bank," said Lisa brightly,
letting the self-confidence show.

Weiss looked at her carefully. A good investment for the bank?
Forget it. For himself in his capacity of lender of the bank's
money? Maybe. Just maybe. He peered at the sharp nipples,
blinked, and then swallowed nervously. There was a way of handling this one, but it was littered with minefields. One wrong foot
and he'd blow it.

"Suppose you fill me in on some of the details of your business
proposition." The avuncular look didn't quite come off. There was
definitely some sort of a leer.

Lisa was well prepared. What bankers liked was sheets of paper.
Things to look at that could be shown to other people. She'd
brought plenty of that, character references, photographs of the
prospective premises, estimates of probable income. She passed
the envelope across to the banker with a few words of explanation.
For a minute or two Weiss ran through them.

When he looked up his smile was sly. "This is pretty impressive,
Lisa—if I can call you that—but what seems to me to be missing
here is any reference to training in physical education." He waited
for a split second before deciding to go for it. "Although I suppose
one might say that your . . . aaaaaah . . . superb bodily condition
is evidence of that."

Once again the creepy eyes lasered in on Lisa, darting around her breasts, aiming down to the flat stomach, heading lower still.

She was quite unable to control the blush. Christ, he was coming on like gangbusters.

She laughed nervously and played it as straight as hell. "I'm afraid they haven't gotten around to giving out diplomas in stretch and aerobics, but I could for sure get references from the place I teach now."

As she spoke she knew that Weiss's remark hadn't meant that at all.

Weiss's laugh crackled disconcertingly. "No, I'm sure that side of things isn't a problem. I'm certain the physical side of things would be no problem for you. No problem at all."

Inside he felt the adrenaline begin to hum. How much did this little fox want her gym? Because if she really wanted it there was only one way she was going to get it. One way alone. Twenty thousand bucks for some crappy studio that would close down in six months? It was laughable. But a twenty-thousand-dollar screw at the bank's expense—who knew, perhaps several screws—that might not be such a bad deal. It wouldn't be the first time, and, he fervently hoped, it wouldn't be the last. So what that it would be a bad loan, and he would lose a few points? Everyone was entitled to the odd mistake. He would be forgiven. No question. Anyway this girl was *young,* and *stacked.* He would use a modified version of the same basic speech, the one with the good track record.

"Lisa, I must be quite frank with you. I am afraid my experience tells me this loan wouldn't be at all safe. There are several reasons. You're young, very young, with no track record in business. And the exercise thing—fashionable though it may be at the moment— is hardly 'money in the bank.' "

Weiss laughed heartily at the weak joke, as he picked up on the disappointment in the beautiful eyes. The trick was to beat them down into the dust before picking up the pieces. "The truth of the matter is—and I am sorry to be so pessimistic—I can't see any bank taking on a loan like this." He shook his head sadly and made a little clicking noise with his tongue. "Can't see it at all," he added unnecessarily.

Lisa watched it slip away from her, as the dread welled up within her. She had been so certain, so sure. In the past, her desire for something had always been enough, the instant ticket to her destination. Ambition plus effort had equaled success. Now, for the first time in her life, she was about to be thwarted. This man Weiss was standing in her way, and predicting, quite plausibly, that there would be other Weisses who would do the same if she tried to go elsewhere. The worst thing of all was that Lisa *knew* the gym would be a success, but how on earth could she hope to convince a banker of that? All he could see was her inexperience and naiveté.

But Lisa was wrong. Weiss, his eyes blinking excitedly behind the thick glasses, could see a very great deal more than that. He leaned forward into Lisa's almost palpable disappointment and threw her the lifeline. "However." Weiss repeated the word. "However, I'll be quite honest and say that I like you, Lisa. I like you very much, and I admire . . . what you have done and what you plan to do."

The long pause was full of hidden meanings, as he willed Lisa to get the drift. "Perhaps I *can* help. Perhaps we can work together on this one," he said at last. Weiss smiled an oily smile. Still a bit too oblique. How much needed to be spelled out? He waited for a sign of encouragement.

Lisa's friendly smile was strictly neutral, but her mind was suddenly on red alert. Not yet in the forefront of consciousness she had a subterranean awareness of what was going on. Some atavistic instinct told her that Weiss was up to something, and that it was nasty.

"What I suppose I'm trying to say," Mr. Weiss murmured, "is that it would be nice if we could kinda keep in touch—maybe on a social basis—while we have the loan out to you. If, of course, I were to decide to go ahead." There. He'd done it. It was on the table. You screw me for twenty thousand. It was as clear as daylight.

Lisa watched the play and knew at once what he was saying. She wasn't surprised, and that in itself she found surprising. As little grenades of revulsion exploded deep within her, she kept her face deadpan for the reply. "Well, I'd certainly welcome some fatherly advice along the way. I'd be very grateful for it."

Immediately she regretted her remark. She was walking a tightrope, and the safety net was conspicuous by its absence. Weiss wanted her to come on to him, and she had more or less told him he was a dirty old man—old enough to be her grandfather. The twenty thousand, which a second before had dangled in front of her nose, had gone swinging away again.

Weiss laughed uncertainly. Could she be that innocent? Or was she saying "no way"? "What I really mean is, perhaps we could go out to dinner from time to time—get to know each other." There was a hint of desperation in his voice.

Lisa knew she was about to make one of the most important decisions of her life, and she hadn't a clue which way it was going to go. She had two alternatives. Either she sold herself to this ridiculous old man and got the money she needed, or she walked away empty-handed into a teaching career. Whore or respectable pillar of the establishment. Palm Beach or Minneapolis. Danger or safety. She hovered in an agony of indecision.

Through clenched teeth Weiss said, "What do you say?"

For what seemed like an age Lisa said absolutely nothing.

The thoughts came in like gunfire. His disgusting thing inside her proud body, polluting her, violating her, owning her forever as he took her virginity. But it would be only a short moment of time, gone, forgotten, erased from memory by a mighty act of will as the fruits of her ordeal smoothed the path ahead to victory and glory. Her self-respect lost forever as she sold herself to the devil to get what she wanted. But a solemn promise to her dead mother fulfilled as she moved toward paradise. "Only a bridge away . . . only a bridge away . . ." In her nostrils was the scent of burning flesh, as she peered through suddenly tear-filled eyes at her potential tormentor, at her potential savior. Devil or angel—which was he?

Weiss watched the turmoil in the liquid eyes as Lisa struggled with her conscience. The message had gotten across at last. It was out of his hands. He had only to wait. In delicious anticipation he sat back in his chair and savored the delectable feeling that was beginning to course through him.

"I'm not quite sure what you have in mind," Lisa heard herself say. She was playing for time, fishing for anything that would help her to make the decision.

"I think you know what I have in mind," said Weiss quickly. She wasn't getting off the hook.

By fair means or foul. Lisa had promised herself that a few brief minutes before. Had fair means been exhausted? And, if so, how foul could you get?

A passionately interested observer of her own mental processes, Lisa watched herself in fascination to see what she would do. Her soul seemed to hover over her, a passive spectator as, like a sleep-walker, she stumbled onward.

The speech when it came was delivered in a firm, defiant voice. "Mr. Weiss, I think I *do* understand what you are saying to me. You're saying that you will lend me the money if I make love to you, and *only* if I make love to you." She stopped, and when she began again there was a catch in her voice. "Well, you must know that I don't want to do that and I think it's very wrong of you to ask it and to want it. But I do need the money—I need it desperately because I want so much from life. So if you want it I will make love to you, but on one condition—that we do it here, now, this very minute. And then you give me my money. All of it—in a certified banker's draft."

Slowly, deliberately, with her mind on fire, she stood up.

The mighty wave of guilt crashed over Joe Weiss, extinguishing the dancing flame of passion with the ease of a tornado blowing out a candle flame. Torrents of the purest shame rushed and raced, dampening his base desires. Joe Weiss, the father of his children, the husband of his wife, the son of his mother, was reincarnated and he struggled for the words that would best show his atonement. Before him Lisa Starr stood stock still, offering herself as a glorious sacrifice, an embodiment of magnificent determination and single-mindedness.

And then the guilt in old Joe Weiss was replaced with another feeling—admiration—and quite suddenly he laughed his first genuine laugh of the day.

He had been outmaneuvered, outgunned, outplayed by this beautiful seventeen-year-old girl—and he laughed because for some extraordinary reason he didn't mind a bit. That just had to be the definition of charm. Until this moment he hadn't thought for one second that her business had a snowdrop's chance in hell.

Now suddenly he wasn't at all sure. The one thing he'd learned in the money-lending business was that you lent bucks to people, not to ideas, and this person had a bankable personality quite apart from the more obvious ready assets.

"Lisa Starr," he said, "you get the money, and let me tell you this for nothing: you're going to go one hell of a long way."

In all of his sixty-two years Joe Weiss had never been more right.

Bobby Stansfield's face peered back at him from the hand-held mirror, and he liked what he saw. The Florida suntan seemed to have been painted on, a deep rich all-over brown relieved only by the tiny white streaks in the embryonic wrinkles around the shining, laughing eyes. From long practice Bobby made the inventory fast. Start at the top. The sandy hair, lustrous, exuberant, was suitably untidy—its self-confident, orderly chaos hinting at the harmonious marriage between boy and man that the voters had learned to love. He shook his head from side to side, encouraging the wayward curl to fall forward over the right eye before flicking it back again with the sweep of an impatient hand. The nose, cracked neatly by the side of a loose surfboard so many years before, gave an appealing lack of conformity to the otherwise all-too-perfect face. Endless Stansfield conferences, political and familial, had debated the advisability of plastic surgery. Now, and on a hundred previous occasions, he thanked God that the verdict had been no go. He needed the nose. It had become a trademark, a symbol of virility, a statement that Bobby Stansfield, despite all other appearances to the contrary, was very far from vanity. Mouth? Closed—just a little too thin, intimating the possibility of coldness, if not of cruelty. Open—incredible, a perfect frame for the sculpted, pure white teeth. The chin was smooth and square, with no hint of a vote-losing shadow. Great. The box of tricks was looking good. He allowed the face to smile its self-satisfaction, the smile widening in positive feedback as it contemplated itself.

"How do I look, Jimmy?"

"Knicker-wetting good," laughed the short, squat man by his side.

Despite the joke, Jimmy Baker's professional eyes checked the Stansfield visuals below the neck. Dark blue ribbed silk tie with a subdued crimson diagonal stripe; standard-issue Brooks Brothers suit, navy blue and not too well cut so as to avoid the aroma of smoothness that would be the kiss of death to the people's choice; black Gucci loafers, their leather soft as a baby's bottom. It was all there and all hanging together. Candidates had become instant history for crimes no more heinous than an unzipped fly. In this life there was no relaxing.

From the wings both men could see the stage and the rostrum. More important, they could both hear and feel the excitement building in the hotel auditorium. The characterless room, its decorations derived effortlessly from airports and waiting rooms all over the world, throbbed with eager anticipation as three thousand women, and a handful of males, prepared to meet their man of destiny. Over the stage somebody had hung a banner bearing the legend THE MAN YOU KNOW.

Standing at the rostrum, some faceless party hack was making his pitch, basking in the reflected glory of the bringer of good tidings.

"And now, ladies and gentlemen—the moment we have all been waiting for. It is for me the greatest pleasure to introduce you to a man who needs no introduction. Ladies and gentlemen, the man who—though he doesn't say it himself—will one day be president of these here United States, Senator *Bobby Stansfield!*"

At the mention of his name, Bobby took a deep breath and launched himself into the sea of noise that erupted all around him. Looking neither to right or left he negotiated the blinding lights and achieved the floodlit rostrum. Now at last he could make contact with the audience, begin the ritualized love-in that was so important to both him and them. The smile was deprecating, the head held low in the universal gesture of humility, but the thrill ran through him. In his ears ran the mealymouthed platitudes of the introduction. He had heard words like that a thousand times in a thousand dreary halls, but he never tired of them. As his father had before him, he loved every single one. Stansfields didn't need food, drink, and vitamins like other mortals; they ran on a different

kind of fuel. What they needed was appreciation, noisy appreciation, public appreciation. It didn't matter what people said and it
didn't matter who said it. The phrases and sentiments were meaningless and irrelevant. The vital thing was that they should be an
expression, however inadequate and unimaginative, of unconditional love.

Bobby held up his hand wearily to stem the flood of enthusiastic
approval. He didn't mean it to work and it didn't. The applause
rolled on like a river, punctuated now by shouts and whoops as
the women went into their act.

"We love ya, Bobby!"

"We're with you, Bobby. All the way. All the way to the White
House!"

The boyish smile played hesitantly around his lips, turning up
remorselessly the sexual rheostat of the audience. A quick movement of the head sent the curl downward on its predestined journey to meet the tidying fingers and, in the intensification of the
applause that the gesture brought, he stared straight back at them,
the suddenly glistening eyes showing that the love was getting to
him, touching him, that he was *theirs*. Again the hand raised to
stem the floodtide of adulation, the mouth opening and closing as
if to speak. The smile again. The laugh. A sideways glance. A
shake of the head.

He was talking to them, but he wasn't speaking. I'm overwhelmed by your welcome, said the body language. Overwhelmed
and deeply touched. I've never been greeted like this. It's the first
time. You're all special. Special people. Special friends. Together
we will march to glory. Your glory, my glory.

This was the point when the aides got into the act. From either
side of the stage, immaculately suited young men burst from the
wings, gesticulating to the audience, pleading with them to allow
the ritual to proceed to the next phase, the one in which the hero
was actually going to *speak*.

Bobby played the resulting silence like a soundless Stradivarius
violin. For long seconds he said nothing. The suspense built. Then
from the back of the auditorium a lone female—fat, fair, and fifty
—told it like it was.

"I love you, Bobby."

Now they could hear the laugh. It was a sort of a chuckle, deep, gurgling, reassuringly genuine, frighteningly charming.

"Well, thank you, ma'am," came the stylish reply. The syllables were cut short, except for the very last word, which went on forever, like a stripper's legs. Patrician, Old World, the gentleman from the southern plantation. Rhett Butler time.

Once again the audience dissolved in a demonstration of collective love. The wit of the man. The intelligence. The brilliance of the repartee. He would eat those Russian peasants for breakfast, castrate the international bankers, make Fidel Castro curse his mother for bearing him.

When the laughter and clapping died down at last, Bobby seemed hesitant, nervous, a little boy lost, tossed on the ocean of the audience's enthusiasm. He straightened the already straight tie and gripped the rostrum firmly in a gesture that said he was going to need all the help and support he could get. All around the crowded room maternal instincts made their appearance, merging in titillating alliance with the sexual ones.

The voice was pitched low, now—deliberately downbeat, leaving lots of space for the long journey to cataclysmic climax when he would make his audience explode in ecstatic joy as he loved them and left them.

"Ladies and gentlemen, you have made me very happy tonight . . . by the warmth of your welcome. I thank you all from the bottom of my heart." Head bowed, Bobby felt the love go out to them, feeling it, being it, as the delicious tears welled up in his shining eyes. The next words positively vibrated with the genuineness of his emotion.

"In Savannah one expects courtesy and good manners—sometimes seems to me Georgians invented those—but I get the feeling tonight I'm among close friends. And, if I may, that's the way I'd like to talk to you."

His voice firmer now, he mouthed the familiar words like a litany.

"The great thing about friends is that you can speak freely to them because you know that at heart they share your values, and that you will not be misunderstood. You may disagree over the little things, but deep down you know you are on the same side. I could give you a list right now of the truths you and I know. Self-evident truths in which we believe passionately . . . but which our enemies disavow."

Bobby loved the next bit. In a way it summed up his very essence. The strength of his belief illuminated the words, and in turn the words invigorated the sentiments.

"We believe in the sanctity of the family . . . in the greatness of our beloved country. We believe in God and in the Christian morality of the Bible. We believe in being strong so that we can protect freedom. We believe in the individual and in his right, unhindered, to do the best for himself and his loved ones."

One by one he ticked off the items on his beloved agenda, punctuating each one with the wave of an outstretched hand, his finger a stabbing emphasis of each point. In front of him the audience hummed with pent-up passion at this appeal to their most basic beliefs, feeding back the enthusiasm of the converted to the preacher.

First establish the mutual interest, the shared creed. Then to identify the enemy.

"But you and I know that some people . . . fellow Americans . . . are working day and night to undermine those institutions and beliefs that we hold so dear. They are the doubters, the pessimists who let no opportunity pass to sneer and scoff at our patriotism. They neglect our defenses, preferring to see us weak in the face of the threat from without. They seek to strip the religion from our schools, to allow the destruction of the innocent unborn, and everywhere they encourage perversion and pornography in the name of their beliefs. Professing faith in freedom, they strive night and day to take away our right to determine our own future—building always the government and the faceless bureaucracy which they themselves seek to control. We, however, are vigilant. We know of their ambitions. We understand Big Brother's plans."

The roar of the applause submerged the words. In the lull they allowed, Bobby searched the wings of the auditorium for Jimmy. Even the stupendous audience feedback was hardly enough for him. He wanted the professional's accolade, too.

Jimmy Baker caught his eye immediately and made the thumbs-up sign. If it was possible, he was somewhere above the seventh heaven. The whiskey sours before dinner may have helped, but it was the way these folk were going for the "candidate" that had provided most of the uplift. For a blissful moment earlier on he had wondered briefly if Bobby Stansfield might be able to get through the entire twenty-minute slot without actually saying anything at all except his courteous response to the lady in the audience. It would have gone down in the record books as the " 'Well, thank you, ma'am,' speech." Now, his professional campaign manager's mind was assessing the phenomenal vote-pulling power of the Stansfield persona.

Jimmy's restless eyes peered into the back of the hall and found the NBC crew. Great. They were catching the action, immortalizing on tape the throbbing excitement his boy could generate. It had taken some doing to persuade the network that the speech would contain a fireworks display that they would need to cover. They seemed to have gotten the message, if the quality of the field producer thay had sent was anything to go by.

The speech was heading for its climax now, and all around the room the emotions surged and raged as Bobby took the audience with him. It was a virtuoso performance, and, suddenly, in the crash of thunderous applause it was over.

Bobby came off the platform almost at the run. All souped up on adrenaline, he was also bathed in sweat, overdosed on attention.

"Great, Bobby. That was just great. NBC got it all in the can. I've never seen an audience like it. Better than Orlando."

Bobby looked relieved. He wiped a weary hand across the famous brow. "They understood, Jim. My kind of people," he said. "Where is it we go tomorrow?"

3

The powerful probing fingers darted mercilessly into the small of Jo-Anne Duke's back, and the shock waves of exquisite pain went roaring into her mind, cold, clean, and invigorating as a line of the purest pharmaceutical coke.

"Oh, Jane, baby, you're strong today," she moaned, half in reproach, half in admiration.

The lithe, muscular masseuse didn't let up for a second. Biceps and triceps rippling, she played the sleek, oiled body like a musical instrument—torturing it, caressing it, controlling it—oblivious to the pleasurable anguish she was causing. Her laid-back voice, soft and confident, provided the running commentary. "What we're doing here is moving the tissues to a new place—allowing the energy work to travel the body. We reorganize the tissues so that the gravity field reinforces the body rather than breaking it down."

"Fer sure," murmured Jo-Anne, luxuriating in the feeling. "Feels like I'm dancing the masochism tango."

Jane didn't laugh. Rolfing was no laughing matter. It was a religion, an article of faith, a way of life. Jokes were just inappropriate.

Her right elbow replaced the unforgiving fingers as her chosen instrument, punishing Jo-Anne for her unwarranted levity, her insufficient respect for the great Dr. Ida Rolf. She leaned in hard on the slippery, suntanned back and smiled grimly as she elicited the first small squeak of pain.

"It's a question of alignment. The body must be aligned with gravity. What we call 'grounding.' As the biological system becomes more stable and orderly your emotions will become more fluid, more free."

The clipped, patrician voice cut into the psychobabble. "Surely you can't believe all that crap."

64

Peter Duke had had enough. It was one thing to watch your wife being massaged poolside in the open air by a long-legged girl with an ass like a dream, but he didn't see why he should have to put up with all the verbal shit. He clinked the ice in the tall glass and sipped moodily at the rum punch as he waited to see the effect of his observation.

Jane tossed her shoulder-length hair petulantly, but said nothing. She reached out for the bottle of moisturizing cream and poured a generous portion onto Jo-Anne's splendid back.

From the prone figure came Jo-Anne's languid drawl. "Oh, Peter, why is it that everything you don't understand always has to be described as *crap?* Couldn't it just be rubbish, or nonsense or something?" Jo-Anne felt like quarreling. It cleared the air like the late afternoon thunderstorms that dropped the unbearable temperatures of the Palm Beach summers. And afterward, sometimes, they would make love, angrily, hungrily, punishing each other's bodies as they ground themselves together. It was about the only time they got to do it nowadays.

"It's crap because it comes out all the time and because it stinks. That's why." Peter stood up. Like the spoiled child he was he wanted the last word. Turning on his heel he disappeared into the shady recesses of the vast house. Over his shoulder, winging like an arrow, came his Parthian shot. "I don't know why you two bull dykes don't just cut the cackle and get it on. That's what it's all about, isn't it?"

The muted whir of the pool filter was the only sound to disturb the lakeside silence as the two women digested Peter Duke's barbed verbal missile. For a minute or two neither spoke, as each wondered how best to use the remark to her own advantage.

"Don't take any notice of him. He's been in a filthy mood all day." It was a sort of apology, and an invitation to a female alliance against men in general and Peter in particular.

Jane was all too happy to join in on that.

She removed the elbow that had been wreaking such havoc with Jo-Anne's vertebrae, and with the flat of both hands swept up and down the statuesque back in the motions of Swedish massage. From her position beside the firm naked buttocks she leaned forward, sending her strong hands north to grip the square shoulders, drawing them back again down the full length of the spine, letting them linger briefly on the perfectly rounded cheeks of Jo-Anne's bottom.

"He seems a little hostile," she agreed. "But it doesn't worry me. I get that all the time."

The long slow strokes continued remorselessly, making twin tracks of oil on the supple, suntanned skin.

Jo-Anne moaned her pleasure.

The massage had surreptitiously changed its character. No longer were the fingers aggressive, invasive, cruel. Now they were capricious, daring, innovative, and Jo-Anne's appreciative response was asking that they stay that way.

Jane was intending to grant that request.

"You're not overheating, are you?" she asked solicitously, her voice warm and caring, wafted on the sandalwood-scented breeze.

"No. I'm fine. Just . . . fine." Jo-Anne drawled the words as she luxuriated in the delicious feeling. This was how she liked it best. Being massaged in the direct sun was the ultimate experience as the ultraviolet rays merged with the infrared ones to unknit the muscle knots and melt the tension. All over her perfectly proportioned body the little beads of sweat fought to escape the thin film of oil that covered her, before exploding into nothingness under Jane's powerful touch.

Sometimes Jane's long soft hair would fall forward like a waterfall onto Jo-Anne's smooth hot skin, sending a tantalizingly ambiguous message into her tingling psyche. Jo-Anne flowed with the rhythm of the massage, in perfect harmony with the knowing hands that worked her body. At times like this she knew she was in paradise and she would allow her spirits to fly away, soaring like an eagle, free and unfettered while down below, spread out like some exotic Persian carpet, lay her life.

In the bleak streets of the truculent city, it had been far from easy. Mostly it was temperature rather than hunger that she remembered. In the Big Apple you were always either too hot or too cold. In the unforgiving winter everything froze and even the restless roaches slowed down. In the steaming cauldron of summer, one's body became a sponge, enervated and flaccid, as it indulged its voracious appetite for the liquid whose only purpose was immediate escape. The money to buy food had always been scarce, but the fingers to take it had been nimble and Jo-Anne had never failed to find the fuel for the awesomely beautiful body that she had somehow known from the earliest times would be her salvation.

And so it had been. Of course, her stepfather had been first. Drunk and horny he had taken her roughly, standing up against the living-room wall. It was one of the great mysteries of her life that she had never suffered the emotional pain that everyone assumed must flow from this presumably traumatic event. Even now she could remember the scene perfectly. It had hurt a bit going in, but not as much as the other twelve-year-old street children predicted. Once inside, it had been a little like having a mild itch scratched— sort of nice but not terrific. The main problem had been her stepfather's precarious balance, helped by neither the position nor the alcohol. Jo-Anne remembered surreptitiously propping him up as she produced the dutiful tears and protests that she felt the situation demanded. The worst thing of the whole business had been the poisonous fumes of the stale breath that had engulfed her; the best part had been the quality of the scene when her mother had walked in to discover them. After that her stepfather had not tried his luck again. For a week or two afterward she had been mildly disappointed. Had she been deficient in some way? Hadn't she given him a good enough time?

Then the whole business had faded from her mind. In the ghetto you didn't have the luxury of indulging in emotional amateur dramatics. There was the business first of survival, and then, in Jo-Anne's case, of advancement. That was another mystery. Where the hell had she discovered ambition? Certainly she hadn't gotten it from her drunken stepfather, her slatternly mother, or the two older brothers who had fingered her in exchange for candy and makeup before she finally walked out on the whole motley crew at the tender age of fourteen.

It had been one small step for Jo-Anne to prostitution, and she had worked her way through the business from the bottom up. In that brief year of scratched existence she had done it all, and in some remarkable way she had managed to keep her feelings out of it, had existed always on some emotional automatic pilot. Come to think of it, that had never changed. It was as true of her now as it had been then, and sometimes she wondered what this thing was that others called conscience. Certainly *she* had never found it a problem.

A pusher had put her in touch with the Upper East Side madam who had smartened her up and fed her before putting her to work in the city's high-class call-girl system. She had been a natural. Her fifteen-year-old tits, pink, pointed, perfect, had slain the businessmen in their hotel rooms, and as her percentage of the take mounted remorselessly she was increasingly able to call the tune from her pretty, one-room studio on Madison. The jocks got grander, the accents tighter, the pricks limper, and the tastes more jaded.

It was around that time, somewhere between the Madison Avenue studio and the apartment on Fifth with a view of the park, that she had discovered girls. The Racquet Club member whose request had resulted in Jo-Anne's first double act had one hell of a lot to answer for. In the musky, sweet scents of the female body, the silky softness of the warm flesh, in the gentle intimacy of a woman's arms, Jo-Anne had found herself. On leaving the Pierre suite where she had first experienced it, she had invited the svelte Jewish girl back to her apartment, and for the first time in her life Jo-Anne had made love with the earth-shattering intensity of the virgin who had discovered how to give not only her body but her soul. For two years she and Rachel had been lovers. By day they had worked as a team doing for money what at night they did freely for each other, and Jo-Anne had been faithful.

Ambition, however, had not slept. The modeling world was the passport to a different society. Men married models. Seldom did they knowingly marry prostitutes. Every afternoon, as Jo-Anne saw in a thousand hotel mirrors the superb body that she was selling for peanuts, she vowed that one day she would flog it for megabucks. One hundred dollars to make some middle-aged lush come. A million big ones to move the cosmetics of some tycoon like Estée Lauder off the drugstore shelf.

Well, she'd gotten there. Right now Estée Lauder's oceanfront estate was only a rifle shot away.

Breaking into the modeling world had been the second step. Jo-Anne had bided her time and sharpened her image. She had spent her money wisely on the right clothes, read everything she could on etiquette and manners, eaten clever food, gotten lots of sleep, exercised fanatically until she looked as good as the best of the girls who stared at her from the covers of *Vogue* and *Cosmo*. It had been a question then of getting the "in." Pauline Parker had been the passport. Something of an institution in the modeling world, Pauline Parker was quite shameless about using her position as head of the prestigious Parker Agency to indulge her passion for beautiful women. Short and stocky, she scored zero out of ten for looks, but at the interview, as she sat in amazement behind the big desk, Jo-Anne had turned her on like a neon sign. Spoiled by oversupply, Pauline came across few enough girls who could do that. She had instantly taken the phenomenal-looking girl onto her books, and, in exchange for the ditching of Rachel, and her moving in as live-in lover, Pauline had set about turning her into a star.

The rest had been easy. A top model met anyone she liked. It was just a question of sorting out the sheep from the goats and not doing anything stupid like falling in love, or going for some cheap con man's line.

Peter Duke had not been a con man and was a card-carrying fully paid-up member of the sheep species. There hadn't been a goat in the Duke family since old Teddy Duke, who had bought the scrubland under which the large proportion of Louisiana's oil lay. Disgustingly rich, spoiled, and headstrong, Peter Duke had fallen hopelessly in love with Pauline Parker's girlfriend, and after a few short, spine-tingling weeks during which he had discovered the meaning of sexual ecstasy, he had proposed to her.

Fearing the overzealous investigations of more circumspect Duke relations, Jo-Anne had capitalized on Peter Duke's self-confident spontaneity. She had spirited him away to the Dominican Republic and married him the next day on the beach, to the exuberant strains of a mariachi band and to the congratulations of two Army generals, one owned by Gulf and Western, the other by the CIA.

The inquisitive finger, racing down the slippery back, seemingly overshot its destination. It plunged precipitously into the cleavage of the tight buttocks and hovered encouragingly on the edge of the erogenous zone—cutting short Jo-Anne's reverie and precipitating her back into the suddenly more interesting here and now.

Jane's voice cut through the mists of memory. "I thought I'd lost you there." Was there an iota of reproach in the remark?

"Just daydreaming. I'm back now."

"Sometimes the Rolfing gets you going down memory lane. Sort of lets you dare to remember." The gentle insinuation that Jo-Anne might need courage to remember was a shot in the dark, but Jane was intuitive. Massage made you like that. You got to know bodies, and from there it was a short step to getting to know minds.

Once again the fingers overstepped their mark in the ambiguous gesture. Was it a mistake or a mistake on purpose?

Jo-Anne pushed it.

"Mmmmmmmm. That was nice."

It was Jane's turn to think. What was she doing? What did she want? What did Mrs. Duke want?

She had been mildly irritated when her client had drifted away from her. Her fingers had summoned her back. But why had she chosen that particular method to regain her attention? Jane had worked the bodies of Palm Beach for nearly three years now, and she was far from insensitive about what was required of her. Massage was relaxing therapy, but beneath the surface, the spark of sensuality danced. Some people liked it to be ignored, others for it to be gently fanned, while a small, but far from insignificant minority wanted the spark to become a raging fire, stoked and banked by the masseuse's fingers until it burst through in the prancing flames of overt sexuality.

It was vital not to get it wrong. With some of her clients, but not all, Jane was more than prepared to go all the way. This was only the second time she had been to the Duke home, but with a little thrill of excitement Jane realized that Jo-Anne was indubitably in that last category. It wasn't her husband's scornful remark, not even the enthusiastic response to her hands' daring. There was something else. Something indefinable, yet instantly knowable. The exciting aura of a woman who liked women. It was as real and as alluring as the warm, perfumed air.

"Does your husband have a fantasy about women making it together? A lot of men do, you know." Somehow the time gap between Peter Duke's remark and the present didn't seem important.

Jo-Anne knew. Firsthand. That was nice. Jane was softening up.

70

Jo-Anne squirmed obviously beneath the pleasing touch and laughed. Soon this thing could be out in the open.

On one level Jane's question had been irrelevant. She didn't really want to know the answer, but she was drawn toward a discussion of the topic. That was the oldest trick in the book. Thinking and talking about things was so often a prelude to action. But to Jo-Anne the question was interesting. What did her husband want?

In the early days in the Big Apple he had seemed so straightforward. Poor-little-rich-boy time. He was suntanned and sexy, preppy as hell, in love with vodka, in love with life, the accelerator firmly pressed to the floor. Like everyone else in his group he had been lazy, spoiled, was in love with his mother, and fought like a dog with the father whom he so exactly resembled. In short, Peter Duke had been typecast and Jo-Anne had made a special study of his category. There had been nothing she hadn't known about him, from the latent homosexuality to his abhorrence of men who wore white shoes and jewelry. In those days he had just loved to screw but he hadn't had a clue about how to do it, and he had never tried it when he was even halfway sober. She had been able to provide a crash course of instruction and he had gone for it.

Before she had scored the marriage certificate and the meal ticket for life, she had played it as straight as lace. No funny stuff to offend patrician susceptibilities. Later on, as the novelty of the toy had begun to wear off and boredom, the curse of his class, had showed its ugly head, Jo-Anne had begun to improvise. In those days he certainly had liked to watch her with girls, and he hadn't had to fantasize about it either—it had been gritty reality. But now? It was difficult to say.

One thing was certain. He wasn't into her anymore. For the last year or two there had been nothing but arguments. Only then did they have sex and on two occasions just a little bit of violence.

To Jo-Anne that was pretty much par for the course. She had never believed in such bourgeois concepts as married bliss, and in her experience knights on white chargers had a way of metamorphosing into bloated toads or worse. No, Peter Duke had already done his bit, and for that she would be eternally grateful. He had married her. She was a Duke. Could anything else possibly matter? And the Dukes were rich. Seriously rich, and certain to remain so.

They had long since diversified out of oil and now the money was everywhere, woven into the very fabric of America, in rolling Texas acres, in rolling stock, in long-term Treasury bills, in Manhattan office blocks. The Duke position in General Motors alone would have financed the deficit of a medium-size banana republic, while the Palm Beach estate, stretching from ocean to lake at the southern end of the island below Worth Avenue, just had to be worth ten million. That wouldn't be a bad marital home to cop if it ever came to divorce. Not that Jo-Anne contemplated divorce. There was no way to follow a Peter Duke. Richer Americans could be counted on fingers, and mostly they were spoken for.

So Jo-Anne had been careful. In Palm Beach society, in which the Dukes were substantial stars, it didn't do to play around—at least with men. There was one thing alone that the American aristocracy could not stand and that was the thought of their wives getting it from another man. The Europeans didn't share that prejudice. For them a young lover and a lot of discretion was often more than acceptable. It took some of the heat off husbands in whom both the flesh *and* the desire had weakened.

So in Palm Beach if you wanted to stay close to the real money, you didn't mess with the tennis pro. Going up market was marginally less dangerous, on the principle that fraternity relationships were as thick if not thicker than blood, and that a man to whom you would cheerfully lend your golf clubs could probably be forgiven for borrowing your wife. Still, with a billion dollars at risk it didn't do to take chances. Which left a problem: what to do about the zipping hormones, the urges of incredible strength whose power could neither be repressed, sublimated, nor wished away.

Jo-Anne had found her solution, and it was the one that had always worked so well for her. Women. Now, in the heady social atmosphere of Palm Beach charity galas, in the smooth, slick ambiance of the Bath and Tennis Club, in the smartly decorated salons and bedrooms of the sleek oceangoing yachts, she indulged her illicit desires. Bored, underoccupied, neglected by their husbands, not daring to risk the divorce that a heterosexual affair might threaten, the wives of the richest society on earth succumbed in turn to Jo-Anne's charms.

Did Peter know about it? Jo-Anne had often wondered. If so, he was apparently more than prepared to turn a blind eye. Perhaps, as the masseuse had suggested, he still got a vicarious thrill out of imagining her with other girls. Certainly his last remark hinted at something like that. Whatever. By his silence he had condoned it. She was in the clear. Nothing else mattered.

Well, something else did.

In Jane's electric fingertips Jo-Anne could detect the early signs of panic. Floating, drifting up and down her back, the friction was now reduced, and her skin rather than the firm underlying muscle was the target. The nails touched her lightly and the center of operations moved inexorably lower as the fingers became more bold, roaming longingly over the proud upturned buttocks, sometimes pushing down hard, crushing Jo-Anne's pelvis against the black leather of the massage table.

Slowly, surely, Jo-Anne responded to the new meanings of the touch, allowing her firm rump to ride up to meet Jane's eager hands. At last the two bodies were speaking to each other directly. There would be no need of further conversation.

It was going to happen.

The Negro's deferential voice blew it all away.

"Mr. Duke says to tell you you're running late for the party." Standing at his mistress's head, seemingly oblivious of her nakedness, the white-coated servant delivered his message with total impassivity.

Suspended in space in the jingle-jangle moment of sexual arousal, Jo-Anne cursed openly. As the pile of carefully constructed bricks of passion toppled about her, irritation filled the gap so recently vacated by desire.

Screw them all. Peter, Jane, black servants, the world.

With a fluid, sinuous movement she slipped off the massage table, grabbed the monogrammed rough white terrycloth dressing gown from the hands of the servant, and stalked off toward the house. Over her shoulder, without smiling, she said, "Some other time, Jane. Okay?"

The cold Carrara marble beneath her feet went some way toward calming Jo-Anne's suddenly foul temper. It was cool in here, the unrelenting sunlight blocked out, the air circulated by the eight large ceiling fans. For Jo-Anne it was the best room in the whole remarkable house—the deep, comfortable sofas, the inch-and-a-half-thick glass tables, great bowls of white gardenias—the whites and different shades of oatmeal saved from lack of adventure by the stunning colors of the paintings. Jackson Pollock, Rothko, de Kooning—the best examples of the greatest artists of the Abstract Expressionist movement chosen by her personally from the famed Duke collection in Houston. There was not a museum director in the world who would not cheerfully have given a testicle to possess one tenth of the room's paintings. The curator at Houston had been in tears as Jo-Anne had made her choice, stalking through the high-ceilinged, air-conditioned rooms, legal pad in hand, Tom Wesselman tits straining against a tight T-shirt, Allen Jones legs rearing suggestively out of dangerous Manolo Blahnik shoes. Unfailingly she had gone for the most important paintings—the ones that couldn't be replaced with mere money, and now the results of her expedition were all around her, existing solely for her private consumption, removed from the prying eyes of the Texan hoi polloi forever.

Casting herself down languorously on the welcoming sofa, she stretched herself out—a graceful feline, preening itself in blissful self-congratulation. It was a long way from the hungry, steamy streets. The whole western wall of the room was arranged as electrically operated sliding doors, the smoked-glass panels screening the ubiquitous sun. In the middle they were retracted and Jo-Anne's field of vision was clear to the sixty-foot pool with its separate cabana, the bright green lawns, smooth as the baize of a billiard table, the sensuously rounded Henry Moore bronze sculptures scattered on the grass like smooth pebbles dotted capriciously on a sea-washed beach. By the pool Jane was folding her table crossly—a nomadic Arab packing away her tent before moving on—her back bent in the graceful curve of a Modigliani line drawing.

Jo-Anne sighed appreciatively. It was good, all of it. The art, Jane's body, the landscape, the life she had won for herself. Nobody would take this away from her. Not a living soul. Certainly no soul who would not die in the attempt. That much she swore to herself. No, the problem, if there was one at all, was where to go from here. Hanging on to what you had was about as exciting as hearing her husband's views on the likely course of interest rates. Okay, so she tried to inject a little danger into the proceedings from time to time, but compared to the survival game on the Big Apple's streets, it was the softest of softball.

In Palm Beach the hottest game in town was social climbing. There at least people got hurt. They didn't bleed openly, but they made up for that in the quantity and quality of their tears. Jo-Anne had learned the game's rules in a long afternoon and was now a past mistress of it. The trick was to keep your ass and your shoe leather in the faces of the people on the rung below. A few rungs below that you could give people a leg up, aiming always for the downward displacement of those who aspired to one's own position. Once one had achieved that objective, the former allies would themselves become fierce adversaries as they tried with all their might to steal your rung. The higher you got the more difficult, and the more desirable, became the upward mobility. In that, the climbing game resembled real life. Peter and Jo-Anne Duke of course were already in the rarefied stratosphere when they had, at Jo-Anne's instigation, begun to play.

Still, once you were in the contest you had to struggle onward, bravely, courageously, employing cunning, dirty tricks, and very large quantities of money, ignoring the emotional or financial cost until the top of the mountain had been reached. And at the top of the mountain, high above the clouds, beyond the racing of the rats, at the right hand of God the Father Almighty, was Marjorie du Pont Donahue. The queen of Palm Beach. The one Jo-Anne Duke wanted to *be*.

Jo-Anne let out a deep sigh and hugged the dressing gown close to her. Some raddled old trout with varicose veins like a relief map of Europe and the mind of a black widow spider: Marjorie du Pont Donahue, the rat-bag with the fortune that made even the Dukes look like small time, the bag of bones held together by leather skin whose offhand remarks could cut an unlucky social mountaineer in two.

Nobody knew why she was the queen. Nobody knew how she had gotten there. But the players of the game all knew that she *was* the queen, and the only queen, and they all paid homage at her court. Marjorie Donahue was the first thing they thought about in the morning, and their last shining vision before they went to bed at night. In between the darkness and the dawn they would dream of her—of her dinner-party invitations arriving on the silver salver, of her crackling voice on their cordless telephones, of the rasping touch of her wrinkled hand.

Unbelievably, Jo-Anne herself had been drawn into the spider's web. The game was no longer absurd. Instead, it was all-consuming. As a fish swimming in Palm Beach waters, one became oblivious to the reality of the world outside. Jo-Anne was more than happy to be one of them, just as long as she was the hunter and not the hunted—that her teeth were sharper, her bite more deadly than that of the other inhabitants of the aquarium. So far it had been just that.

Tonight there would be another round. The Planned Parenthood Victorian Picnic. Jo-Anne didn't even try to suppress the smile at the thought of it. Charity dances were a joke in themselves, but Planned Parenthood? In a way she supposed she ought to have been considered a charter member. In prostitution there were two "no-no's"—pregnancy and the pox. Both reduced one's income-making capacity, that ultimate sin. Jo-Anne shuddered to think how many men had been inside her—a thousand, two thousand? —but not one of them had succeeded in impregnating her. Planned Parenthood indeed. Planned Parenthood owed her a medal. Perhaps she would arrange a special announcement. "Ladies and gentlemen. May I have your attention please. Jo-Anne Duke has had more screws than you've had hot dinners without getting pregnant. Planned Parenthood would like to recognize her services publicly by . . ."

Jo-Anne laughed out loud at the outrageous thought. Boy, that would really be dropping it on the fan. For years she had worked to bury her past, and she had been completely successful. Not a whisper had survived. Not a single rumor had found the fertile soil in which grew the Palm Beach grapevine, and she prayed that it would stay that way. She couldn't help feeling that now she was in the clear. The Duke name and her Donahue friendship were the most powerful possessions. With those two talismans a girl could enter the very gates of hell unafraid.

Contentedly Jo-Anne gazed up at the brilliant de Kooning. Why was the girl with the big tits smiling like that as she stood next to her bicycle? She looked mighty pleased with herself. Had she just spread her legs for the bank manager and bought the bicycle with the proceeds? Little things, little minds, she thought absent-mindedly. What was *her* bicycle? The sleek hundred-and-twenty-foot oceangoing Jon Bannenberg yacht bobbing on the waters of Lake Worth just the other side of the twelve-foot ficus hedge? The sky-blue Lear jet soaking up the sun in the Bennett Aviation compound at the West Palm International Airport? Or perhaps it was her splendid-looking husband himself, six feet of fifty-year-old muscle and breeding, and with just a touch of blood in his vodka-filled veins.

Damn. The thought of Peter clouded her mood. Really, he had been impossible lately, rude and indifferent, his previously reliable sense of humor absent. Perhaps it was the drink. *Palm Beach Life* said it made you irritable.

For sure it wasn't a shortage of sex. It was no secret that he screwed everything that moved and even, in Jo-Anne's opinion, one or two women for whom any movement at all had become difficult. But that had never been a problem. It was often irritating but not a problem problem. To hell with it. She needed a drink if she was going to get through this evening.

She hardly raised her voice. Certainly didn't bother to look around. There would be a servant there. Hopefully, Caesar. He seemed to understand about caiparinhos.

"Can somebody make me a caiparinho?"

A minute or two later the glass was in her hands. Sometimes she preferred the tequila base, but today she was glad it was white rum. The shiny green crushed limes nestled in among the chunks of ice and she drank deep on the bittersweet liquid. The Brazilians called it a peasant girl. Well, she liked the taste of peasant girls, Brazilian or otherwise. Taking a deep breath, and revitalized by the first warming sensations as the strong spirit hit her empty stomach, she stood up and walked toward the marble staircase.

In the master bedroom on the first floor the angry colors of the Abstract Expressionists were merely an exciting memory. Here all was pastel peace—gentle Renoirs, soothing Manets, a deeply relaxing Pissarro. The huge four-poster bed dominated the room, its football-field size allowing exotic acrobatics, or almost total privacy from one's bedmate. Recently it had been the latter.

Jo-Anne looked around. Peter was in here somewhere. In his dressing room? On the fifty-foot veranda with its view of Lake Worth and the mainland?

She heard the click of the replaced telephone receiver.

"There you are. About time. The cars are organized for six thirty. What a time to fix a massage." The aggressive, truculent voice drifted in through the open window.

"Oh, fuck off, Peter. Don't give me a hassle. Who the hell wants to get to this ridiculous party before eight o'clock anyway? Riding on carousels and having my fortune told I can do without. When I want to know my fortune I call the accountant."

Jo-Anne stalked through the open doors onto the balcony. Peter was all dressed up. Standard Palm Beach evening wear. Kilgour, French and Stanbury navy-blue double-breasted blazer, Everglades Club buttons, sky-blue-and-white dotted silk tie from Turnbull and Asser in London, Gucci loafers worn without socks, dark gray razor-creased worsted pants. The sunburned face, greased hair, graying slightly at the temples, and a vague but indefinable flavor of the most understated cologne made up the picture of plutocratic excellence.

He looked great. It was just a drag that there would be two hundred Identikit look-alikes under the big top at the Flagler Museum. Sartorial daring was no part of the Palm Beach picture, and people had been socially extinguished for crimes no greater than the wearing of white shoes or synthetic-fiber shirts.

Peter Duke snarled back, "Believe it or not I am not a carousel fiend either, but we are meeting Marjorie *and* Stansfield and we said we'd be there at seven. I realize of course that doing what you promise to do is not something you learned on mother's knee. However, I was always brought up to keep my word."

Bastard, thought Jo-Anne. That was hitting low. It wasn't like Peter to throw the class thing at her. Something was definitely up.

Still, trading insults was something of a specialty for her. She had for sure learned *that* from her mother. She let rip.

"Frankly, I'm surprised you have the nerve to bring *your*

mother into all this. Everyone says the old lush hardly knew your name, and that you were farmed out to all those English nannies. The only thing you ever learned from her was to drink too much."

Peter stood stock still. Knuckles white, his face suffused with blood, he pulsated with anger and hatred.

Jo-Anne wondered momentarily if she had gone too far. Employing the old Arab ruse of insulting an adversary's mother could always be relied on for strong reactions, but she hadn't expected this.

"You tramp," he managed at last, spitting the words out through clamped teeth. "I'll bury you for that. Do you hear me? *Bury you*." His voice rose to a crescendo, cracking with the strain of the violent emotion that shook him. "Don't you ever dare mention my mother again. Do you hear me? *Do you hear me?*"

Me and the rest of Palm Beach, thought Jo-Anne. "Oh, why are you always such a *child,* Peter," she said aloud, in apparent despair as she turned around and walked back into the bedroom.

Jo-Anne was laughing helplessly. Tears had appeared to order and her whole body shook with uncontrollable hilarity. But the really funny thing was that Marjorie's joke hadn't been funny at all. Marjorie Donahue had long since ceased to care about counterfeit emotions. She had been dealing in that currency for far too long, and now she had even lost the facility to recognize the real thing. For her the important element was power. When people failed to laugh at her dirty stories it didn't mean they were lacking in humor—that was irrelevant. The significant message would be that her power was on the wane, that her courtiers were on the verge of some violent palace coup. So, she laughed back at Jo-Anne and filed the information away in the ancient but still awesomely efficient filing cabinet that was her mind. Jo-Anne could be counted on. Jo-Anne was loyal. Jo-Anne would still get favors. Jo-Anne's enemies would be her enemies.

"Oh, Marjorie. Why can't I tell jokes like that?" Jo-Anne forced out the words through the gales of laughter.

Marjorie Donahue preened herself, while around the table the other dinner-party guests mentally reached for the vomit bag. They'd all laughed at the queen's joke too, but none of them had been as willing or as able to go so convincingly far over the top as Jo-Anne. All had made the fatal mistake of underestimating a successful person's vanity. Jo-Anne alone had recognized that in the department of flattery nothing succeeded like excess. It was only the moderately successful people in life who affected a dislike for sycophants. The real winners couldn't get enough of them.

The Duke table was very definitely the top spot for the top dogs, and all around the lesser players craned their necks to see what was going on and to identify those who by their presence among the mighty were on the up and up. Jo-Anne stared proudly back at the envious heads, shouting a welcome here, delivering a glassy rebuke there, as she reveled in the public demonstration of her social-climbing skills. The heady feeling gripped her, as she saw the envy in a hundred eyes. And not just any eyes. This was not the untutored, unconditional adoration of common people for some movie idol. These eyes had class. There were Vanderbilts out there, and Fords, as well as sleek counts of obscure Italian origin; the inevitable English, poor as church mice but dramatically well dressed, sponging like hell off everyone in return for a few finely turned phrases; and a group of truculent Frenchmen, perpetually irritated by the fact that nobody could or would speak their half-dead language. All of them would have given whatever they had to give to be sitting at Jo-Anne's table.

Marjorie Donahue peered suspiciously around the table at her courtiers—a bit like a lion tamer in a circus cage.

"I do so *enjoy* dirty jokes," she said to no one in particular. "Makes a change from talking about money and servants, although sometimes those are rather cruder topics."

Jo-Anne laughed loudly.

"You're so right, Marjorie. You should hear Peter on interest rates. It's positively disgusting."

She made a face that managed to suggest that her husband discussing any topic at all was positively disgusting.

He scowled across the table at her.

"Well, dear, if it *has* to be money I'd like to hear what the senator has to say about the budget deficit." Ostentatiously she stifled a yawn. At this table and in this town she was the boss and she wanted everyone to know it. If that meant poking a little gentle fun at the powerful senator, then so be it.

Bobby didn't mind one bit. The self-confidence was armor-plated.

"Funny you should say that, Marjorie." Bobby Stansfield's voice was calm, and around it danced the ghost of a dry humor. "You know, if you and Jo-Anne got together and made a small contribution from your personal funds, I think we could solve the deficit problem right here."

That was nice. They were all rich as well. Rich, beautiful, and successful. The mood of mutual self-congratulation hung heavily in the air, merging easily with the scent of the fifty white gardenias that floated in the Irish Waterford glass bowl in the center of the table.

Bobby turned to Jo-Anne.

"Would you like to dance?"

"Why, thank you, senator."

Jo-Anne mimicked a Southern belle drawl.

He smiled across the table at Peter Duke.

"You don't mind if I borrow your wife? I might never bring her back."

Peter Duke joined in the general laughter, but inside he wasn't laughing. You can take the cunt. She's just about what you deserve, you self-satisfied, stuck-up, pompous ass, he wanted to say. Since childhood days Dukes and Stansfields had enjoyed an uneasy friendship. In many ways they had a lot in common—old, patrician, Republican Palm Beach families, with vast fortunes and shared prejudices. There were, however, two problems that tended inevitably to sour relationships. The first was that the Dukes were much, much richer than the Stansfields. The second was that the Stansfields were far, far more successful than the Dukes.

The bone of contention had two infinitely gnawable ends. Dukes were jealous of the Stansfields' power, and the attention that power brought. To compensate they accused the Stansfields of being common, lacking in class, courting media attention, being overactive philistines who didn't know how to behave. The Stansfields were envious of the phenomenal Duke wealth and of their nationwide reputation as sophisticated patrons of the arts. To get even, they accused the Dukes of being self-centered layabouts who asked not what they could do for their country, who drank too much and did too little, who thought a great deal of themselves for no better reason than that their ancestor had locked into Louisiana's oil.

That having been said, the families were too alike to afford to fall out openly. Palm Beach was a small town, and there were other enemies who could only profit from a Duke-Stansfield vendetta. Teddy Kennedy, for example. When old Stansfield had died, his eldest son Bobby had inherited his well-oiled political machine and, soon after, his Senate seat. Bobby was flashily good looking and the standard bearer of the Stansfield political dynasty; some of the more aware pundits were already muttering about his making a bid for the presidency. It was likely that in the future his Democratic opponent might be his North Ocean Boulevard neighbor, Teddy Kennedy—the memories of Chappaquiddick perhaps dulled by the passage of time and by sterling work in the Senate.

No true Palm Beacher who was welcome in the Everglades Club viewed the disturbing possibility of a second Kennedy presidency with anything but naked horror. Kennedys were Democrats and Democrats were socialists, who were, of course, the next best thing to communists. All ranks would have to be closed to defeat a Kennedy. The result of all this was that although Peter Duke's thoughts about Bobby Stansfield were seldom charitable, he had actually donated to his Senate election campaign. In turn Bobby had not only accepted the gift graciously; he had on more than one occasion intervened in Washington on behalf of Duke business interests, despite his personal dislike of Peter Duke—a dislike that in no way included his pretty, vivacious wife.

Bobby threaded his way between the closely packed tables toward the dance floor. It was a regal progress. Everyone fought for his attention—hands reaching out to grab the sleeve of his immaculately cut dinner jacket, the rasping welcomes of the gravelly voiced society matrons, the raucous jokes of the good-ol'-boy battalions, their tongues well oiled by the predinner martinis. Bobby swam effortlessly across the sea of popularity, an impressed Jo-Anne following in his wake. For every remark, he had the appropriate one-liner, pitched at just the right level, matching ounce for ounce the seriousness or frivolity of those who had made it. In the short time it took him to reach the floor he had smiled and frowned, charmed and flirted, made promises and accepted them. As Jo-Anne watched the strong back with its wide, sculpted shoulders, she was lost in admiration of the performance. This was the art of the born politician. He had offended no one, massaged egos, consolidated votes. In his position, Jo-Anne would not have resisted the temptation to spread a little pain with the pleasure. That was the difference between the professional and the amateur.

On the edge of the dance floor he turned toward her, his arms held out to take hers. The smile was warm but with an edge of humor. It said that he was attracted to her, and that she was about to have to deal with that fact.

Jo-Anne smiled right back. Handling men had never been a problem. In this case it was going to be a pleasure.

"Do you know this is the first time we've danced together?" Bobby pretended to be hurt.

"Surely you weren't too shy to ask. God knows you've had enough opportunity. Sometimes I think the only damn thing we do in this town is dance."

"Well, you know what they say—you don't go to a ball to dance. You go to look out for a wife, to look after a wife, or to look after somebody else's wife."

Bobby looked right into her eyes as he said that, and swirled her self-confidently into the mainstream of dancers. On the bandstand, Joe Renée and his orchestra, veterans of a thousand Palm Beach balls, told Dolly for the umpteenth time that she was looking swell.

"Are you looking after somebody else's wife right now, Bobby?" She squeezed the strong hand and moved in a little bit closer, conscious of the eyes upon them. Flirting on the dance floor was permissible in Palm Beach. That was one of the reasons there were so many dances.

In answer, he bent forward and whispered in her ear. "We should have an affair, you know." That was the Stansfield way. Up front. No time wasted. The smell of self-confidence all over the place.

"I don't cheat on my husband." Jo-Anne laughed flirtatiously as she moved in closer.

"There's always a first time."

"Not for me. Until death us do part."

"Maybe we should try to arrange that."

They both laughed as he swung her exuberantly across the room. Both Joe Renée and the endless Dolly were still going strong.

God, you're attractive, thought Jo-Anne. Fabulous looking. Famous as hell. A man of the future who knew how to make the present sparkle like diamonds. But, compared to Peter Duke, a pauper. Richer by far than most Americans could ever hope to be, here in Palm Beach he was a financial minnow. What a pity. God, in his wisdom, had dealt fairly, and Bobby Stansfield missed by that all important card the royal straight flush. Which was why a flirtation was all he would ever get from her, as long as she was Mrs. Peter Duke.

"Come on, Bobby, stop practicing your charms on a married woman. Let's go and have a ride on the carousel. I'd never get Peter on it. He'd be sick, or something boring."

Outside the marquee, in the grounds of Henry Morrison Flagler's museum, a fairground setting had been created for the Planned Parenthood ball. There were jugs of ice-cold martinis on long, white-linen-covered trestle tables, a fortuneteller and a palmist, and a sparkling, magical carousel, its red-and-white horses rising and falling to the evocative sound of an old fairground organ. The cream of the town's society mingled beneath the palm trees, many of them dressed in the Victorian costume that was the "picnic's" theme, the men wearing the traditional straw boaters that had been given to them on arrival.

Jo-Anne had ignored the fancy dress on the principle that modern women had on the whole done better than Victorian ones. She wore a knee-length Anne Klein silk crepe dress of the purest white, slit to the calf on one side and covered in bugle beads that shimmered and shone as she moved. From time to time a long brown leg flashed interestingly, and the rest of her, dramatic and alluring, was hardly concealed at all by the flimsy material. Jo-Anne didn't detract from the beautiful sexual simplicity of the dress by wearing jewelry. In that she was almost alone. All around her the rocks of the plutocracy flashed and sparkled, but Jo-Anne, who could have afforded any of them and all of them, confined herself to simple one-carat diamond-stud earrings.

On the carousel, jammed tightly against her in the wooden saddle built for one, Bobby Stansfield didn't give up. Stansfields never gave up. "We bachelors get lonely, you know."

"That's not what I heard. Word is there's more ass up in the North End on the weekends than Heinz has varieties."

Bobby Stansfield's laugh was almost the best thing about him. It was wicked, and uninhibited, charming and totally real. Jo-Anne felt the danger signs within her. This man was just a bit too attractive, and the stakes were high. It would be safer back at the table.

When the music stopped she was firm. "Come on, Bobby. Time to eat. I could eat a horse, I'm so hungry."

Taking his hand in hers she lead him back to the marquee.

Horses not being evident among the courses on the menu, Jo-Anne had to struggle through a sumptuous cold buffet of Scots salmon flown in from the Dee that afternoon, Maine lobsters, Florida Bay prawns, cracked crab, sliced filet mignon, and crisp apple pie. There was a Bâtard Montrachet 1973 with the mollusks, the crustaceans, and the fish, a mouth-watering Chateau Beychevelle 1966 with the beef, and a Dom Pérignon '71 with the pie.

With the coffee the party began to go liquid in more senses of the word than one. During the "picnic" the tables had more or less hung together, the members of each dancing and talking among themselves. Now, as the alcohol liberated the party's collective psyche, lines of communication between the guests loosened up, and that well-known species, the table hopper, began to appear. The old hands recognized this as the most dangerous, but also the most promising, time of all for a little judicious social climbing. The booze had injected courage into the socially fainthearted, but it had impaired judgment, too, and the floor of the tent was positively littered with banana skins for the unwary. During this stage the "haves" sat tight as they prepared to receive homage from the "have-nots." The aim of the upwardly mobile parvenus was to secure a seat at the table of a group of their social superiors. The game plan of the top dogs was to repel boarders as far as possible except in those cases where it had been decided that some protégé needed a visible "leg up" the ladder. The Duke party was the honey pot around which the most ambitious bees buzzed. Marjorie Donahue's presence always guaranteed that.

Two or three unlucky Palm Beachers had already gotten their coded messages to "walk on" by the time Eleanor Peacock arrived. Eleanor was a difficult one. A fully paid-up member of one of the town's oldest families, she had, however, never quite made it in the social swim. Her parties were unexciting, and her food and flower arrangements were as dull and lacking in inspiration as her placements. Also, the Peacocks were not rich. Well born certainly, and members of all the right clubs, but the North End house wasn't on the beach or the lake, and the summer trips to Connecticut were shorter than was strictly desirable. And Arch Peacock worked. That in itself was not a disaster, but it certainly didn't score bonus points in a town where the smart thing was to inherit old money and spend one's time looking after it, or rather supervising others as they looked after it.

The fact that she was not a top dog in Palm Beach society irritated Eleanor Peacock, and she had scratched at the itch until it had become an angry, livid sore, painfully obvious for all to see. Sometimes she would cover it over, all sweetness and light, as she fought for the place in the sun that she felt was rightfully hers. At others she would lapse into a cynical, explosive aggression during which her bile would be directed menacingly at those she felt had wrongfully taken her place. Jo-Anne was an obvious target. Obscure origins, and too good looking by half. On several occasions Eleanor had tried to take her on, but she had always come off the worse in the clinches.

Tonight, however, she reckoned she had some very special ammunition and she was going to fire it to maximum effect. Both Peter Duke and—far more important—Marjorie Donahue would be there to watch her deliver the broadside that would sink Jo-Anne Duke for good. All evening she had savored what she knew would be her triumph as she had tucked into the wine. Now in full sail, her white taffeta dress billowing in the breeze created by her confident approach, she bore down on the Duke table as heads craned to see whether she would do better than the three aspirants who had already failed.

Jo-Anne saw her old adversary coming and noted the red flush on the chest bone above the ample if shapeless bosom and beneath the rather mean diamond choker. Her nose scented trouble. A veteran of a thousand such skirmishes, Jo-Anne sought out her most powerful ally. Tonight Peter would be no help at all. He had been scowling at her all evening.

Leaning across the table she laid her hand on Marjorie's weath-erbeaten forearm, kneading the wrinkled skin. "Oh, Marjorie, I'm *so* glad you could come tonight. I haven't laughed so much for *weeks*—since the Heart Ball."

Marjorie had been at their table at that one, too.

"Hello, everyone."

Eleanor Peacock's forced bonhomie broke over the table like a big wet wave. With various degrees of enthusiasm, none of them substantial, muttered welcomes were returned.

"Marjorie, you're looking wonderful as usual," Eleanor lied in-gratiatingly. The old bag looked as if she had some terminal dis-ease.

Taper at the ready, she prepared her salvo as she turned threat-eningly toward Jo-Anne.

"Oh, Jo-Anne, I didn't see you there," she lied. "Do you know I met the most *extraordinary* person in New York the other day? He said he used to know you really well." To everyone at the table with the glaring exception of Jo-Anne, Eleanor Peacock's words were completely innocent. It was a standard table hopper's open-ing gambit. Eleanor was about to ingratiate herself with her social superiors by claiming a shared friend. The more alert might have wondered about the word "extraordinary," but nobody did.

The effect on Jo-Anne, however, was electric. Any mention of New York made her nervous as hell, and from the lips of Eleanor Peacock the mention was grotesquely significant. Jo-Anne alone picked up on the cruel smile and the horrendous innuendos. The "know," for instance, had been given almost biblical connota-tions, and the "really well" meant *really* well.

For the first time in years, Jo-Anne Duke felt the emotion of fear. It rushed through her body like a tidal wave, blotting out everything, washing away all thought, paralyzing her with its dreadful force. Oh, God! Not now. Not here. In front of the queen. In front of her husband. In front of Senator Stansfield. She felt the blood drain from her face and watched her right hand move in slow motion toward her untouched glass of water as if by this unneces-sary movement she was proving to herself that she still had some control over her destiny. In blissful ignorance of the drama that was being played, the rest of the table carried on as if nothing had happened. Eleanor Peacock was being "endured." General con-

versation wouldn't be interrupted for long before Marjorie Donahue would "move her on" with a few placating phrases. It was the
sort of minor irritation that was part of the onerous burdens of
social superstardom.

The thoughts were coming together again now and Jo-Anne
fought to organize them in the milliseconds left before disaster
struck. What did this dreadful woman know? How much, and in
what detail? And if she knew it all would she say it now? All of it?

"Oh, really," her voice said.

As she spoke Jo-Anne took in the Teflon determination in the
Peacock eyes, the glassy patina painted on by the white burgundy
and the claret. Dear God. This was it. She was going to be exposed.

"Yes, it was really interesting. It was at a charity gala for the
New York police department, and I found myself sitting next to
this character called Krumpe . . ."

Krumpe. Krumpe. Krumpe. The name rolled around in Jo-
Anne's mind like an undetonated mine. Krumpe. Fat and mean.
Krumpe, cruel and revengeful. Krumpe who'd screwed her in exchange for his silence. Lieutenant Krumpe of Vice. On the wings
of memory she soared like an eagle over the sordid fields of her
past, and beneath her, scurrying about like a rat in a sewer, was
Leo Krumpe. Krumpe had blown away the morals charges, tipped
her off about the drug busts, protected her from violent pimps and
outraged johns. But he had exacted a terrible payment. In exchange he had demanded and received the run of her body, and
even now at the top of the Palm Beach pinnacle she could feel the
fetid, alcohol-sodden breath on her skin, the rough touch of the
stubbled cheek, the dreadful heaviness of the short, squat body as
it straddled her. When Peter Duke had entered her life, she discarded Krumpe like a used condom, and almost certainly he had
never forgiven her. Now from the grave of her past his evil finger
was reaching out to touch her.

She was at the interface. Up till this second she was in the clear.
A good friend in New York called Krumpe. Dear old Leo. I hope
you gave him my love. No relation to the Palm Beach plumbers of
the same name. Ha! Ha! Haven't seen him in years. Always remember his wonderful Polish jokes. But in a few seconds the cat
would be out of the bag and a lifetime's work would be destroyed.

She must play for time, summon allies, call in I.O.U.'s.

Her unsteady hand found the glass of water, brushed against its side, and sent it crashing from the table to the floor. At the same time she turned to Marjorie Donahue and allowed her stricken face to do the talking. No actress had won an Oscar with a better performance than Jo-Anne's now. Everything was there in her eyes. The fear, the helplessness, the awful need. She was white as a sheet and her lip was trembling as her left hand felt for the scrawny forearm of the only person who could save her.

Marjorie Donahue saw it all, and the ancient mind weighed it up. Jo-Anne was in mortal danger. And the threat was coming from Eleanor Peacock. That much was immediately clear. But what threat? It was impossible to say. She hadn't really been listening. One never made a point of listening to Eleanor. Something about New York. Some mutual friend? The hand that gripped her and the face that beseeched spoke of the urgency. The urgency for her intervention. But why? What was to be said? Time was clearly of the essence. She would have to rely on her social instinct; seldom had it let her down. Jo-Anne was a friend. She laughed at her jokes; she flattered her extravagantly. At her age and in her position, what more could one ask for? Eleanor Peacock, however, had never been a fawning courtier. While far from being an enemy, she was a million miles from the inner circle. She had tried to play the game all right, but there had always been something held back —almost as if she subscribed to the heretical idea that there were other things in the world besides Palm Beach and its social scene. And no money to speak of. Perhaps if there had been charm and good looks in sufficient quantities to offset the disadvantage of relative poverty, she might have been forgiven. But in those departments she was deficient too. No, in the stone, paper, scissors game that they played in this town there could be only one winner in a confrontation between Peacocks and Dukes. Jo-Anne must prevail. No question.

Eleanor puffed herself up like a balloon as she prepared to launch the missiles that would destroy Jo-Anne. But before she could speak, the queen spoke, and it was with all the sweet reason of a nice old lady.

"Eleanor, dear. I'm glad you popped by. You remember I mentioned the possibility of your doing the junior chairman stint for the Red Cross Ball next year. Well, on more mature reflection I think you're a bit inexperienced for it. So I think we'd better forget it. Oh, and thank you for that invitation to drinks next week, but I'm afraid I won't be able to come. I'm surprised you chose next week for your party. What with everything else going on, I'd imagine quite a lot of people won't be able to make it.''

Everyone saw the blood leave Eleanor Peacock's face as they witnessed the social execution. Apart from Jo-Anne, all were unaware of the cause. As far as the rest of the table were concerned this was public retribution for some prior crime, Marjorie Donahue's meting out justice for some peccadillo—Eleanor's befriending of a Donahue enemy, a treacherous remark of Eleanor's finding its way back to the Donahue ear. Something like that. All were far too caught up in the guts and the gore to recognize that Jo-Anne herself had had a significant part in it.

No ritually slaughtered lamb could have bled so fast and so comprehensively as Eleanor Peacock. The social lifeblood drained from her at the touch of Marjorie Donahue's deft dagger, and nobody doubted that her days in Palm Beach society were gone forever. Her ''party'' next week would be as well attended as a wife-swap evening given by a host who was rumored to have the clap.

In case there should be the merest shadow of doubt, the queen turned the knife in the wound. Overkill.

''Anyway, Eleanor dear, I'm sure we are all thrilled you enjoyed New York. I suspect that in the future you'll be spending *much* more time there.''

4

*T*he excitement in the air crackled like electricity. On the surface nothing much was happening; the girls stood around on the wooden workout floor chatting nervously, giggling occasionally. From time to time there was an extravagant yawn— always a sign of tension.

Lisa was no exception. She, too, was affecting a nonchalance she didn't feel, a bravado she imagined the occasion demanded, but inside all was turmoil. Perched on the edge of the receptionist's desk, long legs dangling aimlessly, she smiled down at Maggie.

"Well, Maggs, a few more minutes and then . . . instant fame."

She laughed and looked at her watch for the hundredth time. They were ten and a half minutes late.

"You don't think they'll cancel," said Maggie dubiously.

"No way, sweetheart. My gym's news, and they need news. We're doing them a favor." Even Lisa had to admit that didn't ring true. West Palm TV's "Focus" program could almost certainly struggle on without Lisa Starr.

"Does everything look all right?" Maggie peered unhappily around the glittering, gleaming gymnasium. The question, of course, was superfluous, but at moments like this the free-floating anxiety needed a home and the mind searched desperately to find one.

"Oh, come on, Maggie. Everything's immaculate. You know it is."

That was true. Old Weiss's money was scattered all over the room, but it wasn't in dollar bills. The shining Nautilus machines, closely resembling fiendish instruments of cunning Medieval torture, took up the whole north wall of the oak-floored exercise area. They had been delivered factory fresh the week before—twenty thousand dollars' worth of mechanical pain. There were biceps machines, triceps machines, stomach flatteners, trapezius strengtheners, and all were arranged in strict scientific order, each of the body's muscle groups catered to in turn.

To reach them you had to cross the aerobics floor, its highly polished wood brand new, not yet scuffed and mellowed by the assault of a thousand pounding sneakers. All around, the mirrored walls threw back the reflections, pandering to the narcissistic element that seemed such a vital part of all bodily endeavor. In corners, scattered in apparently orderly chaos, were piles of foam-rubber exercise mats, and stacks of dumb-bell-shaped weights for the aerobic routines.

In the back portion, entered by a long corridor, was a different world. If the front of the gym was blood, toil, sweat, and tears, in the back all was soft seduction, an air-conditioned retreat from the harsh realities of routine. The Finnish sauna was big enough to lie down in, welcoming and womblike. On its floor the wooden bucket was permanently filled with the delicious pine essence whose scent would fill the suddenly damp atmosphere as it was poured over the white-hot coals. Outside in the sitting area, there were oatmeal-colored deck chairs beside which lay columns of magazines, shamelessly up market: *New York* magazine, *Architectural Digest, Town and Country*. Rough, white towels lay in neat, serried ranks, a superabundance of plenty, giving an aura of effortless luxury. Farther down the narrow corridor, doors led to the soundproof massage area, and the mosaic-tiled Jacuzzi. The entrance foyer in which Lisa and Maggie sat doubled as a boutique for the dance-wear. The sexy, skimpy, brightly colored workout clothes were everywhere—festooned from each available ledge and corner, their straps and bodices leaving nothing at all to be imagined, hymns of celebration to the beauty of the female body. There were leg warmers, flesh-colored body stockings, pastel-shaded dance shoes, pink plastic hair clips, hand weights, terrycloth head and wrist bands, and bottle after bottle of vitamin pills.

"I don't know how you do it, Lisa. I guess some people are just born lucky."

"Screw luck, Maggie. It wasn't just that. I telephoned that producer every day for a week, until he finally agreed to see me. And then he said no at first. So I hung around that sandwich shop he uses eating rubbish and drinking shit until he finally surrendered."

"And now he's in love with you, I suppose."

"Who knows or cares? I got the spot. This place is on the map and the paint's hardly dry." Lisa laughed at the sound of herself. So tough, so ballsy. But why the hell not? If you believed in yourself enough, then everything was up for grabs. It was a question of daring to reach for the sky, of blocking one's ears to the propaganda of those who believed that some things just weren't possible.

In her stomach, however, the butterflies were playing and her mouth was as dry as the desert. She mustn't blow it. She must get the message across.

The arrival of the mobile television crew was always something of a spectacle, enjoyed most of all by the TV people themselves. In latter-day America, media men were gods incarnate as the citizens fought tooth and nail for their fifteen minutes of instant fame. Jim Summerford, relaxed but businesslike, led the way. Behind him trooped a gang of laid-back professionals—cameramen, lighting men, sound men. The greetings were friendly but he obviously wanted to get down to work. "I thought we'd start by having the class work out with these hand-weight things. Then we could cut to you pumping iron on those machines. We wrap it up with the interview in which you lay down the philosophy of the gym and explain how it differs from the mainstream gyms. How does that grab you?"

"Sounds fine to me."

The film crew worked fast setting up their equipment, and soon everything was ready for Lisa to give the signal to begin.

Bathed in the unforgiving heat of the arc lights and pushing themselves to the maximum, Lisa's girls gave it their best shot. The cameras lingered lovingly on the dancing, waving bodies, tracing the erotic contours, peeping shamelessly into the wet feminine recesses, playing lasciviously over the thrashing limbs. Hungrily the tape recorders lapped up the slashing rhythm of the electrobeat music as the frenetic arms and legs whipped up their owners' sweat into a rich lather of effort and ecstasy.

Jim Summerford raised both thumbs in the air as his daring cameramen waded into the cauldron of bubbling feminine flesh, their phallic lenses leering lecherously at smooth damp cleavages, at parted lips, tasting the abandonment, the total commitment to movement and work. Across his face was the smile of a man who had gotten what he wanted—a turn-on for his male viewers to which wives and lovers could not possibly take exception.

"Okay. That's it. I think we have it," he screamed above the music. "Let's move on."

Coitus interruptus. The cameras withdrew at the conductor's command, leaving the collective female psyche stranded on a plateau of unfulfilled expectation. Somebody threw the switch on the music, and the dancing limbs began dejectedly to wind down, marionettes of whom the puppeteer had tired, clockwork figures whose time was up. This was television, and what television wanted television got.

To Lisa, strapped into the hip adducer machine, it seemed everything was going well. The girls had looked great, and the pretty ones in the front had, as was intended, gotten all the attention. Now it was her turn. First the visuals, then the verbals.

She had chosen the particular Nautilus machine carefully. Its purpose was to exercise the muscles that drew the legs together. Starting with her legs splayed wide apart she would draw the two platforms to which they were attached toward the midline against resistance, before allowing the force of the machine to snap them apart once again. The camera angle was full frontal, the camera lens peering unashamedly straight between her spread-eagled legs. The effect, blatantly erotic, was heightened by Lisa's choice of clothes. A daringly brief jet-black singlet, its tantalizingly thin strip of black cloth barely covering her crotch, was superimposed over a skin-colored one-piece body stocking.

To all but the exercise cognoscenti it looked as if she were wearing hardly anything at all.

Jim Summerford was not complaining. "Lisa, that looks wonderful. Tell us what you're doing. Let's have a commentary."

As Lisa's powerful legs opened and closed in front of the camera's unblinking eye, her voice was confident, assured, showing no evidence at all of physical exertion. "The basic difference between my studio and the others is that I have the Nautilus machines. I don't just rely on aerobics. The beauty of the Nautilus program is that you can complete the circuit in twenty minutes. Ideal for a lunch break. And you only need to do it three times a week. In fact, you shouldn't work out on the machines more than that.''

Her legs scissored effortlessly in and out as she spoke, the sensuality of the movements seemingly at odds with the matter-of-fact delivery of her words.

"You start slowly, lifting only the weight you can manage. Then you build up gradually until you move mountains.''

The dazzling smile burned into the videotape as Lisa's legs made short work of the formidable pile of iron ingots. "The circuit is arranged so that all the different muscle groups are dealt with in order. You keep a record of the weight you move on each machine, and increase it gradually as you get stronger. You do fifteen actions on each machine. No more. No less. I guess that's my fifteen now.''

Languorously, she unstrapped herself from the Nautilus, disentangling her legs from the platforms, sitting upright now, hands clasped demurely in her lap, as she waited for Jim Summerford's approach.

"Well, Lisa Starr, that was pretty impressive. But I expect our viewers might wonder if this sort of body building gets one musclebound.''

"Do I look musclebound?''

Lisa did not look musclebound. The fantasy of some daydreaming anatomist? Yes. The answered prayer of any heterosexual who liked his women fit? Certainly. Incredible hulk? No way.

"I think we'd all agree you look great, just great, Lisa.''

The camera roamed lovingly over the magnificent body.

"What I am trying to do here is a whole new concept in body maintenance. I call it body sculpting. Being fit isn't enough anymore. It's good, essential even, but it's not enough. What we women need is to get strong as well as get fit. To be strong and beautiful. That's what we aim for here. When we do aerobics we carry weights—and every other day we work out on these machines. The body building helps with the exercise and stretch, and vice versa.''

In Lisa's eyes shone the spark of the zealot, and for a second she stopped as the glorious vision played around in her mind. A sea change. A fundamental realignment of attitudes and expectations. Strong women. Physically strong women. The emotional and intuitive strength now allied to a firm, hard, efficient body—a body that could lift things, carry things, *do* things. And then it would be but a short step to real meaningful parity with men, and an end to second-class citizenship which at the bottom line stemmed from female weakness.

As if reading her thoughts Jim Summerford went for the obvious question.

"And what about us men? Are you hoping that women are going to make some sort of takeover bid for territory that has always been ours?" Jim Summerford smiled to himself. That was a question that might have gotten him fired in New York or Massachusetts. But you couldn't get farther south in the U.S.A. than Florida. This was chauvinist country.

"I want women to compete with men, and on equal terms. I don't want women to fight them. They're not our enemies. We love ya'll." The dazzling smile cemented the truce between sexes.

No action in flogging that line, thought Summerford. "And I believe you suggest that psychological problems respond to this fitness discipline. Could you tell us about that?"

"Certainly they do. My program is guaranteed to cure the blues. Far better than the couch or the medicine bottle. But it's not all work. We offer saunas, Jacuzzi, steam heat, body massage. Once a month every woman should take a morning off and really pamper herself."

Get in the sales pitch. Do the commercial. Christ, this was going to go out into people's homes, into *Palm Beach* homes.

Then Lisa leaned in closer, and her eyes bored into the camera as she forced her thoughts into the minds of her future listeners. "There's no doubt at all. It can change your life," she said. "It's changed mine."

5

Jo-Anne Duke was having a very bad day indeed. Waking up had been a problem, opening her eyes an effort, getting out of bed a seemingly insuperable task. Now, as she sat moodily on the veranda still swathed in the pure silk Christian Dior negligée she had worn all day, she wondered why she had bothered. Sleepers and sedative antidepressants spaced out judiciously every few hours would have kept her near enough to unconsciousness to miss out on the angst that nagged and pulled at her. She could have given the whole damn day a miss. Passed on it. Started again with a clear slate tomorrow. The sun was getting low, its red fingers beginning to explore the surrounding sky. Usually the Lake Worth sunset was something that was guaranteed to lift her spirits. This evening it seemed to have all the soul of a gaudy picture postcard.

Jo-Anne wandered aimlessly back into the bedroom, and for a minute or two she stood in front of the long looking glass. God, she looked awful. The depression seemed to have painted her gray. Gray hair, gray face, gray eyes. Intellectually she knew that her mood's distorting spectacles were playing tricks with her perception, but intellect was the slave of emotion, and she felt that she looked awful. Nothing else mattered. In vain she concentrated on the jutting breasts, the billiard-table-flat stomach, the high, self-confident bottom. Filtered through the all pervading gloom that engulfed her, the body that could drive all humanity wild looked to be fit only for the glue factory.

Days like this happened from time to time and there was nothing that could be done about them. In the Big Apple the moods had sometimes lasted a whole week. She would shut herself up in the apartment, refuse to open the door, and take the greatest pleasure in living like a slut. She'd eat chocolate and junk food, let the dishes pile up in the sink, and wallow around in the slough of despond. Jo-Anne used to call it "housecoat weather." What was it now? Finest-silk-negligée weather? For sure the surroundings had changed, and the dishes got done. But feeling blue under a Renoir was much the same as feeling fed up under a bullfight poster.

It was pointless to speculate on what had caused the black mood. There were several candidates: Peter's bloody-mindedness, the near disaster at the Planned Parenthood thing, and Mary d'Erlanger's failure to call up after the mind-bending afternoon in the rented room at the Brazilian Court. But on other days she could take little local difficulties like that in her stride. Today she felt she could have a nervous breakdown if she found a spider in the swimming pool.

A tiny squirt of energy appeared from nowhere and fed itself into her bloodstream. Almost as a disinterested observer she discovered that she was going to phone that bitch Mary. Talk about bad manners. The least she could have done was to call and say she'd enjoyed the screw. Moodily she drifted across toward the telephone and punched out the familiar number.

The strange metallic click had been there before. From time to time over the last few months it had been quite noticeable. A click, and a kind of a hollowness on the line, as if you were speaking in a public lavatory. There was obviously something wrong with the damn telephones. She kept meaning to mention it to the housekeeper.

Mary d'Erlanger's voice was just a little cool. Friendly, but at the same time distant. It hadn't sounded like that in the bedroom of the Brazilian Court. Jo-Anne pictured the long, thin fingers, the delicately manicured nails as they caressed the telephone. The ones that had left marks on her back.

"Jo-Anne, darling. How are you? I've been meaning to call you."

"What stopped you?" Jo-Anne wasn't in the mood to pussyfoot.

"Oh, you know how it is. I've been so busy. Sometimes I just don't know what happens to my day."

"Well we both know what happened to your day last Wednesday afternoon, don't we?" The anger and the irritation were right up there on the surface. Mary would already be dressed for the evening. A little Givenchy number. Black and simple. Great pearls, great legs. The ones that had wrapped themselves tightly around Jo-Anne's body when she'd come.

Mary d'Erlanger's sigh was one of resigned disappointment. Why was everything a problem? Why did *everything* have to be paid for? "Don't be like that, Jo-Anne. It was fun, but it was silly. I wouldn't want it to happen again."

Jo-Anne felt the fuse blow within her. The stupid, vacuous cow. Who the *hell* did she think she was playing with?

"Fun, but silly. *Fun but silly!*" she screamed into the telephone. "You lie there on that bed like some beached whale pleading with me to make you come and now you call it funny but silly? Well, let me tell you one thing, Mary d'Erlanger. In bed you stink. You couldn't fuck your way out of a paper bag. No wonder that impotent lush of a husband of yours can't get it up. If I was a man I wouldn't have been able to either."

Jo-Anne heard the gratifying gasp of horror at the other end of the telephone as she slammed the receiver down. "Okay, Mary d'Erlanger. You're history," she said out loud to herself. Great! That was better. Some of the angst was out of her. Suddenly there was a gap in the little black cloud that had been sitting on her head all day.

She stalked across the room to the drinks tray and paused for a minute. Decisions. Decisions. Why were they always more difficult when you were down? Scotch on the rocks? With water? With soda? With nothing. She splashed a generous measure of Glenfiddich into the bottom of the big crystal glass and walked over to the sofa. She looked at her watch. Cartier said it was 7 P.M. Cartier was never wrong.

Drawing up her long legs beneath her she nursed the drink. Damn. She had lied to Mary. It wasn't true that she was bad in bed. She had been unbelievable, amazing. Now she was over. Jo-Anne drank long and hard of the smooth amber liquid, allowing it to burn the back of her throat before swallowing it down, feeling the warmth of the malt whiskey as it hit her empty stomach. She exhaled and shuddered with the momentary pleasure. Leaning out she reached for the remote control device and touched the Channel 5 sensor. A few feet away the Sony Trinitron flickered into life.

God Almighty. Jo-Anne sat up straight. She was peering between the legs of the most attractive girl she'd ever seen in her life. With consummate ease the legs opened and closed, seemingly oblivious to the pile of black weights that tried pointlessly to impede their progress, as their owner extolled the virtues of the Nautilus program.

Eyes on stalks, Jo-Anne took in the earnest, enthusiastic message, the dramatic facial features of the messenger.

"Body sculpting . . . to get strong and beautiful . . . want women to compete with men, and on equal terms . . . guaranteed to cure the blues . . ."

Hey, this was exactly what she had been waiting for. This girl had it right. You only had to look at her, to listen to her, to know that. The vitality, the charm came beaming off the screen. It zapped you right between the eyes.

And then quite suddenly Jo-Anne realized that the cloud had lifted. It was gone, vanished into the heavy atmosphere, dispelled effortlessly by the vision in the black singlet. A thoughtful expression appeared in the beautiful eyes, and a smile of anticipation began to play around the full lips.

Lisa Starr knew the very second she saw her. This girl was the *real* thing. It wasn't the cream-colored open Mercedes roadster, or the casual, even aggressive way it had been parked—one wheel on the pavement, the rear jutting dangerously into the road. Nor was it the quality and shape of the clothes—the almost square shoulders of the Calvin Klein jacket, the waspish waist, the matching oatmeal-colored linen skirt showing perfect, bronzed legs. It was none of these things, but at the same time it was all of them. The manner, too, screamed Palm Beach. Jo-Anne came in at a rush, her hair flying behind her, giving not a backward glance to the soon-to-be-ticketed car. Her whole attitude proclaimed that as far as the Mercedes was concerned any juggernaut was perfectly welcome to eat it for breakfast.

She walked right up to the receptionist's desk where Lisa sat, and her face dissolved into an enormously attractive smile.

"Hello, Lisa Starr. I'm Jo-Anne Duke and I saw you on television."

The thrill of adrenaline shot right through Lisa. To announce yourself as a Duke in this part of the world was like saying you were a Rockefeller in New York. Or a duke in England, for that matter. But somehow the girl's open manner, her transparent friendliness, forced all hierarchical thoughts out of mind.

Lisa laughed at the directness of the approach. "Welcome to my gym, Jo-Anne Duke," she said in mock formality, her smile encouraging, warm. "I won't ask which program, because I've only done one," she added.

Jo-Anne waved an arm in the air dismissively, and Lisa caught the flash of the four white-gold Cartier love bangles—the ones made to be screwed on by your lover with the sapphire-studded screwdriver.

"I've come to join your gym. I want you to cure my blues and to turn me into superwoman."

Lisa wasn't at all sure why that made her blush, but somehow it did. And when Lisa heard herself saying "Well, my initial impression is that it'll only take about ten minutes," she felt the color deepen.

"Thanks for the compliment," came Jo-Anne's straightforward reply. "But actually I feel like shit." Again the laughter bubbled and gurgled. Then it stopped. The next line came across dead straight.

"I want to look exactly like you."

Lisa couldn't think of any answer to that at all. Compliments she could usually handle—from men, from girls like Maggie. But coming from a girl who made a *Playboy* centerfold look like a secondhand rose, it was a fast ball. Clearly she had lost all control of her facial blood vessels. She could swear her cheeks were beginning to *pulsate*.

Again the laughter, the head thrown back, as the Duke girl enjoyed her confusion.

"Come on. I'm only joking . . . sort of, anyway."

The apparent disclaimer only served to reinforce the truth of her originally expressed desire, as it was meant to. Lisa covered her confusion by getting down to business.

"I'd sure like to have you as a member here. Would you let me show you around? Classes don't start for another half an hour, but you could look at the saunas and Jacuzzi.''

"No, I don't need to see it. I just want to join it. Let's do it now.''

"It's a hundred and twenty bucks a month, but you can take out a year's membership for nine hundred dollars. That's the best value.'' To a Duke that had to be insultingly little, thought Lisa. She didn't yet understand the habits and attitudes of the stinking rich.

"Hmm. Expensive,'' said Jo-Anne. "For West Palm,'' she added as an afterthought. "I'll take out a month's membership for now, and see how things go.''

The gold American Express card floated down onto the desk, and Lisa thanked God that she had signed on with the company. She'd thought twice about it.

"Do I get you for that?'' Both girls laughed at the apparently unintentional ambiguity. It was obvious what Jo-Anne meant, but on another level it wasn't clear at all.

"Oh yes, I'm here all the time,'' said Lisa, allowing herself a neutral smile.

"Great. Now let me tell you, Lisa. You were terrific on that show. I was feeling really low, and you picked me right up. This place is going to be a goldmine. All my friends will be screaming to get in. I'm going to pass the word. That's if you don't mind a whole lot of neurotic, sex-starved troublemakers with more money than sense.''

Lisa didn't mind. It was what she had prayed for, dreamed about, and now this fairy godmother was waving her magic wand and promising her paradise. And she liked her. They would be friends. Good friends. Her mother would have been so pleased, so proud.

Jo-Anne picked up on the suddenly wistful, distant expression, saw the mark of pain's touch. "They're not as bad as all that,'' she joked, well aware that it was not her disparaging remarks about her Palm Beach neighbors that had caused the momentary hurt.

"No. No. Of course not. I'd love to have any of them,'' said Lisa, forcing the sad thought from her mind. "Come on, Jo-Anne Duke,'' she said suddenly, springing up and taking her hand. "I'm going to put you on the rack—see what you're made of.''

Jo-Anne smiled and ran a tongue over already moist lips. "Sugar and spice of course," she lied, "like all the very best little girls."

Stretched out on the Nautilus machine that specialized in quadriceps contractions, Jo-Anne, it turned out, was made chiefly of beautifully constructed, if a little underworked, muscle, ligament, tendon, and bone. Aerobics had kept her fit, massage had made her sleek and smooth, but she was short on strength.

"No problem. No problem at all," Lisa said. "Two weeks and you'll be pushing seven, maybe eight, weights on this one."

Lisa took her slowly through the circuit—demonstrating the exercises, making sure that Jo-Anne knew how to do each correctly. It was vital to get it right. Bad habits could creep in, and once one started cheating and the muscles did the wrong work then the whole carefully calculated program fell apart, and the beneficial effects were lost.

By the end of the course Jo-Anne knew she was hooked, and in more ways than one. Muscles she didn't know she even had were speaking to her at last. It would be a whole voyage of bodily self-discovery. Her posture would improve, and with it her spirits. The excitement that coursed through her had a focus, too. Lisa had been the pathfinder, the guide, and her almost obsessional attention to detail had been almost as impressive as her startling physique, as alluring as the coolness of her strong hands. And she had a terrific sense of humor too. Bright as a button, sharp as a knife, fresh as a daisy: the old phrases were always the best ones. It was a combination for which Jo-Anne had all the time in the world.

In the shower Jo-Anne had felt her spirits sing, had even managed a bar or two of the dreaded "Hello, Dolly," which Palm Beach bandleaders always insisted on playing. Was it imagination or could she see the protuberance of a new muscle high up there on her arm? The mirror said "yes," but then yesterday's mirror had told her she was gray all over. Mirrors, like men, could not be trusted. She dried and dressed quickly. Outside she found Lisa organizing the tapes for the first aerobics workout of the day, bending down low over the tape deck. She laid a hand on one of the rock-hard gluteal muscles.

"Lisa Starr, will you have lunch with me?" she asked.

Lisa turned and smiled. "Sure, I'd love to," she said, only subliminally aware that Jo-Anne's hand was still resting on her bottom.

"How do I look, Maggs?" Lisa twirled in front of her girlfriend, half joking, half deadly serious. A Palm Beach lunch with Jo-Anne Duke was about as excitingly unpredictable as playing "lucky dip" with a diamond in one box and a rattlesnake in the other. Lisa hadn't a clue what to expect. She had remembered her mother's intense monologues, but they weren't any help; such vital details as what one wore to lunch and how one understood a French menu had been left out of the general and highly romanticized picture. Would it be a sit-down lunch for twelve in the Duke mansion, a buffet poolside with chicken legs and glasses of wine balanced precariously on knees—or perhaps it would be a restaurant thing? There was no way of knowing and Lisa had instinctively felt it would be desperately uncool to ask. So she had gone for the woman-of-all-seasons look, and she felt it worked. The faded blue jeans were immaculately pressed, downy soft, and offset perfectly by the expensive cream silk shirt and the wide-shouldered Diane Von Furstenberg jacket, which she had discovered on special sale at Burdine's. Including the black patent-leather pumps and the Christian Dior tights with the raised heart motif, the whole outfit had cost less than a hundred bucks, but the total effect was that of understated elegance, of throwaway cool. The Levi's were a bit of a gamble, but then so was life.

"You look like a dog. A great big, ugly dog." Maggie made a face. "Lisa, I really don't think you should go out like that. You might frighten the horses."

Through the skin-tight trousers the graceful limbs twisted and strained as Lisa struck a carefree pose, hands on hips, head thrown back, ass jutting up toward the ceiling. She laughed at her friend, and at her own silly feelings of insecurity. "Okay, Palm Beach.

I'm ready for you. Do your worst," was what she said, and was trying to feel.

"What time is she picking you up?"

"Picking me up? Picking me up? The Dukes don't pick people up. They *have* them picked up. The limo comes at one."

Lisa bowed extravagantly from the waist, the years of stretching allowing the raven hair to sweep down low to the floor, the knees ramrod straight, the arm extended in the graceful gesture of a ballet dancer.

"Well, all I say is make sure you're back before the clock strikes midnight, Cinderella—and don't let Prince Charming screw you on day one."

Lisa went for the mock drop kick to Maggie's plump bottom, but the horseplay was cut short by the arrival outside of the biggest black limousine either girl had ever seen. The Dukes' stretched Mercedes was intimidating transport indeed, and was intended to be. Chivers, the dove-gray-uniformed English chauffeur, was no less impressive. Holding his peaked cap beneath his arm he oiled his way into the gym.

"Miss Elizabeth Starr?" The jaw dropped away as he drooled Lisa's last name, so that no possible hint of an *r* remained.

"I'm Lisa. Are you taking me to lunch with Jo-Anne Duke?"

"Mrs. Duke has asked that I take you to meet her at the Café L'Europe." He said that as if the restaurant were about as familiar as the Eiffel Tower to a Parisian, the sort of place Lisa ate every other day.

"Take me to your leader," said Lisa, winking hugely at Maggie as she set off toward the limo, trailing a marginally chastened Chivers in her wake.

In the air-conditioned womb of the mighty car Lisa stretched out her legs and tried to relax. That was what the damn thing had been designed for. No way could one have had an adequate game of mixed doubles in there, but eight people could happily sit down for after-dinner drinks. The cushions seemed to want to devour her. It was like quicksand—the sensation of being sucked down into a vortex of naked luxury.

Lisa laughed out loud at the theatricality of her thoughts, causing Chivers to chance a look over his shoulder to investigate the cause of the levity. Finding none, he slipped into the safety of the servant role. "Should you like some refreshment you'll find the bar in the cupboard in front of you. There's fresh ice in the bucket and mixers in the refrigerator."

Lisa's initial inclination was to refuse, but quite suddenly she changed her mind. Hell. Why not? If this was the *dolce vita* maybe she should make hay while the sun shone. Rich people had a way of tiring of new toys, even if she had scarcely been unwrapped.

She reached forward and opened the Aladdin's cave that was the bar. There wasn't a bottle in sight. Everything was decanted into flat-bottomed ship's decanters of the finest cut glass. Around the neck of each hung a silver label on which the contents were described in a rich, intricately engraved script. She poured a half inch of vodka into one of the heavy goblets and scooped a handful of ice on top. The color was confined to the cooler section below. Every conceivable drink was there. A jug of iced tomato juice, Miller's Lite, Carlsberg, what looked like fresh orange juice again in a tall jug, a bottle of Taittinger Rosé, another of hock, Tio Pepe sherry, a plate of sliced limes. Resisting the temptation to embark on the construction of a bloody mary, Lisa reached instead for the iced Martini and splashed a minimal amount onto the vodka. Ignoring the elegant silver stirrer she stuck her finger irreverently into the drink and whisked it around. Mustn't get too carried away.

The cold spirit on the warm stomach lining had messages for the brain. Lisa felt the rush almost immediately. Drinking was not really her bag, but today was special. She was going across the bridge at last and in the style of which her beloved mother had dreamed. Okay, so white chargers were conspicuous by their absence, but since the first sip of the vodka martini she could have sworn she'd heard a choir of angels warming up. Again she chuckled to herself as the golden-coach substitute purred down Royal Palm Way into the heart of Palm Beach. The sign in the stockbroker's window in the "400" building told her that the Dow was off 19.48 points. Oh, dear. What a pity. The rich had gotten just a little poorer. Would that mean pasta for lunch?

The crowd waiting to get into Doherty's as they made the right turn onto South County hinted that the town's residents were putting a brave face on the stock-market fall. Nor did the people on Worth Avenue look downhearted.

The big car swept into the Esplanade complex as if it was returning home; a gaggle of valet parkers clustered around it. Chivers spoke imperiously. "If you look after it for a minute or two I'll be back immediately." He decanted himself from the front seat and opened the back door for Lisa. "If I may I'll take you to Mrs. Duke."

Lisa was only dimly aware of her surroundings as she made her way up the Spanish steps of the Esplanade's staircase, her eyes fixed on Chivers's rather ungainly bottom. He looked a bit like a Confederate soldier in some made-for-TV Civil War rehash, she couldn't help thinking. At the top of the stairs the signs on the doors said Café L'Europe, and Lisa took a deep breath and thanked God for the vodka as the improbable duo made it inside. The maître d' seemed to have been waiting for them.

"Is this Mrs. Duke's luncheon guest?" asked the heavy French accent. "Please follow me, mademoiselle."

Lisa fought back the idea that this seemingly endless process of being transported into the hallowed presence of Jo-Anne Duke might well go on all day. At the table there would be a black major-domo who would transport her by waiting helicopter to a yacht where the bearded captain would sail her to a submarine . . .

With the vague impression of mountains of colorful flowers and of even more colorful people, Lisa allowed herself to be wafted across the beautiful restaurant.

Jo-Anne was sitting alone at what was clearly the best table in the room. She stood up at Lisa's approach and held out a long arm. The smile was warm, but was there just a hint of patronization in her opening words?

"My teacher, my guru. Great to see you, Lisa."

"Wow," said Lisa, sitting down gratefully. "Are you in the magical mystery tour business?"

Jo-Anne laughed.

"Yeah, the limo's a little far out, isn't it? Chivers, too, for that matter. Still, I always say, if you've got it, flaunt it."

Jo-Anne did always say that, and as far as possible she always *did* that. Maybe when she was old and gray she'd play the under-stated high-class game, like the Hobe Sound crew, but for now she wanted to get as far from big-city blowjobs as it was possible to get.

"I'll drink to that," said Lisa, reaching for the glass of chilled

champagne that seemed to have been poured her while she was
midway between standing and sitting down. The bubbles went
right up her nose. That was nice. It was funny, now that she was
there all the doubts and fears were gone. Already she was enjoying
herself. Just the two of them. Good. Jo-Anne seemed real nice.
She peered around the room at the flora and fauna of Palm Beach,
as the reality met her fantasy.

Jo-Anne looked at her proudly. Christ, she was a magnificent
specimen. Ballsy as hell and with the looks of a goddess. What did
she want from life? That was the secret it would be the luncheon's
purpose to answer. If you knew what people wanted, where they
went to in their beds at night as they dreamed their wildest dreams,
then you were well on your way to controlling them.

Jo-Anne felt the throb of the engine inside her as the machinery
started up. Control. Domination. The scheming of schemes. Forget the champagne, forget the beluga. They were sideshows to the
main attraction. "So what do you think of the show so far?"

Lisa wasn't quite sure. "Who *are* all these people? Let's have
the guided tour, Jo-Anne. You must know everybody."

"Are you really interested, Lisa? For sure they could all use a
subscription to your gym."

"Oh, I'm just fascinated by the whole Palm Beach trip. Ever
since I was a little girl I've felt like that. My mom used to work
over here, as some sort of a ladies' maid for the Stansfield family
—you know Senator Stansfield. She loved it so much and never
really talked about anything else. So I guess I sort of inherited the
interest."

"No, how *fascinating*. That's really interesting, Lisa." Jo-
Anne's mind churned up the information as she fed it into her
mind's computer. The girl was totally unaffected and refreshingly
naive. The fact that your mother had been a maid was not something that most people would have wanted to advertise. Also it
appeared she was a little star-struck; the brainwashing process
seemed to have substituted the Palm Beach plutocracy for the
celluloid meritocracy. She smiled to herself and then at Lisa. It
was all encouraging information.

"Well, let's see. I guess you've heard of Estée Lauder. She's
the lady in the sequinned top. Next to her is somebody called
Helen Boehm. She makes porcelain and runs the most successful

polo team. The good-looking guy on Boehm's right is quite interesting. He's Howard Oxenberg—very attractive to women. On his other side is his wife, Anne, who's a real doll—beautiful and charming. Howard used to be married to Princess Elizabeth of Yugoslavia; they have a wonderful-looking daughter, Catherine, who acts. The Oxenbergs live out at Wellington part of the year at a place called the Palm Beach Polo and Country Club."

Jo-Anne smiled at Lisa's look of total concentration. To anybody who knew the Oxenbergs intimately, as she did, they were lovely, ordinary people whose comings and goings were totally taken for granted—unremarkable, hardly worthy of comment. But as part of a *People* magazine-style commentary they sounded undeniably glamorous. Perhaps a little influenced by Lisa's powerful reactions, Jo-Anne's attitude toward her old friends underwent a subtle shift as she saw them anew in the light of Lisa's enthusiasm.

"Tell me about this Wellington place. I've seen all the TV ads for the polo. Who lives there, and why?"

Jo-Anne began to feel a bit like a sociology major. How to define the delicate difference between the Polo Club and Palm Beach proper? It took a remarkably gifted social animal with a nose closely attuned to the ever-changing scents and aromas of societal intercourse to pinpoint the characteristics that divided the two communities. But in a way she *was* the expert. Lisa couldn't have asked a better person, with the possible exception of Marjorie Donahue herself.

"The obvious differences aren't the important ones. Wellington is fifteen miles from the sea. The emphasis is heavily on sport— golf and tennis as well as polo. I guess it's a younger place. Certainly a newer one. And it's very pushy. They're spending a fortune trying to make it the slickest place in America for the young, sports-loving group, and they *are* succeeding. But they haven't *quite* succeeded. A hell of a lot of Palm Beachers go out each Sunday for the polo, but the rest of the week during the season the Wellington crowd is eating and swimming over here. Of course it's cheaper there. You can get something for around five hundred thousand that's halfway decent. At that price you'd get a rabbit hutch in Palm Beach.

"I think the real thing is the race thing. In this town the WASPs and the Jews don't mix. It's like apartheid. Estée Lauder wouldn't be welcome at the Bath and Tennis Club for instance, although B and T members would be more than happy to go and drink her champagne if she gives a big charity reception. The Polo Club is much more free and easy, more democratic, more liberal. Perhaps you'd like to come with us all this Sunday. You could meet my husband, Peter. We usually have a big lunch first, then there's a box in the grandstand where we drink too much Pimms and catch the action.''

"That sounds great, Jo-Anne. I'd like to see that.''

Lisa sat back on the comfortable banquette and allowed the relaxation and the champagne to flow through her. None of the feared horrors had materialized. The menu had turned out to be an easily negotiated hurdle—a mixed salad followed by a minute steak—and Jo-Anne, too, had been totally charming, with no sign of the airs and graces that could so easily have been a by-product of her almost indecent wealth. So far Palm Beach had certainly lived up to Lisa's inflated expectations.

It was just about to exceed them in a way that would change her life forever. "Hey, look, speak of the devil.'' Jo-Anne's voice was suddenly full of excitement as she gesticulated toward the door of the restaurant.

Lisa did as she was told, but Satan was not at all what she saw.

The initial reaction was almost entirely biochemical. Later there would be words to describe it, rationalizations to explain the great surge deep within her. But now there was just the rush of feeling, the weird shift of emotion as a hornet's nest seemed to empty itself into the center of her gut. Something was happening to her, she didn't know what, and the appearance of a remarkably attractive man in the doorway of the Café L'Europe was the cause of her discomfort.

As her shocked intellect began to reassert control over the raging torrent of body chemicals, Lisa tried to work out what it was she was seeing. There wasn't a satisfactory answer. Okay, so he was incredibly good looking, but that wasn't exactly unique. It was something much more important than that—something disturbing, dangerous, exciting, inevitable. And it wasn't just coming from him. It was an interaction—a reaction, something between her and this stranger that added up to a total greater than the sum of the individual parts. Far from sure what it was, Lisa watched and waited, Fate's hostage, as the man left his position at the door and headed into the restaurant.

One thing was immediately obvious. He had about him success's sweet smell, the heady aroma of concentrated charisma, and all about him lesser mortals were sniffing at it. The maître d', businesslike on Lisa's arrival, had degenerated into a hand-wringing hunchback as he ushered the man between the tables. All around the crowded room necks of rubber twisted and turned as the Palm Beachers shamelessly eyeballed the handsome newcomer, and the clatter of conversation stilled noticeably as elbows dug into ribs and fingers found wrists to alert the unwary to the clearly formidable presence in their midst.

Lisa turned helplessly toward Jo-Anne. The question didn't need to be asked.

Jo-Anne smiled back at her. "Bobby Stansfield," she said simply. "And that's his mother, Caroline Stansfield, behind him."

Lisa felt the strength go out of her. This man was a Stansfield. *The* Bobby Stansfield. Impressive to anybody. A mythical superhero to Lisa—standard bearer of the Stansfield dynasty, that fabled collection of Titans that had populated her beloved mother's romantic fantasies. No wonder she had known him instantly, recognized immediately at a subconscious level his phenomenal importance for her. The inexplicable was instantly explained, but the knowledge was no help at all.

And then there was Caroline Stansfield. Her mother's employer. The spirit of Palm Beach, the epitome of the magical world across the bridge. God Almighty! The mixed emotions struck up their raucous cacophony. Lisa fought to make sense of them. Bobby Stansfield, this beautiful, desirable, famous man, who could one day be president. Caroline Stansfield, who had fired her mother and ruined her life, and had been turned into a goddess as reward for her lack of charity. Did Lisa worship or hate her? It was impossible to intuit the answer to the question. As the mighty adrenaline flow sucked the color from Lisa's cheeks, she sat stock still like some frightened animal hypnotized by the headlights of the oncoming car—unable to move, unable to think. Dimly, through the mists that had engulfed her, she took in the fact that the Stansfields were heading directly toward her.

"Jo-Anne Duke? A girl's lunch? Well, well, I should get out more often." The twinkle in the voice said much, much more than the words. The baby-blue eyes fastened on Lisa's. "And may I be introduced to your very beautiful friend?"

The smile was still there, but somehow the voice had gone deadly serious.

"Oh, Bobby, this is Lisa Starr. Senator Stansfield. Lisa has just opened the most marvelous gym over in West Palm. She's going to change my life, turn me into a female Adonis, if such a thing exists."

Both Lisa and Bobby missed the delicate flavor of patronization. There were other things on their minds.

"I'm very pleased to meet you, Lisa Starr. Maybe if you've any spare time you could change my life a bit, too."

Lisa blushed deeply at the suggestion as the wonderful eyes probed her soul. Dear *God,* he was attractive. Disgustingly attractive.

"Mother, you know Peter Duke's wife, Jo-Anne. And this is Lisa Starr, who, I'm ashamed and unhappy to say, I've never met before."

Like a conjurer revealing the rabbit, he stood back to display Caroline Stansfield. Her weary smile said it all. Table hopping at a thousand-dollar-a-plate political dinner was business; table hopping in a restaurant was a perversion.

Caroline Stansfield extended a frail hand and both Jo-Anne and Lisa stood to take it. Yes, she knew Jo-Anne Duke. Hooker with a heart of brass, or some other unpleasant metal. Lisa Starr? Sounded like an actress. Surely no relation to the Philadelphia Starrs. But those beautiful eyes, the high cheekbones. They were distinctly familiar. Reminded her very much of someone. Damn. Her memory was all shot to pieces these days. Who on *earth* was it?

"Lisa Starr," she said thoughtfully as she shook hands. "I feel sure I know you from somewhere. Have we met before?"

There was so much to say, a lifetime of anguish, ambition, of joy and heartache to discuss—but, of course all of it was impossible. "No, I am afraid we haven't," was the only possible reply, and so Lisa said just that.

"Come on, Bobby. I'm starving. Are you going to buy me lunch or not?'' Caroline Stansfield's command, as always, was instantly obeyed.

Bobby's arm assumed the steering position as he gathered up his mother for the resumption of their journey. Over his shoulder he said insistently, ''When are you going to invite me over, Jo-Anne, or are the Dukes economizing? Give me a call. Bye, Lisa Starr. I hope very much we meet again.''

The throaty, bantering laugh crept right inside Lisa's heart and immediately made itself a home.

6

For the first time in weeks Lisa was totally relaxed. The sauna had taken all the surplus liquid from her body, had cleaned the pores and sucked the tension from her tired muscles. Now the Jacuzzi was rounding off the process. Warm jets of water played firmly over her, massaging, soothing, kneading the flesh. There was no sound except for the gentle rush of the scented water, and the lights were turned down low to minimize all sensory input. At last Lisa was free, free to unwind, to feel, to enjoy the delicious sensations of the present. But her restless thoughts refused to be still. So much had happened. In such a short time she had traveled from tragedy to the edge of sublimity, but it had been a tiger ride, exhilarating, frightening, dangerous—and she herself had been part driver, part driven.

Before there had been safety, comfort, love—and of course her parents, who had represented all three. The aching sense of loss had lessened now, as time's balm worked its healing way, but the memories lived on, real and alive. Mostly it was her mother whose presence she felt, whose warm, reassuring scents she missed. The flames had eaten away her dreams, but had they, in Lisa, lived on, transmuted, transplanted into the body and mind of a new and worthy standard bearer?

Lisa sighed as she wiped a bead of sweat from her brow. She had given up her ambition of going to college and becoming a teacher. Was her discarded life a cause for regret? In a vacuum, maybe. But the vacuum had been filled. Now she was queen of her own domain, not a lowly courtier in the kingdom of someone else. It was an infinitely smaller fiefdom, but she ruled it. That it was already a success was obvious for all to see. The membership applications were flooding in and the list was on the verge of closure. But it offered so very much more. It was a way to give to her mother the ultimate posthumous gift. On Sunday she would sit with the Dukes in their private box at Palm Beach polo, not as a servant but as an equal. At a stroke she had achieved Mary-Ellen's impossible dream. Okay, so for now it was only a tenuous foothold on the ladder, but for sure she hadn't started at the bottom.

Nor did she intend to rest on her laurels. She would consolidate her position like some invading army, build up her reserves, before breaking out of the beachhead on a campaign of conquest that would leave Palm Beach helpless at her feet, its unspecified delights surrendered unconditionally to Lisa Starr. She savored the delicious thought, but even as she did so sorrow crept in at the edges to sour its flavor. Damn. It was so unfair. If her mother could have lived to have seen it. If her father, and granddad. . . . But they were all gone away, and there was nobody to watch the first tentative steps.

She was all alone in the world of danger and difficulty with only her wits, her beauty, and her shining vision to help her. Suddenly Lisa felt the self-confidence slip from her tight grasp, and the lump in her throat found a companion with the emergence of the tears in her eyes. "Yours enemies, my's enemies"—that was what Grandpa Jack had liked to say. "Some boah don't treat you right, Lisa, you be tellin' me. He won' be chewing steak so good." And then they would always laugh, but the truth was Jack Kent had broken jaws before, and for some real or imagined slight to his beloved granddaughter he would probably have exacted a far more fearsome retribution. With that kind of man on your side there wasn't much to fear. With old Jack's meanness, and her father's enormous fists, Lisa's childhood had been totally secure. No fresh black boy along the block had ever dared to give her lip, no booze-sodden wino ever risked a suggestive remark when her tits had begun to sprout, no boyfriend had ever pushed his luck when the answer had been no. Then in a few wicked minutes they had all gone away and left her alone. A motherless, fatherless child.

A big tear rolled gently down Lisa's flushed cheek, picking up the moisture of her sweat, and she reached up to smooth it away. In Palm Beach nobody would use fists against her, but they would possess words as sharp as any dagger. Their defenses would be lawyers, money; their allies the cunning tongues of their friends. Competing in that world would be far from easy, very far from safe. Somehow that thought pleased Lisa. After all, Jack Kent's blood ran in her veins, and if there was one thing that invariably cheered him up it was the prospect of a good fight, preferably with the odds against him. Her father had not been quite like that, but she had seen his eyes light up in Roxy's when the beer had begun to flow and when some raw youngster had decided the time had come to chance his arm against his elders and betters. She would take them all on, and she would win in the process. No matter how big the guns she would find a way to return a more withering fire.

As if to exorcise the rapidly lifting despondency, she dipped down into the bubbles, lowering her head into the warmth. When she reemerged her old self-confidence was back.

She began to think about Sunday. What would it be like? Who would be there? Bobby Stansfield? The thought came through like the rays of the sun through a thick cloud—suddenly, unexpectedly, and with the same warming, uplifting effect. Stansfield. The name with the power to concentrate the mind, to tie the loose threads into the coherent whole. It was the code word for everything—for her past, for her present, and, she dared to hope, for her future. Maybe he was only a symbol for the world she sought, but his was a frighteningly potent image, one of flesh, and of blood.

Mmmmmmmmmmmmmmm. Now the sunlight played on Lisa as on the petals of a flower ready to open, and in response her legs splayed wide open, and she pushed her pelvis out toward the satisfying jets of water. In her mind was the memory of bright blue eyes and a lilting voice that had dared to admire that which she knew to be admirable. It was true, thank God, that she was beautiful, but then so was he. Everything her mother had predicted, and more. What would happen now? Would she see him again? On Sunday? If not, then maybe at another of Jo-Anne's parties. His last words at the restaurant had contained the unmistakable message that he was hoping for such a meeting.

Would he want her? Would he like her? Could he love her? Make love to her? The delicious speculation went on and on as the column of water pushed at her, playing delightfully with her most precious place.

Before now, her desire had not been for warm bodies, for the comforting touch of lovers. That sort of thing she had always thought of as a sideshow. It would happen when the rest of her life

was in place. Then it would be an amusing, even a fascinating
diversion, but it would be a leisure-time pursuit—somewhere between Tennessee Williams's plays and live country music on a
Saturday night in the hierarchy of pleasure. Lisa had never been
able to understand the people whose lives were controlled by love.
It seemed so inefficient, so fundamentally self-indulgent. For her
control was the thing. Control over herself. There had been boys,
but they had never been her *life,* and their inexpert fumblings and
unpracticed lips had never tempted her to let them have what they
all so desperately desired. One day it would happen. But she was
more curious than impatient.

Gently Lisa eased herself off the Jacuzzi's seat. She advanced
delicately on the column of water, which pleased her, savoring the
more insistent touch as she approached its source. Now, both
hands on the side of the sunken tub, she pressed herself against
the orifice, luxuriating in the delectable feeling of the water's pressure against her. She sought sweet words for the sexual poem she
was about to compose. Hard and strong the water stroked her,
long and lean it lapped at her, shameless, invading, it took her.
Through parted lips Lisa breathed in deeply. Careful. Not too fast.
Lisa swiveled her hips to disengage the instrument of pleasure,
allowing the confident stream to play over her hard lower stomach,
to hose the sweeping lines of her inner thighs.

Then, very slowly, as if unwilling to disturb or discourage her
watery lover, she turned and gave it her back. It rushed in eager
torrents into the welcoming cleavage of the rounded buttocks,
searching out the shy entrance—loving it, pleasing it, with a firm
touch. Little packets of explosive pleasure discharged their contents into Lisa's mind and she moved to intensify the feeling.
Bending at the waist, her spine perfectly straight, she brought her
chin to the level of the water's surface at the same time thrusting
hard against the wall of the Jacuzzi. In blissful collusion with the
daring water jet, she allowed it to ravish her. But in her mind she
had achieved the fusion she sought. The lifeless, mechanical thing
that thrust so aggressively at her had magically acquired life. It
belonged to Bobby Stansfield.

Into the steamy vision, unwanted, unmistakable, intruded the
doorbell's tactless ring.

Christ! Damn!

She tried to block it out, to hold on to the fragile fantasy that promised so much.

As she struggled to capture the elusive dream the ringing stopped. Great! A few more seconds and the moment would have been gone. Lisa repositioned herself to reclaim the divine stimulation, but even as she did so the unknown finger disturbed the work of the watery one. This time the bell was more intrusive. Its truncated rhythm said that the intruder knew there was somebody inside to open the door.

With a sinuous movement she extricated herself from the womb-like waters, and grabbing a towel, she padded through the gym toward the street door. "Who on earth is it?" she shouted through the bolted door.

In West Palm you didn't open the door to strangers. "It's me— Jo-Anne," came the confident reply, unfazed by the distinctly irritable tone of the question.

"Oh, Jo-Anne. Hang on a second while I open up. You've got me out of the Jacuzzi."

Again Jo-Anne refused to be discouraged by the underwhelming enthusiasm of the greeting. Lisa Starr recently emerged from a Jacuzzi was to her a choice morsel indeed. As the door opened and the truth was confirmed she made her pitch. "I was just passing by, and I saw the lights on. Wondered what you were up to."

Jo-Anne looked straight at Lisa as she told the lie. This part of Clematis Street wasn't on the way to anywhere. During the last day or two she'd made a point of checking out the gym when she happened to be over the bridge. It looked as if her scouting efforts had paid off.

Lisa knew the geography; it was unlikely to be coincidental that Jo-Anne was standing on her doorstep, although the reason for her presence was far from clear.

"Well, aren't you going to ask me in? I could catch my death of cold out here."

They both laughed. The West Palm temperature was pushing eighty-eight degrees.

"Of course, come on in."

"Hey, Lisa, don't let me disturb you. You'd better get right back into the health-giving waters. Come to think of it, I might join you. That's if you don't mind, of course."

"No, I'd like that. You can fill me in on what to expect on Sunday." An uninvited guest in what was supposed to have been a solitary hot tub was *not* what she needed, but she hadn't forgotten that Jo-Anne was the open sesame to the Palm Beach cave. Better to give in with grace.

Purposefully, Jo-Anne lingered a step behind on the short walk to the Jacuzzi. In front of her a dripping, betoweled Lisa led the way. Mentally Jo-Anne checked her out. Big, square shoulders, rounded muscular calves, delicate, beautifully arched feet, immaculately pedicured toes. The long, dark hair, wet and untidy, rushed over the shoulders on which beads of moisture—sweat? water?—still glistened. Lisa walked with a swinging, easy gait—perhaps just a tiny bit butch, certainly athletic, not typically feminine. Inside her Jo-Anne felt the little rush of excitement as the familiar feeling began to build. In a second or two the sculpture would be unveiled. It was not difficult to predict that it would win prizes.

It did. For one brief, blissful second as the white towel made it to the mosaic tiled floor Lisa Starr stood naked at the brink of the Jacuzzi. The lights, still dimmed, gave to the visual an ethereal, detached quality—a latter-day Victorian photograph, a bather caught unawares on the banks of some lazy Indian river at dusk. The body, of course, was magnificent and it was held momentarily in the relaxed pose of the professional athlete, one leg pushed forward in front of the other, the subdued light able to pick out the edge of the smooth quadriceps muscle group, the perfect triangle of dark and infinitely interesting hair, the undulating sweep of the tight stomach. Her right hand dangled delicately, fingers in the repose of some Greek goddess; the left was held up high at shoulder height attached by the well-formed pectoral to the sublime breast. Was it the heat or the pummeling of the water jets that had stimulated the erectile tissue in the delicate pink nipples—or did the girl always look like this, her breasts permanently conical, perfect pyramids, demanding attention, commanding admiration, haunting in their loveliness, daring the adventurous touch?

Jo-Anne's eyes lingered longingly over the transient vision, trying to capture it for the album of her mind. Then, it was taken from her as Lisa stepped into the foaming water.

As Lisa did so she was mystically aware of the greedy eyes that had fed from her. Far from conscious of the muted music of desire that all around her was beginning quietly to play, she somehow felt that the water was a safe haven from an alien, exotic thing at once alarming and alluring. Its bubbles touched the skin that Jo-Anne's eyes had touched and inexplicably sent little shivers up and down Lisa's graceful spine.

Lisa turned her face upward toward Jo-Anne, her expression curious, questioning. Women always had a passing interest in the appearance of each other's bodies, and Lisa, a professional in the field, was no exception. But somehow, somewhere there was something else. For a second she looked away as an inexplicable embarrassment gripped her, but then her eyes were drawn back again by some force field of magnetism of which she was only subliminally aware. Jo-Anne was staring at her, and there was a hypnotic quality in her gaze. It was lazy, laid back, reassuring, and yet frighteningly powerful, and impossible to ignore.

I'm fully clothed, and yet soon I'll be naked. I want you to watch me undress, said Jo-Anne's eyes—and unable, unwilling to resist, Lisa found herself obeying. On a thousand similar occasions she had witnessed the same happening, but now it was charged, invested with an altogether indefinable flavor of illicit voyeuristic coercion. Try as she might, Lisa could not get the idea out of her mind that she was peeping through a keyhole.

The fingers played with the big brass buckles of the two thick brown leather belts that straddled Jo-Anne's tiny waist. Patiently, gently she pushed downward, peeling back the blue denim trouser tops, easing down the white silk briefs. Her eyes were laughing, now, teasing, mocking, daring Lisa to transfer the center of her gaze from the knowing smile to her most secret place.

Lisa felt the moisture in her throat begin to dry. Self-consciously she tried to swallow, suddenly aware of a difficulty in doing so. Then, seemingly unable to resist the unspoken command, she looked down, her eyes playing helplessly over the pubic hairs, framed like some priceless painting by the turned-down jeans. Seemingly aware of the beauty of the effect, Jo-Anne made no effort to lower the jeans any farther. Instead her hands moved higher to the buttons of the sky-blue man's silk shirt against which her stiff nipples already strained. Dancing to the string of the expert puppeteer, Lisa's gaze was once again dragged upward to pay homage to the arrogant, self-confident breasts.

The silence had gone on too long for comfort, and yet somehow there was nothing to say. Already an unholy alliance was in its earliest stages of formation, but its purpose was ill defined, scarcely to be admitted. With mounting horror Lisa realized that the appalling dryness of her mouth was being balanced by the beginnings of wetness elsewhere.

Jo-Anne sensed it all, saw it in the confused eyes. So often it had happened like this. The alien act, undreamed of, unwanted, translated into abandoned desire by the art of the seductress. Quickly now, she slipped off her trousers, panties, and ankle-length cotton socks and slid smoothly into the water. Still she didn't speak. No words must disturb the magic.

Sitting opposite her prey in the bubbling foam, Jo-Anne waited and watched for the moment she knew so well how to recognize.

Slowly, like the rising sun, the realization of what was happening came to Lisa. For the very first time in her life she had been turned on by a woman, by a supremely beautiful and powerful naked woman who sat inches from her in the swirling, sweet-smelling currents of her own hot tub.

But why? Was it just a hangover from her own interrupted attempt at self-gratification, her aroused senses searching desperately for an object to focus on. No. It wasn't just her. Jo-Anne was a far from passive participant in whatever it was that was happening. Waves of sensuality were beaming from her, creeping under Lisa's skin, vitalizing her nerve endings. There was a fullness in her breasts, an empty void in her stomach and the far more significant feeling of emptiness between her legs.

Jo-Anne's laughing eyes bored into her, understanding her dilemma, mocking what was rapidly becoming her need, at the same time encouraging it. Then, with her reassuring, knowing smile still playing around her parted lips, Jo-Anne crossed the short space into intimacy.

The kiss was an age in coming. It started as a slow, lazy thing with all the time in the world. The nuzzling lips, warm, soft, and dry as the desert's air, did not touch her at first. They hovered, suspended in space and time, inches, and then less than inches, from Lisa's own. Through them came the hot, scented breath, fanning her face, creeping delightfully into her nostrils, evaporating the moisture on her skin. Then, in swoops and darts, they descended on her, delicate, calm, on their mission of mercy and conquest. Lisa felt her back turn to liquid as the extraordinary lips traced the borders of her own, exploring, curious, tenderly spelling out the unspoken language of love. Still it was not a kiss, but it was a treaty, an unbreakable alliance in what promised to be a voyage into the uncharted seas of sexual ecstasy. Soon, mercifully soon there would be the tongue. Lisa for the very first time in her life was a helpless passenger; whatever deed would be done, she had in some way agreed to it. The passive acceptance of these lips was final as the signature on some ghostly contract.

As if acknowledging the capitulation Jo-Anne moved to consolidate her position. Resting her lips on the corner of Lisa's half-open mouth, she licked at her, running a wet, sweet-tasting tongue along first the upper and then the lower lip, moistening the dry skin with saliva.

Lisa stifled her low moan of pleasure as the wetness exploded deep within her. She leaned back against the wall of the Jacuzzi and let her long legs stretch out before her as she opened herself up.

Jo-Anne saw the gesture of acquiescence and moved to take advantage of it. Beneath the water her fingers sought and found the rock-hard nipples, playing over the firm breasts in wondrous reverence as her mind's eye compared the messages of touch to the remembered vision. Gently, but insistently she squeezed the tight flesh between her thumb and forefinger as her tongue traced the contours of Lisa's teeth, before plunging in deep to taste the delicious secretions of this beautiful girl's mouth. Now she concentrated everything on the kiss. Jo-Anne's body had effectively disappeared. It was a mere appendage, a superfluous adjunct to her conquering mouth. Her hands moved gently to frame Lisa's flushed cheeks, and always her tongue, inventive, unpredictable, wise in the ways of arousal, moved subtly to fan the flames of Lisa's rampaging desire. Her forearms strongly flexed, she drew the younger girl in toward her, her right hand reaching behind Lisa's head, buried in the damp hair as she forced her mouth onto her own. Sometimes there was desperation in the embrace as the lips were crushed together, as the tongue sought to merge with the deepest recesses of Lisa's throat. Then it would be playful, teasing as it licked and tickled, luxuriating in the lascivious wetness. Occasionally there was the sharp touch of teeth, and the momentary excitement of delicious pain as Lisa fought back for her share of ecstasy, taking the aggressive tongue between the pure white teeth, nipping, nibbling, disciplining it before succumbing once again to its infinitely welcome dictates.

Lisa was lost hopelessly in the battlefield of the kiss. It was war, life, love. Nothing else mattered. No ambition, no memory, no happiness. It was not a prelude, not a conclusion. It was instead the only reality, the distillation of the present, the very essence of bliss.

Long, and thin, now Jo-Anne's tongue reached into her, its strokes slow and deliberate. Lisa loved it, braced herself to receive it as she tried to ease its pleasure-giving progress, willing it to penetrate her head, to creep further into her mind, to reinforce the wild riot of joyous feeling that roared out of control within her.

Jo-Anne sensed the approach to the plateau as she held the vibrating body in her arms. The fresh innocence of this girl had primed her for this headlong descent into abandonment. Lisa Starr, the ripest and the best. Her beautiful virginity there to be taken, wide open, asking, begging, demanding for satisfaction. She was a gift, a divine sacrifice to the passion gods, whom Jo-Anne Duke served.

Not yet. Not yet. Jo-Anne forced the decision, willing herself to do the impossible, to brake the careering, all but uncontrollable wagon of mutual desire. With very nearly every fiber of her being she wanted the sweet conclusion, as Lisa jerked and twisted her way into ecstasy; but there was a sinewy, steel thread of determination in her as well.

With the effort of the superhuman she turned down the rheostat of raw desire and slowed the pace of the kiss, licking tenderly now at the hungry, suddenly insecure mouth. Jo-Anne moved the forefinger of her right hand to separate their lips, leaving it in place on Lisa's as she pulled hers away. She looked down tenderly at the eager face, allowing the love light to shine through concerned eyes. Then, still silent, she eased herself upward to a standing position on the ledge on which Lisa sat. Towering over her would-be lover, straddling her, she stood, tall and splendid, unpredictable, magnificent.

Lisa felt the thrill of anticipation collide with the sudden doubt.

Before her eyes was the prize and the cause of her predicament. The hairs shone with moisture, the pouting pink lips mimicking the promise of the ones she had loved but a few short seconds before. She lifted her head, her eyes questioning. In reply, Jo-Anne spoke for the very first time. "Not now, Lisa. Not now, my love."

In a second she was out of the water, once more the tantalizing but distant vision. She swooped down gracefully to pick up a towel, and in a few moments of mind-numbing disappointment she was gone.

As the Duke limo sped along Forest Hill Boulevard toward the polo fields of Wellington, Lisa's thoughts were in turmoil. Things seemed to be happening too fast. Good things, strange things, frightening things. She herself all but seduced by the sweet-smelling, sweet-talking billionairess who now sat by her side. From the start Jo-Anne had played it cool. When Lisa had climbed into the cavernous limousine Jo-Anne had pecked at her cheek as if she were a favorite niece. Clearly the party line was to carry on as if nothing had happened. That suited Lisa down to the ground. As far as she was concerned Jo-Anne Duke's lips had been revealed a dangerous weapon, and an action replay of her near fall from grace was the very last thing she wanted, now, or ever for that matter.

Lisa breathed in deeply and tried to keep the excitement inside her. She was riding in the fast lane at last, living in the middle of her Palm Beach dreams, and although it was wonderful it was terrifying, too. Bobby Stansfield had also been invited. She was going to meet him again. Please God he'd be there. A man like him was more than capable of canceling at the last moment. A crisis in South America. Some problems with interest rates, and maybe he'd be called away. Bobby Stansfield. In his eyes she had seen him want her, as in hers she had signaled her desire. When they met the heavens would move. It was as simple as that. Apart from one dreadful thing. She had been conned into wearing all the wrong clothes.

It was the oldest trick in the feminine book and Lisa had fallen for it. What should she wear, she had asked earlier in the week.

"Oh, anything, darling. It's not at all smart. We don't dress up," had been Jo-Anne's confident reply. Lisa had taken her at her word. From her limited wardrobe she had picked out a simple cotton sundress, ending at mid-thigh. A pair of white rubber-soled dancing shoes and the faithful conch belt, once her mother's pride and joy, made up the formidably casual ensemble. Bare legs. No jewelry. In dramatic contrast was Jo-Anne's double-breasted Yves Saint Laurent suit. Tapering down from wide shoulders to a narrow waist, the navy-blue material hugged the curvaceous body, ending precipitously at the knees, where a frontal vee flashed visuals of the inner thigh. The big brass buttons, bright and gleaming, were offset beautifully by pure white gloves. The color was provided by two silk scarves of red, white, and blue—one peeping stylishly from beneath the coat just in front of the left hip and cascading down the upper thigh, the other knotted carefully around the neck, held in place by a vast amethyst brooch surrounded by an exuberant cluster of diamonds. The earrings were smaller versions of the same design, sparkling and shining against the background of a stunning red-and-black striped turban whose tail spread out in an Egyptian-style fan across the formidable shoulders.

She looked like far more than a million dollars.

The breathtaking outfit had taken the wind right out of Lisa's sails at the very moment when she most needed flying speed. At a stroke she had been relegated to country-cousin status. The initial feeling of panic had given way to mild irritation at being so comprehensively set up. Now it had been replaced by the to-hell-with-it-all attitude that was par for her course.

The enormous car sailed grandly through the gates of the Polo Club, the driver waving imperiously at the obsequious guard whose duty it was to vet intruders. There was the shortest of waits in the semicircular entrance driveway and then the valet parkers were clustering around like puppy dogs at a bitch's teat. In the cool of the foyer Lisa braced herself for the plunge into the deep end. Here it was at last. The gates of paradise. In the role of Archangel Peter, the maître d' rushed forward to greet the party, abandoning the lectern at which he presided over the table bookings.

"Mr. Duke, Mrs. Duke. Welcome. Your table is ready, and

Senator Stansfield arrived only a minute or two ago. I hope you enjoy your lunch. Follow me please.''

Lisa was only vaguely aware of her surroundings. It was the sound of her heart leaping about in her chest that preoccupied her most. At the waiter's mention of Bobby's name it had started its wild war dance, and it showed no signs of slowing down. He was *here*. Over there by the window, already beginning to get up as he saw them across the crowded room. Some enchanted evening. It felt like that to Lisa. She had been cast headfirst into the romantic deep end, and all the clichés in the world had come true. So this is what it felt like to walk on air. On either side the bronzed and alabaster faces peered up at her—white for women, brown for men —with the interest of regulars for a stranger in their midst. But Lisa didn't see them. On remote control she steered herself around the groaning buffet and headed for the Duke table, the place of honor in the middle of the picture window with its panoramic view of the cool green polo fields.

Bobby Stansfield was on his feet to greet them.

His first words were infinitely reassuring. Dressed with confident casualness in an open-necked gray-and-white striped Lacoste shirt, gray worsted pants, and a pair of black Cole-Haan loafers, he fastened his disturbing eyes on Lisa. "How wonderful. Lisa Starr. The girl who changes lives.''

He continued to watch her as he ladled out far less substantial greetings on the Dukes. Peter Duke in particular, immaculately blue blazered and white-duck trousered, scored a pointedly cool reception.

If Jo-Anne was undermined by the relative lack of warmth at her arrival she wasn't in the business of showing it. "Sorry we're late, senator. It's Peter's fault. He's so vain, you know. Takes far longer to dress than I do.''

Both Lisa and Bobby laughed at that. Peter Duke looked as if he had just accepted the invitation to be pallbearer at a close friend's funeral. Lisa immediately stopped laughing when she saw that the butt of the joke wasn't enjoying it, but Bobby didn't. She got the picture right away. It wasn't going to be a cozy foursome at all. Bobby and Peter Duke were quite clearly in the middle of a cold war. Jo-Anne was at best neutral, but probably inclining against her husband. For Lisa herself, Bobby seemed already much more than an ally, and Jo-Anne was a far from certain friend if the dress ploy was anything to go by. Damn. She'd imagined that the tricky part would be relating to the outsiders. Now it looked as if the hard ball would be played right there at the table.

An uneasy truce descended as the wine waiter hovered over the table. It didn't last long.

Bobby turned toward Lisa, helpful, solicitous. "The champagne's fine with orange juice, but I wouldn't drink it on its own." Somehow the way he said it didn't sound pompous at all. At least that was what Lisa thought. To her champagne was fizzy, expensive stuff that you drank to celebrate something. But to people like Bobby, who obviously drank it all the time, it was presumably possible to make all sorts of subtle distinctions between one type and another.

"I wouldn't drink it at all, with orange juice or anything else for that matter," said Peter Duke grandly, his lip curling with acid condescension. "That Spanish rubbish produces the worst hangovers in the world. The next day is a total write-off. I'd stick to the bloody marys, Lisa."

His remark said a lot. In the Duke household the champagne was always French, invariably vintage—1971s and 1973s at the moment—and of the very finest marques—Krug, Louis Roederer, Bollinger. A bottle of the Spanish Cordorniu that was being served at the Palm Beach Polo and Country Club Sunday brunch would have been about as welcome in the Duke cellar as a cockroach in a jar of face-cream.

Peter Duke's purpose was not merely to establish himself as a connoisseur. What he meant was that Bobby Stansfield was not only a Philistine, but an impoverished one at that. Stansfield could not afford to buy his way out of vicious hangovers. He was prepared to drink filth and to hide its taste with orange juice. The nuance was there for all to see. Dukes could buy Stansfields at any hour of the day or night.

Bobby got the message. Politicians of his caliber, however, were not fazed by puny javelins of the type Peter Duke could throw. "Must be pretty vital, Peter, for you to be on top form first thing in the morning." Bobby Stansfield's apparently flattering observation was about as innocent as a Chicago politician counting dollar bills in a smoke-filled room.

127

Peter Duke's face reddened as he picked up on the rebuke. Mornings these days tended to start late, and it was a problem filling in the couple of hours before one could decently start to drink again. There was a limit to the amount of time that could be spent on the telephone to the broker finding out if the market movements of the day before had left you a few million dollars richer or poorer.

Jo-Anne didn't help matters by laughing outright. "Listen, Bobby. Poor Peter's mornings are a write-off anyway. I don't think it's the quality of what he drinks—more like the quantity."

Lisa fought back the desire to laugh. Already she had Peter Duke's drift. He was a lazy, pompous incompetent whose most significant achievement had been the accident of his birth. Money was all he had.

Nobody was prepared for Peter's reaction.

First he changed color completely. High up on his cheekbones twin dots of red began to spread like the bloodstains of a disemboweled Samurai warrior. Then, throwing the crumpled linen napkin onto the table in front of him, he stood up suddenly, shaking the china and the cutlery with the violence of the movement.

"Listen, you fucking cow. Don't you ever speak about me like that again. Especially in front of your gym mistress and some clapped-out poseur of a politician." He didn't speak at the top of his voice, but everyone within twenty feet with waxless ears caught the speech. Abruptly, he proceeded to withdraw facilities. Turning his back on the surprised trio, he stalked out of the crowded restaurant, ignoring the two or three would-be friends who tried to talk to him on the way.

For a brief moment the babble of conversation slowed. Not for long. The Polo Club crowd were used to this sort of thing. Too much booze? Somebody caught cheating on his wife? Coke paranoia? Whatever. In seconds they were concentrating on their own lives once again.

"I'm so sorry. I don't know what's gotten into Peter lately. He's as antsy as hell these days."

"He's an asshole," said Bobby simply, and Lisa was more than inclined to agree.

They all ordered champagne and orange juice as a gesture of solidarity.

128

"Come on, Lisa, let's get you some food. All that exercise you do you must burn a lot of fuel." Bobby Stansfield stood up, and he held Lisa's chair for her as she did the same. Jo-Anne had to make it on her own, and for the very first time her expression registered displeasure. Hey, wait a *minute*—it seemed to say. This hick kid is *my* production. You can look but don't touch—and don't forget *I'm* the star around here.

Bobby and Lisa didn't see it at all, and both were already at the stage where they wouldn't have cared if they did. As far as Lisa was concerned, he didn't have to do a thing, and anything he did would be all right. But Bobby wasn't used to the passive role. From the moment he had set eyes on the beautiful young girl, all his most potent instincts as a hunter had been aroused. Okay, so he had a lot going for him in the seduction stakes, but he couldn't know the conditioning process that this one had undergone. So he pulled out the stops and piled on the Stansfield charm, far from suspecting that it was overkill.

Several things were obvious to him. First, from the social point of view Lisa was in way over her head. The clothes said it, the manners confirmed it. But at the same time she was far from over-awed. A little uncertain now and again maybe, but not thrown by the heavy hitters who now surrounded her. Then there was the unmistakable feeling of anarchic strength that hung around her like an aura. This girl would not be pushed around, by people, by conventions, by life itself. Bobby had always been drawn to that. Most politicians, adventurers at heart, were.

Standing in line at the magnificent buffet laid out on the vast T-shaped table Bobby protectively guided her through the social minefield.

"The thing to do is to make several expeditions. Start with some gazpacho maybe, and then come back for the shellfish. The cracked crab is just delicious. Some people just pile it all on their plate, and end up eating roast beef covered with apple pie."

Behind him Jo-Anne's temperature was beginning to rise. She had already lost her husband from this party. Now it looked as if she were in the process of losing one of the best-looking girls she had ever come across. It was time to reassert a bit of her authority, to crack the ringmistress's whip. She looked around for a blunt instrument.

A small man, looking a bit like a tired schoolmaster, scurried past. Snakelike, Jo-Anne's arm shot out to grab the only arm he possessed.

"John, wonderful to *see* you. I must introduce you to my new discovery. Lisa, this is Lord Cowdray. He's on the board of governors here, and just about everywhere else I should imagine. You must have heard of Cowdray Park in England. That's really the Mecca of the polo world."

Lisa reached out a hand. She'd never heard of Cowdray, never met an English lord before, didn't at all like being introduced as Jo-Anne's "new discovery." Rubbing in salt, Jo-Anne bubbled on. "Yes, Lisa runs a little gym in West Palm. We all go there to work out. Isn't that cute?"

Behind the spectacles, John Cowdray had acquired a hunted look. He hardly knew Jo-Anne Duke, and what he had seen of her he was inclined to dislike. Nodding politely, he offered a word or two of small talk before engineering an escape.

Bobby Stansfield, busy plate filling, missed the exchange, but Lisa felt Jo-Anne's wave of patronization break all over her. For some reason the girl who a day or two before had almost seduced her clearly didn't like her at all. Mentally she put up her defenses. Jo-Anne was obviously a very dangerous lady.

Back at the table, Bobby Stansfield was on top of the world. "The thing I always feel is that the people here miss the point. I like to come out here to watch the polo, not the damn people. I can't think why everyone dresses up like it's some fashion parade. Now, you and I, Lisa, have it just right. Casual, nice and cool, comfortable. That's the way to dress in this weather."

"Oh, Jo-Anne told me to dress like this. I'm real glad she filled me in," said Lisa with the innocence of an asp.

Bobby looked at Jo-Anne first in disbelief and then with quizzical interest. Feminine games were clearly being played.

Jo-Anne, looking like she had just gotten off the runway at the Paris collections, stared back evenly. Touché.

"Senator, Jo-Anne, looking indecently lovely I may say. How are you all?"

"Hello, Merv," said Bobby. "Have you allowed yourself a weekend off? I thought you TV superstars were too busy making money to relax."

Merv Griffin laughed good-naturedly. He had been one of the first to buy into the Polo Club. "You're quite right, senator. Actually I'm working right now. Came over to ask you on the show. We need a class act to shore up the ratings." Both men laughed. It was only half a joke.

"Now, Merv, if you want to go through the top on the Nielsens, the person you want is sitting right here. Lisa Starr, meet Merv Griffin."

"Tell you what, senator. You marry her, and we'll have you both on as a double act. How about that."

Lisa felt the blush explode all over her cheeks.

Bobby threw back his head and let out the well-known Stansfield guffaw.

"Well, now we might just do that. Might just get around to that. What do you say, Lisa? Would you take on a confirmed old bachelor like me?"

It was with only the bare minimum of surprise that Lisa realized that, yes, that was exactly what she would be prepared to do.

7

The vein high up on Peter Duke's forehead had quite definitely begun to pulsate. Jo-Anne had only seen that happen once before, and it was not a good omen.

"Shall I tell you what I want. *Exactly* what I want," he yelled at the top of his voice. "I want a fucking divorce, and I want it quick."

There weren't many words that Jo-Anne Duke found really dirty, but divorce was undoubtedly one of them. Divorce, from a Duke. That was a real obscenity. She felt the color drain from her face.

A distant voice, presumably hers, said, "Oh, don't be so silly, Peter. If there's a problem we can work it out. We always did before."

"You're a tramp, Jo-Anne. You know that. You were a whore when you hooked me, and you're still one today. I want out, and I want out now. Do you hear me?"

Jo-Anne struggled to make sense of the earth-shattering message she was receiving. If the decibels were anything to go by, it looked as if he were serious. The fact that it was ten o'clock in the morning meant that he wasn't drunk either.

Jo-Anne tried to lighten it up. That had worked before. It didn't now. She managed a hollow laugh. "You'd be lost without me. You know you would." Sitting on the end of the big bed, she languidly drew on a silk stocking.

Peter Duke took two steps toward his wife, until he towered over her, an unforgiving mountain of hate. The spit that cascaded from his mouth as he fought to wrap his tongue around the venomous syllables filled the air above Jo-Anne's head. "You filthy bitch. How dare you suggest I need you. I need you like I need

brain cancer. I'll step on you like the roach you are. I'll bury
you.''

He was on the verge of physical violence. Jo-Anne knew the
signs. In the old days the hookers who cared about their looks had
learned to read their johns right.

She said nothing at all.

"And when I've gotten rid of you, I'll be free to marry someone
who's as pure and clean as you are totally *disgusting*." He stepped
back, a pleased look of neat spite all over his face.

Jo-Anne struggled for words. She could hardly believe her ears.
This was the ultimate danger. Another woman? Who, what,
where?

"You've got somebody else," she managed at last.

Peter smiled wickedly. "Pamela Whitney. We love one another.
You were too busy whoring to notice."

Christ! Jo-Anne couldn't take much more of this. Pamela Whitney. Face like a doughnut, ass like a sponge pudding, pedigree as
long as the yellow brick road. Of course, it made sense. A dynastic
marriage, like the ones the medieval princes arranged. You take
my daughter, and we merge our kingdoms. Dimly, through the
mists of horror, she began to see the enormity of what faced her.
Together the Whitneys and the Dukes would eat her for breakfast.
Between them they must own more lawyers than the Justice Department. She'd be lucky to get out of the marriage with anything
more than the exotic underwear that had been her sole material
contribution to it.

"Listen, Peter, I think we should talk about this."

"We *are* talking about it, sweetheart. At least I'm *telling* you
about it. There's not a lot you can say that'll interest me."

Jo-Anne couldn't help herself. She just had to test the water, to
see how bad things really were. "If we do split up, I guess there'll
be some sort of settlement."

She sounded far from certain.

"Right on, there'll be a settlement. Do you want to know what
it'll be? I can tell you right now. You get to pack a suitcase, just
one, and you get to call a cab—and then you piss the hell out of
my life, back to the gutter you came from. Understand? Maybe,
just maybe, if you act real nice I may let you take the Mercedes."

It was Jo-Anne's turn to laugh. "You've got to be joking, Peter. This isn't the Dark Ages, you know, or Saudi Arabia. If I go, then I *take*. Do *you* understand? I'll cut your fucking fortune off at the knees."

"Hah." All the scorn in the world was packed into Peter Duke's derisive exclamation. He had the look of the man who was holding all the trumps. "That's for a court to decide, isn't it. And a *Florida* court. More specifically a Palm Beach County court. Do you know what that means, Jo-Anne? Dukes have been around here a long time. They've got some powerful friends, and in this part of the world the good ol' boys have a way of sticking closer together than copulating dogs—or haven't you noticed? When I said I'd bury you I wasn't joking. Sweetest thing is, you gave it to me on a plate."

Jo-Anne had never heard a nastier laugh. What the hell did he mean?

"Yes, sir, I'd sure like you to see what I've got sitting in old Ben Carstairs's safe. Just about the juiciest dossier a man could read. If I ever get short of cash, I might just go right on and publish it. Should be worth millions."

The dreadful fear rushed through Jo-Anne. "What dossier? Have you been spying on me?" Even as she asked the question, she knew the answer was yes. God! How could she have *been* so stupid? She'd thought she'd played it safe, covered her tracks, avoided the heterosexual affairs that were always supposed to be the dangerous ones. She had heard the metallic click of the telephone, the hollow sound when she spoke into the receiver. Peter had bugged it. For months all her most secret conversations had been going down on tape.

"I've got transcripts of conversations that would make a seventy-year-old judge's false teeth fall out. I swear I thought old Ben was going to come right there in his pants when he heard you sweet-talking that Mary d'Erlanger. And you know those photographs of the pair of you walking out of the Brazilian Court—boy, I've seen some wrecked ladies in my time, but you two looked as if you needed crutches. Somehow, I don't think the court is going to look too kindly on your claims on my assets."

Of course he was right. No way he wasn't. But suddenly Jo-

Anne didn't mind at all. Already she was one step ahead of poor Peter. Always had been. Ice cold inside, she knew exactly what she would do.

"What was he *like,* for Chrissakes?" Maggie looked ready to explode with curiosity.

Lisa reached down and picked up her leg as if it were a totally foreign object. Putting her right knee on her cheekbone she straightened it and pointed the big toe directly at the ceiling. As she did so she thought about Maggie's question.

"I guess I'm in love," she laughed.

"Oh, I know that. Of course you are. But what the hell is he *like?*"

"Well, if you want me to be serious, let's see. He's incredibly good looking, which isn't exactly the latest news, I guess. He's kind, sort of sensitive. You know, puts you at ease. Protective, you could say. Oh, and he's funny, very funny—and incredibly self-confident. Like you know he wouldn't take any shit from anybody. He really carved up that Peter Duke guy. Put him through the mincer."

Maggie leaned forward. It wasn't nearly enough. "But did he come on to you? Is he going to *call,* for God's sake? How did you leave it?"

Lisa's expression was reflective. "He could call. I'm sure he liked me. But I just don't know if he has time. He must be worked off his feet."

Lisa retrieved her limb, removed her bottom from the corner of the desk, and stuck her foot in the small of her back.

Looking envious, Maggie went right back to gnawing the bone. "Listen, baby. It doesn't take that long."

Lisa laughed wickedly. "Yeah, maybe he'll stop by and try me out on the Nautilus machines."

"Okay. Well, I bet he makes a move. Anyone would."

"Thanks, Maggs. But seriously, I just can't be his type. You know, a guy like that. I mean he's so sophisticated. He knows everything, everyone. I mean he probably calls up the president to check what's on TV if he's lost the newspaper. What the hell have I got to offer him?''

"I can see a couple of things right now," Maggie said. "That body stocking is *evil*, Lisa."

"I think somebody like Bobby Stansfield is into minds more than bodies. All those political groupies, with their master's in philosophy and politics."

"I know we all try to forget brains around here, Lisa, but you're really bright."

"If he *does* call, he's going to wait a day or two, so there's no point us getting too excited just yet."

Six inches to the right of Lisa's crotch the telephone rang.

She smiled as she picked it up, flushed as she heard the voice.

"I can tell that's Lisa Starr I'm talking to. Bobby Stansfield. What are you doing for lunch?''

"Oh, goodness. Hello. How are you? Lunch. God! What's today? Yes, of course I'd like to."

"Great. We were all sitting here around the pool trying to think of what we needed to make good things even better, and I hit on you. Have you got wheels? I can send a car. Come as soon as you like—it's paradise over here, and we're drinking the neatest margaritas."

Lisa's head had begun to throb. The compliment was nice, but it was something else he'd said. Paradise over here. Paradise over here. Paradise over here. She opened her mouth to speak, but the words wouldn't come.

"Are you still there? Do you know where to come? You turn left at . . .''

"It's okay. I know the way. I can find it." I've been there a thousand times in my dreams.

"And you don't need transportation?''

"No. I'd like to cycle over."

"God! In this heat? Boy, are you exercise freaks into punishment. Anyway, hurry, and don't melt before you arrive. I want to see all of you."

"I'm on my way."

Lisa put down the telephone. For a second the two friends stared at each other, saying nothing.

Maggie broke the ice. In an exaggerated stage voice she intoned, "Ladies and gentlemen, please make way for Senator and Mrs. Robert Stansfield," as Lisa threw at her four pens, six paper clips, an eraser, and a small Japanese calculator.

Lisa pedaled hard as she crossed the dangerous North Flagler intersection. Her experience had been that accidents tended to take place around where she was; that she herself might possibly be the cause of them had not occurred to her. The disinterested observer would not have made that mistake. She was all in white, from her Adidas sneakers and ankle socks to the shorts and loose T-shirt under which her mind-bending breasts surged and reared. Her long firm legs stroked the pedals with seemingly effortless ease.

Across her back was the white plastic beach bag, a rope from each end snaking out around Lisa's torso and plastering the T-shirt flat between the conical tits. There wasn't much inside. She had packed fast. The only real problem had been the swimsuit. The ones she possessed were just fine for the *Sports Illustrated* beachwear editions, but were hardly, she imagined, standard issue around the Stansfield swimming pool. Still, there hadn't been time for a shopping trip, or indeed the inclination. Lisa was intelligent enough to know that in this life you scored few points trying to pass yourself off as something you were not—especially to the Bobby Stansfields of this world.

The jet-black skin-tight suit she had selected would have been a wow on Copacabana and Ipanema. One piece, it was cut away sharply at the crotch, front and back, to show all but the most private aspects of the anatomy. So far she hadn't had any complaints, and she didn't anticipate any now.

Once across the bridge, she made the left turn onto the Palm Beach bicycle trail. Running along the borders of Lake Worth, the five-foot-wide tarmac pathway rambled for seven miles past some of the most beautiful, and expensive, houses in the world. It was a magical thoroughfare, closed strictly to motor vehicles of every kind and yet, despite its flavor of total exclusivity, it was open to the public. Here different worlds could meet as cyclists, joggers, and hikers were able to peer at the pools of the rich. Somehow, though, it never happened like that. The bicycle trail was a closely guarded secret, and those sophisticated enough to have discovered it were discreet enough to respect the rights of others. For Lisa it was enough to speed past the sleek yachts moored at the bottoms of their owners' gardens, past the thick banyan trees, the banks of sweet-smelling jasmine ivy, through the rich aroma of sandalwood and frangipani blossoms, past the tall ficus hedges of those who valued their privacy more than their view. She remembered her mother's words, "The higher the ficus, the richer the man." Would, one day, her ficus hedge be tall? The street names at the intersections said it all—Tangier Avenue, West Indies Drive, Bahama Lane. Farther north there would be Tradewind Drive, Orange Grove Road, and Mockingbird Trail. How easy it would be to love a place like this. How easy it *was* to love it. And the people who lived in it.

On purpose Lisa overshot the Garden Road turn that would have taken her directly to the Stansfield house. She often did that. Instead she took the right on Colonial that brought her to the gates of the Kennedy home. She paused briefly. Was Rose in there now, insulated at last from the ongoing tragedies that history seemed determined to heap on her family? In the parking lot stood the battered family Buick, desperately unpretentious. Who could have thought a few years ago the car park had been created as a helicopter pad for the most powerful man in the world? Even then Palm Beach had made it hard on the Kennedys, and it was only with the utmost reluctance that the town council had made a special exception to the strict rule that forbade any flying craft to land within the town's borders. The brick-red paint on the Mizner gem was peeling unselfconsciously, and the two signs that read hopefully NO TRESPASSERS and BEWARE OF THE DOG had long outlived their usefulness.

What trick of fate had thrown the Kennedys and the Stansfields together, separated by only half a dozen houses on the long, lonely beach? Two great political dynasties, one Democrat, one Republican, neighbors and foes, one day perhaps to be locked in battle for the greatest prize of all. It was a potent thought. The two potential opponents could near enough have enjoyed a game of Frisbee without ever leaving their respective front lawns. Within a few years, North Ocean Boulevard could once again number a president of the United States among its residents, and casual bicycle rides of this sort would be very strictly curtailed. Lisa allowed herself to imagine it: the traffic diversions, the lean, hard men with their suspicious eyes, the aura of latent excitement and danger. And maybe, God willing, it would be Bobby. Bobby Stansfield. Her host for lunch. She was to be an honored guest in the mansion where her mother had been so proud to work.

The police car rolled by, its driver checking her out quickly. She was used to that. Every other car in this town belonged to the police, and the three-and-a-half-mile strip of the North End was probably just about the only place on God's earth where *everybody* kept to the speed limit. Most of the residents liked it that way. People didn't lock their doors in this part of town. Lisa shook her head in disbelief, half admiration, half horror as she thought about the town's excesses. They'd recently passed a bylaw that made it compulsory for the people who worked in the town without living there—the gardeners, cleaners, etc.—to carry I.D. cards at all times and to give mandatory fingerprint samples. That just *had* to be unconstitutional. But Palm Beach didn't mind. Palm Beach did things its own way. Even now, some liberal was taking the town to court to contest the rule. Lisa hoped he had deep pockets; he'd need them. Then there was the jogger, arrested and charged for being indecently dressed. The poor guy had taken off his T-shirt. Perhaps if he'd been female . . . Lisa laughed out loud at the thought. Then the laugh died in her throat. She was cycling through the big gates of the Stansfield mansion.

Lisa was hardly ready for the white-uniformed maid who opened the heavy, carved oak door. For a second she stood there, immobile, as the bittersweet memories came flooding back. How well she had grown to love that uniform. How proud her mother had been of its immaculate whiteness, of its symbolic meaning. All those years it had lain there in the closet, laundered faithfully from time to time and kept scrupulously pressed. Occasionally Mary-

Ellen had taken it out and put it on to show the young Lisa the glories of her former position as trusted servant in the Stansfield house. Did the young girl in front of her feel the same way about her job? Unlikely. For a start she was black, and for blacks it was unwise and unprofitable to dream dreams in Palm Beach.

Lisa pushed the unwelcome thoughts from her mind. There were other emotions to be dealt with besides nostalgia. Life had to go on. To go upward. "I think Senator Stansfield is expecting me. I'm Lisa Starr."

The maid inclined her head backward and made a sort of a sniffing noise. The look said, Senator Stansfield is always expecting pretty young girls. Don't you go getting ideas above your station.

"Theyse all out by the pool. Follow me, Miss Starr," was what she said.

Lisa was inside at last—a child in the toy shop of her dreams. Wide eyed, she tried to imprint everything on her memory as she followed the maid through the dark old house. They passed along a Spanish-tiled cloister, both sides of it opening through archways to immaculately landscaped terraces, thick with greenery—bougainvillaea, tecoma, and wild orchids nestling in Spanish moss—and the sound of tinkling water from cleverly placed fountains. Long oak sideboards, dark and intricately carved, containing silver bowls of long-stemmed flowers and smaller bowls of pink and white azaleas, lined the walls. A huge still life of fruit and flowers painted in the style of the Dutch School was lit by an ancient picture light.

Gloomy, thought Lisa. But incredibly stylish. Pure and unadulterated Mizner—the whole house reeking of twenties Palm Beach when its rich had ruled the world and imagined that they would do so forever.

Before her the soft-soled white shoes padded over the highly polished tiles as her mother's had once done; again Lisa fought back the wave of sadness that threatened to engulf her. At the end of the cloister was a big, black wrought-iron gate, its brass doorknob highly polished. Through the delicate patterns of its design Lisa could see a stretch of green lawn beyond which was the sea, its waves rolling in lazily toward the breakwater.

"I'll leave you here, Miss Starr. You'll find the senator and his friends over there by the pool."

As she approached, Bobby Stansfield uncoiled himself from a toweled sun bed, rising to greet her.

"Lisa. Lisa. Just what we needed." He turned to his friends. "There you are. I promised you an angel and now I deliver one." His smile was as warm and welcoming as sunlight on soft skin. "Lisa, this is Jimmy Baker. Knows everything in the world about politics. I hope! Not much about anything else."

Jimmy smiled carefully at the jocular introduction, as he stood to shake Lisa's hand, his cunning eyes reaching into her. How would she affect his boy? Was she good news or bad news? A cheap trick or a respectable girl? How could she be *used?*

Lisa looked him up and down in distaste. If he ever got around to shaving his chest he could go into the doormat business.

The other two men seemed to be less important, more deferential, eager to please.

"Now, Lisa, can you handle a margarita? I'm afraid we started without you—if I may understate the case a bit." He threw back his head and laughed. A little boy owning up to a raid on the cookie jar? A fun-loving man of the world who was not afraid to enjoy himself and needed a partner in crime? An old-style aristocrat who knew a thing or two when it came to mixing a cocktail? There was an element of all three in his remark and in his laughter, and Lisa wasn't at all sure which she found the most attractive.

He steered her toward the bar area of the poolside cabana. "The secret of a *really* good margarita is always to make it yourself," he said in mock seriousness. "Glass in the icebox, of course."

Like a conjurer he extracted two frosted, V-shaped cocktail glasses from the freezer compartment of the refrigerator. He emptied a pile of salt onto the white marble slab and smoothed it flat with his hand before dipping in the rim of each glass.

Bobby filled the two glasses from a large jug, and handed one to Lisa. "Tell me what you think of that." On his face was a playful expression of concern.

"Mmmmmmm. That's delicious," said Lisa. "What a way to go."

Bobby laughed as he led her away to a table some distance from the other three men. Lisa felt the alcohol pass straight through her stomach lining and into her bloodstream. He was even more attractive than she had remembered, if that was at all possible. Sort of

craggy rather than muscular—a body that looked as if it had become fit by being used for things other than just constant exercise.
There was enough hair on the chest, but not too much. Nice feet
and, thank God, well-manicured toenails. Few men realized how
important that was. The face of course won medals, but then that
was common knowledge from the redwood forests to the Gulf
Stream waters. It was difficult to separate the man from what he
meant, from what it was possible he could mean. Bobby Stansfield
wasn't just a good-looking jock hanging out poolside and getting
gently stoned in the sun. He was a symbol. More self-confident
than the old conservatism, the philosophy he embraced had struck
a vein of feeling right across the country, and if he was able to
mine it well he might draw the ultimate dividend. That made him a
figure of awesome potential power, which acted in synergy with
his abundant physical attractions. Anyone would have felt that.
But Lisa wasn't just anyone: she was Mary-Ellen Starr's daughter,
and if the pun could be forgiven, she saw him through starry eyes.

"Listen, did you bring some swimming things? If not, I'm sure
we could fix you up. There's usually a pile of my sisters' stuff
around."

"Sure. In here." Lisa patted the bag. "Where do I change?"

"Use the cabana."

By the time she had returned Bobby had stretched himself out
on the sun bed and, eyes closed, was soaking up the sun.

Standing over him she cut out the sun's rays. Bobby sat up,
aware of her presence from the sudden darkness. He opened his
eyes, filling them up with the erotic vision of a lifetime. For the
first time in an age he was at a loss for words. "Christ," he managed at last.

Lisa laughed, pleased at the effect she knew she was having.

For a second or two she let him feast upon her, his desperate
eyes sliding all over her flowing body. Then she turned on her heel
and ran the few steps to the pool's edge. In one liquid movement
she arced through the air and, making no splash at all, disappeared
into the drinkable blue water.

She knew he would follow her, that he would be drawn into the
water by the magnet of her body. She had seen it all in the eager
eyes. Lisa swam the length of the pool before breaking the surface,
her lungs more than capable of providing the oxygen for her pow-

erful underwater breast stroke. As she emerged from the depths she tossed back her head, sending the wet, black hair behind the strong shoulders. With her right hand she smoothed errant strands from her eyes as with her left she held on to the blue mosaic tiles of the pool's edge. She looked for Bobby. He had vanished.

For a second her heart skipped a beat. He'd gone. Gone to get himself another drink? To talk a little more politics with his poolside cronies? To answer the telephone?

Like an otter, slippery, muscular, the dark form rushed up between her legs. He was very close, his hands tracing the contours of her body, of her ankles, her calves, her outer thighs, the fine line of her buttocks, the sweep of her waist. In one lingering second of delight the confident hands touched the line of her breasts, before reaching for their final destination—in the pits of her arms.

The underwater lap of the sixty-foot pool had not caused Lisa to lose any breath at all, but she lost it now. As Bobby's head emerged into the sunshine inches from Lisa's own, his laughing smile promising the world, he lifted her up, strong and mischievous, until she herself was propelled from the pool by the crane of his arms, forced to sit on its side, her knees dangling in the water, framing Bobby's head as he smiled up at her.

There, silhouetted against the wild blue of the Florida sky, he allowed himself to worship at the altar of her teenage beauty as Lisa, the breath coming fast now through parted lips, gazed back at him, the excitement shining in her eyes at the contemplation of the desire in his.

Something would happen. Both knew it.

For an age they savored the moment—the first delicate moment of the journey to intimacy when everything is new, all is supercharged with the mystery and danger of passion.

Bobby's arms snaked upward to encircle each of Lisa's upper legs and he drew himself in toward her, forcing the delicious flesh hard against his head, his lips centimeters from the place she already wanted to be his. Again he looked up at her, his chin touching the material of the bathing suit, its delicious pressure caressing her at the most vulnerable part of her being. Once again the baby-blue eyes questioned her, reassured her, tantalized her. Then she was being pulled forward, her bottom losing its precarious seat at the pool's edge as he drew her toward him into the water. Her momentum carried her down deep, and Bobby went with her, his hard body plastered against hers, held rigidly against her by the ropelike arms.

Like the drowning man whose life is supposed to flash past in the seconds before destruction, Lisa's mind kaleidoscoped the events which had led to this most wanted moment. She was gone, lost, spinning in the vortex of lust, and love. That was it. She loved this man who held her. Loved him physically and mentally as she had been programmed to do. He was everything. Her mother, her ambition, her future. And he was here now. Holding her tightly in his arms beneath the surface of the Stansfield swimming pool a few feet away from his friends.

For a desperate moment she felt the need to escape, to collect her chaotic thoughts. Soon they would be lovers, but there was a no-man's-land to cross.

Like a mermaid she slipped away from him, searching for the safe haven where she could rediscover her mind, the clarity of her thoughts. Without looking back she was out of the pool, and running toward the cabana.

It was dark in the changing room. Cool and dark. As good a place as any to try to get a hold on runaway emotions. Lisa was wet, and she shook from head to foot. Every single nerve ending was shouting, screaming for some sort of release from the unbearable tension that gripped her body. She backed up against the white tile of the shower, grateful for its cold touch against her skin —for any touch at all. All the time she fought to grip the reins, to slow the chariot of desire that careened dangerously within her. On her thigh she could still feel the imprint of Bobby's urgent strength, the mind-stopping feeling of him crushed against her in the deep blue waters. God, how she wanted him. It was crazy to want like this, and so ludicrously sudden. Then, with the shock of joy she realized that she was no longer alone. Her eyes tightly closed, she felt his hand on hers, and her mind stopped as her body crashed on. It was a beautiful dream, a wonderful fantasy, as he placed her hand elsewhere. She could feel it throb, expanding, rearing, twitching beneath her hot fingers. Still she kept her eyes closed, unwilling to disturb the magic of the moment that she knew now would come. She heard her low moan of acquiescence, as the material of the swimsuit was drawn away from her body.

Beneath her hand the penis moved, a living, wanting thing, desiring conquest and possession. Lovingly she traced its contours from the proud, smooth head along the rock-hard shaft to the jungle abundance of its base. Still her eyes remained closed as she prepared herself to receive the offering. From her parted lips came a shuddering sigh of ecstasy as she readied herself, and she flexed her powerful pelvic muscles, bending very slightly at the knee as she pressed her back against the shower's wall.

The two hands of the lovers worked in union to guide the invader to its destination. Pausing for the briefest of moments at the wet, anxious entrance, it plunged gratefully into its rightful home.

Lisa let out a short, sharp cry as the delightful thing moved within her. Like a traveler in a strange land it was first cautious, unsure of itself as it explored the unfamiliar surroundings, but slowly it began to gain in confidence as it established a rhythm of its own.

Only now did she open her eyes.

"How did you know it was me?" he whispered tenderly.

Lisa tried to speak as she moistened dry lips with a partially dry tongue. She smiled back at him, saying nothing, as he pushed gently into her.

"I wanted you since the first time I saw you," Bobby said.

"You can have me. Like this. Anytime. Anywhere." Thrusting downward she gripped him in the vice of her passion, guarding the willing prisoner, crushing its abundant strength with the power of her own need.

Her tongue reached out for his, ravenous for him, hungry for his taste, as her mind willed the impossible merger of bodies, of souls. It seemed to Lisa as if whole parts of her had ceased to exist. From her mouth to her vagina, all the feeling, the wanting, the living and the loving concentrated at the point where Bobby had entered her.

"Do you want it here? Like this?"

The question was concerned, urgent.

Lisa felt the panic rush into the battlefield of her mind. "God yes. Don't stop, Bobby. Don't dare stop."

All she wanted was his climax. Later there would be time for anything and everything, but now she wanted his seed inside her. Nothing else mattered, not her own body's satisfaction, not tenderness, not understanding, not even love.

Her hands found the thrusting buttocks and she pulled at them in the desperation of desire, forcing him deeper inside her as she added her own strength to his. Her back jammed tight against the wall now slippery with her sweat, she withstood the heavenly onslaught as she prayed for its sweet end.

She saw it first in his eyes, the faraway look, the almost dreamy detachment, the intensification of the thrashing love dance in her belly. Like a clarion call from the clearest of trumpets it summoned the reaction in Lisa. Together. It would be together, and they would always be together. Locked in love. Locked in each other's bodies. She stood up on tiptoe, making him reach for her.

"Oh, Lisa."

"It's all right. I'm ready. I want you, Bobby. God, how I want you."

And then Lisa's mind took off, wandering, drifting, dreaming on the sea of detachment as the wave of sublimity engulfed her. Shaking with the rumbling tremors of her own orgasm, she tried, too, to experience his. Feverishly she attempted to call her brain to order, to shine the spotlight of sensation on the event that was happening inside her. She was being cleansed, washed clean of her past, as Bobby bathed her with his passion. Bucking, rearing, forcing himself deeper into her, he shouted triumphantly as Lisa's feet left the ground, a butterfly pinned to the wall by the exploding instrument of desire.

Head bowed on her streaming chest, Bobby shook in the aftermath of love.

Tenderly Lisa cradled the nuzzling head, as she felt the triumph in her soul. And there was another feeling too, mad, impossible, but absolutely certain. One fine day she would have this man. Have his love, his name, forever.

Peter Duke could hardly believe it. Beneath the Egyptian cotton sheets his wife's hands were all over him. For a second or two he lay there like a log as he tried to make sense of it. It seemed to be about breakfast time from the chinks of sunlight visible through cracks in the heavy curtains. But why? They hadn't made it for months, except after quarrels. Giving Jo-Anne her marching orders was unlikely to have made him more attractive in her eyes. Masochism had never been her bag.

Then Peter Duke smiled to himself. Okay, he had her number. Boy, she must have thought he was a real sucker. She was trying to win him back by turning him on. He wanted to laugh out loud. God, the transparency of it. Jo-Anne was disappointing him. He'd expected more from her. Some smart legal moves, perhaps, and a brash determination to brazen it out, to drag the Duke name through the courts and, incidentally, the mud. To avoid that he'd certainly reach for his checkbook. The old Jo-Anne wouldn't have missed that sort of a move. But this? Wow.

Whatever the motive she certainly hadn't lost her touch, and it was impossible to avoid the comparison with Pamela Whitney, who'd never had the touch in the first place. Certainly the first time with his bride-to-be had been a complicated failure. He'd had all the potency of a noodle soaked overnight in condensed milk, and concluded that the act of lovemaking for a female Whitney was about as unimportant as forgetting to carry I.D. to the bank when cashing a check. No, Whitneys relied on other charms. Like money, superior genes, and all those extraordinary *horses*. Breeding horses and breeding children. Those were the sorts of things they were good at. Soon there would be a clan of pint-size Whitney Dukes, a gaggle of little preppies to run the businesses, join the clubs, and irritate the stockbrokers.

Jo-Anne Duke went about her work with the expertise of the true professional. There was no pleasure in it, none at all, but there *was* purpose. Afterward Peter Duke would unwind a bit, bend a little, be marginally more prepared to fit in with her suggestions. That was important if she was to avoid the ultimate disaster. Not for one moment did she imagine it would change his mind. Dynasties and dollars had been in his eyes when he had talked of divorce, and the cold, calculating way he had snooped on her over the months argued that the whole thing had been premeditated. Her objective was a lesser one.

After she had achieved it Peter Duke lay back on the pillows and watched his beautiful wife with suspicious eyes.

"Was that okay?" He couldn't resist fishing for the compliment.

"Only the greatest," she lied. Jo-Anne put out a hand and touched his arm. "You know, Peter, we shouldn't fight."

She laughed the attractive, flirtatious laugh.

Peter smiled back knowingly. It was bad manners to kick somebody in the mouth who had recently been the source of so much pleasure. He fought back the desire to tell her that nothing had changed, that she was still out on the street without a bean, that blowing him was blowing in the wind.

"I guess I can't argue with that," he said.

"You know, I've been thinking, Peter. I've been thinking a lot about everything. About us. The divorce." She watched the interest spark in him as he waited for her to make her pitch. It was clear that he expected bargaining. If you give me this, you can have that. In exchange for the jewels, I'll . . .

She went on. "I came to a strange conclusion, really. I think it's been my fault all along. I blew it. I guess I always have. Perhaps it's just the way I am. Anyway, what I want to say is that I'm sorry for everything. I'm not going to contest the divorce, and I don't want anything for me. I'm best like that, on my own, looking after myself, fighting my own battles. No responsibilities. Kind of like a child of the universe, doing my own thing."

Peter's eyes narrowed. He could hardly believe this. There just had to be an angle. No free lunches.

Jo-Anne plowed on in the pregnant silence.

"I guess I realize you're holding all the cards, but playing them would make a great big mess, for both of us really. It wouldn't help anyone. Who knows, maybe you'd think that was worth something."

Peter saw the play. It wasn't such a bad move, but it was a trusting one. She would go quietly, and in exchange he would do the decent thing and smooth her path with a generous settlement. Effectively, she was throwing herself on his mercy.

Peter Duke liked what he heard. He was at heart a bully, and there was nothing on this earth he enjoyed doing more than exploiting weakness. He would appear to fit in with her plans. Make her sign all sorts of things, and then, when it came to signing the settlement check he would laugh in her face, slam the door, then change the locks.

"That would be very decent of you, Jo-Anne. You could count on my recognizing that, once things had been sorted out."

Jo-Anne let the relief shine out through her eyes. "Oh, Peter, that's great. Just great. I hoped you'd see it like that. So we don't fight anymore. Okay? Listen, I've got a wonderful idea. Let's go waterskiing. Like we used to. I haven't driven the boat in an age, and the ocean's flat as a mill pond out there. I checked it earlier."

"Hell, why not. It might be fun," said Peter Duke.

"Are you ready?" Jo-Anne shouted the words above the gentle thud of the Riva's powerful engine.

Across the smooth, still waters off the North End beach, Peter Duke's reply was clearly audible. His yes drifted through on the breezeless air.

Jo-Anne reached down, pulled hard at the throttle, and the great boat lurched forward as the engines let out a mighty roar.

Peter Duke arose from the calm waters with effortless ease, rock steady, hardly moving from side to side. Right away it was obvious to the lazy sun-worshipers of the nearby beach that this skier was no novice, and the impression was confirmed when he headed immediately toward the speedboat's wake. Arms stretched out fully in front of him, he leaned well back, body straight and inclined at a forty-five-degree angle to the sea surface. As his speed increased he hit the waves of the wash and was momentarily airborne, before crashing down into the flat water beyond. Now, almost parallel with the Riva's side, his forward velocity slowed, allowing him time for a cheery wave to Jo-Anne, before he braced his legs for the turn.

This was the part he liked. Beneath his feet he felt the enormous upward force as he twisted the ski in opposition to the water. The muscles of his forearms stood out like steel spans as the tow rope pulled at him, and the high column of seawater splayed out satisfactorily from the edge of the ski as he made the turn.

Now, he raced across the stern of the boat. Two wakes to jump as he crossed to the other side. He was dimly aware of his wife's long hair waving in the wind created by the Riva's speed.

This was what it was all about. A man pitting himself against the elements, using his skill and determination to stay upright in a situation in which all the cards were stacked against him. In this life the list of his achievements was not a long one, but he was good at this. No question. It had been a great idea of Jo-Anne's.

For a second as he sped along through the salt-sprayed air, he allowed himself the luxury of a moment's regret. Somehow he couldn't see Pamela Whitney in the role of furious chariot driver that Jo-Anne filled so well. She would have other charms, but driving his ski boat wouldn't be one of them. Still, it looked as if they would part as friends. Maybe he'd slip her a million or two for old times' sake. At least it would keep her off the streets—the cheaper ones anyway.

Hey, hang on there. Concentrate. Nearly lost that turn. Twisting and turning like an unleashed rocket on the Fourth of July, the Riva was tracing crazy patterns all over the sea. Peter smiled to himself. Good old Jo-Anne. This was the spirit he admired in her. Nothing she liked more than competition. Her powers as a driver against his as a skier. It was the best way. He gritted his teeth and tensed his muscles for the battle.

Jo-Anne's mouth, usually sensual and full, was now a thin pencil line across her face. Her eyes, normally sparkling, were cold and dead as she gripped the leather-clad wheel. This way and that she turned the sleek vessel, carving and churning at the soft ocean; like a Navy Phantom caught in the guidance system of a heat-seeking missile, she tried for the totally unpredictable turn, the cunningly deceptive change of speed.

Behind the boat Peter Duke held on grimly as he tried to antici-pate her movements. As the minutes clicked by his muscles began to tire with the strain, and his mind to slow with the effort of bodily coordination. Okay, Jo-Anne, that's about it. Enough is enough. Don't let's overdo it.

But the boat didn't stop. If anything its movements had become even more frantic as it leaped and bounded over the sea surface in its effort to shake off its load. Peter Duke fought to stay with it, a fisherman determined not to lose a record catch, as it raced all over the ocean to defeat him. And then, quite suddenly, it was all over. As he went into a turn Jo-Anne cut the throttle. As he came out of it she opened right up again, wrenching the wheel to the right as she did so. Game, set, and match. With rueful resignation and not a little relief, Peter Duke let himself go, arcing gracefully through the air, as the smooth blue surface rushed up to meet his face.

Wipe-out. That was what the surfers said. Well, beneath the water it was cool and quiet, a welcome contrast to the struggle of the fifteen-minute contest. Lazily Peter Duke headed upward.

When he broke surface the boat was just finishing its turn, its bow settled in the water as the big propellers ground the seas at idling speed. Sixty, maybe seventy feet away, and the bow was now toward him. Lying on his back, kicking gently at the warm ocean, he planned his greeting.

Were you trying to kill me back there? Yes, that would do. A humorous response to his wife's little victory. Thirty feet away. Jo-Anne was totally invisible behind the looming prow of the boat with its steel-edged V and sloping mahogany walls.

Careful, Jo-Anne. You should be in neutral now. Swing around a bit to give me some room.

Peter Duke opened his mouth, "Were you trying to kill . . .''

With an angry roar the Riva's engines howled into life. Like an arrow the bow came at him. No time to act. No time to think. The gleaming wood smacked into his shoulder, and the shuddering shock of the terrific blow seemed to loosen all the connections in his body. Down, down he went, his senses pained by the drowsy numbness of a dimly remembered poem. Fractions of time away, the burnished, razor-sharp blades of the propellers churned in eager anticipation. It was a funny sensation. Jingle jangle—a bit like driving over a bumpy road. No pain. Just a strange whirring in the head as the screws rearranged his formerly neat body, spilling his blood, his tissues, and his guts all over the ocean. And then there was nothing really, except perhaps the mildest sense of irritation at the inefficiency of it all, as Peter Duke started out on his unplanned trip to eternity.

"Eternal Father strong to save . . .''
Through the black lace veil, Jo-Anne could see that the whole of

Palm Beach had turned out for the funeral. She had never seen
Bethesda-by-the-Sea so packed. Not at the Phipps wedding, the
winter fête—not ever. But then they would come, wouldn't they?
After all, a Duke was a Duke. Of course, nobody had really *liked*
Peter—except presumably for the grotesque Pamela Whitney, visible out of the corner of her eye, back as straight as that of any
Marine honor guard, upper lip as stiff as a surfer's penis on Saturday night, as she "suffered in dignity." Christ! Those two sure
deserved each other. They could have lain in bed for the rest of
their lives playing with each other's pedigrees. Every now and
again she would have turned on her back and thought of the flag
while Peter grunted and groaned on top of her to produce a few
more little Dukes for the *Social Register*.

". . . those in peril on the sea."

She had asked specially for the song. Good enough for President
Kennedy. Good enough for poor old Peter. Apt, really.

She looked around. It was going off well. The Jackie Kennedy
bit. The grieving widow. Jo-Anne didn't have to look behind her
to know that there wasn't a dry eye in the church.

"Glad hymns of praise and victory . . ."

That was nice. Yes, it had been her victory all right. No other
word for it. Victory snatched in the nick of time from the gaping
cavern of defeat's halitosis-ridden jaws. Peter would have gotten
his divorce, and she would have been drummed out of the town
with hardly the price of a Greyhound bus ticket. From paradise to
Queer Street at the direction of a good-ol'-boy judge. But now she
was smiling beneath the black veil at his funeral, and maybe later,
when no one was looking, she'd go out and dance on his grave.
They had all underestimated her, her determination, her ruthless-
ness, her willingness to do whatever it took to maintain her position—and now they were all having to pay for their oversight. Jo-
Anne Duke—the respected, grieving widow, overtaken by tragedy. Pure as the driven snow, a lady in white cruelly forced into
the black of mourning.

Old Ben Carstairs had nearly had apoplexy at the reading of the
will. A hooker had triumphed—but there was absolutely nothing
he could do about it. Peter's last will and testament had been made
years before in the halcyon days after the honeymoon. When she
had asked exactly how many millions there were, nobody had been

able to say. It apparently depended on all sorts of things like changing property valuations, exchange rates, and things like that. It was the moment Jo-Anne had known that she was seriously rich. If you couldn't count it you were in megabuck territory for sure.

Almost as an aside she had demanded Peter's dossier.

"Shortly before he died my husband told me you were holding a private and personal file of his. I gather from the will that all his personal possessions are now mine. Perhaps you could get it for me."

With a face as black as the late-afternoon thunderclouds of the Palm Beach summer, Carstairs had done as he was told. Jo-Anne had spent the whole afternoon going through it, playing the tapes, marveling at the efficiency of the detective work, the sound quality of the recorded telephone conversations. The Mary d'Erlanger one had made her quite horny. No wonder poor old Carstairs had gotten off on it. Mary d'Erlanger would have to be resurrected. No question. It had seemed such a pity to destroy it, but she knew how to learn from the mistakes of others. Getting anal about things like that hadn't done the Nixon presidency any good at all.

Jo-Anne's eyes rested briefly on the polished wood of the coffin, and she thought briefly of the grisly contents. Was there any regret? Any warmth, any tenderness toward the thing that had been her husband? No, there wasn't. Turning the other cheek was for girls who hadn't had to give blow jobs to tramps in exchange for a few miserable pieces of candy. When Peter Duke had used his power against her and tried to throw her back into the gutter from which she had crawled with such difficulty, she had positively enjoyed unzipping him like a banana with the Riva's propellers. He had never known who she really was, had never bothered to find out—and the oversight had turned him into underdone hamburger meat. There was poetry in the justice.

Things seemed to be winding down. It was time to face the people outside. The tear-stained eyes, the studies in sympathy— "If there's anything we can do, anything at all, please don't hesitate . . ."

Were there suspicions in the eyes of the milling, mourning-clothed crowds on the lawns outside the church? For the paranoid, undoubtedly. But Jo-Anne wasn't paranoid. She was deliriously, deliciously happy. "Accidental death" had been the verdict, and nothing else in the whole wide world mattered. Nothing at all. People could whisper to their hearts' content, but if Jo-Anne knew the fellow citizens of her town, nobody would argue with her Duke name, still less with her Duke fortune.

There was only one question of any importance at all. Where did she go from here? She was one of the richest and most powerful women in America, bearing the proud name of one of its oldest families. She was also single again. A glorious widow, her feet loose, her fancies free. What the hell did she do for an encore? For a second or two she stood there, oblivious to the mouthed condolences, as she pondered her enviable dilemma.

The voice cut into her reverie, the hand squeezed insistently at her arm. "Jo-Anne, I'm desperately sorry. I'm thinking of you."

It provided, of course, the simple answer to her simple question. It was easy, really. Why on earth hadn't she thought of it before? This man was the answer, with his soft voice and sexy eyes. There was only one person in Palm Beach, in the whole of America even, who would be at all possible after a Duke. After a decent interval, whatever that was, she would marry Bobby Stansfield.

8

*T*he setting sun had only about ten minutes to go before bedtime, and at the controls of the twin-engine Beechcraft Baron Bobby Stansfield was worried. He had no time to take in the haunting beauty of the sunlight on the aquamarine sea between Bequia and St. Vincent, still less to pick out and identify the extraordinary houses set like jewels in the rich landscape of the island below. All he cared about was that the airstrip on Mustique had no lights, and he had to land before dark. Damn. He was cutting it close. He reached up to adjust the trim, cut back on the throttle, and twisted the stick to the left as he went into the bank. Only one chance at the runway. Why the hell hadn't they stayed in Barbados? They could have been hitting the planters' punches in Sandy Lane by now, not dicing with disaster in the depths of the Caribbean. Pan Am and their damn scheduling; the flight from Miami had given them the minimum possible time to reach Mustique before nightfall. It was always a gamble, but this was the closest yet.

Next to him Lisa sensed the tension without knowing its cause. Bobby had been quiet on the forty-five-minute flight from Barbados' Grantley Adams airport. A couple of times he had spoken to draw her attention to a beautiful cloud formation or a school of flying fishes frolicking in the warmth of the pale blue ocean below, but he kept looking at his watch, and from time to time a frown puckered the bronze skin of his forehead. Lisa was supremely unworried. Bobby Stansfield was at the controls—of the airplane —of her life. That was enough. And if the Lord in His wisdom decided to take them both here and now, well, what a way to go— locked in the arms of a man she had learned to love with an intensity she had never dreamed possible. Over the last few weeks the Florida weather had gone over the top with record heat and prize-winning humidity: she and Bobby had done little to cool things down. From the first earth-moving lovemaking in the Stansfield cabana to last night's mind-bending sailboat ride on the edge of the Gulf Stream, their bodies had fanned the furnace of the Florida heat wave, their sweat running together as their minds clashed in the steambath of ecstasy. Even now Lisa could feel her body humming like a taut clothesline in a high wind. She was all tensed up, vibrating like a snare drum in response to the closeness of her lover. It was nothing less than a magic swirling trip of delight and she prayed to her God it would go on and on.

To cap it all, he had invited her to Mustique—the most exclusive private island in the world. And they wouldn't be staying in some hotel. It was incredible, almost totally unbelievable, but Lisa was on her way to stay with Princess Margaret, sister of the queen of England—and in her own house. She had known that the Stansfields mingled with the rich and famous, *were* the rich and famous, but this was ridiculous. Yet Lisa wasn't worried. She was so far removed from the social game she had never had a chance to cultivate a fear of the players. To her, foreign royalty were a different world, exotic animals who aroused curiosity rather than apprehension.

In case she was nervous Bobby had played the whole thing down.

"She's really not too bad when you get to know her. Rather more fond of amusing young men than good-looking girls like you, I'm afraid. We all have to sing for our supper, sometimes quite literally, but it's a beautiful house and it's a great opportunity for me to meet Mark Havers. I get these invitations from time to time. We all do. The bottom line is she just can't *bear* to be alone, and so if the house looks like it's going to be empty she puts out distress calls and we all have to rally round. Being close by in Florida often means I get the first call! Anyway, it'll be amusing. Quite an experience. And Havers is going places in England right now."

That, it transpired, had been the important factor. Mark Havers was the blond-haired, sharp-tongued rising star in Britain's Conservative Party, and a great favorite of Prime Minister Margaret Thatcher. He had been a friend of the princess's for many years and was to be a fellow house guest. It was an important opportunity for Bobby to meet him and vice versa. If the dreams of the two men were ever to become substance, they would then meet in very different circumstances. A friendship cemented here would stand each in good stead later.

There was, however, from Lisa's point of view, a fly in the ointment.

Behind the two lovers, legs stretched out over the neighboring seat, sat Jo-Anne Duke.

Lisa couldn't quite understand why Jo-Anne had been invited, but she was enough of an innocent and sufficiently in love not to question Bobby's motives. Actually, it was quite straightforward. When Bobby had received the princess's distress call to fend off loneliness he had been asked to bring people on a "more-the-merrier" basis. Feeling sorry for Jo-Anne in her supposed grief, and genetically attracted to fortunes of the size she now possessed, she had been the obvious person to invite. The fact that Lisa and she were friends and fellow exercise fanatics made it that much better.

Although Jo-Anne looked relaxed, actually she was hard at work, her mind racing as she schemed to catch her prey. This invitation had been an additional stroke of good luck, and everything else had dropped neatly into place: Peter's coffin into the soft earth of the cemetery, his stupendous fortune into her eager lap, his dangerous dossier into her fire.

Only one thing had gone wrong, but it was already beginning to look like a blooper of monumental proportions. The maddening thing was she had brought it entirely on herself, although even with the benefit of hindsight it was difficult to see how she could have predicted the disaster. Bobby Stansfield and Lisa Starr were busy screwing each other's brains out, and to Jo-Anne's practiced eye it looked like far more than a casual affair. In the ordinary way that would have been merely irritating. After all, she'd been planning Lisa for herself. On Bobby she had had no territorial ambitions. Not while her husband still wanted her to be his wife. Now, however, things had changed dramatically. Little bits of Peter Duke were still feeding the fishes off the North End beach. That left Bobby Stansfield—a great big target slap bang in the middle of her sights. Somehow she would have to have him. He would have to be persuaded to see things her way. After all, politicians needed two things—money and status—and she had bags of both. Luckily Bobby Stansfield had liquid ambition running in his veins. He was programmed to want, to need, to grasp at anything that would push him higher. Jo-Anne intended to be that object. Of course he would have to be reeducated with regard to Lisa Starr. He would have to realize exactly what she was. A passing ship in the middle of the night. Nothing more, nothing less. To Jo-Anne, Lisa was a nobody. A peasant with the body of an angel who would be cast aside like a broken doll, as Bobby and she marched on toward a White House destiny. At this most appealing thought Jo-Anne pushed out her long legs in front of her and eased herself backward in the comfortable seat.

Buffeted by the rising currents of hot air from the ground below, the Beechcraft bucked and reared as Bobby straightened her up for the landing. As he felt the wheels slap down on the tarmac he could sense the sun slipping below the horizon as dusk began to fall. He had made it with nothing at all to spare.

He taxied toward the thatched hut that served as the customs and immigration building. As he cut the engines and pushed open the door a tall, diffident, and effortlessly good-looking man walked across to greet them.

"Hi, Bobby. Welcome to Mustique."

The English accent was recognizably upper class.

"Only just made it. You know you've got to get this strip lit, Brian."

"Afraid the residents won't play. Frightened of being kept awake all night."

Bobby grunted. Screw the residents. He'd just had a hairy half hour. He made the introductions as Lisa and Jo-Anne clambered out onto the tarmac.

As he sipped the traditional Mustique welcoming drink—a pure white concoction on which an equally white hibiscus flower floated, he attempted to suppress his irritation with small talk.

"These white hibiscus are rare, Brian. Just like you English to go for the sophisticated understatement. White on white."

"Nothing sophisticated about the effect—white rum, dark rum, banana liqueur—it's all in there."

"Great," said Bobby, cutting him short. "Let's get this show on the road. I could use a shower, and I bet the girls could, too."

They piled into a red jeep, the luggage stacked in another one, and the convoy set off into the gathering dusk. It was an incredibly bumpy ride.

"Mustique Company doesn't run to tarmac yet I see," said Bobby.

"It's an effective speed limit, and the Europeans don't seem to mind. Probably because they're used to it."

Bobby changed the subject. "Have the Haverses arrived?"

"Yup, they came in yesterday morning. P.M.'s on good form, and Patrick Lichfield's here with a load of people, so your end of the island should be busy. Mick Jagger and Jerry are staying with Patrick for a couple of weeks. Mick's going to build here, you know."

Jo-Anne perked up at the mention of the rock star. To Lisa, Jagger was about as interesting as Bing Crosby, but Jo-Anne's age group had been weaned on Stones music.

"How did he come to invest here?"

"Quite interesting actually," said Brian. "Around the time he was getting rid of Bianca it looked for a moment as if he were going to get stuck for a load of alimony. Bianca had hired that Mitchelson chap. Mick's business adviser, a guy called Prince Loewenstein, was a friend of Colin Tennant, who used to own this island, and they got him residency of St. Vincent in ten days flat. Apparently it saved him a hell of a lot of money. He had to own a house here to satisfy the residency requirement, so he bought a plot on the beach at L'Ansecoy Bay, and lived in a run-down beach house that happened to be on it. Now he's building a fantastic Japanese-style house with a croquet lawn."

The night smells of the Caribbean drifted over them as they peered out into the blackness. Occasionally the car's headlights illuminated something, a shed full of bulldozers, a native family walking by the side of the road, banks of wild bougainvillaea. It looked far from the manicured paradise that Lisa and Jo-Anne had expected. A million miles from Palm Beach.

Then quite suddenly they were traveling up a steep incline that led to a straight road, on either side of which the land fell away into darkness. Over to the left were the sparkling lights of a rambling yellow-painted house, a feature of which was the large pagodalike building standing like a gatehouse guarding the causeway over which they were crossing. Directly ahead were the lights of another house. Low slung and built on one level, two symmetrical wings flanked a central terrace and courtyard that led up to the front door.

Lisa took in the flamingo-pink stucco exterior, the bugs dancing in the beams of the headlights, the faint sounds of big band music. So this was it. Princess Margaret's house. Her own home for the next three or four days. God!

Brian Alexander shut off the engine. "Here we are. Les Jolies Eaux."

"What does that mean?" said Jo-Anne. French had been in short supply on the streets of the Bronx. At least the *language* had.

"Beautiful waters." Lisa helped out.

The black servant opened the door.

"What the hell do I call her—'Princess'?" whispered Lisa urgently.

Bobby laughed as they were ushered into the living room, but he didn't answer.

Lisa looked around her. Not at all what she'd expected. Pretty, rather than formal or grand. Cane furniture with fitted cushions, two stainless-steel frame chairs—the sort of thing they had at Jefferson Ward, a light-colored wooden writing desk on which two colorful porcelain parrots stood guard. The lamps were standard island design, raffia shades, patterned coral bases. Over to the right of the room was a dining table, seating eight. Orange candles protruded from glass candle holders complementing, no doubt, the far from expert painting of an orange fish. Otherwise there were the sorts of things she had in *her* room—lots of tattered paperbacks in a bookshelf, a ton of music cassettes, a cheap and rather ancient black-and-white color television. The architecture was infinitely superior to the room's contents, from the concrete floor with its geometrical design, to the white bleached wood of the V-shaped ceiling. But the real point of the room was obviously its view. Lisa's eyes were drawn irresistibly through the theatrical French windows out toward the floodlit swimming pool—the one in which Prince Andrew had seduced Koo, or had it been the other way around?

"Bobby, how lovely to see you."

The voice was deep and throaty, legacy of too many cigarettes, the hint, perhaps, of the odd late night.

"Wonderful to see you, ma'am." Bobby leaned forward to brush the proffered cheek. One each side—European style.

"And these are my two friends. Jo-Anne Duke and Lisa Starr."

As she shook hands, Lisa tried to analyze her first impression. Petite, small, definitely—dare one even think it?—squat. Princess Margaret waved a long tortoiseshell cigarette holder from her left hand as she said her hellos.

"Well, ma'am, it's a great relief to be here. We only just made it before sunset."

"I'm glad you did. We are all going over to Patrick's for dinner. He's got a house full of people. Mick Jagger and his 'lady,' and lovely David Wogan. I can't remember whether you met him before. The Haverses are here, but they're resting. We had ratner a hectic lunch down at Basil's."

Lisa was prepared for the sleeping arrangements. There were only four bedrooms, and overt cohabitation of unmarrieds was apparently frowned on. She had to share with Jo-Anne.

Already she sensed a chill in the air. Since the lunch at the Polo Club, Jo-Anne had been less than friendly. She still came to the gym, but the girls' lunches had dried up, and when they spoke there was a reservation that had not been there before. Lisa had been too preoccupied to think much about it. After all, Jo-Anne had just lost her husband, and in the most horrific circumstances imaginable, and she herself had been far too busy falling in love to worry about anything at all. It was a big drag that Bobby had taken pity on her and invited her along to this party, but then that was just like him—kind, thoughtful, generous.

"I think she gave us the goddamn servants' room," said Jo-Anne, flicking the hair from her eyes in a gesture of irritation.

Lisa felt the sharp pang of hurt. She had moved so far and so fast, remarks like that really got to her. In her world there had been nothing wrong with being a servant. She had always seen it through her mother's eyes as a wonderful profession. Presumably people like Jo-Anne, probably even Bobby, had a different view-point. She felt almost furtive, an interloper who had infiltrated the ranks of the aristocracy by false pretenses. It was ridiculous and untrue, but for the very first time in her life she felt she had some-thing to hide—a strange and alien emotion of shame at something of which she had formerly been proud. Was that what these people did to you? Was it the first subtle step in a campaign of humiliation that would leave her riddled with secret fears, her self-confidence destroyed as she fought to appear to be something she was not? No way. Not Lisa Starr.

She drank deep on the rich rum punch the black butler had poured for her and headed for the bathroom. If these were the servants' quarters she was going to apply for the job. The house seemed to be predominantly orange, which was clearly Princess Margaret's favorite color. The towels in the bathroom, however, were sludge green. Lisa let out a little yelp of glee.

"Oh, Jo-Anne, *look*. The label on these towels says 'Royal Fam-ily.' Look, right here. Cannon beach towels. Royal Family. That has to be some sort of a joke, doesn't it?"

She waltzed into the bedroom brandishing the exhibit.

Jo-Anne fired from the hip.

"Really, Lisa, I think you ought to try to have a bit more re-spect. I know it's a little strange for you to be here with us all, but it isn't a game you know." Jo-Anne's voice was heavy with pa-tronization as she fiddled with Jeep curlers.

"Well, screw you," said Lisa shortly, and walked straight out of the door.

Bobby's room was directly opposite across the tiled terrace, both rooms having doors that opened outside the house. She didn't knock.

He was wet from the shower, a towel slung casually around his waist. Lisa felt her batteries recharge just looking at him. "Hi, senator—or should I say Mr. President. Thought you might need some assistance after your shower."

Bobby smiled his lazy, sexy smile. He placed a finger on his lips and pointed at the closed communicating door.

"I'm next to the master suite," he whispered.

As if in confirmation, the faintest sound of the royal baritone could be heard singing in the bath. "I'm siiiiiiiiinging in the rain, siiiiiiinging in the rain. What a glooooooorious feeling I'm haaappy again . . .''

"I think she'd really like to have been a nightclub act," said Bobby. "In fact, in a way I guess she *is*."

Lisa smiled as she moved toward him. Gently, but firmly, she pushed him back onto the bed.

Mark Havers, his lustrous blond hair ruffling slightly in the welcome breeze, was making his point strongly. He waved his gin and tonic to emphasize the words.

"I just think it's a little naive to see the Soviets as being intent on world domination. History tells us they are terribly insecure. They're so frightened of being attacked that they have adopted offense as the best method of defense. By saber rattling we bolster that sense of insecurity, and turn them into some dangerous cornered animal. The other place we tend to take issue with you is the actual scale of the threat they pose. We see them as a nation with very serious problems—economic, political, and military. They haven't been very successful in the Third World, and if it's world domination they're after they appear to be blowing it."

Bobby leaned back in his chair and smiled gently. "Well, that sure seems to be the European position right now," he drawled. "I don't agree with any of it, but you put it very eloquently." He was formidably polite, the Stansfield charm wafting out across the space that divided the two men, to compete with the force field of Royal Yacht hair lotion that surrounded the Englishman. Havers wasn't sure whether he had been complimented or not.

"Of course from our vantage point here in the New World," Bobby continued, "we see you Europeans as being a little too obsessed with the so-called lessons of history. I tend to agree with the guy who said that history was bunk. You can read it any way you choose, just like statistics. To the average American, your so-called dialogue with the Russians smacks of appeasement. Quite rightly you're anxious that Europe shouldn't be turned into a nuclear waste dump. Talking endlessly to the Russians may not be the best way to avoid that."

"Better jaw-jaw than war-war."

Bobby leaned forward and fixed his blue eyes on the Englishman's. "Sometimes jaw-jaw is the very best way to get war-war. As an example of the lessons of history of which you're so fond, what about Munich? Talking to Hitler hardly led to 'peace in our time.' He took it as a sign of weakness and went right on building up his military machine."

The complacent smile that had been hovering around Havers's lips vanished in a hurry. This character was no pushover. He might have adopted the rather simplistic American right-wing position toward Russia, but he certainly knew how to argue his corner. Munich was always a sore point to an English Conservative. It had been far from their finest hour.

He fell back on his second position. "But it seems to us your position is a little paranoid. Russia simply doesn't have the resources to control the world, and if you look back over the last forty years you see that in fact their frontiers have remained static, with the exception of Afghanistan."

Bobby couldn't resist it. The politician in him produced a smile of dazzling brilliance to offset the unkindness of the words he was about to use. "I think you Europeans have every reason to be grateful for our so-called paranoia, even perhaps for our so-called naiveté. You're totally correct when you say that the Russians haven't been that successful so far. Let me tell you why: because of our half million men in Europe, and because of our nuclear umbrella, under which you people shelter. And I'll tell you another thing. Those defenses are paid for by American tax dollars, at a time when the budget deficit is causing high interest rates and widespread unemployment. The most difficult thing I ever have to do is to explain to my constituents why they have to pay out all that money to protect a whole load of foreigners who demonstrate against our missiles, bad-mouth us in their newspapers, and refuse to pay a reasonable contribution toward their own defense."

Havers gulped at his drink.

Seeing the effect of his words, Bobby moved fast to defuse any hostility they might cause. "Of course, you know and I know that our interests are your interests. I'm telling you this to give you an idea of public opinion in my country. As you know I was totally against the Senate threat to withdraw troops from Europe unless the Europeans contributed more to defense costs. I realize, too, that England is not guilty in that area. I'm a great admirer of your prime minister—Americans know she's not soft on communism, that she sees the threat.''

By ending with a fulsome compliment Bobby poured soothing balm over any hurt feelings. It had been a useful conversation, since it was always as important to get your own view across as to listen to the other man's. Prime Minister Thatcher would get a report on this exchange of opinions. Bobby hoped the report would be that he was a man whose right-wing views were not only from the heart but had been well thought out, too.

Princess Margaret's voice cut into the debate. Framed in the French windows she shouted out to the thatched poolside gazebo in which the two politicians sat. ''Come on, you men. We'll be late for dinner.''

Dinner, as far as Lisa was concerned, had not been a success, and just about everyone was to blame. Jo-Anne, for instance, was rapidly turning into Public Enemy Number One. She had been seated at Bobby's right and throughout the meal she had been all over him like a bad attack of hives. Her restless fingers had never left him alone for a minute. As she laughed up into his face at his every remark she had reached out constantly to touch him, caressing his wrist, grabbing enthusiastically at his arm to emphasize a point, and on at least one mind-stopping occasion she had allowed her fingertips to rest briefly on the nape of his neck. To Lisa she was as innocent as a fox in a chicken coop, and just about as welcome. At first she had hardly been able to believe her eyes. It was so totally unexpected. But then, as the outrageous flirting became more and more overt, she wondered why she had been so naive. It was obvious that Jo-Anne had engineered the whole thing. Her husband was still warm in his coffin, and she was busy on the trail of a replacement. It all made perfect sense. Bobby Stansfield was one of the most eligible bachelors in the universe. To somebody like Jo-Anne Duke, he would be the ultimate prize.

The whole business had put Lisa right off her food, as the alien emotion of jealousy had eaten away at her guts. Bobby had been hers, *was* hers. But it sure didn't look like it from where she sat. Jo-Anne Duke had acquired the capacity to make her blood run cold. Jo-Anne Duke, whose lips had brought Lisa to the verge of sexual surrender in the foaming waters of the Jacuzzi. Jo-Anne Duke, with the splendid body, the Midas fortune, the aristocratic name. It was difficult to conceive of a more dangerous and powerful rival. Damn it to hell. She had fallen in love for the first and only time in her life, and already it began to look as if she had a battle on her hands—and one in which the heavy artillery belonged to the opposition. Already it was possible to see the direction in which the enemy offensive might go. Bobby Stansfield's political ambitions.

From her position on Bobby's left, Princess Margaret had leaned across and said, "Tell me Jo-Anne, do you support Bobby politically? I'm told running for office in your country is ruinously expensive. You ought to make a campaign contribution."

It had been clear to Lisa that the princess was hoping to create a marginally difficult situation for the stunningly attractive Jo-Anne. Her remark had put Jo-Anne on the line. If she wanted to pass herself off as a political soulmate of Bobby's, she might now feel obliged to put her money where her mouth was. Unwittingly she had played right into Jo-Anne's hands. The gift horse had not been looked in the mouth.

"I'm glad you mentioned that, ma'am. Actually I haven't told Bobby yet, but I've been talking to the Duke Foundation about doing something clever for his campaign—that's if he decided to run of course."

Everybody laughed. Except Bobby. Stansfields didn't laugh about things like campaign contributions. After all, one didn't play touch football in church. For a long moment he had stared at her, as if seeing her for the very first time, in an entirely new and comprehensively favorable light. Across the table Lisa had watched it happen, and it had frightened the hell out of her. Straightaway afterward they had begun to talk serious turkey, as Jo-Anne had floated the megabuck bait at Bobby's voraciously eager mouth. Once or twice he had caught Lisa's eyes across the table and smiled the warm, reassuring Stansfield smile. All Lisa had been able to see in the baby-blue eyes had been dollar signs.

Mick Jagger, on Lisa's right, had been as much use as a fart in a four-acre field. For some extraordinary reason best known to himself he had imagined that Lisa might be interested in cricket, a passion of his. After forty minutes of her glacial disinterest, he had tried her on croquet instead. Wipe-out. On her left David Wogan had been much more use. A lovely, bubbling, gurgling Irishman well known to be Princess Margaret's best friend, or B.F. as he liked to describe it, he was in the process of doing what his countrymen did better than anyone. He was getting drunk. From what Lisa could gather, this had not been a process started during the course of dinner, or even during the cocktails that had preceded it. No, David's voyage into foothills of oblivion had apparently started with the Buck's fizz before lunch.

In a stage whisper David produced the lowdown on the cricket- and croquet-loving pop superstar.

"Somewhat inferior manners, me darlin'." He took a deep breath and burped theatrically, incurring a frosty glance from Princess Margaret. Unfazed, he continued. "Don't know why P.M. puts up with him. Probably 'cos her cousin was best man at his wedding to Bianca."

Lisa laughed, and the laugh made her feel just a little bit better, if such a thing was possible. The hell with it, nothing was lost yet. If Jo-Anne wanted to make a play for Bobby Stansfield then she would be given a run for her money that would leave her fighting for breath.

Lisa sipped at the red wine, sighed deeply, and tried to enjoy herself. This should have been paradise—mingling with the mighty in perhaps the prettiest home on the most beautiful island in the world. She looked around her. Patrick Lichfield's house was a jewel. Painted canary yellow, it was built in the Oliver Messel style —theatrical, wide open to the Caribbean breezes, and with stunning views and vistas. The house itself was constructed on several different levels, and so far four had been completed, although Patrick apparently had plans for more. At the pool level a large semi-circular poolhouse had been fitted out as a video area, with a beige-cushioned half-moon banquette arranged around the Sony VHS system. Later that evening they would all watch a movie. Now, in the round dining gazebo she could look out at the lush, subtly lit landscape, the sparkling forty-foot pool, and smell the heady scents of the Grenadines, as she listened to the hum of polite conversation, the chink of fine china, the ceaseless sound of the crickets.

The booming voice picked her out like a searchlight on an escaping prisoner. "Tell me, Lucy, how exactly did you meet Bobby? I'm always so intrigued to know how people met."

Could one decently tell a princess she had gotten your name wrong? Lisa felt the answer was probably no, especially as the odds were it had been done on purpose.

Princess Margaret, wielding her tortoiseshell cigarette holder as if it were an offensive weapon, leaned across the table for her answer. The full lips, bright lipstick, and mahogany suntan made her look more like a Miami Beach manicurist than the queen of England's sister, thought Lisa.

"I was introduced to him by Jo-Anne." In retaliation Lisa had left out the "ma'am."

The royal eyes hardened at the oversight. Princess Margaret took a long sip at the dark brown malt whiskey which had appeared unbidden with the coffee. "Have you and Jo-Anne been friends for long?" The questioning was taking on a relentless quality. After this one there would be another, and another, until Lisa had been forced to say something embarrassing.

Pretending to be the friend she no longer was, Jo-Anne came to Lisa's aid. "Lisa runs a gymnasium in West Palm Beach, ma'am. We met there."

The laughter resembled the sound of a broken fingernail being drawn slowly over a microphone.

"A gymnasium? A gymnasium? What an *extraordinary* thing to do. And in Palm Beach, too. I thought everyone there was far too old to exercise."

Lisa took a deep breath.

Around the table two people tried to help out, with hopefully defusing exercise jokes.

"I'm with W. C. Fields. Whenever I get the urge to exercise I lie down until it goes away," said David Wogan, looking and sounding as if an hour or two on the horizontal were exactly what he needed.

"The only exercise I take is playing chess in front of an open window," offered Patrick Lichfield.

Lisa was grateful for the attempts, but she knew she mustn't avoid the confrontation. Any weakness now would be paid for with interest later on. "Exercise is very good for you, ma'am. You should try it sometime."

An ominous silence descended.

Mentally Lisa packed her bags. How did one get a flight out of Mustique? For a second her fate hovered in the balance. In this atmosphere, surrounded by her courtiers, the faithful members of her most recent "set," a heavy rebuke from "P.M." would transform her at a stroke into a nonperson, condemned to walk forever with the social "undead," an outcast, a pariah. If she was unable for some reason to fly away, she would be in for the stickiest few days of her life.

Princess Margaret let the malice flow from her eyes as she considered how best to deliver the *coup de grace*.

Lisa stared evenly back at her, defiant, unafraid. In the eyeball-to-eyeball confrontation it was the older woman who looked away.

"I've far better things to do with my time," she said at last, taking a petulant swig at the Famous Grouse Scotch.

The distraction from Lisa's small but far from insignificant victory was not long in coming.

Muttering, "I'm not feeling well. Not at all. Not at all," David Wogan struggled to his feet and, before anyone could come to his aid, lurched out into the night. A minute or two later a short sharp cry was followed by the sound of crackling vegetation and then complete silence.

It had taken the men ten minutes to find him in the darkness, fast asleep and lodged firmly in the branches of a deep purple bougainvillaea bush, fifty feet down the hillside.

Somehow, and none too soon as far as Lisa was concerned, that seemed to bring dinner to a close.

"They all laughed at Chris-to-pher Co-lum-bus
When he said the world was round . . ."

Lisa could hardly believe her eyes or her ears. The whole thing had clearly gone right over the top into the realms of black humor. And the funniest thing of all was that she seemed to be the only person who had noticed it.

The little group clustered around the piano in Basil's Bar on the Mustique beach of Britania Bay didn't see the joke at all. They, like the royal performer to whom they listened with such rapt attention, were playing it straight as hell.

"They told Mar-co-ni wire-less was a pho-ny
It's the same old cry . . ."

Princess Margaret was shamelessly soaking every last ounce of up-tempo jauntiness from the old Gershwin tune. She wrapped her full, ripe lips indulgently around the syllables, milking them of their humor, as she rolled her eyes toward the ceiling. Her voice was surprisingly, almost disturbingly deep—a bit like Betty Bacall on a bad day—and it tended to wander around like a leaf on a Chicago street when it went for the higher notes. The accompaniment was standard saloon strum, the left hand pumping backward and forward. There were missed notes, and missed words, and the two seldom coincided.

From the looks on the faces of the audience, however, this could well have been Rubinstein in full spate, Streisand in top gear. They crowded around deferentially, attempting to swing and sway in time to the uncertain rhythm, to catch the eye of the royal cabaret artiste as her turretlike eyes swirled and swiveled to identify who was with her, who against her.

On the top of the battered black piano stood the glass of Famous Grouse, the ashtray with its cargo of long cigarette holder and wispy, burning cigarette.

In midsyllable the maudlin song was interrupted. "Damn! I've forgotten the words."

Lisa's mouth dropped open. This just couldn't be for real. Could this *happen* in the twentieth century? She fought back the overwhelming desire to laugh.

"Something about Hershey inventing the chocolate bar, I think, ma'am."

"*Thank* you, Patrick." The tone was accusing. The schoolmistress irritated that the class had been slow in answering her question. Had they been *attending?*

Once again the assault on the soundwaves continued.

For a second Lisa allowed herself a guided tour of the company assembled around the piano. Royalty might not have much real power anymore, but clearly, like the Almighty, it moved in mysterious ways, its wonders to perform. An old Harrovian photographer aristocrat, an Irishman who, it was rumored, had once been the conductor of a London bus, a glamorous Texan model and a pop superstar, a British cabinet minister and his wife, an American heiress, and a potential contender for the Republican nomination for president of the United States. There had been two unlikely additions to the party who had made it down to the beach bar after the sumptuous dinner: a dusky South American called Julio, a regular at the bar, and a rather blowsy but pleasant redhead who had been introduced as Contessa Crespoli. Julio and Contessa Crespoli were clearly close "friends," leaning against each other for support as if each would be unable to remain upright without the other.

Lisa caught Bobby's eye, and seeing the look of amazed amusement on her face, he winked broadly at her. Lisa smiled back at him. Thank God somebody around here still had a sense of humor. On "Saturday Night Live" this would have brought down the house.

"Who's got the last laugh now?"

From the thunderous applause it was clear the song was at an end.

"My word, you sing that well, ma'am," said somebody, enthusiasm dripping from the syllables.

Quite suddenly Lisa had had more than enough. She wanted to be away from all these people with their alien values and weird attitudes. They were Martians to her. Well meaning, perhaps, but way beyond her experience. Their world wasn't her world, and she wanted out.

She moved quickly in the excited confusion caused by the agreement that the next song should be "Hello, Dolly." Apparently that was something of a royal show stopper.

Lisa hurried along the wooden catwalk, half expecting to hear barked commands in her wake as the hounds were sent chasing after the defector from the royal audience. What crime had she committed? *Lèse majesté?* Would they telegraph to prepare a room for her in the Tower?

She kicked off her shoes as she made it to the sand, still warm from the sun's heat. God! That was better. This was what it was all about. Soft sand, the gentle lapping sounds of the Caribbean, the smells of native cooking from the pine trees behind the beach. Seventy yards from the shore half a dozen yachts bobbed on the insistent swell. Some were lit up like Christmas trees, their owners dining ostentatiously in the stern as crewmen padded the decks, catering to their every whim. Others carried minimal navigation lights only, their passengers obviously dining ashore, with Colin Tennant perhaps, or one of the many Guinnesses who had houses there. Mustique. An island of crazy contradictions. Which was the real Mosquito Island? The jade-green mountains, the pearl-white beaches, the aquamarine sea, the pink conch shells littering the Caribbean-lapped shores? Or was the essence of the place best summed up by the uncertain strains of "Embraceable You," now unhappily audible on the scented night air—embodiment of all the worst excesses of English snobbery, as it polluted the natural beauty of the environment it had so capriciously taken over?

Lisa sat down on a piece of driftwood and tried to gather her surging thoughts. Where was she going? What was *happening?* Until this evening there had been no time and no reason to think, as she had immersed herself in passion, in her magnificent obsession. There had been no time to doubt whether her love had been returned. Lisa had, subconsciously, taken that for granted. Now, alone with her thoughts on a beach in the Grenadines, she dared to wonder if her oasis of ecstasy had been an illusion constructed from shimmering sand, about to vanish from view, leaving behind nothing but a bittersweet emptiness. From the corners of her eyes two large tears broke free and rolled down her cheeks at the awful thought.

The soft voice at her shoulder stole into her consciousness. "Lisa Starr, I had no idea you weren't a music lover."

Lisa had to smile through the tears, but it was gratitude more than humor that allowed her to do so. He had followed her. He cared. He loved her. "Oh, Bobby. Can we go back to the house now? Just you and me, and split this scene."

"We're on our way," he replied, and leaning forward tenderly, he licked away her tears.

Lisa looked up at the star-filled sky and breathed in deeply. The moon was almost full and it cast a magical light across the rippling waters of the pool. Bobby knelt beside her on the steps, his hand resting gently on her strong shoulders.

"I guess pools are a bit special for us," she said at last, and her laughter, soft, tinkling, carried with it hints of suggestion as well.

Bobby chuckled. "Moonlight swims. Sure takes me back."

Lisa aimed a mock blow at his arm. "I was talking about *us,* senator." She pretended the jealousy. "You know, this is the most beautiful place on the island. I mean right here in this pool. It's like swimming on the edge of a cliff. The house I don't really go for—although the commemoration plates of the family are quite sweet. She sure didn't have an interior decorator do it. White vinyl furniture and brass knobs. Yuk!"

"I don't think you'd make a good courtier," said Bobby. "Not enough *reverence.*"

"Doesn't it stick in your throat too?"

"Listen, when you're a politician you'd better be able to massage egos. Anyway, meeting Havers has been useful. That was the bottom line."

"Are we the bottom line, Bobby?"

He didn't answer her. Instead he reached for her.

Lisa tumbled into his arms, letting the water's buoyancy take her. She felt like a gift, a beautiful naked present, the sort that was far too good to be wrapped.

Bobby lifted her up toward him, bending down to receive the parted lips. His action would answer her question. There was no need for words. But he knew as he kissed her that the choice of words would not have been easy, that at some level he was avoiding them because he didn't know which ones to use. Lisa Starr. What was she to him? A lover certainly. Never before in his far from insubstantial experience had he enjoyed making love to somebody as much as he did to Lisa. And then there was her mind, pure, forceful, unsullied by the bitterness of life's defeats—a far from cockeyed optimist who saw the best in people because she chose not to dwell on the worst. Her vibrating enthusiasm had lifted him up, a tonic for his jaded palate, and he had felt the cloak of cynicism in which he so often wrapped himself fall away under her liberating influence. He had, during these last days, begun to see life anew as he peered at his world through her eager eyes. All that was true. But what did it amount to? Was this love? If so, it was his very first experience of it. Stansfields had never been encouraged to fall in love. That was rather an irresponsible thing to do, often unlocking a Pandora's box of nasty tricks that had a way of screwing up the really important things in life. Of course his father had "loved" his mother and vice versa. It went without saying. Husbands and wives loved each other until the divorce. Being "in love," however, was an entirely different ball game, a world of Barbara Cartland novels where handsome princes fell for servant girls and gave up their kingdoms for their passion. Yes, that was part of the definition. You had to be prepared to give something up. Something important. Something like his political ambition. As Lisa's tongue squirmed deliciously in his mouth Bobby felt the potent pang of guilt as he realized that his was a Judas kiss.

As Bobby wrestled with his doubt Lisa felt hers melt away. She would merge with this wonderful man, become him. Their bodies had already fused, two burning liquids joined in the same container, entering each other, passing through each other, pouring themselves into each other. In marriage the world would see the unnecessary evidence of the mystic, sweet communion that joined their souls and cemented their flesh. Someday, a child would come as the consummate blessing, the living proof of their need to become one. Her child, his child. Their child.

She wrapped her legs tightly around him, crushing herself against him as, in joy, she felt the familiar stirrings. Still she explored the well-known mouth, retracing lovingly the memory-illuminated paths, the little pockets of pleasure, the silky softness of his tongue. They would make love here, in the pool, her body light as a feather in the warm water, her soul soaring above them both, witnessing the desire, the need, and the passion.

Bobby hovered on the brink of her, feeling her open up to him, as he luxuriated in the delicious anticipation of entry. Then, unable any longer to prolong the sensation, he pushed himself upward into the depths of Lisa's being as she closed herself gratefully over him. For a second he didn't move as his mind received the delightful messages of pleasure, then as his senses acclimated to bliss, he began to move within her.

Lisa leaned back, her arms around his neck, her legs straddling his waist as he pushed at her. She wanted to watch his eyes, to see his face. In the moonlight she would experience it all, the love, the glory—as the life-giving fluid bathed her body.

As he thrust into her she rode him, her body reeling with the power of his rhythm, and all the time she watched his eyes as her muscles tensed around the pleasure source. It was the look of sleepiness that prepared her to receive the offering—the eyelids suddenly hooded, the gleam in the eyes dulled, the breath coming faster, lips parted, the tongue forming the shout of ecstasy. At her back she felt the desperate fingers bury themselves into her, beneath her heels she felt the buttocks harden, summoning their remaining strength for the star burst that would soak her soul.

She took his head between her hands, using her legs alone to hold him to her. Tenderness and force, the love light burning, the beauty of wholeness. He was almost there.

She felt his legs go weak, and she watched him intently, her eyes hungry, determined to capture this moment for eternity. Whatever happened, nobody could take this away.

Through the still night air the cry rose up to the cloudless sky, abandoned, shameless, unmistakable, as the two lovers howled their passion at the moon.

$$9$$

For Jo-Anne it had been pretty much of a normal Palm Beach day. She had woken early, around seven o'clock, and breakfasted in bed. Earl Grey tea, a bowl of fresh fruit, some thinly sliced toast, a single pink hibiscus flower floating in a small Sèvres bowl as decoration for the tray. More important than the breakfast had been the immaculately folded copy of the Shiny Sheet. The blue and white *Palm Beach Daily News* that got its nickname from the high quality of its glossy paper was the most important single factor in the high-stakes social intercourse of Palm Beach, and had been ever since its establishment in 1894. There were three basic ways of playing the Shiny Sheet game, and Jo-Anne was thoroughly conversant with all of them. First, there was no other way to the top in the town's society than through constantly repeated presence in its columns. A thousand glazed expressions conjured up by a thousand impudent flashbulbs was the considerable price of social glory. In order to achieve that glory, the most important thing was "being there." Endless charity balls had to be religiously attended, some far grander and more prestigious than others. The Heart Ball, the Red Cross Ball, and the American Cancer Society Gala were the most important of all, and to miss them was socially irresponsible, but others were moving up fast—Planned Parenthood, for example, and the Norton Gallery dinner dance. As a rule of thumb for novice climbers, diseases ranked above culture—the Retina Research Institute Gala, known affectionately as "the Eyeball," for instance, counted for more than some orchestra or ballet benefit.

But being there was not enough. You could be there and yet not really "be there." No, the important thing was to be "seen" to have been there, and that meant celluloid evidence. Somehow the photographer had to take the picture. That was hurdle number one.

176

Next, the photograph had to be selected to appear in the paper itself. That meant being favorably regarded by the powerful social editor, Shannon Donnelly, and the even more powerful publisher, Agnes Ash. In the very early days when Peter Duke had introduced his young bride to the deeply paranoid Palm Beachers, Jo-Anne had been considered guilty until proved innocent. That was par for the Palm Beach course. Every social parvenu, gigolo, con man, and phony European aristocrat in the Western Hemisphere worth his salt had tried his luck on the WASP natives, and they were naturally suspicious. Starting at the bottom, Jo-Anne had begun work on the photographers. One in particular had been identified as a target. He had been young, gullible, and horny—a superb combination for a girl whose total experience had been exclusively in the art of turning men on. Poor John Destry had been a pushover. From the first mind-bending kiss behind the Henry Flagler railroad car on the grounds of the Flagler Museum, while Palm Beach society danced and pranced a few nerve-racking feet away, he had been in love with her. She had played him like a fish, keeping the line taut and the hook firmly in place, and throughout two seasons he had taken photographs of hardly anyone else. The social arbiters in the Royal Poinciana offices of the Shiny Sheet had been more or less forced to include her against their own better judgment, and by the time Destry's partiality had been exposed and he had been "let go," Jo-Anne's feet had been firmly on the ladder. From that moment on she had consolidated her position, dressing carefully, never deviating from the mainstream in public, keeping her makeup as simple and straightforward as her standard-issue right-wing Republican political views. Over the years the policy had paid off. No matter that from time to time the female chairmen of the charity galas—there being no chairpeople, chairwomen, or other such nonsense in Palm Beach —would occasionally drop their pants for her. What mattered was that in public Jo-Anne Duke's image remained as pure as a nun's underwear.

The next and ultimate step in Palm Beach society seemed on the surface to be somewhat paradoxical. In a few years she would resign from the Shiny Sheet's pages altogether. In the rarefied atmosphere at the very top of the tree where the Maddocks and the Phippses lived, all publicity was bad publicity—even in the otherwise hallowed pages of Agnes Ash's newspaper. It was strange, really, but in other ways it was a bit like life. You served your apprenticeship, immersed yourself in the rat race, desiring only to reach a position in which you could turn up your nose and scoff at the contestants whose ranks you had so recently deserted.

As a background to her professional analysis of the changing fortunes of the players of the Palm Beach social game, Jo-Anne had flicked capriciously backward and forward between "Today" and "Good Morning America." That was where she acquired most of her information. There and in the pages of *Town and Country, Vogue,* and *W.* She had dressed at a leisurely pace—a plain white Calvin Klein suit, perfectly tailored, a splash or two of Joy, chosen because she didn't want to smell like all the other Palm Beachers of her generation who seemed at the moment to favor Opium— and walked downstairs to the vast marble hallway where the head chef had been waiting for her. In her book-lined study they had gone over the menus for the evening's dinner party—a smoked salmon soufflé, beef Wellington, a mango sorbet. The head butler had joined them for a discussion of the wine. In that department she had to rely heavily on the Englishman's expertise—a dry Corton Charlemagne 1973 with the fish, Latour 1961 with the meat, a 1975 Krug with the dessert, or what the upper-class English and their servants preferred to call the pudding.

"I'll leave the flowers up to you," she had said over her shoulder as she made her way toward the Rolls. "Get them sent over from the Everglades Flower Shop. Those lilies were nice last week."

In the hallowed precincts of the world's finest jewelers at 340 Worth Avenue, Jo-Anne had not messed around. In thirty minutes in the private room at the back she had gone through three hundred seventy-five thousand dollars.

The Cartier manager, Jill Romeo, had not batted an eyelid when Jo-Anne had said she would wear the ring and the sapphire-and-diamond-studded leopard bracelet immediately. Nor had she asked for any payment, not even the signing of a receipt when Jo-Anne had gotten up to leave. As far as Cartier was concerned, knowing their customers was everything. A Duke could pay. A Duke would pay. Most important of all a Duke would come back . . . again and again.

On a whim she had decided to stop at the Armonds Nail Salon. She liked having her fingers fiddled with. An hour later, blood-red talons super-glued in place, she had been ready for the light Petite Marmite lunch—steamed stone crabs and a green salad with a genuine French vinaigrette dressing—with Inger Anderson and her attractive husband, Harry Loy.

By two o'clock it had been time to enjoy the high point of the day so far. So now here she was tucked comfortably into the red plastic swivel chair of the Domani hairdressing salon as Dino ran appreciative fingers through her long blond hair. Dino was great. He was above all safe, and he *understood*. What was it about hairdressers that made them so knowing? The fact that they saw the face behind the mask? That they caught you when you were most relaxed? The intimacy of the close bodily contact shorn of its sexuality? Most of it anyway. It was difficult to say. The smooth, firm fingers plowed knowingly through Jo-Anne's lustrous locks, occasionally catching an earlobe—the touch professional, totally expert. Sometimes Dino would gather up a whole bunch of hair and hold it up for a second as he watched the effect in the mirror before casting it down again, like the discards in a game of canasta. Jo-Anne felt deliciously like an object, not really a person at all but more a collection of bits and pieces that needed to be rearranged to produce a more pleasing appearance. If any other man in the world had made her feel like that she would have gone for the jugular. With Dino it was just fine.

"I haven't seen you since the day of the funeral. You're looking very wonderful, Jo-Anne."

Jo-Anne appreciated that. It was charming. Delightfully European. *Bellissima signora* and all that jazz.

Boy, had Dino done her proud for the funeral. Everybody had agreed she looked the personification of widowhood, the hair piled up high, severe, minimalistic. But there was something else in his remark. He had picked up on the buoyant sense of freedom, of triumph, that bubbled throughout her soul. Some of it undoubtedly shone through her eyes. Perhaps some, too, was palpable beneath the practiced and mobile fingers. Dino was probing. He had her number. He knew the grieving-widow bit was window dressing. Jo-Anne's antennae sensed danger, but immediately she rejected the thought. She was safe. She had it all. The three hundred seventy-five thousand dollars' worth of Cartier jewelry was caressing her skin, the tangible proof of her victory.

She smiled a wicked smile and allowed the flavor of conspiracy to leak out. "One must struggle on," she said. "I'm sure Peter would have wanted that."

Like hell he would, ran the subterranean thought. He must be the unhappiest man in heaven right now. Fuming and spluttering with his mighty rage. The Cartier trip would have made that little vein in his forehead jump around like a jack-in-the-box.

"If this is you struggling, then I'm thinking when the sailing is plain you'll be looking a million dollars."

Jo-Anne laughed. "Only a million dollars, Dino? Forget it, baby, that's the small change in the Duke family."

It was the Italian's turn to laugh, but it was a respectful one. In this country, and especially in this town, one didn't laugh too loud and too long about money.

"So, what are we going to do with it today?"

"I want that Eton crop look. Short at the back, long and straight on top. Do you know the one I mean? Not very Palm Beach, but screw that."

"Sure, I know it. It'll suit you fine. Let's get you washed."

For Jo-Anne, Dino did his own washing. It was one of the subtle little messages that created a hierarchy among his customers. They liked that.

Back in the cutting chair, Jo-Anne was totally relaxed. Like some body slave in ancient Rome, Dino sensed what was needed. He sent his fingers into the firm back, pushing at the muscles of the shoulders, massaging away any lingering tightness.

Behind closed eyes Jo-Anne's mind worked on. Already she was looking forward to tonight. The telephone conversation last week still reverberated in her mind.

"Bobby? Jo-Anne. Listen, I've been doing some work on the campaign thing we discussed in Mustique. I wonder if you could make dinner one evening to discuss it. I have a couple of the Duke trustees staying, and I've done a little work on them. If you could come yourself, and perhaps bring some of your people, we might be able to get it all sewn up. I'm afraid that it'll be a dead loss socially. They're boring old farts. That's why I haven't invited Lisa. She'd feel pretty out of it."

"Sounds wonderful, Jo-Anne," Bobby had said. "I'll bring Baker if I may. Can't guarantee he'll know which knife and fork to use, but he's hot shit politically."

Tonight he would sit on her right-hand side at dinner. And Jo-Anne would buy him as she had bought the Cartier jewels. Oh, it wouldn't appear she was doing it. The language would be businesslike, the sentiments expressed lofty. She would intimate that it would be in the very best interests of the Duke Foundation for it to find a way to support the Stansfield campaign with heavy cash. The Democratic threat, the debasement of American values, etc. But at the end of the day she would own a part of him and would be well positioned to make a takeover bid for the rest. And maybe, after dinner, when the exquisite Napoleon brandy, 1805, the Trafalgar year, made its appearance, Bobby Stansfield would be in a mellow mood. First she would let slip a couple of choice pieces of information about Lisa . . . and then, who knew?

As the hands moved from her back to take up the scissors, and as the gentle snip, snip, snip of the sharp blades sent her blond locks to the floor, Jo-Anne kept her eyes shut. She was far from being asleep, but she didn't want any words to disturb her delicious anticipation of what was to come.

Bobby Stansfield held the paper-thin brandy balloon between thumb and forefinger and pressed gently around the rim. The glass bent satisfyingly in toward the center. He lowered his head appreciatively toward the rich amber liquid, taking in the smooth, caramel aroma. Unbelievable. Divine. Next he swirled the glass around, the heavy spirit clinging like glue to the walls, and only then did he allow himself to taste it.

Across the room Jo-Anne smiled back at him as she saw the enjoyment written all over his face. How handsome he was. The dinner jacket so very well cut, the bow tie small, hinting that it had belonged to his father, even his grandfather—the patent-leather opera pumps formidably correct. Even the cuff links, thin, plain gold, the initials RS engraved with understated elegance, were absolutely right. Bobby Stansfield had class. He would look terrific at the altar.

Jo-Anne waited for the moment. About the time the brandy hit the stomach wall. "I'm sorry Lisa couldn't be here tonight," she lied.

"Mmmm," agreed Bobby absent-mindedly. God, this brandy was good.

"Amazing girl, Lisa." Jo-Anne sharpened the knife.

"You'd better believe it," agreed Bobby with enthusiasm. "You sure did me a favor making that introduction."

"Yep, she's a surprising lady. I was really amazed to find out she cuts both ways."

"What do you mean?"

"You know, that she's AC/DC, bisexual."

"What!" Bobby sat up in his chair. "You're joking," he added.

"You mean you didn't know? I imagined it was part of the thing you had going together."

"Not only did I not know, but I don't believe it. Who on earth told you that?"

Jo-Anne had expected the irritation. She moved quickly to produce her "evidence."

"It's firsthand. Lisa tried to seduce me. It was quite embarrassing actually. You know—I almost felt it was rude to refuse." Jo-Anne laughed. The liberal lady. Intrigued, surprised but not shocked by another's little weakness.

Bobby could hardly believe his ears. He took a long hard swig on the brandy. The connoisseur had been replaced by the man who felt he needed a drink.

"When? Where? In Mustique? Are you sure you didn't get it wrong?"

Great, he wanted chapter and verse. "It was some time ago. When we first met. We were in the Jacuzzi, and she just asked me straight out if I wanted to screw her. You could have knocked me over with a feather. I said it wasn't my bag, and I was sorry, and she put her hand right between my legs—just like that. I gather she has quite a reputation at the gym. You know, 'we aim to please' taken just that little bit further."

Again she laughed, to avoid the suspicion she was dishing the dirt on Bobby's girl.

182

"I can't *believe* it."

"Do you mind?" Jo-Anne asked. "Surely it's no big deal." Was he ready for the double whammy?

"It's just an incredible surprise. I mean, I'm really close to Lisa. She never gave me any idea. I'm sure she'd have told me if she was gay." Unusually for him, Bobby's words didn't seem to be coming at all easily. He was obviously flabbergasted.

"God, Bobby—it sounds as if you've got it bad. I never thought I'd see you, of all people, go overboard for the daughter of the hired help."

"The hired *what?*" he spluttered.

"Christ, don't tell me she didn't mention *that?*" Jo-Anne looked incredulous. "You must know her mother used to be a maid working for your parents."

"Who on *earth* says so?"

"She does, Bobby. It was one of the very first things she told me. In fact I think she told me that day at lunch when we met up with you in the Café L'Europe. Don't you remember? You were there with your mother."

Jo-Anne looked down at her red nails as she spoke. They were a little too much really. Maybe she'd go back tomorrow and have them filed off. When her eyes locked back on Bobby's, the change in him was immediately apparent. He was slumped in his chair, his face a complex mixture of emotion. Most of the ones that Jo-Anne had intended were there—surprise, hurt, perhaps even the beginnings of anger—but there were other feelings, too: sorrow, disbelief, and, around the corners of the mouth, determination. Jo-Anne read them all. But what the hell was he going to do with that determination?

Jo-Anne moved toward him quickly, the ancient bottle in her hand.

"You look as if you could use another drink," she said, running a moist tongue over her lips.

Caroline Stansfield rather enjoyed old age. Not many people recommended it, but she found it restful. Most of the things it had forced her to give up she had given up anyway—through choice. Sex. Drinking and eating too much. Exercise. She didn't even mind the physical decline. She had never been vain, and the slack skin, liver spots, and gray hair didn't bother her at all. The failing eyesight was a bore, as that interfered with her tapestries, and so were the increasingly arthritic fingers—but those were small things. On the other hand the advantages of old age were quite substantial. She had always been the family's gray eminence, and now that she actually *looked* like one, her influence was even more powerful than it had been in her youth.

"What did you want to see me about, Bobby?" Her tone sounded positively matriarchal.

"I wanted some of your famous advice, mother."

She smiled back proudly at her eldest son. There was no mistaking his charisma. Even though she was his mother she could be objective enough to recognize that he possessed the X factor. Poor old Fred had never had it, and despite the energy and cunning with which he pursued his political career, he was never able to make it to the ultimate goal. But Bobby was different. He had star quality. Her bridge partners at the Everglades thought the sun shone out of his backside. They were always twittering on about a nephew who had heard him speak in Boston, a cousin who had read his book in Saratoga, a grandson who had been impressed by him on "60 Minutes." Yes, a shot at the presidency looked entirely possible. And yet . . . there was possibly a little something missing. Did he have the killer instinct? Or was he just a mite too gentle, a touch too sensitive? Fred Stansfield had done his best to thwart those instincts in him, and certainly he had been partially successful, but the doubt remained. Only time would tell.

Caroline Stansfield arranged the tapestry in her lap, and waited.

"I've fallen in love, mother."

"How very nice, dear." She plunged the needle into the beige background of the tapestry like a Sioux warrior dispatching a cavalry scout with his spear.

"Anyone we know?" she added as an afterthought.

Bobby felt the burst of irritation rush through him. His mother could produce this response in him with effortless ease. What the hell did she mean, "*we* know?" It was insufferably condescending, the more so because she had gone right to the core of the problem.

"We" didn't know Lisa Starr. "We" wouldn't want to know Lisa Starr. "We" wouldn't cross the road to piss on Lisa Starr if she was on fire.

Damn. He wasn't going to get what he wanted. She was going to say it wasn't on, could never be on.

Bobby wished the color wasn't burning on his cheeks.

"Her name is Lisa Starr. I believe you met her once when lunching with me at the Café L'Europe. A very beautiful, wonderful young lady. I'm very fond of her, mother."

"Who is she?" Caroline Stansfield had had a lifetime's experience of cutting through the shit. He's going to get angry, she thought, picking up on the twin spots of red high up on her son's cheeks, and caring not a bit.

It was pointless to pretend to misunderstand the question, to reiterate that her name was Lisa Starr. His mother hadn't meant that at all. Bobby tried to minimize the damage. "She's from West Palm. Runs a business there." Even as he spoke he knew that, far from minimizing it, he had compounded it.

"Yes?" The word said it all. West Palm for a Palm Beacher had all sorts of hidden meanings. After all, the town across the bridge owed its existence to Palm Beach. It was where the black servants lived. Nowadays they had been joined by a crude assortment of carpetbagging riffraff, retirees from the North, the ubiquitous lawyers and dentists and God knows who else, but to Caroline Stansfield it was a ghost town, inhabited by specters, people without substance, without significance. Intellectually she knew that it was no big deal for a politician's wife to be born in a place like that. Americans in general wouldn't understand the significance. But emotionally the idea filled her with horror. A daughter-in-law from West Palm. It was unthinkable. She cocked her head to one side and repeated her loaded affirmative. "Yes?" she said again.

Bobby looked out of the window for inspiration, for rescue. A water skier, a man in a rowboat hauling in what looked like a pretty decent fish, two or three busy sea gulls. Hardly the Seventh Cavalry.

His mother was not about to be fobbed off. She wanted *information*—the page number of the *Social Register,* the Dun and Bradstreet report on the business, the brief biographies of the more substantial relatives, a thumbnail sketch of the most disreputable of the family black sheep. So far one thing was globally clear. She was not impressed. Apparently Lisa's face was not to be found in the Stansfield memory bank, and that was ominous. She had made it her life's work to know of everybody who was anybody, who had *been* anybody.

Caroline Stansfield explored one last cul-de-sac, knowing as she did so what the answer would be. "Nothing to do with the Philadelphia Starrs?"

"No."

For what seemed like an age his mother was silent. One thing was crystal clear. This was not the range. Discouraging words had been heard. At last she spoke, and as she did so, she single-handedly proved the validity of extrasensory perception.

"How old did you say she was?"

"I didn't," said Bobby unnecessarily. He paused. "She's very young, mother."

"Very young, and no money." It was a statement.

"Yes, she has no money, and I guess you'd have to say she's not exactly our class, but she has very many wonderful qualities and I love her. I'm thinking of marrying her. I believe she'd even be a great asset to my career. You know, the working-class vote, the young . . ." He petered out. He was scarcely convincing himself.

"Baloney." Caroline Stansfield didn't bother to hide her scorn. Bobby was talking nonsense. Marriage to a moneyless, familyless child bride from West Palm might just be all right for a Democrat, but for a right-wing Republican it would be political and social disaster, and Bobby knew it. It was insulting that he tried to pull the wool over her eyes.

She looked down and sent the needle darting into the material with renewed vigor, as if into the heart of the adventuress who had dared to make a play for the standard bearer of the Stansfield political dynasty.

"Love's one thing. Politics is another. Frankly, the money thing is the most powerful objection of all. To get to the Oval Office you need more than we Stansfields have. It cost me a small fortune to keep your father afloat, and there isn't enough left to give you the push you need. Don't kid yourself. Unless you can marry it you're not going to get it. Please yourself, but don't make the mistake of believing you can have your cake and eat it. That's just not practical.''

Lack of practicality was for Caroline Stansfield a cardinal sin. Still, she had come on a bit strong. Bobby would have to be talked out of this. He was no longer a child, and although he would listen to her, he was headstrong. She would have to tread carefully. Her sixth sense, far better preserved than her failing eyesight, told her there was more. "Anything else I should know about her?"

"There *is* a slight problem." Bobby hesitated.

Caroline Stansfield watched and waited, fighting back the desire to say something like, "Go on, Bobby, cough it up. That's a good boy." How many times had she used those lines when he'd been sick as a child?

"It appears that her mother once worked for us as a servant. A maid, I think. I'm not sure what her name was."

Caroline Stansfield fought back the impulse to laugh out loud. That would be quite the wrong thing to do, but it was difficult to resist.

A Stansfield had never yet been president, and Bobby would look so good on the Capitol steps, taking the oath. He had such a marvelous speaking voice. And at the White House receptions everyone would say how distinguished she looked. She'd be where she belonged at last. Then, quite suddenly, it wasn't funny anymore. The glorious dream was in deadly danger. Marriage? To a penniless young girl from West Palm of all places, and the daughter of a former servant? It would be a disaster. But how to tell Bobby so that he believed her. That was a problem. He was already beginning to bristle at her lack of enthusiasm.

"Well, Bobby, how can I advise you about the person you love? Love is everything. You must follow your heart." Somehow she made love sound like a dangerous drug in which only the weak-willed and feebleminded indulged. Certainly Bobby picked up that message.

"What I meant, mother, was how do you think it would affect me politically?"

"Ah. That's quite a different thing altogether, isn't it? Well, she's poor apparently, and unknown. And very young, you say. The daughter of one of our servants. I wonder which one. Mmmmmmm. It doesn't sound as if it's the cleverest match in the world—politically speaking, of course. But then, does it matter, Bobby? Do you really want to go any higher than the Senate? It should be enough for most men. It was for your father. He got used to it in the end. We all did. You see, the presidency is a vocation. You have to want it, to need and to dream it if you are ever going to be it. And you have to put up with all the hardship and the sacrifice, because you know you can serve your country, your fellow Americans. That has always been the Stansfield way —but then you are already in service, Bobby. You have done enough. I don't think Lisa Starr would hurt your reelection chances in the Senate, and if you hang on long enough you should get the chairmanship of a good committee. Agriculture, or even Foreign Relations.''

Bobby's face was going through the floor as Caroline spoke, and one by one, she watched her clever bombs strike home. Noblesse oblige. Ask not what your country can do for you. The greater good, the wider picture. Its significance in comparison to the paltry lusts and personal desires of the individual. She knew Bobby wanted the Oval Office the way he wanted air to breathe. She and Fred had personally supervised the placing of the desire in the depths of his mind. But how great was the need? Less than his need for Lisa Starr? More?

"You think she'd be no good for the presidential nomination."

"She wouldn't be any good for that. You know that, Bobby, don't you?"

"It would be the popular wisdom." Bobby sounded ungraceful on purpose.

His mother didn't care. The stakes were far too high to worry about little things like that. She played a trump. "Really, though, you shouldn't be asking me. What do I know about politics anymore? I'm old and passé. What does that awful Baker man say? I must say I can't stand his manners, but I've a healthy respect for his political judgment."

Bobby looked miserable. He had never met anyone with the political nose of his mother. Baker ran her a close second. He hadn't dared to ask Baker's opinion, because he knew in his heart exactly what it would be. He would have said what his mother had just said, with a piquant sauce of the more fashionable and cruder swear words thrown in for good measure.

Like a wise old owl Caroline Stansfield watched her son struggle on the horns of his dilemma.

"It would be political oblivion," said Bobby, almost to himself. Inside the questions milled around. Did that matter? Weren't there more important things in life? Like Lisa?

"It's one of the marks of greatness to have the ability to make sacrifices. We are all so unimportant in relation to the common good. It's the cross you have to bear in public life."

"You make yourself very clear, mother. I shall have to give this matter a great deal of thought."

Caroline Stansfield smiled her gracious smile, the one that went down so well at charity functions. It was not exactly a racing certainty, but she was pretty sure she had won. She shifted her tack. The negative must always be balanced by the positive. When you took something away you should always try to replace it with something of value. "I hope you won't mind my saying this, Bobby, but as you know, I've always spoken my mind. Too old to break the habit now." She laughed the tinkling laugh that all Stansfields had come to value for its rarity.

"It seems to me that poor Jo-Anne Duke is a marvelously attractive person. So dignified at the funeral. So *very* good looking. Apparently Peter Duke left her everything—control of the foundation, the entire fortune. And I'm told she's very ambitious . . ." She tailed off as she cast the seed. Would it fall on fertile ground? The ground on which she had just so effectively doused the flames of Lisa Starr.

Bobby managed a laugh. Really, his mother was incorrigible. He couldn't resist drawing her out a little more. "Mother, you're wonderful. But I can't say I know an awful lot about Jo-Anne Duke's past. Do you? Rumor has it she was some sort of model in New York when Peter Duke found her."

"The point is she was *found,* dear. And by a Duke. And what's more, he gave her his name. That makes her one of us. At a stroke. She bears his name, controls his money, and looks the part. I don't think one could ask for much more than that."

Bobby fell silent. The Duke money . . . and the Stansfield machine. The one oiling the other. It was quite a thought. Quite a thought indeed.

Caroline moved to consolidate her position; she seemed to be talking to herself. "So much sense," she murmured. "So much sense." Out loud she added, "But of course it's the heart that's important. One should always do what the heart dictates."

She watched her son carefully. What *did* his heart dictate? Were the genes, the careful upbringing strong enough to undermine his infatuation with the nobody who had captured him? Her instinct said they were. They had better be. Because around the corners of Caroline Stansfield's canny mind scurried a very disturbing idea.

10

*L*isa and Maggie peered into the mirror with a studied intensity that suggested that the secrets of life itself were about to be revealed.

"There's nothing there," said Lisa. It was difficult for her to catch the feeling conjured up by the words. Relief? Disappointment? Relief mixed with disappointment?

There was no doubt at all about Maggie's response. "Well, thank *God* for that."

Maggie's satisfaction seemed to push Lisa off the fence of indecision. "But I've *never* been late before. Usually you can set your watch by me. I know I'm pregnant. I can feel it. That time in the pool in Mustique. I just *know* it. Perhaps we did something wrong. Let me look at the instructions again."

Maggie laughed in disbelief.

"Lisa, really. You sound as if you *want* to be pregnant. You ought to be thanking God that the damn thing's not positive."

It had never crossed Maggie's practical mind that anyone who wasn't married or engaged to be married would actually want to be "in the club." She had seen more than enough soap operas to know that the traditional masculine response to learning that fatherhood was in the pipeline was shock/horror followed quickly by anger/irritation and blame/abuse. Somewhere around the third stage came the veiled accusations that some Machiavellian schemer was trying to trick him into marriage. Invariably it was followed by a dry little speech about getting rid of the baby, and then the relationship. That was the reaction ordinary people expected, and whatever else she wasn't, Maggie was certainly one of those.

The look on Lisa's face reflected the indecision in her heart, and Maggie's gut response amplified it.

Did she want to be pregnant? It was almost impossible to say. A beautiful baby by the man she loved. Her life changed at a stroke by the intervention of Fate's cruelty. Or was it kindness? Around and around the emotions whirled as intellect attempted to inject order into the chaos. One thing was certain: it had not been done on purpose. That was not her style. She simply hadn't considered the possibility. Of babies, of marriage. Of anything like that. In the awesome intensity of the love boat ride to bliss, such mundane things had been forgotten in the excitement of the glorious present. But now reality was intruding on the dream, with its own demands, and Lisa fought to make sense of it. But it was still uncertain. The bridge loomed up, but it had not been reached. Maybe it never would.

She didn't respond to Maggie. Instead, for the twentieth time that morning, they pored over the blue Daisy 2 booklet. They hadn't made a mistake. An imbecile couldn't have screwed up. Early morning urine specimen. Don't shake the tube after mixing the urine with the chemicals. Read the result only from the mirror on the test kit stand. Don't read the result until exactly forty-five minutes had passed. Well, of course they hadn't obeyed *that*. They had sat, side by side, eyes glued to the mirror, waiting for the black ring to appear from minute one.

"Maybe if it's going to appear at all it sort of comes suddenly at the end of the forty-fifth minute, and it's not a gradual thing at all," said Maggie.

Even as she spoke, she was aware that there had been a subtle shift in her attitude. Lisa could do things like that. Lisa had intimated that pregnancy would not necessarily be a total disaster and Maggie's psychology was already beginning to shift to accommodate the alien idea. But although emotion had moved, intellect was still rock solid. Bobby Stansfield would not like the idea of Lisa's carrying his child.

Lisa saw it first.

There was excitement in her voice, but a careful, reserved kind of excitement. The sort you experienced when something of awesome importance occurred whose effects were uncertain. Possibly good. Possibly bad.

"Look, Maggs, it's forming. Can you see it? Can you see it? There, that blackness. It's round isn't it? Like a halo? Christ!"

She turned to look at her friend, her expression questioning, as if she hoped for some lead as to how she ought to feel.

Maggie felt acutely uncomfortable. Should she share her misgivings? The bearers of bad tidings tended to get a bad press. Sometimes, as now, the duties of friendship could conflict. Should she be there with reassurance and support, or was a little reeducation in the unfortunate ways of the world in order? "Will Bobby be pleased?" she asked lamely, as a sort of a compromise.

Now Lisa's face registered open disbelief. Dear God, *that* wasn't the problem. It was *her* feelings she was worrying about, not Bobby's. She hadn't reckoned on being pregnant, and now she was. It took a bit of dealing with. "Maggie, what do you mean? Of course he'll be pleased. Surprised as hell, like me, but pleased for sure. It's *his* baby, silly."

The laugh was all mixed up with the words. It was unlike Maggie to fail to get the point.

Maggie couldn't give up just yet. "But . . . I mean . . . some men . . . feel, you know . . . that girls should be sort of responsible for taking precautions . . . and if they don't . . . well, you know, it's like a back-door way of getting them to the altar."

For a second Lisa looked thoughtful. She hadn't really confronted that one. Not consciously anyway.

"Oh, Maggie, Bobby's not like that. I mean, he loves me. We love each other. He'd never react like that. He just couldn't. Not Bobby. Anyway, he knows I'd never even *think* of doing a thing like that on purpose."

Maggie took a deep breath and plowed on. "You mean he'll marry you."

"Well, I guess so." Suddenly Lisa didn't sound quite so sure. "There isn't an alternative, is there?" she added quietly.

"Some people get rid of the baby."

"No!" The exclamation shot from Lisa's lips, and its force blew away the doubts and fears that had been hovering around the edges of consciousness. Maggie had voiced the unthinkable, and clarified the confusion in Lisa's mind.

She spoke fast. "Maggie, that's just ridiculous. Bobby and I aren't 'some people.' We never have been and we never will be. He's a totally responsible person, and so am I. He'd always do the right thing."

Maggie could feel herself giving in. Like Custer she had made her last stand against "head-in-the-clouds" attitudes, and now it was time to relinquish the role. Maybe Lisa was right, anyway. One thing was certain: Stansfield would have to be a moron to turn her away. The girl was as near to perfection as it was possible to be on this earth, and a man of his experience would recognize that. Wouldn't he?

"Of course he will, Lisa. Hey, this is *exciting*. You a senator's wife! Do I get to be maid of honor?" With a certain lack of conviction Maggie attempted the role change from doubting Thomas to cheerleader.

But Lisa was scarcely listening. She sat up straight and ran her hand over the superflat stomach. "Bobby's baby. Growing in here. How *weird!*" The sudden thought rushed into her mind. "There's no chance it could be wrong, is there?"

"It says it's ninety-eight percent accurate." Maggie laughed in the more comforting part of co-conspirator.

Flinging her arms around her friend's neck, Lisa let it all surge out, and, as within the tube her human chorionic gonadotrophin, a special hormone of pregnancy, reacted with the HCG antibody of the test kit to form the black ring, she burst into floods of tears.

Bobby Stansfield's heart was breaking. In front of him stood Lisa, her beautiful face beginning to drain of color, her hands gripped tightly, her knuckles white. God, how he loved her. He wanted her now, even this minute while his words tortured her, but there was the steely Stansfield part of his soul, and he was letting it ride roughshod over his emotions. Over the last few days he had rehearsed this moment in his mind, but he was still unprepared for the reality. Lisa was carrying his child. She had walked through the door as if floating on air and had told him the news with all the excitement and wonder of the young, and deeply in love. It had never occurred to her that he wouldn't share her joy. It was occurring to her now. Before his eyes she was teetering on the brink of tears.

"Lisa, I don't want you to think what we've had together hasn't been important to me. It has. We both know that. You're a sweet and wonderful person, and I'm very, very, fond of you . . .''

He moved to the window, and for a second his broad back was toward Lisa as he fought to find the words that would lessen the pain, that would excuse him from his dreadful guilt.

Lisa stared at him, her face blank with the beginnings of shock as she tried to understand what she didn't want to hear. There was something wrong with the script. She hadn't written it like this. Fond? A sweet and wonderful person? Like somebody's favorite great aunt. Christ! He was going to slam the door in her face at the precise moment he was supposed to take her into his heart.

Her voice, small and insecure, shook with words. ''Bobby, I'm pregnant, I said. With our child.'' It was a plea as much as a statement. Maybe he hadn't quite understood what she'd said.

Bobby turned to face her. He splayed his hands open in a gesture of defeat. ''I sort of imagined you'd ah . . .'' His voice trailed off unhappily as he heard the indecision in it. God, this was awful. The guilt was creeping all over him, plucking at his skin with its sharp little fingers.

Lisa sat down heavily on the edge of the old chintz sofa, her knees up to her chin, her face startled, bemused, uncomprehending. She said nothing as she watched her world die before her eyes. He'd imagined she was on the pill. That she'd ''taken precautions.'' What did he think she was now? A West Palm girl on the make. That her pregnancy was part of some deep-laid plot to hook the eligible senator. He was supposed to be ecstatic. She was supposed to be twirling in his arms as he whispered his promises of a lifetime together as parents of the child she would bear him. This wasn't Bobby. Her Bobby. She should call the police and have him arrested for impersonating the man who had fathered her baby.

Bobby tried desperately to find the tap that would turn on the ice-cold water to douse the emotional flames. He had wanted this girl. But her irresistible love had crashed up against the unmovable object of his ambition, and the mighty wave was about to be broken into a fine mist of spray on that massive breakwater. Cruel to be kind. It should be clean. It was the only way for her. He would not turn her into his mistress. He could not marry her. He belonged to America, to his vision of America's future. Lisa Starr would be replaced in his life, but perhaps never fully replaced in his heart. Like the child of Abraham she had to be sacrificed at the altar of the greater need, and Bobby prayed that both he and she would be able to survive it.

"Lisa, I'm afraid marriage is totally out of the question. It always was, and it was wrong of me not to make that clear. God knows I'm not a snob, but there are things that politically just don't make sense, and it's the politics that must always come first with me. Jo-Anne tells me that your mother used to work here in this house. I wish you'd felt able to tell me that yourself. In itself it's no big thing, but it was something I should have known about. The press could hurt me with a thing like that. Believe me, I know the sorts of things they can do. And then there's the whole family thing. My mother, and the Stansfield name. And you're so young. You have so much time. One day you'll find a better man than me and you'll look back on this . . ."

Bobby winced as he made the nasty little speech. Pushing the red button just might be preferable.

"What!" said Lisa.

It was the cruelest and most vicious thing she had ever heard, and it came from the lips of the man she loved. He was as good as telling her that she wasn't good enough to be the mother of his child. She had defiled the Stansfield bloodline, polluted it with her innocent baby. Surely he hadn't meant that.

"What?" she repeated, her mind woolly and numb with shock.

"I think you must know what I mean, Lisa."

He couldn't handle that all over again. He swallowed hard. He had to go the whole way. "And Jo-Anne tells me there's another problem, Lisa. I didn't know you were bisexual. It came as a great surprise. Both personally and politically I'm afraid that's a hot potato, too. As you know I take a firm stand against homosexuality, and I always have. I'd find that very difficult to deal with." That at least was true. In a way it was all true. But the words came from the mind and not from the heart.

A lesbian? Where? Why? How? Who? No answers, but the beginnings of anger. The birth of herself. The rebirth. She would nurture the emotion, cosset it, build it up to replace the numbing unreality that had gripped her.

"Bobby, what the *hell* are you saying to me?"

She stood up, her fingers pushing into her palms, the blood rushing in her ears. There was a funny feeling in her throat.

Bobby watched her. Inside he was beginning to uncoil. He had done the deed. The blood was on his hands. Christ, she was magnificent. The most beautiful woman he had ever seen. Never again would he be asked to make a sacrifice like this. He had given his all, and paradoxically there was pride to be found in that. It was the sort of thing that separated the sheep from the goats. To get there you had to want it enough. You had to be prepared to pay the price.

There was one last thing to be done. "As for the child, Lisa. Well, you know that my stand against abortion is a fundamental part of my beliefs. But the child will be well taken care of. There will be no financial problems for either of you. I promise you that."

Like a can of kerosene poured over a burning match Bobby's words amplified the fire in Lisa's soul. Now she saw it. Saw the snobbery, saw the callous indifference to her and to the truth, saw the hardness of heart. Her eyes rested on the naked ambition, the brutality, the single-minded, undistractible preoccupation with self, and her stomach turned as her mind exploded into hatred.

The rage hovered and slithered about her, creating sparks of electricity as it crackled through the atmosphere.

She took a step toward him. Bobby took one back.

"When I leave this dreadful house, Bobby, do you know what I'm going to do? I'm going to find the dirtiest and most disreputable doctor I can find. I'm going to have him rip this thing of yours out of me and flush it into the sewers. Along with all my memories of you."

Lisa parked her bike right up against one of the immaculate white columns of the Duke mansion façade, taking care to chip the paint as she did so. She walked straight past the pin-stripe-trousered, black-jacketed butler as if he didn't exist. In the marble entrance hall beneath the vast cut-glass Georgian chandelier she hesitated as she looked around. It was eight o'clock in the morning. She took the steps of the Carrara marble stairs two at a time. Jo-Anne's bedroom would not be hard to find.

Struggling in her wake, making little mutterings of protest, his arms waving ineffectually, followed the English butler.

The second door she tried led her to her quarry. Jo-Anne lay back queenlike in the huge bed, a Crown Derby cup of exquisite delicacy raised to her lips.

Lisa stood at the end of the bed white with fury, her body quivering with anger. Behind her the butler had made it to the door. "Madam, I'm so sorry. I wasn't able to stop her."

Jo-Anne put down the teacup. She was rather looking forward to this. It began to look as if she had won. Mrs. Bobby Stansfield's former name would be Duke, not Starr. Served the little girl right. Nobody got in her way. Nobody should dare to try. But what a pity she hadn't made hay while the sun had shone in that damn Jacuzzi. She'd never get around to experiencing that amazing body now.

"It's all right, Roberts. I think you'd better leave us alone. It looks as if Miss Starr has a thing or two on her mind."

"You're too right there's something on my mind. You set me up, you bitch. What the *hell* are you trying to do to me?"

"My dear Lisa, there's no need to be melodramatic. Listen, sweetheart, you've been setting *yourself* up ever since you set foot in this town. Who the hell do you think you are?"

"I know exactly who I am and I know exactly what you are. You're a vicious, disgusting liar. You told Bobby I was a lesbian. You know that's not true."

"Truth? Truth? You naive little fool. What the hell do I care about truth? Anyway, for someone who's not a lesbian, you sure kiss like one."

Lisa shook her head in disbelief. Somehow she hadn't expected this reaction. Jo-Anne was actually enjoying it, goading her, ready to add to her humiliation. She was totally at sea when confronted by the pulsating force of pure evil.

"Why did you do it to me, Jo-Anne? Did you want him for yourself? Or was it to get at me?" The anger was receding. Now she was puzzled, desperately hurt but wanting to know the reason why, to understand the wickedness that had broken her heart and ruined her life.

"Why did you lie to him, and why did you tell him about my mom? I wanted to do that myself. It was a terrible thing to do."

Jo-Anne lay back on the cushions as the purest malice shot from her eyes. The girl had shown weakness, and she was trained to go for the kill in its presence. Her voice was low as she spoke, but the words dripped with the poison of her sarcasm. "You really don't understand, do you? You walk into this town, all bright eyed and bushy tailed, and expect everyone to forget where you came from and what you stand for. Don't you realize, Lisa Starr, you're just a nobody, a great big zero with no past, no present, and no future? You don't count here. You come from a sleazy part of town, from sleazy parents, and yet you dare to walk into our world and pretend you're an equal. Bobby Stansfield is a prize around here, you know. He's ours. Or at least mine. Baby, you never had a chance. Okay, so I helped blow you out of the window, but you were never anything more than a slow, comfortable screw, so I didn't have to try very hard. Your grave had been dug before you were even born. You should have gotten wise and chosen less beat-up parents."

Lisa stood there as the acid words burned her soul. There and then she felt her world change. Nothing could ever be the same for her again. A metamorphosis had occurred and now she was different. Lisa Starr had died. Lisa Starr had risen.

Her voice was quiet when she spoke, but it turned Jo-Anne's stomach and sent icy fingers dancing up and down between her shoulder blades.

"For what you have just said, Jo-Anne Duke, I will bury you. I will destroy you and everyone and everything you love, if it takes me a lifetime to do it. Never, never forget this promise."

She turned and left, but when Jo-Anne had reached out for her tea, her fingers had seemed to have a mind of their own. The Crown Derby cup and its pretty saucer had gone crashing all over the place, leaving Jo-Anne with the discouraging thought that their destruction could just have been a symbol of Lisa Starr's spine-tingling vow of vengeance.

Jo-Anne sipped gently on the ice-cold fino sherry, allowing the arid dryness to scourge her tongue. It was a delicious penance to drink it, atonement for more simple and straightforward pleasures. She kicked off her shoes and hoisted her bare legs onto the oatmeal hessian sofa, allowing her eyes to roam around the elegantly decorated Jon Bannenberg yacht. It had been a good move to get him to do the interior. He wasn't the most original choice, but more than any other boat designer in the world he knew how to achieve the delicate marriage of good taste and expediency that was so necessary in a private transoceanic vessel. Beneath her she could both sense and hear the reassuring throb of the twin 1,280-horsepower General Motors turbodiesels as the 120-foot motor yacht *Jo-Anne* edged out from the dock into the smooth waters of Lake Worth.

Absent-mindedly she reached out to the nearby brushed-chrome control panel and flicked casually at a switch. It took her three tries to score the Vivaldi. Just what one needed to complement a mood like this. Soothing, yet uplifting. A present for the senses of a hooker who was in the process of landing the biggest and best catch of them all.

Everything had gone like clockwork. A virtuoso performance, the logistics impeccably handled. God, she was a winner. She brought the treble up a bit, turned down the base. Mmmmmmmm. The sound was full and rich. Just like her. In the blue stateroom Bobby Stansfield would be changing for dinner. Slipping into that dinner jacket that he wore so well. Probably splashing on the Eau Sauvage that all men of his class seemed to prefer. Later they would drink the dryest of martinis, Tanqueray gin, a Spanish olive, on the afterdeck and watch the spectacular Lake Worth sunset. Oh yes, it had all been stage managed, the timing orchestrated by the conductress's baton with nothing left to chance. Dinner would be open air, *à deux,* bobbing on the Gulf Stream by the light of the silvery moon. Owl-and-pussycat time.

The white-coated steward cut into her reverie. "May I get you another glass of sherry, Mrs. Duke? Or perhaps a canapé."

"No thank you, James. I'll wait for the senator. Was the chef able to get the swordfish steaks I asked for?"

"He certainly was. And I think I can say that the sauce Bearnaise is the best I have ever tasted. Roberts has organized the wine. Le Montrachet 'seventy-six with the fish."

"Marvelous, James. Make sure you keep a close eye on the senator's glass. Oh, how are we doing for breakages on the blue Sèvres dinner service? I think it was for sixteen originally."

"It would certainly cover fourteen now. No problem. Tonight I laid out the Meissen. That was what you ordered."

"Yes, that's fine. Flowers?"

"Four single birds of paradise as a centerpiece. White orchids on the serving table."

Jo-Anne was really just checking. Everything was shipshape. The troops responding like automatons to her general's command. It was things like that that made the difference between success and failure. And tonight was special. Quite apart from anything else it was day fourteen of her menstrual cycle, and she fully intended to make maximum use of that.

She fingered the buff folder on the heavy glass table in front of her. No need for another look. She knew its contents intimately. Six legal methods of short-circuiting the rule that said no individual's contribution to a political campaign should be more than one thousand dollars. All skirted the borders of legality, obeying the letter if not the spirit of the law. As a result all were a little dubious, laying one open to the criticism that play had not been entirely fair. That could cost votes in a close-fought campaign. Jo-Anne's way was a better one altogether. It had the virtue of simplicity and it tied up all the loose ends. On the day of her marriage to Bobby Stansfield she would write him a check for five million dollars. A simple gift from a loving wife to her much-loved husband. That way he could spend it as he wished. No law forbade a rich man from financing his own run for the presidency. But although it was a "no-strings-attached" gift, it would also be a fee. Jo-Anne Duke would actually be buying the Stansfield name.

She stood up and walked over to the mirrored wall. A simple
pure silk dress. A single strand of the Duke pearls. White shoes.
No stockings, no bra. White silk briefs. Nothing else at all. He
could have her wherever and whenever he wanted. As long as it
happened, Jo-Anne didn't mind. Once the game was on, she was
its mistress. She could do everything because she *had* done everything. Practice had made her perfect.

The swordfish, lightly grilled, had been a dream, its flesh firm
yet moist. And the white burgundy had set it off to perfection.
Bobby hadn't held back on the martinis and he hadn't held back
on the classic wine either. Over the delicate, frothy chocolate
mousse she had cast her fly and like a salmon on the rainswept
Spey in August he had risen to take it. She hadn't actually proposed to him—some things, not many, a man had to do for himself.
But she had put her proposal to him. The difference had been
largely one of semantics. As the moonlight had caught the surface
of the warm water, as the soft, salt breeze had played across their
faces and the delicious wine mellowed them, she had leaned across
the polished mahogany and let him see her tits as she had offered
him the power of her huge fortune, and the delights of her voluptuous body. She had watched the mighty battle being fought in his
eyes as his ambition had gone to war with his finer feelings, and
she had known that she had won. The real decision had been made
a day or so earlier when Bobby had sacrificed happiness for the
ultimate goal.

Now he smiled across the table at her. Shy, debonair, infinitely
appealing, he allowed her a sight of the Stansfield grin, universally
described as boyish from *People* magazine to the acerbic pages of
the *National Review*. But there was a sadness about him, too.
Unmistakable, and appealing in its challenge. Lisa had gone.
Clearly, though, she was not forgotten.

"I think we maybe should get married," he said at last.

"I think that certainly we should," agreed Jo-Anne. She stood
up. The contract needed to be signed in the most meaningful way
she knew how.

Holding his hand in hers, she took him below, steering him past the Erté watercolors and the gorgeous set of original Diaghilev stage designs, past the Epstein bronzes recessed in alcoves and lit by hidden spots, to the place where her best deals had always been made. Her bedroom.

11

*L*isa wanted to be sick. She wanted to lie down right now on the polished wood boards with all the heaving flesh dancing around her and puke until her soul had come out of her. She wanted to spill her guts, vomit until she was empty, blow her insides all over the gym. And they called it morning sickness. What a grotesquely inadequate description for the hell on earth she had experienced these last few weeks. Why did women keep this one quiet? Were they frightened that if the truth came out the human race would end then and there, stopped in its tracks by the universal knowledge of this most dreadful experience? With quiet desperation she forced herself to concentrate on the music. They said the first three months were the worst. Well, it was almost twelve weeks since she had stared with such misplaced joy at that black ring and she had had enough.

"And eight more . . . one and two and three and four . . . Come on go for that extra bit . . . work those bodies . . ."

Lisa pushed herself harder. Maybe the exercise would do what she had found herself unable to do. Three times she had made the appointment. Three times she had canceled it as she had fought back the temptation to sacrifice the unborn child on the altar of her hate. Now it was too late. Bobby Stansfield's baby would see the light of day after all. Conceived in love, it would be born in an atmosphere thick with the smoke of loathing, the sky dimmed by the black cloud of revenge. Sometimes when she woke bathed in the swirling mists of nausea, Lisa Starr looked in horror at the person she saw in the mirror. Outwardly little had changed, but inside her mind it was another planet. There was a stranger there living in her brain, an alien creature, foreign and fearsome, feeding on bile. Already the invader was taking over, as it redesigned her memories, redefined her beliefs, recast her ambitions. Already the fruits of its handiwork were subtly visible.

In front of her the bodies tortured themselves, twisting and straining as they fought for physical glory. But they were not the same bodies. Cheap sweat shirts, torn tights, Swiss-cheese leotards, grubby sneakers were nowhere to be seen. Nor were haggard faces, cheap hairstyles, Timex watches. The lingering smell of stale sweat was gone too, together with the cheap beach bags and dirty towels that previous patrons had left littered around the edge of the exercise floor as they sweated out their grinding routines. The colors now were brighter, the fabrics of the workout clothes of a noticeably higher quality—Barely Legal, Body Electric, Dance France. Through the air thick with the smell of Joy, Opium, and Giorgio, Cartier and Piaget watches flashed and darted in time to the rhythms belted out from the state-of-the-art Fisher sound system. A coal miner from Kentucky would have missed the point. To him it would have been a tits and ass show—"Solid Gold" dancers in the flesh. The point that he would have missed however was that this class was different in that it *had* class. Inside the tits the blood was blue, and the ass was pure old Palm Beach.

Lisa watched them as she orchestrated the group effort. It was working beautifully. From across the bridge the Palm Beachers were flocking to Clematis Street as she had intended: a few cunningly worded ads in the Shiny Sheet, her personal touch, and the word of mouth which crackled like wildfire around the tiny town. Already she was something of a celebrity. An outsider of course, and likely to remain one, but more than useful to make up numbers when house guests arrived in Palm Beach from the North, when nephews were on vacation from Princeton or the University of Virginia.

Lisa smiled grimly to herself as mercifully the nausea began to pass. She was getting there. Slowly but surely the first part of her life plan was coming together. Already she was learning the rules of the complicated social structure, her antennae sensitive to the vaguest nuance that could point the way forward. It was a deadly business and no book of etiquette was of the remotest use. You were allowed few mistakes, and beneath the precarious gangplank on which one walked, the water was stiff with the sharks, their razor teeth poised to rip the socially unwary wide open from top to toe.

The blood that had formerly run in her veins, warm and loving, had been replaced by another liquid, cold and unforgiving. It was exactly what was required for Palm Beach survival, and more important for Palm Beach advancement, and now she knew not only who was important to her, but, just as vitally, who was not. Now there were a group of people to whom she didn't talk; not large admittedly, but it was a start. The West Palm people, of course, had gone first. It had taken a few barbed comments, a few public quarrels, but they had been cleared out eventually to the continual protests of the ever-faithful Maggie. Into the vacuum created by their departure had come the "quality," with their high-pitched laughs, their "in" jokes, their endless gossip, their boundless self-confidence. Lisa knew them all—the girl with the funny name who was actually a Vanderbilt by birth, the one who was married to a Greek but whose children were called Phipps, the older woman with the toothpick tits whose daughter was a leading light on the junior committee of the Bath and Tennis Club.

They were a funny lot. Martians at first, but she was getting to know them—what they liked and didn't like. First, they didn't like any sign at all of weakness, of deference, which might hint that you needed them. The moment they sensed that, their lips would curl in condescension, as they sharpened their tongues for the slice-up job, an art they practiced effortlessly and with surgical precision. Second, they were more than prepared for a hard time, superb masochist material, quite happy to endure the pain and the insults as Lisa revved up their screaming bodies and forced them toward the muscle "burn." That had been unexpected. Somehow she imagined the upper classes to be without spines, effete and ineffectual. Maybe they were, but on the workout floor they went for it as if their lives depended on it, and she had to admire that.

Never for one moment, however, did Lisa make the mistake in believing that just because they allowed her to scream at them, that she was one of them. In Palm Beach nobody was given instant access. It took time. She would be on probation for years. There was one and only one way to shortcut the process, apart from marrying into the town's aristocracy. If she could somehow get hold of a sponsor—a patron who would look on her as a protégée, somebody powerful enough socially to insist that her friends became Lisa's friends. That was what she needed. She had found it briefly with Jo-Anne Duke, and it had ended in tragedy. But now Jo-Anne was a bitter enemy who could be relied upon to bad-mouth her at every opportunity, and the rumors of impending marriage to Bobby Stansfield had strengthened her already almost invincible position. Without a protector, Jo-Anne would murder her in Palm Beach society, and without her infiltration into its ranks revenge would be impossible.

More than anything, Lisa needed friends in the big league whose social cannons could outgun Jo-Anne's. But who? And how would she meet them? How could she befriend them? There were so many unanswerable questions.

"Okay you guys, let's unwind—relaxation, deep breathing, stretch it all out."

Lisa looked down at her forearms. Only the thinnest film of sweat. In front of her the class looked like it had been under a shower. That was what fitness was all about, and Christ, was she in top condition, her skin shining with the patina of robust health, her body a superb machine . . . with one small blemish. Damn. The child. How soon before it wrecked her body and disfigured her sculpted abdominal musculature? The child of the man who had more or less told her she was inferior goods, that his bloodline deserved a better baton carrier. Well, damn them all. She would work out until she dropped the little bastard.

The cake was unashamedly traditional—huge, and layered—the initials of the happy couple intertwined on top. Apart from the size, a little too large for Palm Beach purists, it was understated. Snow white, the icing intricate, the proportions perfect. It stood all by itself on a long table at the end of the pink-and-white marquee that had been erected on the lawn of the Duke mansion, and many of the guests had already admired it as they had the ice sculptures that were scattered strategically among the groaning buffet tables. Typical of these was an enormous American eagle, powerful and predatory, which hovered over the white damask tablecloth as the tent's air conditioning fought a losing battle to keep it alive, its body dripping away gently onto the immaculate linen. The beluga had a separate table all to itself, and the finest Iranian caviar, both black and red, free of its unhappy homeland at last, lay in huge inviting mounds on ice beds in the silver serving salvers. It was here, and around the champagne bar, where a Taittinger Rosé 1976, the color of crushed rose petals, was being poured into elegant Baccarat wineglasses, that the crowds were thickest.

"Can I get you a little caviar, Aldo? Some chopped egg or chives with it?" Jo-Anne spooned a mound of the improbable delicacy onto a Limoges plate.

"Just a little lemon. Nothing else, thank you." The elegant old Italian showed his traditionalist colors. Dr. Aldo Gucci, like the merchandise he sold, was interested only in undiluted quality.

She looked around the tent. It was magnificent. The perfect wedding reception after the fairy-tale wedding. Even the hard-bitten Palm Beachers had been touched by the emergence of happiness from the ashes of tragedy, although there were more than a few who had commented on the indelicate speed of the process and others who had smiled behind their hands at the ostentation of the caviar and the ice sculptures. Whatever they thought, they had all showed up—the aristocrats, the politicians, the fashion people, the displaced Europeans. Palm Beach was on the map again, and nobody was quite sure why. It had never really changed, but the world around it had. Both money and conservatism were fashionable, and Palm Beach had buckets and buckets of both.

Across the room Jo-Anne saw Ralph Lauren locked in conversation with Laura Ashley, the hugely successful British designer who had recently bought a house in the town. Ralph, it was rumored, was planning a "Palm Beach look" for his next collection.

In another corner was Ted Kennedy, floating his formidable charm over house guest Beverly Sassoon. Bobby might despise him, but only a few hundred yards of North End beach separated the Kennedy house from the Stansfield home. It would have been impossibly churlish to have failed to send an invitation. Actually Jo-Anne herself was rather drawn to him—that braying self-confidence, the skill with the Frisbee in the surf, the eyes that said their owner liked women more than men. Whatever else you could say

208

about the Kennedys and their socialist politics, you had to admit they had style. That was a cliché, but it was true. The North Ocean Boulevard home, for instance, was a tip. Jo-Anne had been there once with Peter in the days when Rose had given the occasional party. The carpets had been threadbare, the furniture damaged irreparably by the corrosive sea air, the ancient fifty-foot pool requiring all the considerable skills of C and P Maintenance to save it from algae, frog spawn, and nameless creepy-crawly things. The windows didn't open and close properly and the whole house needed a coat of paint. But the Kennedys didn't mind things like that. They were above it, no longer interested or aware of what others thought. And they displayed the true patrician disinterest in conspicuous materialism. Despite their wealth they looked after the pennies. In the kitchen the refrigerator was so old that once a week the maid had to defrost it by hand. To them the vast 1923 Mizner home on North Ocean Boulevard was just a beach house, and they treated it as such. She had to admire that.

Jo-Anne smoothed her hands over her stomach. It was such a funny feeling being pregnant. So much was going on in there, but there was so little to show for it. In vain she had waited for the morning sickness, for the food fads and all the other little happenings that seemed to figure so prominently in other people's pregnancies. It looked as if she were going to sail through her nine months with no problems and no discomfort at all. What had she done to deserve the prizes that were falling so readily into her lap? It was almost as if the Lord in His wisdom had decided to make it up to her for all the bad times, for the cold, for the hunger of the Big Apple days. She had wanted Bobby, and wanted to be pregnant as a method of increasing her hold over him, and she had gotten both. How lucky could you get?

Thank God she hadn't messed around with the wedding dress. She had played it straight and gone for Dior. Traditional elegance, sweeping lines, the finest stitching, obsessional attention to detail. If she was filling out below the waist it wouldn't show in this creation.

The voice whispering in her ear cut into her thoughts. "Congratulations, honey. 'Mrs. Robert Stansfield' sounds even better than 'Mrs. Peter Duke.' " Mary d'Erlanger smiled the smile of the person who had seen through the charade.

Jo-Anne laughed openly. What the hell did it matter anymore? She'd made the home run. She was the girl with the perfect batting score. There was only one important secret, and that had died as the blood had risen in Peter Duke's drowning throat. No longer did she have to play the part of the grieving widow. She didn't even have to pretend that she loved the man she had just married. At last she could let it all hang out. It was with a glorious feeling of liberation that Jo-Anne Duke Stansfield realized that she didn't give a fart.

"The problem is I have nothing left for the encore."

"Oh, come off it. Jo-Anne. I'm counting on you for the White House dinner parties. I've already started to read *Time* magazine at the hairdresser so that I'll know what to say to all those foreign politicians."

Again Jo-Anne laughed. People always got it wrong. The presidency was Bobby's trip, not hers. Nobody seemed to realize that. The truth was she was hooked on another game, the one they played here in the town of Palm Beach. For years she had crept higher up the social ladder, dislodging the incumbents on the rungs above as she sabotaged the progress of fellow-traveling glory seekers. It was in her blood now, an addictive drug whose withdrawal would be extraordinarily difficult if not impossible. There was absolutely no doubt about it. What she wanted right now was not the worldwide fame of the first ladyship. That could come later. Now she wanted the crown of Palm Beach. She wanted to park her pert rump on the throne on which Marjorie Donahue sat so regally. She wanted to pry the wily old bird's wizened fingers from the top-rung perch. For far too long she had been a princess, the jam promised tomorrow but never had today. But nothing lasted forever. It could be done. She could make it happen. The queen is dead. Long live the queen.

There was a wistful look in the eyes of Jo-Anne Duke Stansfield as she looked across to the corner in which Marjorie Donahue was holding court. Around her clustered half a dozen socially ambitious, attentive courtiers wrapping their tongues around the compliments—shameless in their sycophancy. In a minute or two Jo-Anne herself would be among them. A first among equals maybe, but still nothing more than an ass-licking parasite.

Marjorie, what a *brilliant* dress. How dare you shame me on my wedding day? Where on earth did you get it? That would just about do for openers. Christ, what a terrible dress it was. The sort of thing you got in a thrift-shop clearance sale. Jo-Anne fervently wished it were a shroud. She turned to her "friend." "Come on, Mary, we'd better go pay our respects. A thousand dollars for the most flattering lie!"

As she walked toward her social superior, Jo-Anne felt the irritation rise within her. This was *her* day. *She* was the star. Why the hell was she doing the walking? Who did this superannuated geriatric think she was fooling? A chemical fortune married to department store megabucks was pretty impressive, especially when allied to a diamond-sharp tongue, but what right did she have to exact subservience and obedience from a person like Jo-Anne, who would spend the next forty years dancing on her grave? The feeling of dangerous exhilaration coursed through her as she realized what she was going to do. She would open hostilities. Fire the first shot in a long, cruel, but infinitely exhilarating campaign. Everyone would be forced to take sides, as the town split across the middle, like Virginia families in the Civil War.

The moment of truth was approaching, after which nothing would be the same again. Jo-Anne could feel the color rising in her cheeks as the burst of careless self-confidence exploded within her. Was it the wedding? The Taittinger? The hormones of pregnancy? Impossible to say. It was an emotional thing, not rational, hardly wise, but it was symbolic of her new-found power. For the first time she had the ammunition and big battalions on her side. The all important bit players who would be the troops in the coming conflict would expect payment and protection from their general. The Duke money and the Stansfield patronage would provide for them, and as her husband's star rose across the firmament of America, she would prevail in the real battle, in the one in which her heart was involved. It would start here. Now. She would insult the queen.

The gaggle of courtiers parted to allow Jo-Anne's approach.

"Jo-Anne dear. What a wonderful day. Such a brilliant wedding. A marvelous day for us all, and for Palm Beach."

Jo-Anne's lip curled in condescension as she let fly the arrow. It was Pearl Harbor. The crucial element of surprise. All who were present at the opening skirmish of the war agreed later that Jo-

Anne had been victorious. "My dear Marjorie, where on earth did you get that absolutely *dreadful* dress? The Church Mouse or that other little leukemia thrift shop in West Palm?"

Later opinions differed as to the nature of Marjorie du Pont Donahue's expression as the verbal missile struck home. Some said her mouth dropped open and her eyes widened. There were others, however, who told a different story. Some went for malice rather than surprise. A few for incredulous humor, at least one for a hint of tears. As always when momentous events occur unexpectedly, the reported details got blurred, but, strangely, most observers agreed on the substance of what had actually been said.

"What did you say?" had been the initial response as Marjorie had played for time to regain her composure.

Jo-Anne had just smiled back at her, enjoying the confusion.

Marjorie, however, was not the queen for nothing. In a split second she had seen it all. This was a palace revolution. A courtier had become too powerful, too successful, and was making a play for her title. It had happened before, but it always came with the element of surprise. Jo-Anne had been a favorite. Et tu, Brute? Damn. She had allowed herself to become too complacent, to be lulled by the flattery, to believe in her own P.R. That was how empires fell, as ancient rulers lost their grip and fell into bad habits, allowing the cutting edges of their swords to become blunted, the strength of their sword arms to wane.

She knew immediately that she had been badly wounded. This was all happening before a big audience, and deep down every single one of them wanted her to fall on her face. She had laid herself wide open by not anticipating the threat. She had given politeness and enthusiasm and received open hostility in return. That made her look weak and ingratiating. And any comeback now would be of necessity contrived and artless. Yet she would have to respond.

The ancient neurons worked at high speed as she sifted through her most potent armament—her global information system. "My dear Jo-Anne, I'm surprised you think I shop in West Palm. I haven't even thought of the place for years, although lately friends have been saying I ought to go and check out some gymnasium run by a very close friend of your husband's. Lisa Starr I think she's called.''

She made the most of the "very close friend."

It wasn't the best she had ever done, but in the circumstances it was creditable.

But Jo-Anne was impervious to insult and insinuation. She was flying high on an adrenaline surge. Already she could see the admiration and wonder creeping around the mouths of the younger observers.

"God, Marjorie, you mustn't go anywhere near Lisa Starr's gym. At your advanced age you'd almost certainly drop down dead, and we'd all have to get out those dreary little black dresses for the funeral.''

As she turned her back and walked away, Jo-Anne wondered if anybody would walk with her. Mary d'Erlanger was still by her side. So was Pauline Bismarck, and one of the Boardman girls. The queen would forgive none of them. They were bound to Jo-Anne at the hip. The Palm Beach wars had begun.

Lisa powered the vintage 1966 Ford Mustang across the Southern Boulevard bridge. It had been her present to herself. Some small compensation for the collapse of her future. Charlie Stark from Mustang Paradise had picked it out at a bank foreclosure sale. It had been a bargain then at six thousand dollars, but her old friend had sharpened it up at no extra charge. Red leather upholstery, immaculate bright white body work, thin black stripes strategically placed to mark the aerodynamic flow of the wind. The expensive Sony sound system was tuned as always to the Country K and Emmylou Harris was telling the world it was going to be all right in her dreams. Well, for sure she was the lucky one. In Lisa's dreams things looked about as bleak as a nuclear winter.

Until last night's telephone call, that is.

The accent of the caller had been the purest of prep. Female. In her thirties. "I am calling on behalf of Mrs. Marjorie Donahue, for whom I work as social secretary. Mrs. Donahue has asked me to say that she has heard a great deal about you from mutual friends and would very much like to meet you. Would you be available at around eleven o'clock tomorrow morning?''

Like the offer from a godfather, it was not one that could be refused. Nor did Lisa want to refuse it. A royal command appearance. It just had to be significant. But what did it mean? What would the mighty Mrs. du Pont Donahue want with her? Hardly a course of aerobic instruction! Whatever, Lisa had agreed there and then. Somebody else could take her class. Yes, most certainly, she would be at the Bath and Tennis Club at eleven o'clock sharp.

She eased the convertible across the roundabout and through the gates of the B and T. It was the first time she had been through the portals of the Palm Beach social Mecca, but then the air was thick with ''firsts'' these days. Thank God the awful sickness seemed to have passed. Throwing up on the floor of one of Palm Beach's grandest clubs would score no points at all.

The bellhop who parked her car liked it as much as he liked its driver. But why the hell did everybody know she wasn't a fully paid-up member of the Palm Beach ruling class? Lisa would bet a hundred bucks he didn't wink at a Vanderbilt. Through the doors and up the steps, and the first hurdle. The lady with the severe glasses at the reception desk looked about as welcoming as a starved Doberman Pinscher. Like the parking attendant she seemed to have advance warning that Lisa didn't ''belong.''

''How can I help you, ma'am?'' The tone was not nearly as deferential as the words implied. There was a definite note of irritability there, and a touch of mockery about the ''ma'am.'' Christ! Was she wearing her ''other side of the tracks'' sign? Were the words flashing in neon across her chest? What was the matter with the open-necked cotton shirt and matching mid-calf-length skirt? She'd purposefully given the blue jeans a miss.

''I have an appointment to meet Mrs. Donahue here at eleven.''

The words ''open sesame'' could scarcely have had greater impact. In the haughty receptionist there was a breathless change. Usually when strangers stated their name and business she would peer maddeningly at the crumpled pieces of paper in front of her as she pretended to look for the name of the visitor on some mythical list. That little charade could reduce even the most self-confident visitor to a twitching heap of groveling uncertainty as he or she contemplated the possibility of the oversight that could lead to instant rejection.

"Ah, Mrs. Donahue's guest. Of course, of course. Miss Starr. We've been expecting you. If you wouldn't mind just waiting here a minute, I'll call through to Mrs. Donahue's cabana and have somebody come down to pick you up." She spoke quickly into the telephone.

Within what seemed like seconds Lisa was following a Lilly Pulitzer wrap-around skirt through the long green-carpeted corridor off the B and T main drag. A right turn took them out to the Olympic-size pool, its clear blue water sparkling like Evian. Delicately they threaded their way through the studious millionaire sunbathers as they picked over the by now bare bones of the previous night's party. In Palm Beach midnight was Cinderella time, and that allowed an early start the next day.

Up some stairs carpeted with Astroturf, a left turn along a balcony, and they had arrived. The Donahue cabana, or rather cabanas, were a completely different world. Lisa couldn't know of the years of political in-fighting that had allowed them to be so. The essence of a Palm Beach club was that within it all members were treated equally while collectively being able to look down their noses at outsiders. It hadn't been enough for Marjorie Donahue, who considered equality to be the enemy of her own excellence. So when she had asked the committee to allow her to knock three cabanas into one, they had refused. Over the next few years of social bloodletting, thirty percent of the committee had eventually been replaced by Donahue lapdogs. She had gotten her way. "If one can't have one's way over little things like that, then there's no point in having any influence in this town," she was fond of saying. She never referred to herself as the queen.

Lisa could hardly believe it. The green synthetic-grass-lookalike floor covering had been replaced with black and white marble, checkered like a chessboard. It was not impossible to imagine the floor being laid out, after lunch, perhaps, with social pawns, bishops, and knights as the queen herself dictated the play—the courtiers hopping lightly from square to square as they demolished the opposition. Black and white was clearly the theme of the décor. There were black-and-white awnings, black-and-white zebra-skin rugs, black-and-white coverings on the sofas and chairs.

On the walls were the most extraordinary black-and-white paint-ings, in which twisted faces and scenes of dreadful carnage figured prominently. They looked vaguely familiar to Lisa.

Marjorie du Pont Donahue lay like a Dugong on a black-and-white terry-covered chaise longue basking in the direct sunlight. Clearly she was used to it. She looked like a raisin, a dried-up prune—black and baked by the years of exposure to the ultraviolet rays. There was not an inch of her body visible whose elasticity had not been eaten up by the sunlight, and any moisture or liquid that her skin contained quite obviously came out of bottles. Cac-tuslike, she could have existed for days out alone in the Sahara. Effortlessly she would have been the survivor on an unsheltered life raft after the shipwreck. She disproved by her very existence the link between sunbathing and skin cancer. Around her three or four women rushed about like roaches as they scurried and crept from the sunlight, hiding under huge hats and judiciously posi-tioned parasols.

Lisa stood there and took it all in. Marjorie Donahue was talking on a white telephone. She had signaled for Lisa to wait. Nobody spoke while the queen spoke.

"Yes, Fran. The most extraordinary behavior. In all my years in this town I've never heard anything like it. One always gave poor Jo-Anne the benefit of the doubt with regard to her back-ground—for Peter's sake as much as anything, but I am afraid this marriage to Stansfield has taken the lid off the can of worms. What was the name of that nice young man who always maintained he had seen her 'perform' at some bachelor party up North? I am afraid I was rather harsh on him. I fear now he might have been right all the time. I'm sure we should all put him back on our party lists. I should tell you he's certainly back on mine. Yes, my dear, you're quite right. That's the point. What are we all going to do about it? Well, I'm sure the very first thing is for us all to cancel our tables at that ball she's running for the leukemia people. I think that between us we can guarantee that party will be the non-event of the year. I suppose it's a bit hard on the cancer people, but personally I'm going to make an anonymous donation to their cen-tral fund to make up for it. I don't think she'll be getting any ball chairmanships after *that*. Oh, yes, Fran, and I want you and your crowd to come to the drinks party I'm giving next week for

Eleanor Peacock. *Such* a wonderful person, Eleanor, don't you think? Yes, dear, I do so agree. Such a *good* friend." As she spoke Marjorie stared hard at Lisa, who got the message loud and clear. This telephone conversation was in part directed at her.

"Good, darling. Marvelous. I knew I could count on you. You're a wonderful friend, Fran. In fact, the more I come to think of it, they should have asked you to do the leukemia thing in the first place. Let's see what we can do about that next year. Yes, I'm sure we could fix that up. No, you'd be perfect. A great pleasure. Yes, darling. And be sure to pass the word, won't you? I don't want any of our friends at that party of Jo-Anne's. I can't think that anybody who shows up will have any future in this town. None at all. All right, sweetheart. Bye, darling."

She banged the telephone down, a look of triumph on her face.

"Put Fran Dudley down on the 'definitely with us' list," she barked at a pale girl wielding a large yellow legal pad.

Once again the gimlet eyes fastened onto Lisa. "How very nice of you to come, Miss Starr. Your fame has spread across Lake Worth, and I wanted to meet you so that I should know firsthand who everybody is talking about." There was a twinkle in the eyes. It was as clear as the sunlight that beat down on her tortured body that Marjorie Donahue was motivated by something more than just curiosity.

Lisa, whose training on the streets of West Palm as a child had taught her a thing or two about human nature, was beginning to get the drift. Marjorie Donahue and Jo-Anne Stansfield had, for some as yet unknown reason, fallen out in a substantial way. The cabana already resembled some command bunker in the front line. Reinforcements were being mobilized on the telephone, aides-de-camp were taking notes. It had the look of a pretty substantial operation. Somehow this cunning old fox had learned of Lisa's feelings about Jo-Anne. Most likely she knew too about Lisa's recent relationship with Bobby. Was it possible she even knew about the child? She had kept it secret from everyone except Maggie. But doctors at the Good Sam knew . . . and nurses . . . and presumably secretaries . . . maybe cleaners. Lisa didn't care, for in the back of her mind a particularly wonderful picture was beginning to form. In it she saw the beginnings of the most beautiful alliance. A friendship with Marjorie Donahue based on the total destruction of Jo-Anne Stansfield. It was exactly what she needed. With the Donahue protection she would possess an asset with which she could walk through the gates of hell unafraid. The queen's protégée would swim without a backward glance through the predator-infested Palm Beach waters, and she needed to do that before she could even contemplate the achievement of what had become her life's ambition—to revenge herself on the Stansfields who had so hurt and humiliated her.

"It's a great honor to meet you, Mrs. Donahue," said Lisa as she walked over to take the gnarled hand. Marjorie Donahue cocked her head to one side as she sized her up. Stunningly attractive. An open smile. Self-confident, yet sufficiently deferential. She would make a promising ally. Yes, a great deal could be done with this girl. Really, a very great deal.

"I'm surprised our paths haven't crossed before, Lisa. At the Stansfield wedding yesterday, for instance. It seems we have so many mutual friends."

Again Marjorie looked quizzical as she attempted to read the effect of her words in Lisa's eyes. That she and Bobby Stansfield had had an affair was common knowledge. How it had ended was not. It was far from impossible, however, to speculate on how things might have become unstuck. A young girl with more enthusiasm than experience caught in the spider's web of the Stansfield charm. A beautiful young innocent who had underestimated the power and cunning of a scheming rival. After all, Marjorie herself could still feel the mark of Jo-Anne's dagger between her shoulder blades. This girl would have had no chance at all.

Lisa stood her ground, but said nothing. There would be more cards laid on the table. Her eyes began to sparkle as she thought of what might happen.

"Yes," Marjorie continued reflectively. "So many mutual friends who go to your gym. I say they're committing aerobicide." She laughed a jolly laugh in which Lisa joined.

Any minute now it would come. Marjorie seemed to be talking almost to herself. "And possibly we may have shared enemies."

Suddenly the air was thick with the aroma of conspiracy, the sense of common purpose overpowering. Lisa knew she had been propositioned. It wouldn't be spelled out any clearer than this. She had to give some sign that she had accepted the terms of the alliance.

"I'd like to think that I see people the same way that you do, Mrs. Donahue."

But it was Lisa's expression more than her words that told Marjorie Donahue what she had wanted to hear.

One thing was crystal clear. This perfect-looking girl had learned how to hate. It was more than likely that Jo-Anne had taught her.

It was time for a little small talk, before the telephone marathon continued once more as the troops were summoned to do battle, and the social I.O.U.'s were called in. "Good, good, Lisa. Now tell me, what do you think of the throbbing heart of Palm Beach?" She flung out a scrawny arm to indicate her surroundings, the pool, the club, the people who inhabited them.

Lisa, whose mind was full of stimulating visions of fire and brimstone falling all over her enemies, was caught temporarily off guard. "I think these paintings are very interesting," she managed at last.

"Supposed to be Goya. His black period, you know. Aren't they wonderfully gloomy? Quite mad when he painted them. I just love depressing art, don't you? So uplifting. Of course they're all fakes. Everything I ever buy seems to turn out to be a fake in the end. One of the disadvantages of being so terribly rich. Not that I mind anymore. In fact, it's rather fun. I sold a Renoir I didn't like the other day, and it turned out to be genuine. For two whole weeks I was walking on air. Never would have gotten such a charge out of it if I didn't always expect the worst."

Lisa laughed at the cheerful irreverence and was at the same time awed by the vast wealth that allowed it. It was a side of Marjorie Donahue she had not imagined would exist. This old girl was formidable, but it seemed like she was fun, too.

"I'm afraid I've never been able to afford to buy a painting." The way Lisa said it didn't sound at all self-pitying.

"Ah, Lisa. When I was your age I'd never bought one either. But let me tell you something, my dear, and remember what I say . . . you will, you will."

It seemed to Lisa as much a promise as a prediction.

The audience was clearly at an end, but not the relationship.

"Anyway, Lisa, I've very much enjoyed meeting you, as I imagined I would, which brings me to something else. I wondered if you would like to join my party to the first night of the new Neil Simon play at the Poinciana Theater. We all go on to dinner at Capriccio afterward. Cocktails at my house at six thirty sharp. Nothing dressy."

That was it. Passport to paradise. Multiple reentry visa to the Palm Beach inner sanctum. Lisa didn't have to ask where she lived. She could have walked there blindfolded. But it was with something close to desperation that she contemplated the "nothing dressy." She had been caught like that before. Where the hell in West Palm did you rent a tiara?

12

It was only the second time that Lisa had met Vernon Blass, but already she was beginning to warm to him. The first meeting, at the Donahue dinner party, had not been a success. During the cold Madras soup he had ogled her shamelessly, scarcely bothering to reply to her attempts at conversation. Over the broiled grouper he had propositioned her with all the delicacy of a New York taxi driver, and in response to her haughty and disdainful refusal, he had bided his time before plunging his hand between her legs as they prepared to attack the orange sorbet. Lisa had been appalled, not so much at his behavior, as at the fact that a seventy-one-year-old Palm Beacher of the most impeccable social credentials could stoop so low. On more mature reflection she had come to the conclusion that it wasn't so strange. Jo-Anne Duke, Bobby Stansfield, and now this Vernon Blass. It began to look as if her mother's P.R. had been the bummest of bum steers. She had delighted him, and incidentally her host, by responding in no-nonsense fashion. Without thinking twice she had emptied her gelatinous water ice into his lap, where for several blissful seconds it had clung to the immaculate navy-blue trousers in the region of his fly, its intense cold symbolically cooling his misplaced ardor.

From that moment on, his attitude toward her had changed dramatically. No longer did he see her as a cheap and cheerful import from the other side of the tracks who might provide some scratching for the endless itch that plagued him. The girl had spirit to go with the dangerously attractive body that so excited him. And, apparently, she had for some reason the most powerful of friends. As he had attempted to remove the sticky dessert from between his legs Marjorie du Pont Donahue had pitched into him, using humor and ridicule as her weapons.

221

"Lisa Starr, *now* I know where you got your marvelous name," she had boomed across the table so that everybody in the crowded Capriccio restaurant could hear. "I've been telling Vernon he should have an operation on that prostate gland of his for ages. If he'd have the damn thing out he might be able to keep his fingers to himself."

Vernon had joined in the general laughter at his expense. In part this was because it was almost a reflex action to laugh at Marjorie's jokes, but there was another reason. All his life he had been a bully. His immensely successful father had taught him that. Rich and pampered, he had been the classical spoiled only child, and the years that had passed hadn't changed that one iota. Most people he needed he had bought, and those he didn't need or couldn't buy he had avoided. To be confronted by a girl like Lisa, who had dared to stand up to him at considerable social risk to herself, was refreshing in the extreme. For the rest of the evening he had poured his not inconsiderable charm all over her and by its end he had been forgiven. Over the next few days he had found himself thinking of her all the time—so much so that he had called up Marjorie Donahue and requested a rematch.

This was it.

In the Donahue box at the Palm Beach Polo Club the Pimms was flowing free, and the atmosphere matched the fizzy, colorful drink. Lisa was thoroughly enjoying herself, and *that* was a relief. It had been a bad four months. Growing a child on a diet of hate didn't make for happy days. Still, there had been compensations, and most of them were called Marjorie Donahue. Since the meeting at the Bath and Tennis she had taken a rocket trip into the social stratosphere, and now, like Major Tom, she had almost lost touch with ground control. It had started with the gym. The queen had spoken, and, kamikazelike, the Palm Beach high flyers had responded, taking out memberships in droves. Lisa had kept the lists open to take them and was already negotiating for a lease on the adjoining building. Her stock was rising in every way.

"The thing to remember about polo handicaps is that it's the opposite of golf. The higher the better. That little fella hitting the ball now, is called Alonso Montoya. He's one of the only two ten-handicap players in the country." Vernon Blass leaned in toward Lisa as he spoke. For the past half an hour he had been teaching her the intricacies of polo, pointing out the superb horsemanship, the dangerous and illegal plays, providing biographies of the players seasoned with spicy details of their off-field activities.

"The Argentinians are the best. No doubt at all. And off the field they make love to anything in a skirt as long as it's got money in the bank. They'll go anywhere for a free meal, eat you out of house and home, and knock off your wife and daughter when you go to the men's room."

Lisa laughed. She had the measure of Blass now. He was a dirty old man, but at least he was an amusing one. She liked the way he dressed, too: the Panama hat from Lock's in St. James's, the worn but immaculate white linen suit, the faded, blue-spotted bow tie, the glasslike brown brogues.

"What about those two Englishmen? The Wentworths. I think I rather like the look of them," Lisa joked.

"My dear Lisa. Promise me—whatever you do, never go to bed with an Englishman," he intoned in mock horror. "They don't wash, it takes two minutes if you're unlucky, and afterward they're so proud of themselves they expect applause and a letter of thanks in triplicate they can show to their friends."

Lisa wagged a finger at him. "I hope you didn't find that out firsthand, Vernon."

It was Vernon's turn to laugh. "Never succumbed to the temptation. Mind you, it's been offered once or twice. Something to do with all those public schools, I believe."

Lisa looked around. The stand was packed for the final of the Piaget World Cup, and it looked as if everyone were there. Jo-Anne? Bobby? It seemed such an age since her first visit, when she had played Cinderella, dressed in rags at Jo-Anne's request. God, how naive she had been. Even then, while her husband was still alive, Jo-Anne Duke had been sabotaging the competition. Had she wanted Bobby then? With the benefit of hindsight it seemed far from impossible.

"Come on, Vernon. Tell me who all these people are. Who's that incredible-looking guy with the earring?"

"That's Jim Kimberly. He's my age—seventy-one, going on seventeen. His family founded Kimberly-Clark, so each time you blow your pretty little nose in a Kleenex you make Jim a cent or two richer. Poor old Jim's had a bit of trouble lately. He married a child bride, Jacquie—the one who starred in the Pulitzer divorce. She's just left him. There wasn't another man. She moved into the guest house, the one King Hussein owns, with the housekeeper!''

Vernon Blass's eyes were rolling at her again. The Kimberly marriage seemed to have set off a dangerous thought process.

"Now, now Vernon. Don't make me put the Pimms where the orange ice went.''

A large blond woman shouted over from a neighboring box. "Vernon, you rat. Now I know why you skipped my lunch party. Don't you ever stop? Why don't you give in gracefully and let the younger men have a try?''

"Who is that?'' whispered Lisa as Vernon Blass waved cheerfully, acknowledging the compliment.

"Sue Whitmore, the Listerine Queen. After you've wiped off your Estée Lauder makeup with one of Jim's Kleenexes you can have a crack at the halitosis with some of Sue's mouthwash. Sometimes I wonder what the rest of America would do without the inhabitants of this town.''

"Thanks a lot, but I don't *have* halitosis,'' laughed Lisa.

"Prove it,'' said Vernon with a chuckle, lunging in toward her.

"Vernon, are you molesting my adopted daughter again?''

Lisa heard the music play within her. It was all coming together. All the loose ends. Now she was Marjorie Donahue's "adopted daughter,'' and this cheerful old lecher with his publishing company and his magnificent house on South Ocean Boulevard was eating out of her hand. And she smiled to herself grimly as she thought what she would do with her new-found power.

This was more like it. Lisa hadn't looked at the price tag yet. She was already learning that that tended to spoil the fun, but the dress was one of the most exciting things she had ever seen. It could have been made for her, apart from its understandable failure to accommodate her rapidly growing breasts. All morning she had traipsed around the "acceptable'' Worth Avenue shops with Marjorie. She had been patronized by middle-aged matrons posing as shop assistants in the spacious marble halls of Martha's as she had tried on beautifully tailored dresses from Valentino and Geoffrey Beene. Later, in the Ralph Lauren boutique, which was Marjorie's idea of "young fun," she had been patronized by uniformed preppies as they went through the motions of selling the goods.

In desperation she had gone into Saint Laurent's Rive Gauche where the conspiracy to turn her into a forty-year-old had achieved mammoth proportions and she had been patronized by a French comtesse whose elegant fingers had plucked and picked at her as if she were merchandise at a Roman slave market. The Krizia shop in the Esplanade had provided an oasis of style and originality. The clothes were her age, daring, provocative. There was no built-in safety in the label, no passport to acceptance by the casual dropping of the designer name; only the truly avant garde knew all about Krizia, and when you were wearing one of their eye-catching creations you were out there on your own.

Lisa twirled in front of the long mirror. On paper, the dress didn't look like much. Hundreds of white plastic disks meticulously sewed together, mid-calf length, slit up the side to the thigh. A matching top, the generous slice of bronzed breast, the occasional sight of the already darkening pregnant nipple. God, it looked good. God, *she* looked good. Lisa smiled at her reflection. Marjorie, perched uncomfortably outside on some sharp edge, longing for the comfortable sofas and deferential homage of Martha's, would loathe it. They had had such a funny morning.

Since the meeting at the B and T, they had become close friends. Lisa had soon learned the measure of the tricky old socialite and had discovered the goldmine of her sense of humor. You couldn't hold back on the flattery, but if you looked around there were enough genuine things to flatter. No, the real point about Marjorie was that she was an anarchist at heart. Irreverence for everything and anything, her own person strictly excluded, was what she liked. In response to Lisa's anguished plea to be allowed to look her age, Marjorie Donahue had replied with world-weary wisdom that anyone under forty should be heard but not seen.

"Listen, darling," she had said. "It's difficult enough in this town to keep one's age under reasonable control, especially when one's nephews and nieces all need facelifts. The last thing we need is teeny-boppers with tits."

Well, this teeny-bopper's tits were available for the world to see.

Thank God her stomach was still flat as a board. The unfortunate
child must be paper thin in there, crushed by the iron wall of her
ceaselessly exercised abdominal muscles. Praying that there would
be no males in the shop to catch the potent visuals, Lisa shot out
of the changing room with the high-powered velocity of a model
hitting the catwalk at a Kenzo show.

Straight into Bobby Stansfield's arms.

For the split second that he was just a person, a man who had
gotten lucky, she began to mumble her apology. It stopped when
she saw the blue eyes and felt the strong arms on her shoulders,
when she smelled the familiar smell of him, remembered the mind-
bending taste of him. That was the part that came first. Apparently,
for both of them. The first few bars were the New York Philhar-
monic on a good day, the music pure, clean, crisp, clear. On the
waves of sound were borne the scent of the Caribbean night air,
the moonlight's soft touch on the clear waters of the pool, the
joyful cry of ecstasy as their baby had been created. Then, as if
the conductor had tired capriciously of the beautiful harmonies,
the music was sweet no more. It didn't stop suddenly. Instead it
degenerated, falling apart bit by bit into cacophonous discord and,
as Lisa's mind's ear heard the terrible words once again, she recoiled from him, pushing him away from her, tearing her eyes from
his.

"Lisa."

Politicians weren't supposed to be lost for words. They were
meant to be unflappable, suave, and urbane in the most trying of
circumstances. The public demanded it. But Bobby was on the
verge of losing his cool. Behind him somewhere was Jo-Anne, who
could be expected to view Lisa about as favorably as a hole in a
Renoir, and yet he was seized by an all but uncontrollable desire
to run after her, to take her in his arms once again, to tell her he
hadn't wanted it to end in the way that it had, to dare to hope that
what was past had not ended a possible future. In short Bobby was
in turmoil.

There was another problem. The logistics of the situation posed
all sorts of potential difficulties. The Krizia boutique was in fact a
cul-de-sac joined to a larger area by the narrow corridor that contained the two changing rooms and in which he and Lisa had just
inadvertently embraced. Jo-Anne was hard on his heels, only hav-

ing missed the emotion-laden meeting by seconds. Unless they turned back some sort of confrontation was now inevitable.

Marjorie Donahue stood up awkwardly from her cramped seat on the window ledge as Lisa cascaded into the room. Wise in the ways of the world, she saw immediately that the dress was no longer the point. Lisa was white as a sheet and, a second or two later as Bobby Stansfield loomed over her shoulder, she could see why. But her mind didn't stop there. Bobby Stansfield would not be cruising Worth Avenue dress shops by himself. Any minute now there would be Jo-Anne. A moment later there was.

The minimal advance warning allowed Marjorie Donahue the substantial advantage of first service.

"My, my, the Stansfields on a shopping expedition," she warbled. "How nice to see the two of you out and about. I thought you'd given up going out altogether, Jo-Anne. I never seem to see you at the parties anymore."

Marjorie's social blockade of Jo-Anne had been a conspicuous success. Her invitations had dried up like a fly's wings under a blowtorch as the queen had passed the word that she would not attend any party at which Jo-Anne Stansfield was present, and that she would never invite to her house a hostess who had allowed her through the front door. Within days Jo-Anne had discovered the full extent of her catastrophic miscalculation. Nobody of any importance had rallied to her banner, and those that had had rapidly been made to see the error of their ways. Cleverly Marjorie had outflanked her, concluding alliances with Jo-Anne's initial supporters and offering them a free pardon in exchange for the renewal of their allegiance. It had been a lightning campaign in which no mercy had been shown, and the few revolutionaries who had stayed loyal to Jo-Anne were now themselves outcasts, puttering about on the fringes of Palm Beach society.

To Jo-Anne it was a bit like being mugged from behind in church. She stopped dead in her tracks as the verbal missile snaked out toward her and could only watch in disbelief as it exploded in an air burst over her position. Lisa Starr, standing next to her arch enemy, looked good enough to eat, and her husband's eyes were registering that fact for all the world to see. And Marjorie Donahue was spitting venom from a position of unchallenged strength. There were few things on earth she needed less than that. Thank the Lord it was a small audience. There surely wasn't much else to thank Him for.

"Oh, Marjorie, you know how it is. Small-town politics are so provincial once you've had some experience of the big time. There's a whole world out there. You Palm Beachers are inclined to forget that."

Damn it to hell. If only she could *feel* that. It sounded so sensible, but without the emotion it was as transparent as a glass-bottom boat over the Pennekamp Reef.

"My word, Jo-Anne, it begins to sound as if you and Bobby are beginning to think of moving on. Back to New York, perhaps. One gathers you had a fairly 'colorful' upbringing there. Should be excellent for Bobby's political career."

Jo-Anne turned toward Bobby. It was about time he joined in the battle. After all, his wife had as good as been called a hooker who would destroy his political career. His "putdown" would have to be pretty neat to pull the bacon out of this fire.

But Bobby wasn't really listening. He was staring at Lisa as if he were a prep-school boy at his first strip show, and it wasn't just lust in his eyes. Jo-Anne felt the anger and irritation well up within her. What had happened to everybody? Had they all gone mad? Wasn't *she* the one with the pot of gold that made Croesus look like small time, with the body electric that could light men up like a beacon?

"Oh no, Marjorie, we wouldn't dream of *leaving*. But just because one has a house or two on the island, and the boat's here sometimes, it doesn't mean one *lives* here. Of course it's different for you. An old leopard can't change its spots, can it? But we just don't want to fall into the trap of thinking that the sun rises and sets in Palm Beach. That's all."

Marjorie Donahue changed tack. This was just too good to miss. "Bobby, I was going to introduce you to my good friend Lisa Starr, but I can see from the look on your face that you've met her already. Isn't she just the prettiest girl you've ever seen?" She turned and shot a triumphant look at Jo-Anne.

"Yes, she is," said Bobby simply, turning his wife into an instant enemy. He knew what he was doing, and suddenly, he didn't mind. The hell with it. Lisa *was* the prettiest girl he had ever seen, and he didn't care who knew it. He was already fast tiring of his wife's ludicrous social ambitions. The words she had just been uttering expressed sentiments with which he heartily agreed. Who needed Palm Beach high society when one could be top dog of the whole Western world? But Jo-Anne had caught the Palm Beach bug and the disease looked to be fatal. She was a big girl now, and up to a point he didn't care what she did as long as it wasn't an embarrassment to him, but he was damned if he was going to be drawn into her spider webs. He had better things to do. Like looking at Lisa.

Jo-Anne had had quite enough. That was *it*. Damn Marjorie. Damn Lisa, and most of all damn Bobby. What an asshole! He had dropped her right in it at the moment when she had most needed his support. He'd never get a chance to do that again. And he'd be wiser to give up water skiing.

"Come on, Bobby, we're late. Let's go." She might just as well have run up the white flag. As she retreated she threw a parting shot over her shoulder.

"Love the dress, Lisa. But maybe you should think about having a breast reduction."

Outside on the terra-cotta tiles of the crowded Esplanade, Jo-Anne could keep it inside no longer. It was years since she had been humiliated like that, and the whole point of her enormously successful struggle toward riches beyond avarice's dreams had been to avoid such situations. The man she had married, the man who had been happy enough to share her bed, her body, and her mighty fortune, had stood by while her enemy had walked all over her and hadn't attempted to lift a finger. Worse, he had stared at the girl who had been his former lay as if all he wanted were for her to be his future one, and then had more or less admitted it in front of Jo-Anne.

"You filthy piece of shit," she screamed at the top of her voice. "How dare you treat me like that!"

Bobby's head shot back as if he had been hit on the jaw with a baseball bat. Hey, this was public! The political training flashed the danger signals, as he moved to contain the potentially damaging situation.

"Come on, Jo-Anne. You're overreacting, honey." He reached out for her forearm, as he saw a blue rinse and her portly husband stop and go into recognition mode. "Isn't that Senator Stansfield?'' mouthed the pinched lips as, like a fairground lip reader, Bobby picked up the soundless message.

"Don't 'honey' me, you filthy pervert. Save it for when you're going down on that whore in there.''

Jo-Anne's voice was now shrill and loud. Any minute now it would be a high-pitched scream. Bobby prayed as he thought of the information being fed into the wire services. Even now some bum was probably running to look for a telephone. Out of the corner of his eye he saw the crowd beginning to form like the concentric rings of a pearl growing from a grain of sand. The couple who had recognized him were now firmly rooted to the spot, all thought of continuation on their journey abandoned as they contemplated the delicious domestic accident they had stumbled across.

Bobby wondered briefly whether he could get away with slapping her. It might put out the fire before too much damage had been done, but then again it might be the equivalent of pouring kerosene over it. And zapping a woman in front of an audience, especially when the woman was your wife, tended to be a political no-no.

"Jo-Anne, you're being unreasonable. Let's discuss this at home.'' Once again he attempted to get hold of her arm to steer her toward the stairs.

" 'Discuss this at home.' What home? Do you mean that miserable mausoleum you occasionally come back to sleep in?''

The oohs and aahs whistled around like the wind in the willows. This was food and drink to the handful of tourists and shoppers who now stood two or three deep about the famous couple. The words "Senator Stansfield" and "wife" were now clearly audible. In his mind Bobby was already reading the news story. SENATOR IN FURIOUS PUBLIC ROW WITH WIFE. ACCUSED OF ADULTERY. WIFE SAYS SENATOR A PERVERT. NEWLYWEDS LET IT ALL HANG OUT. A bit like the time Senator Ted Kennedy had left his weekend girlfriend stranded at West Palm International as he and an aide took the only two remaining seats to New York. The lady had not been pleased and had said so in public. Next day, Middle America had devoured the blow-by-blow account.

It was beginning to look as if he had miscalculated. Jo-Anne was unstable. If she could behave like this now, what the hell might she do on the campaign trail when the press would know how many times she changed her underwear? And what about her past? He had been so taken with the money he had ignored that, and turned down Baker's request for an "in-depth" investigation. Certainly the odd rumor had surfaced that suggested there were creepy-crawlies under the stone. Marjorie Donahue's most recent remark about a "colorful upbringing" was a case in point.

Bobby cut short the postmortem. The pressing consideration was how to dampen this thing down. Later he could make plans. Isolate Jo-Anne. Keep her under wraps. He could start to lead a much more separate life. Base himself in Washington and leave Jo-Anne to play her Palm Beach games on her own.

"Jo-Anne, you don't know what you're saying. I know you haven't been feeling well. Calm down." He knew as he spoke that he hadn't found the right button.

"Not feeling well. Not feeling well," screamed Jo-Anne like some demented parrot, as she searched her mind for the most damaging words. "How could anybody feel well with your stinking child inside them. Christ! If the poor little bastard's anything like you and your lecherous old father, he'll probably spend all his days in the state pen as a sex offender."

The red mist sprang up in front of Bobby Stansfield's eyes. More than anything else in the world he wanted to hit her, but he was enough of a politician to know the fatal effect of that, and wise enough, too, to know that it was just what Jo-Anne wanted him to do. The *Daily News* would say something like, SENATOR K.O.'S WIFE IN SHOPPING MALL. The others would dress it up a bit, but the effect would be the same. So he held on to the rage that bubbled within him as he vowed there and then to wipe Jo-Anne out of his life. He would not divorce her, but as a partner she was history. All his life he had dreamed of the presidency. He had given up everything for it. Nothing, no one, would stand in his way.

With bitter determination he turned away from his spitting wife and elbowed a passage through the small crowd.

It hadn't been the easiest of births. On examination, Lisa's hips had looked more than all right. Fetal skull measurements showed that the baby should sail through the birth canal with colors flying, but it hadn't happened like that at all. From the very beginnings Scott had proved a difficult individual. For a start he had decided to meet the world bottom first. For an encore he had gotten stuck fast in Lisa's pelvis like a too-new cork in a too-young bottle of wine.

The wrestling match that had followed had left Lisa as flat as a pancake, and propped up against the pillows in the private room of the Good Samaritan hospital, she looked as if she had gone ten rounds with Doctor Death. All around her the flowers competed for the oxygen, and they were just the tip of the floral iceberg. Palm Beach had emptied its shops of everything that was colored and alive, and there was hardly a patient in the hospital who hadn't benefited from the excess of well-wishing enthusiasm.

Lisa was under no illusions about all this. The reason for her popularity sat in the corner of the simple room, looking a bit like an expensive scarecrow in Adam and Eve's garden. Everyone who mattered knew the score. Lisa Starr was Marjorie du Pont Donahue's protégée and confidante. Some even used the words "crown princess." To ignore the birth of her illegitimate child would be an oversight that could turn the social ladder into a water slide to oblivion for the careless climber. Few had taken the chance, and they had been right not to. Marjorie Donahue had written the names of every flower sender in a little black book, much to Lisa's amusement.

"It may seem a little thing, Lisa," she had said. "But if you catch disrespect early, it's so much easier to nip it in the bud."

Lisa had laughed again, but she had gotten the point. In this life you couldn't be too careful if you wanted to get anywhere. You had to be ceaselessly on your guard, constantly attending to detail if you wanted to make things happen for you.

She looked down at the baby in her arms, and for the thousandth time tried to discover what she felt about him. He was kind of cute. Very little. Perfectly formed. Delicate, of course. Sort of dependent, and rather charming for that. In vain she tried to get past the clichés. There was a sense of having produced something, of having done something worthwhile, but there ought to be more

. . . much more. Maybe it was just too soon. Did they call it the baby blues? But she didn't feel blue, just tired and very sore, and a bit empty. She smiled to herself at the thought of emptiness. That was really crass. The sort of thing people said on the TV soaps. "How do you feel, Mary-Lou?" "Empty, Craig. So *desperately* empty."

She allowed herself to think of the child's father. That was better. Firmer ground. Real emotions. The bastard and his bitch wife. What an incredible, unbelievable, hysterical coincidence that Jo-Anne should be in the room along the corridor teetering on the brink of labor. Two little Bobby Stansfields popping from neighboring pods with scarcely a day between them. It was a great big black joke. Funny and sick at the same time. Hers to all the world a fatherless child, while Jo-Anne's would be as legitimate as the Supreme Court, instantly rich and instantly famous as it choked on its silver spoon. Little Scott Starr, who would never be able to use the Stansfield name that meant so much in the world in which he would live.

Again Lisa permitted herself a bittersweet smile. On that extraordinarily convoluted plant, the nurses' grapevine, she had heard that Jo-Anne's room was as empty as hers was full. Even her husband hadn't bothered to visit. Bobby Stansfield. Okay, so he couldn't know about Scott, but surely he could have looked in on his wife. In the fatherhood stakes he rated top for virility but one great big zero for everything that mattered. Not that Jo-Anne deserved any better. She had gotten what she wanted. Now she would have to learn to like what she'd gotten. All the money in the world and no friends to send flowers. Married to a superstar, and yet with no love. Possessing the body of an angel and yet devoid of heart and soul. It was a topsy-turvy world as God played with his dice, taking with one hand as he gave with the other.

"A penny for your thoughts," said Marjorie.

Lisa sighed. "Oh, Marjorie, I don't know anymore. I was just thinking about Bobby and little Scott, and Jo-Anne all alone in that room along the corridor. It all seems such a mess. I guess the only good thing is that this little thing won't ever know what went down before he was born."

"Of course he won't," said Marjorie in a definite tone of voice.

233

She peered carefully at Lisa. Was this the moment she had been waiting for to make her pitch?

"You know, Lisa my dear. What you need is a husband. In polite society anybody who has a child ought to have a husband."

"Marjorie, you've got to be *joking*. For a start, who'd have me with somebody else's bastard child? And second, the whole love business turns my stomach just to *think* about it."

"Don't be silly, dear. I'm talking about marriage—not love. It's naive to confuse the two. And I'm sure we can come up with somebody who'd be more than happy to have you, child or no child. Anyway, whoever it is can pretend the child is his. It's been done before, and it can be done again. Some nice old codger with a bankroll to match the size of his ego—that's what we need."

Lisa laughed outright. "Okay, Marjorie, who?" It sounded like quite an amusing game.

"I've been giving it some thought, dear. Quite a lot actually. And I have a short list of one. Vernon Blass."

Lisa hooted her reply. "Vernon *Blass*. But, Marjorie, he's *seventy-one*. He told me himself. That probably means he's eighty-five in this town."

Marjorie was not at all put out by the response. She hadn't expected to carry Lisa with her immediately. Like all the best things in life this would take time, careful manipulation.

"One can't have everything in this life, dear. He's old Palm Beach. Everglades Club, and so was his father. And the family publishing business is reasonably profitable, apparently. Nothing fantastic but solvent. Then there's that beautiful house on South Ocean. The business plus the house must be worth about twenty. He's a widower, no children yet that we know of, so you get it all when he goes. He's always banging on about how much he likes you. It would be perfect, darling—a match made in heaven. Can't miss."

By the end of her little speech the enthusiasm was positively dripping from Marjorie Donahue's lips as she contemplated the instant status that her projected match would bestow on Lisa. Mrs. Vernon Blass and her young son Scott Blass. It would be the foundation on which very nearly anything could be built. And it would give her, Marjorie Donahue, that most desirable commodity of old age—an heir presumptive. Lisa could be groomed to inherit her power. It would live on beyond the grave. Immortality. A hereditary monarchy. As senility set in, her crown would not be pried from her grip by upstarts like Jo-Anne Stansfield. She could die with the dignity of her position intact, awaiting the last trumpet in the secure knowledge that her kingdom would not be broken up after her demise—that, in Lisa's capable hands, it would survive unscathed as a monument to her memory.

Lisa had fallen silent. Of course it was all totally ridiculous—the most ridiculous thing she had ever heard. Two words, however, kept reverberating through her brain. Scott Blass.

While young Scott Starr screamed and yelled his anger at the world in his mother's flower-bedecked room, little Christie Stansfield slept the sleep of the blessed in Jo-Anne's monastic suite. Her introduction to the land of the living had been quite unlike that of her half brother, and her birth, like her mother's pregnancy, had been totally without complications. Born in peace as Scott had been born in violence, her tiny face was a picture of serenity.

The scene that was being enacted over her sleeping head, however, was in direct contrast to her tranquillity. Jo-Anne was thoroughly annoyed.

"Listen, Bobby. I know we don't get along. Everyone knows that, and usually I don't ask for much. But I do think that when I'm bothering to go through the motions of bringing your daughter into the world, you might show up to see how things are going. Frankly, I couldn't give a damn, but you might just think about appearances at least. The nurses here can't believe it."

Bobby felt the anger rise in him once again. God, this woman knew how to irritate. Why the hell had he taken her on? Why the hell had he ever had anything to do with the female sex at all? They were nothing but trouble. Always screwing him around. There was a lot to be said for celibacy.

Jo-Anne changed tack. "I suppose you're upset that I didn't give you a boy. That's what you Stansfields always want, isn't it? Then at least when you fail there's someone else to keep alive the dream."

"You know I don't feel like that." But of course he did. Obviously he had wanted a son, and it *was* maddening that she had produced a girl. Typical, but infuriating.

He looked down at his sleeping daughter. A girl! God! Boyfriends and pregnancies. Girls' schools and Barbie dolls. Forget the touch football and fishing trips, the Racquet and the Senate.

There was a long silence as both digested their private thoughts. Jo-Anne broke it. "And to add insult to injury, can you imagine who just produced a son two or three rooms down the hall?"

Bobby wasn't in the mood for guessing games. He shook his head disinterestedly. Jo-Anne and her mindless Palm Beach gossip. She was looking at him strangely though. Somehow what she said next was going to be important.

"Lisa Starr."

"Lisa Starr?"

"Lisa Starr."

"Oh." For some reason, not entirely clear to himself, Bobby said it again. "Oh."

Lisa. Lisa who'd been pregnant with his child. Lisa who'd promised to flush it into the sewer. It had been a terrible, wicked thing to say. A dreadful, evil thing to do. How often during these last months he'd thought of it, and of Lisa. A son. Whose son? *His* son? No, impossible. No, not impossible.

"What do you think about that?" Jo-Anne watched him carefully, picking up on the confusion. During the course of her pregnancy, she had all but forgotten about her defeated rival. As far as she was concerned, Lisa Starr had dropped off the end of the world and been swallowed up in infinity. But for the last couple of days, after she had learned of Lisa's parallel pregnancy, all sorts of disturbing doubts had bubbled to the surface. Was it possible that Lisa had borne Bobby's child? The timing certainly was right. In the scheme of things it wouldn't be a total disaster. After all she was the legitimate wife, her daughter the legitimate Stansfield child, but it was something that needed to be cleared up. She didn't love her husband, but she was enough of a woman to know all about jealousy.

"I don't know what to think . . . I mean, I don't think anything. I'm glad for Lisa. Who's the father?" He tried to make the question as neutral as possible. Like . . . Who was at the party last night? Did the Munns enjoy Lyford Cay?

"Apparently nobody knows. Do you know, Bobby?"

"What do you mean?" Bobby tried to sound irritated.

"I mean . . . is that your baby, Bobby? That's what I mean. Is the little bastard your bastard? That's what I mean. You screwed her, after all, and we've just proved you work." Jo-Anne's voice dripped neat sarcasm as she flipped a casual hand in the direction of her daughter.

Bobby played for time. There were all sorts of ways to react to this. His child? Wonderful! No, a disaster. An illegitimate son. A son! The political fallout if it ever leaked. Some filthy West Palm surfer. His hands all over that amazing body. The love words in Lisa's ears. In the ears of *his* Lisa. The one he had so capriciously given away. The one who had been so terribly hurt.

The answer when it came was spoken with a soft voice. "No, it's not my child, Jo-Anne. It could have been, but it isn't. Lisa was pregnant by me, but she had a termination. I didn't want that, but she insisted. That's what happened."

It was the look of infinite sadness on his face as he spoke that made Jo-Anne believe him. And she did want to believe him.

She almost crowed her triumph. "So, who's the father then? Some cowboy with big balls, no money, and no class I suppose. Loser Lisa. Ha!"

Bobby's face was a mask. "I've got to go now, Jo-Anne. If you like I'll come back this evening. Is there anything you want?"

"Not a thing."

As he closed the door behind him Bobby knew exactly what he must do.

Lisa looked perfect. Fully recovered from the rigors of her labor, the color was back in her cheeks, the gloss in her hair, the glow on her skin. She was looking away from him, the radio playing softly the country music she had always loved.

Bobby stood there for a minute. It was time enough to take in the cot, Lisa's pink gingham nightdress, the sumptuous array of flowers, his own seething emotions.

At last she saw him.

Bobby didn't know how to describe her expression. Surprise, certainly. Confusion, too. Mostly, though, it was the intensity of the look that was its most powerful characteristic. One thing was obvious. She was not yet indifferent to his presence.

She turned off the radio and continued to look at him.

"Lisa. I just heard from Jo-Anne that you were here. I didn't know . . . you were having a baby . . . nobody told me . . ." Bobby searched for the words. "I wanted to know . . ."

"If it was yours?" She finished the sentence for him, her tone flat, matter-of-fact.

Bobby spread out his hands. He needed her answer. Lisa said nothing.

"May I look at him?"

"Yes."

There were no answers from the crib with its tiny bundle of life. Again he turned to her. She had to let him off the hook. "Lisa?"

Scott started to cry.

Lisa stared back at him.

Her voice was ice cold as she said, "Don't worry, Bobby. He's not your child. After what you did I'd never have had your child. Never. You'll know who the father is soon enough. When we get married. So you needn't worry, I haven't polluted the famous Stansfield genes. I got rid of your thing just like I said I would. Now do me a favor and get the *hell* out of this room."

13

*M*aggie," shrieked Lisa. "Help!"

Maggie rushed toward the bathroom. Over the last hour or two there had been half a dozen "crises," each more serious than the last. What would it be this time? A broken nail? Some mascara in the eye? A run in her stockings?

"Okay, Lisa Starr, the troubleshooter is here. Your worries are over."

"Like hell they are. This Carmen roller's stuck."

Stuck it was. The one that did the bangs. Somehow the hair and the plastic had become indissolubly wedded. "It sure is," Maggie said at last after two or three minutes of fruitless fingerwork. "Listen, we'll just have to wet it down, and start again."

"But I'm late already. The car's been outside for hours."

Maggie looked at her watch. Lisa was right. She was hopelessly late, or at least she would be if they started on the hair again from scratch.

The two friends stared at each other—the same thought in both their minds.

"Will you do it or shall I?" said Lisa with a laugh.

"I haven't got the nerve," said Maggie.

"Coward. Okay, Maggs, get the scissors."

Both peered into the mirror to observe the effect, the guilty Carmen with its cargo of hair lying abandoned on the scuffed Formica.

"It's sort of weird," said Maggie uncertainly.

"It sort of is," agreed Lisa.

"Maybe we could cover it up with flowers." Maggie was far from sure.

Lisa was more optimistic.

"Don't worry, Maggs. The veil will cover it up until it's too late to matter.

It had been only a few short weeks since Marjorie Donahue had planted the seed of the idea in the Good Sam hospital room, and it had found fertile soil. As day succeeded day, it had grown and grown in the hospitable environment of Lisa's mind, and the more she had thought about it the more it had made sense. First, there had been Scott. His life would be hard enough without having to struggle through it as a penniless bastard. Lisa had been quite wrong to assume that no man would be willing to lend her son his name. Vernon Blass had been thrilled by the idea and had agreed to the match the moment Marjorie Donahue had suggested it. The beautiful Lisa Starr as his wife? What more could a seventy-one-year-old want, except maybe a strapping baby boy to show Palm Beach that there was life in the old dog yet.

"Are you all right, Lisa?"

"What? Oh, yes. I was just thinking about everything. Do you suppose Mrs. McTaggart has gotten Scott to the church yet? I bet he's howling up a storm in there."

"Aren't you supposed to worry about your husband turning up?"

"Oh, Vernon'll turn up all right. Let's try the veil."

For the tenth time they did just that. It looked like it had the other times. Lisa Starr in the softest of soft focus. A haunting beauty of dramatic loveliness, thought Maggie, about to be sacrificed to a man old enough to be her grandfather. Not for the first time since she had heard the terrible news of the engagement she fought back the revulsion. It wasn't too late. It hadn't happened yet. Her friend was still intact, but within hours Mrs. Vernon Blass!

"Lisa, are you sure this is wise? It's not too late, you know."

Lisa's voice was suddenly a little shaky. "We've been through all that a thousand times, Maggie. Don't bring it up again now . . . of all times."

Boy, had they been through it. Sometimes till all hours of the morning. But the logic had been unshakable. It wasn't just Scott; it was for Lisa, too. She lived now only to get her own back, and revenge she knew was a dish best served ice cold. Marriage to

Vernon Blass was a step toward achieving it. That was the only thing that mattered.

Vernon Blass was an old man. He would not live forever. Another ten years? Fifteen? Whichever way you looked at it she would be mistress of the fabled Mizner house on South Ocean Boulevard. Geographically it was not far from West Palm and Roxy's Bar, but in all the ways that mattered it was a different planet. If she would not necessarily be a merry widow, she would be a rich one. Blass Publishing had quite a reputation, and presumably one day she would control it.

"No, you're right, Lisa," said Maggie with a watery smile. "I guess I just haven't gotten used to the idea of losing you." She put out a hand to touch her friend's arm. "You look wonderful, Lisa. Good enough to eat."

Lisa smiled back at her mistily through the delicate veil. "You're not going to lose me. God, Maggs, I'm going to need you more than ever. It's a snake pit over there. A great big beautiful snake pit, and you're the only real friend I've got."

"Better than Marjorie?" Maggie had always been competitive.

"Marjorie is Marjorie. She's more of an institution than a friend." They both laughed. Marjorie was a bit like that. A vast crumbling edifice, huge and awe-inspiring, housing a fiendishly efficient bureaucracy.

"Come on, let's go. Take me to my destiny." Lisa intoned the words in a theatrical voice, as Maggie manipulated her through the door of the tiny West Palm apartment that had been her home. Lisa didn't give it a backward glance. She was going forward.

In the car as she crossed the bridge to meet her bridegroom Lisa didn't say much, but her mind was far from still. Crossing the bridge to a Palm Beach wedding. Her very own. In the church still warm from a Stansfield wedding. The one when Bobby, her Bobby, had promised to love and honor the woman she despised and detested. How proud her mother would have been . . . of Vernon Blass? Lisa blotted her family from her mind. It wasn't efficient to be sentimental. She would have to grow up, to grow hard. It was too late now to protect herself from heartbreak, but at last she could see through her mother's naive and foolish vision. Palm Beach was paradise all right, but its inhabitants were very far from gods. All she had heard on those front-porch evenings had been myths and fairy tales from the mouth of a dreamer. Now Lisa knew the truth; but hadn't her mother's ignorant bliss been preferable to the folly of her own wisdom, born as it had been in the bitter pain of the cruelest rejection? Bobby Stansfield, who had been her love and was now her hate—who was still in his own way the center of her universe. She had sworn to destroy him as she had his wife, and the holy state of matrimony into which she was about to enter was nothing more nor less than a weapon of war.

The tall royal palms on either side of the road seemed to Maggie like a guard of honor as they drove into Palm Beach. Or were they the erect, well-drilled members of a firing squad? She was far from certain. As if to reassure herself she slipped her hand into Lisa's and squeezed, but Lisa was far away, confronting nameless dragons, anticipating the traps and snares that lay waiting for her.

They were there. Bethesda-by-the-Sea.

"Good luck, honey. I love ya," said Maggie.

"Thanks, Maggie. I've a feeling I'm going to need it."

"Of course they were all thinking that you married me for my money. But only *we* know it was really for my body."

It was the first time all day that Vernon Blass had referred in any way to sex, and Lisa heard herself laugh nervously. From the polished oak table whose ten feet separated husband from wife she could just see the ocean across the lawn. The waves were flecked with white. Wind must be getting up.

Vernon Blass eyed her speculatively. The first night wouldn't be easy. Was she a shallow- or a deep-end person? It was so difficult to know. Other people's feelings. How on earth did you ever know what they were? How did one drum up the enthusiasm to care? He toyed with the glass of claret in front of him. A marvelous wine— 1961 Haut Brion. Somehow it never tasted so good here as in Europe. The distance? The humidity? It was impossible to say. But he was putting off the moment he had been waiting for. He had given Lisa and her son his name, and when he was dead they

242

would have his money. There would have to be a little something
in return. That was life. Maybe she understood that, but then again
maybe she didn't. In his experience people seemed to have an
insatiable desire to get something for nothing. Was his child bride
one of those?

Lisa smiled back at him. With all his millions, Vernon Blass
would not come cheap. It had been cloud cuckoo land to dare to
dream otherwise. Thank God she hadn't held back on the champagne at the reception or the rather good red wine at dinner. It
would be nasty, but it would probably be quick.

You might be called Mrs. Vernon Blass, but deep down you're
just a hooker like all the others, thought Vernon Blass as he began
to psych himself up for the main event. She might not be a slut but
it sure as hell helped to get him up to imagine she was one. He felt
the first vague stirrings. Good. That was better.

"If you've finished, my dear, I thought perhaps we would retire
early to celebrate our wedding . . . if that is what you'd like, of
course."

A headache? A migraine? Too much to drink? Lisa couldn't
bring herself to be so banal. With my body I thee worship. It had
been a contract all right. The minds had met, and she had as good
as promised that the flesh would. She forced herself to think of
something else. Of the Stansfields counting their money and
dreaming their dreams of political and social glory. Enduring the
gropings of a courteous old geriatric was a small price to pay for
ruining them.

"I'll be in my room when you're ready," he said.

Lisa watched him go. Dark blue velvet smoking jacket, formal
trousers, black velvet slippers with the leopard's head embossed
in gold braid. The perfect gentleman. A kindly, generous old man.
Why should he be denied his conjugal rights?

Lisa stared out across the lawns to the waving palm trees, their
leaves indistinct in the gathering dusk. Storm clouds scudded
across an irritable sky. Soon there would be the Florida rain,
soothing the hot land, washing away the dust, cleansing the world.
She suppressed an involuntary shudder. Would she herself soon
need its healing balm? She drank long and hard on the glass of
Hine brandy in front of her, grimacing at the unfamiliar strength of
the hard liquor. She looked at her watch. How long should she

give him? How long could she decently give herself? It could never be long enough. Like some victim of the Spanish Inquisition, Lisa tried to prepare herself for the ordeal—to separate her mind from her body, placing it in some neutral place where fortune's slings and arrows would pass it by. She could do that in the gym sometimes: the screaming, complaining body belonging to somebody else as the spirit soared above the physical, lost in the wonder of transcendence. And so the clock ticked away the minutes of her dying innocence as she sought to escape the implications of the march of time.

She was on her feet. Sleepwalking to the unwanted union. Across the room. Up the stairs. To the room which would be hers. Theirs. For a brief second, for an entire eternity she paused outside the door. She took one last inventory of her emotions and was surprised to find that pity was the most prominent of all. Poor Vernon. Already he would be tucked up in bed, his head poking nervously over clean, white sheets. His "dirty-old-man" role, strictly for public consumption, would be discarded, and now, about to be confronted by the wonders of his wife's body, he would be suitably chastened. Nervous even. He would need reassurance, to be coaxed toward some sort of satisfaction as the reward for the life he had made possible for her. She would turn out the lights for both their sakes, and do what had to be done to fulfill her part of the hard bargain she had struck.

Lisa Blass took the deepest of deep breaths and walked into the bedroom.

Vernon Blass wasn't in bed. Somebody else was.

The girl was very pretty. A pixie face, no makeup, the soft-focus complexion, downy soft blond hair that had never seen the contents of a coloring bottle. The girl was very, very young. She sat there, calm and composed, the sheets covering the lower part of her flat, adolescent stomach, eying Lisa speculatively. With one hand she pushed a strand of hair away from one round blue eye, as she sucked contemplatively on a forefinger of the other.

Vernon Blass stood by the side of the bed, and he didn't look nervous at all. He looked absolutely and completely amazing. The pajamas were acceptable. They looked like standard Brooks Brothers, but his round little face had undergone the most startling transformation. It wasn't so much the heavy mascara, or even the

244

hot pink of the lipstick. It wasn't really the faded ivory of the foundation, or the fact of the cheap costume earrings. It was his expression. It was pure. It was undiluted. It was the face of evil, and the horsewhip dangling from his hand emphasized it.

Lisa stood stock still, as she tried to take in the scene in front of her, and the breath she had taken before opening the door remained imprisoned in her lungs, waiting for the order for release. She had not stumbled on this happening by mistake. It had all been arranged for her benefit. The look on Vernon's face said it all. The expectant look on the teenager's merely confirmed it.

She opened her mouth to say words that didn't exist.

The child on the bed helped her out. "Welcome to your wedding night, Mrs. Blass." The voice was little-girl sexy, provocative, but matter-of-fact. She sounded like a marginally fresh bellhop—Welcome to the Hawaii Hilton. We hope you enjoy your stay.

Lisa found some words. Not the ones she really wanted, but the ones that seemed most available to her tongue. "What on *earth* are you doing here?" For some reason she looked at Vernon as she spoke.

The girl cocked her head to one side, a quizzical expression on a suddenly rather weary face. She, too, looked at Vernon. This was the trouble with all these rich weirdos, her look seemed to say. Too many games. You never knew what was real. What was fantasy. She gave voice to her thoughts. "You mean Vernon didn't let you in on all this? It's like a *surprise!*" Vernon Blass laughed. A nasty, crackling, cackling laugh.

The teenager saw it as her role to salvage what was fast turning into an unpromising situation. She tried to make her voice encouraging, sensual even. But it was the voice of a little girl wheedling. "Well, ma'am, the thing is, Vernon likes to watch. It'll be real fun. You and me, and he watches." Her voice trailed off. She wasn't carrying her audience with her. "The whip don't mean nuthin'. That's just for show," she added as an afterthought.

She apparently decided that actions spoke louder than words. Her trump card usually delivered the goods, and presumably this rich mother *was* into chicks. With a languid gesture she threw back the sheets to show exactly what was being offered.

For one second of concentrated ghastliness Lisa took it all in. The long brown legs, painted pink toenails, small and delicate to match the color of the pubescent nipples, the perfect blond triangle with its shy, half-hidden rosebud lips. In desperation her eyes swiveled back to her husband, demanding, pleading for a lifeline. A dreadful mistake. An intruder. A very badly calculated practical joke. Some amateur theatrical rehearsal. Anything.

Nothing, was the answer in the cruel eyes. It was for real. He'd wanted her to do it. To make love to girl jail bait while he watched, jerked off, and maybe flicked at them a bit with his whip.

Lisa grabbed the frame of the doorway as she backed toward it. In the corridor outside she walked fast, breaking quickly into a run. And after her, like the appalling odor of decay, came the fearsome sound of her husband's laughter.

Outside the rain poured down in solid sheets, providing a double obstacle to vision. The tears and the rain on her wedding night. Christ! Lisa swore out loud as she ground the gears of her Mustang and tried to see the road. She'd had to get out of that dreadful house and away from the repulsive fiend she had married. How could she have made such a comprehensive and terrible mistake? Why the hell hadn't anybody *told* her? Wasn't Palm Beach supposed to *know* about its inhabitants? The anger and frustration rushed through her at the thought of her humiliation and its message for the future. She would have to break it up: the famous Lisa Starr marriage that made the *Guinness Book of Records*. Dead as a dodo in six hours flat. God, the disgusting little pervert, the wicked glee on his face as he had contemplated the horror in hers. She had seen evil tonight in the eyes of the man she had promised to obey and honor until death, in the eyes of the man whom the world now thought was the father of her son.

Over to her left Lisa saw the surf explode against the seawall on South Ocean Boulevard. Not long now and she would be there. The warming brandy, the words of comfort in Marjorie Donahue's snug den. Marjorie would know what to do. She would stay the night with her friend and tomorrow morning the telephone lines would burn as the Donahue lawyers were alerted, as Vernon Blass was exposed.

She peered out into the wet blackness. This was it. The driveway of the Donahue house. But it wasn't dark; it was floodlit, alive with people, and full of cars. A police car's blue light flashed, its driver huddled against its side, talking excitedly into a radio telephone. In the distance there was the sound of a siren, coming closer. Then, there it was. The ambulance, the paramedics jumping from the back. The stretcher. The bottles of plasma. Urgent shouts. The red light of the ambulance at war with the circulating blue one of the police car. And the rain. Slamming down in irritation on Lisa Blass's suddenly upside-down world.

In the house, the pandemonium continued. Lisa grabbed the forearm of a white-uniformed maid as she scurried past at high speed to nowhere.

"What's happened?" she shouted. But of course she knew.

"Oh, Miss Starr, it's madam. I think she's passed away. It was so sudden. When she was having dinner."

Lisa felt the blood run cold within her. Marjorie couldn't die. She wasn't allowed to. It was against the rules. Marjorie had been above such mundane things as life and death.

She took the steps of the big spiral staircase two at a time as the paramedics clattered in front of her. Please let her be alive. Please God. Dear God, please.

Somebody had put her into bed, and Marjorie Donahue was battling to hold on. One side of her face had fallen away like an eroded cliff and she was deathly pale, her breath coming in shallow gusts through the dry, blue lips.

"Looks like a CVA. Put up an IV line, Jim, and get some plasma expander in there. She's in shock. Let's get the vitals going. And whack her with some hydrocortisone. A hundred-twenty-five-milligram bolus into the line for starters."

Lisa stood there helpless as the paramedics went to work. In seconds the straw-colored liquid was pouring into an arm vein, the blood pressure cuff strapped on, the stethoscope taped into place just below the left breast.

The man in charge bent down with the ophthalmoscope. "We've got a chance here. Pupils are reacting to light. But she's bleeding in there. Bilateral papilledema. We may need some burr holes. The sooner we get her to intensive care the better."

Lisa felt the panic rush up inside her. They were going to take

Marjorie away. She must be allowed to go too. To be with Marjorie in the ambulance.

"Can I come too? I'm her granddaughter," she lied.

In the back of the ambulance on the way to the Good Samaritan hospital Lisa cursed the snobbery that had not allowed Palm Beach a hospital of its own. The town was always so proud of things like that, but at moments like this when seconds made the difference, it seemed a dreadful and callous affectation.

In the semidarkness, the blue of the electrocardiograph line danced around on the monitor screen. Even Lisa could see it was irregular as hell, the QRS complexes all over the place like the frantic scribblings of a three-year-old let loose with a felt-tip pen on an immaculately painted wall.

Lisa was startled to hear the slurred whisper. "Is that you, Lisa? Why aren't you at home? It felt like somebody hit me on the head when I was having dinner. Where are they taking me?"

"Oh, Marjorie." Lisa cradled the ancient head in her arms. "Don't speak. Don't say a thing. It's all going to be all right. I promise you."

"I've had a stroke, dear. I must have, because I can't feel my right side." Despite the weakness of her voice, Marjorie sounded quite pleased with her diagnostic skills.

"Just a little one, perhaps. But you mustn't worry. It's going to be fine."

"Nonsense, darling . . . only big things happen to me."

There was a pause punctuated only by Marjorie's labored breathing. Lisa looked at the paramedic for guidance. He nodded to her. The message was unmistakable. Talk away while talking was still possible. It was a lucid interval; she would relapse again into unconsciousness.

Lisa smoothed the sparse gray hair of her friend away from the sweat-stained brow. Already the prayers were winging their way upward. "Don't die, Marjorie. Please, please don't die."

"I'm so glad you're here, Lisa. I feel safe with you." Marjorie's voice was a little stronger, but the words were indistinct and blurred. A drop of saliva formed at the edge of the paralyzed side of her mouth.

"Don't talk, Marjorie. Save your strength. You don't have to say anything."

The knowing eyes turned upward to find her own. The spark was still there, although it seemed to Lisa that a film had formed, a misty veil like a soft-focus lens, over the formerly clear pupils.

"Oh, but I do. I always needed . . . to talk. And I want to tell you something I've never said to you. Come closer."

Lisa leaned down toward the blue lips. With one hand she moved her hair aside to prevent its falling in the face of her stricken friend.

"I love you, Lisa. As I'd have loved a daughter. I admit that in the beginning I wanted to use you. But these last months have been wonderful. You showed me how to laugh . . . again. And how to have . . . dreams."

The voice trailed off. It seemed to be coming from some deeper place now, possessing a disembodied quality, still Marjorie's but traveling from some distance.

"I'm so glad I came to you tonight."

"What? They didn't call you? You came to see me?"

Lisa could have bitten off her tongue. Marjorie had been slipping into sleep. Her remark had been addressed mostly to herself. God! The cunning old fox had picked it up. Half paralyzed and yet still as sharp as a diamond.

"I was dropping by." In a thunderstorm, at ten o'clock on my wedding night. Oh, great, Lisa. Full marks for believability.

Again the restless eyes were searching for hers, peering into the depths of her, reading her like a picturebook. Marjorie had always been able to do that. It was useless to lie to her, and it was the only thing that made her cross. That couldn't happen now. She would play for time.

Through the windows of the ambulance she could see that they had crossed the Royal Palm Bridge and were already turning north on Flagler Drive. They would be in the Good Sam emergency room in about five minutes.

"Why did you come, Lisa? What happened with Vernon?"

"We had a bit of an argument. It was nothing. Don't let's talk about it now."

The stroke had clearly not affected the fabled Donahue antennae. A scrawny arm reached for the flesh of Lisa's strong forearm and the spindly fingers dug into her.

Once again Lisa was drawn in close. This time the voice was

suspicious. "Lisa, tell me exactly . . . what happened." The tone said that time was precious and she would not be fobbed off.

It was pointless to resist. Lisa told her the truth.

"Ah. I see. Ah."

"It's simple," said Lisa. "I'll just get a divorce."

"No!" From somewhere Marjorie summoned the effort to shout the command. At the same time she tried in vain to sit up.

Her grip on Lisa's arm tightened, until the formerly frail fingers were biting into the skin.

The broken voice was difficult to hear, but it was totally insistent, the urgency dripping from the muffled words. "No divorce. No divorce, Lisa. Promise me . . . no divorce."

Lisa nodded her head helplessly. This was the last thing she wanted. The strain on the sick woman was building before her eyes and it was all Lisa's fault.

Marjorie Donahue was speaking from the heart. The physical apparatus was all but ruined, but the sentiments were as strong as ever. Lisa couldn't remember when she had seen her friend so determined to get her message across.

"Too soon . . . all this . . . too soon for you." The good arm waved weakly to encompass the ambulance, her stroke, the broken artery in her brain. "I can't protect you in this town anymore. They'll . . . kill you without me."

"What do you mean, Marjorie? You'll be here. You're not going anywhere. You'll be here."

Lisa repeated the words like an incantation. On the flickering screen the dancing blue lines fluttered nervously.

"Do a deal . . . with Blass. Leave him, but don't divorce him . . . Leave town . . . London, New York . . . Without me they're too strong for you . . . Jo-Anne . . . Revenge later . . . later . . . Revenge."

Two big tears rolled down Lisa's cheeks as her subconscious recognized the sound of the Horseman's clattering hooves. She gathered up the wise old head, cradling it in her arms, her tears splashing soundlessly onto the leathery skin.

"Don't leave me, Marjorie. Oh, please don't leave me all alone."

But Marjorie's effort to summon up the energy to impart the vital wisdom had drained her. Inside her head the aching suddenly became more intense, but mercifully she could feel a muzziness creeping through her mind. Like a fine morning mist in the Blue Ridge Mountains. Rather nice really. Its wet softness blurring the edges of the pain, drawing its sting. Floating, flying. Drifting on the tide. Or leaning on the reassuring arm of old Don Donahue in the stern of the *Bonaventure* in the moonlight off the Grenadines. It was such a relief to be going home at last.

Lisa recognized the insistent high-pitched whine of the EKG machine. And the blue line on the screen was flat, just as it should be when somebody had died.

14

In the passenger seat of Maggie's battered Buick, Lisa was a bundle of contradictory emotions. It was impossible to talk, possible only to feel as the ancient car wound its way, tortoiselike, along the coast road to the Southern Boulevard bridge. The speed limit was twenty-five miles an hour, but they were doing less than that, the way forward blocked as usual by a carload of rubber-necking tourists checking out the mansions, living vicariously as they stared intently at what they could never hope to afford. Once Lisa had been one of them, but what was she now? Was she about to become a sightseer again? Certainly, like the outlaws of old, she was being ridden out of town. Or at least she was getting out while the getting was still good. But despite her tactical retreat from Palm Beach, she didn't feel like an outsider. She had tasted of the tree of the knowledge of good and evil, and she had been Marjorie du Pont Donahue's friend. After those experiences there was no going back.

Surreptitiously she wiped away a tear. Palm Beach. It was so powerful. She no longer idealized it, but it was still a monumental force. It had been her ambition and her dream, and it had turned on her, treated her cruelly, and now forced her away. But Lisa still loved it. She admired its capricious strength. Above all it was mysterious, a creature of infinite difficulty which defied predictions and refused lightly to surrender its prizes. That much she had learned as she had been defeated in the bloody battle. The war, however, was far from lost, and Lisa still had stomach for the fight.

"There's the John Lennon house," the tourists would be whispering to themselves in the car in front. That would be all they knew as they whistled and gasped and fantasized about the mythical superhero who had paced the floor of the first-floor ballroom. Lisa, however, was a member of the club. She could have filled them in on the spicy details. Such as the fact that Yoko Ono had bought the seaside Mizner house for eight hundred thousand dollars and had it on the market for an outrageous eight million. Like the fact that in the few short months he had lived there John Lennon had been having an affair with his secretary, and that the reconciliation with Yoko gave the world the haunting beauty of the song "Woman." Such as the fact that although the house had two swimming pools it had been built as the servants' quarters of the one next door.

Lisa sighed. Where she was going they wouldn't know about Palm Beach. Oh, they'd have heard of it, but they would have never seen the miles of deserted beaches in the North End of town, or walked beachcombing along the soft sand discovering exotic seashells, watching the scurrying crabs, communing with the ever-changing sea and sky, at one with the lazy pelicans as they soared overhead. They would never have cycled along the bicycle trail and experienced the heady scents of the flowers, as the water skiers carved their graceful patterns on the waters of the lake, and the oceangoing yachts drifted majestically down the intracoastal waterway. They would be strangers to the formidable neatness of the tamed jungle, the sparkling cleanliness of the streets and houses, the safety of a town in which to lock your door would be an affectation. Above all they would be oblivious to the undercurrents that swirled and twisted beneath the surface of this paradise on earth, that gave Palm Beach its excitement and its danger, that made the old young, and the young old, that made it the envy of towns like Beverly Hills and Palm Springs, where money and success were the only entrance tickets you needed for the game.

Maggie broke the silence as they approached the bridge. "I wonder what they'll have done to Mar-a-Lago by the time you get back."

She half turned to look at her friend. In some ways she had never seen her look more beautiful. Stricken, but serene. Her fine features colored by the pain, her character forged anew in the flames of the emotional holocaust that had engulfed her. It was one short week since her world had fallen apart for the third time. How much more could she take? Maggie had tried to understand the hurt, but, because she had never known the longing, it was out of her reach. The sympathy was there, but the experience of its cause was missing. All she knew was that for some essentially inexplicable reason Lisa was leaving, and that her interest in the gym that had meant so much to them both was dead. The day before she had signed it all over to Maggie for a nominal sum. It should have been for Maggie the dawn of a glorious new period in her life, but the joy was overshadowed by the sadness of the coming farewell.

Lisa made the effort to answer Maggie's valiant attempt at small talk. "For fifteen million they'll have to sell a lot of houses on the subdivision. Poor old Mrs. Post must be turning in her grave."

Mrs. Merriweather Post. Long before Marjorie Donahue *she* had once worn the crown. The Bath and Tennis loomed low and squat above the high wall on the left side of the road, and Lisa's mind wandered back to the time when she had been summoned for the audience that had had such dramatic effect on her life. Without that meeting her son would have no name, and she would have no future. It was a weird world.

Marjorie Donahue had given her friendship, and now death had taken it away. But she had left her most valuable legacy of all— her advice—and Lisa had followed it to the letter. She would not divorce Blass. Instead she would leave him and spend the days and the nights praying to the good Lord for his speedy destruction. She would exile herself voluntarily from Palm Beach, but, as she roamed the world, a dispossessed soul, she would use the time wisely and well, planning and scheming for a triumphant return. The thought of that would nourish and sustain her in the wilderness as she sought to master the intricacies of the publishing company that one fine day she would inherit. However long it took, Lisa would come to understand it—its weaknesses, its strengths. She would sniff around in its corners and backwaters and poke about in its closets and drawers. Then when the time came she herself would take over its reins, and bend it to her purpose. At the moment Blass Publishing was to her a blank sheet of paper. Soon it would be an open book.

Vernon Blass had been surprised when she had confronted him, coldly, and without apparent emotion. She hadn't tried to condemn his behavior either with a violent outburst of furious abuse or with a "more-in-sorrow-than-in-anger" approach. She had laid it on the line in matter-of-fact tones.

"I won't be living here, Vernon," she had said, forcing herself to look him directly in his gimlet eyes as the sticky fingers of nausea crawled through her. "I think it's best for both of us if I leave Palm Beach for some time. I want to learn about the publishing business. I thought that you could arrange for me to work in the Blass companies in New York and London. Obviously I'd pay my own way out of what I earned. I wouldn't be a drain on profits. I'm quite used to that."

For a second or two she had seen the conflict in the hated face. There was a part of him that wanted to keep her there. To plan new exercises in humiliation and degradation. At the same time he saw, too, that he had gotten her wrong. The girl from the other side of the tracks who might have learned to perform his tricks wasn't that sort of animal at all. He had miscalculated. The girl had balls. She wouldn't play, and she would make him pay. The divorce would be as messy as one could get. It would run on the networks for weeks. No, it was better to cut one's losses as cheaply as possible. To have her tucked away as an office girl or whatever in the furthest reaches of the family business seemed a very tidy deal. The charade of the marriage could be kept going, and people would even be impressed that his young wife was such a serious and hard-working person: "Won't take a penny from me. Insists on living like some student in rooms paid for out of her own salary. Wouldn't suit me, but you've got to admire the girl." The line would go down well at the Palm Beach dinner parties.

There and then he had agreed to write a letter of introduction to the man who ran Blass in New York.

There was also the question of the son. The boy that everybody thought was his. Little Scott Blass, just a month or two old.

He wanted to keep him. As a status symbol. Living evidence of his virility. Would Lisa want to schlep him around the world as she pursued her shadowy purpose?

"I think Scott and the nanny would be better off here, with me," he had said.

A few short weeks ago, knowing what now she knew, Lisa would have as soon left her son at the gates of hell as in Blass's custody, but she had changed. The child knew no one, loved no one. It was merely a bundle of physical needs. In Europe and New York it would be a distraction. Scott would be a weight around her neck far heavier than his few pounds. The Scots nanny was a gem, tough as old boots and yet kind and dependable. Even Vernon Blass was afraid of her sharp tongue. The boy would be safe and surrounded by luxury.

Of course mothers weren't supposed to abandon their young children. But then a lot of things had happened that weren't "supposed" to. Marjorie wasn't "supposed" to have bled all over her brain. Vernon wasn't "supposed" to hire hookers for his wedding night. Jo-Anne wasn't "supposed" to have told the man she loved that Lisa was a dyke. The dreadful cold had run through her veins as she had made the decision.

"Scott can stay," she had said at last as her heart plunged toward the floor. "But Vernon, there's a condition to all this. We both know you're getting off lightly. A divorce would cost you your reputation and a pile of money. If I walk away now and take nothing with me, I want your word that I inherit everything." Vernon Blass's word. It was about as impressive as his morals. Wills could always be changed, but she'd had to take the chance.

For a minute or two Vernon Blass had watched her carefully. There had been a strange look in his eye when he finally said, "I hear what you're saying, Lisa. You have my word."

So here she was flying away to a strange world with nothing but a letter, a Louis Vuitton carry-all, a promise, and a prayer.

On Southern Boulevard she felt the log jam break and the waters of loneliness flow into her soul, filling it with melancholy. Symbolically a dark cloud scudded across the sun, sending a long shadow across the road where they made the left into the airport.

As she turned to Maggie the floodgates opened and, with tears streaming down her face, she said, "Oh, Maggs, I'm going to miss you so much. It's like I'm heading into the darkness."

New York

Lisa's first impression of Steven Cutting was that he was a closet queen, and nothing he said to her, and nothing she later heard about him, gave her any reason at all to change her mind. Behind

the too large desk, in front of the thick glass picture window over-
looking Madison Avenue, he shifted his thin ass in the green
leather chair and twirled his tongue around the lisping syllables.

"Well, Mrs. Blass, it is indeed a pleasure to meet you at last. I
wish I could say I knew all about you from Vernon, but I gather it
was a whirlwind courtship, and that he swept you off your feet."

The laugh was a cross between a snigger and a snort. The implication was unmistakable. She had hooked poor old Vernon. Taken
advantage of a man old enough to be her grandfather. Used her
obvious sexual appeal to do the dirty trick.

Lisa took him in: electric gray hair, a slight but well-exercised
frame, horn-rimmed glasses, standard middle-aged preppy clothes.
A personality as buttoned down as his white broadcloth shirt, on
which the monogramed SC would be in maroon. This guy would
belong to the Union, not the Knick; he would summer in Newport
rather than the Hamptons, and suffer from piles rather than varicose veins.

Lisa couldn't remember when she had disliked someone so
much at an initial meeting. Still, she mustn't let it show. This man
was vital to her. He was the pilot of the Blass ship, and although
Vernon had technical control, he wouldn't override Cutting. To do
that might easily be to lose him, and the last thing that Vernon
needed was the responsibility of running the company.

"What Vernon didn't mention in his telegram was the exact
purpose of your visit." He placed his fingertips together and
smiled a patronizing smile across the red leather surface of the
empty desk.

"I'm very interested in the publishing business," Lisa said. "I
thought I would take advantage of my husband's owning one to
come and pick your brains. I gather you're the man who knows."
The compliment went against the grain, and Lisa didn't quite manage the enthusiasm that she had intended to convey. She stared at
him, her face like a mask.

"Let me think. What can I tell you about Blass Publishing that
you'd be interested in?" Lisa crossed her legs and shifted position
in the ladderback fake Chippendale chair. Usually that had the
effect of increasing male confusion. Steven Cutting was clearly
immune to that sort of thing. He didn't bat an eyelid as he began
to warm to his theme.

"Blass Publishing is a wonderful little company. Vernon's grandfather started it around the turn of the century in England, and his father expanded here into America. Now of course the New York office is the tail that wags the dog. The London office is really a subsidiary, and the Paris offshoot is way down the line in terms of importance. The real action is right here." He waved an expansive hand to indicate what was supposed to be the spinning vortex of the humming Blass Publishing machine.

Lisa glanced around the bare room. It looked like Sunday in Philadelphia.

"Vernon, frankly, has never been particularly interested in publishing," Cutting continued, "and since his father's death the company has been pretty much run by 'professionals' like myself, although the traditions of the firm have been jealously guarded." His voice became suitably reverential as he said this. Keeper of the Faith. Champion of the True Religion. He managed to make "professional" a marginally dirty word that nonetheless possessed minimal entertainment value.

"And what are those traditions?" Lisa felt that she knew what was coming from her analysis of Steven Cutting's persona. Still, she had to keep him talking, had to soften him up for the pitch she would be making later.

Steven Cutting sat up a little straighter. He loved this bit.

He replaced the letter opener at an exact ninety-degree angle to the black, red, and blue pencils that were the only objects on the surface of his desk. As far as Lisa could see, the last thing they had needed was realignment.

"Most of the other publishers both here and in England have become disgustingly profit oriented," Steve Cutting said. "They'd publish Hitler's toilet paper if they thought it would sell. At Blass we're not interested in the bottom line. We publish books because they ought to be published and for no other reason, and we count our profits in terms of the quality of the reviews we get, not the number of books we sell. We feel that is the gentlemanly way. Quality before quantity. Not many people in this business can say that."

Lisa couldn't resist it. "I can't imagine many would want to."

Cutting flinched. He seemed to hiss his next words. "Ah, well, one can't expect outsiders to understand a business like Blass immediately. Vernon has the right instincts. He is in tune with our way of thinking. His heart is in the right place."

The message was clear. Lisa was a parvenu who should enjoy her brief strut center stage while she could. It wouldn't be long before good old Vernon threw her back into the garbage heap from which she had undoubtedly come.

The anger was boiling insistently now, the steam escaping, the lid of Lisa's kettle beginning to dance up and down.

"What people find most irritating is that we don't do so badly with this policy. We have total author loyalty, and we pay that back with interest. Once you are a Blass author you stay that way . . . even after death. And because we deal only with quality, we go to the top of the pile on every reviewer's desk, and our salesmen go to the front of the line when they visit the book sellers." He paused, wishing fervently that the second point was a fraction as true as the first.

It was time for the summary. "The great advantage of being privately owned by a family of what one might call enlightened absentee landlords is that you are free to avoid the strictures of the marketplace which so hamper our competitors."

Lisa had the picture. Blass was owned by snobs, run by snobs, and produced books written by snobs for a readership of snobs. The competitors must be crying all the way to the bank. "How much control does Vernon have?" How much control will I have when I inherit, was what Lisa meant.

How much money is the business worth, was how Steven Cutting read the question. "Vernon still has about sixty percent, but frankly we don't make large profits for the reasons I've described. Businesses like this tend to be valued on the amount of money they make, so his share would be difficult if not impossible to sell. Not that Vernon would contemplate getting rid of it." He smiled a satisfied smile that said he was sure the information would be a big disappointment.

Lisa smiled back. Sixty percent was nine percent more than she needed.

"What kind of books do you publish? I know there are some poetry collections."

"Yes, we make a bit of a specialty of those, both here and in England. Poetry. Serious novels. Biographies of literary figures.

Quite a lot of fine-art stuff, mainly in Paris. You can imagine the sort of thing. All top quality and a joy to produce.''

"Joy to produce" had acquired a sonorous ring. Lisa judged that the time was ripe for her to make her move. "My reason for coming to see you was to ask for a job. Here, in New York.''

"What?''

"A job.''

For a second the blank amazement hovered over the thin, mean features. Then Lisa saw the lips begin to curl.

"Oh dear, no. No. No. Quite out of the question. Ha. Ha. A job? Dear me, no.''

Lisa saw she had blown it. Now she would have to endure the explanation. The face in front of her was alive with a cruel pleasure.

"We at Blass believe in nepotism, of course, but we wouldn't consider carrying passengers. Our duty is to our authors and to the book-buying public, not to . . . dare I say it . . . bored housewives. Then there is the question of propriety. I don't think it fits the Blass image at all well to have the owner's wife *working,* even pretending to work. I can't believe Vernon really wants that, although I'm sure you've been very persuasive.''

Lisa stood up. She had had enough. This man would die for what he had just done. The realist in her saw for now she would not get what she wanted. A man like Cutting would make every minute of her life a misery if she put herself for one second in his power. She had had to leave Palm Beach. Exile from America was next. She would have to crawl away to some quiet place to wait, and learn, to learn and wait. Somewhere like Paris, where they did the "art" books. That would do for starters. For finishers she personally promised there would be Steven Cutting's blue blood on the paneled walls of his patrician office, his guts hanging like Christmas decorations from the dangling bits of the cut-glass Georgian chandelier. He would be thrown out with his pencils and his letter openers to search for a job among the ranks of the publishers he scorned.

"Fix me up with a job in the Paris office," she said. "Do it today. In fact, do it now. If you don't, I will go back to Palm Beach immediately and spend the rest of my life bad-mouthing you to Vernon.''

For a second or two Steven Cutting sat back in his chair. Fish-like, his mouth opened and closed as he sought the appropriate response. But he knew that he would have to do as Lisa said. The risk was too great. Who knew what control she had over the idiotic Vernon Blass?

He picked up the telephone from the side table by his desk, and his voice was high pitched as he shouted into the mouthpiece. "Get me Michel Dupré in Paris."

Lisa smiled. She was beginning to learn how to get her own way at last, and it felt wonderful.

15

Michel was totally still, his eyes tightly closed, legs clamped together, stretched out impassively on the already hot, damp sheets. Deep within her Lisa loved the part of him which lived. Firm and hard it moved against the walls of the prison she had created for it, testing strength, probing for weakness, pushing insistently against the smooth slippery surface. That was it. She was doing it all, having it all, selfish and yet generous in the pleasure she was both giving and receiving. The delicious sensations floated up in her mind. Where did they come from? Not alone from the obvious place. On either side of her prostrate lover's hips Lisa's feet gripped the mercifully hard mattress and her hamstring muscles groaned their pleasure as they strained to lift and lower the full weight of her body over the rigid invader. To Lisa the muscle pain, the oxygen debt of the ''burning'' tissues, was a source of ecstasy inseparable from that provided by the alien that had entered her.

Delicately she balanced herself as the warm wet lips at the core of her being caressed the foreign skin, milking it, squeezing it, vibrating to its rhythm, luxuriating in its arrogant self-confidence. Sometimes she would hover, wrapped indulgently around its tip, daring it to try for escape, willing it to break for freedom, to withdraw from the dark haven in which it pretended to be an unwilling prisoner. Then, hawklike, she would swoop down, an unforgiving jailer, until the captive was forced into the innermost recesses of the sweet dungeon, enveloped and controlled, humiliated and used, gloriously powerless.

Beneath her as he feigned the sleep of the grave, Michel Dupré clung to the physical joy that splashed over him. Seeing nothing, the eyes of his mind, clear and true, showed him the vision of bliss. His nostrils attuned to the wonderful scents of unbridled passion, he allowed his lover to ride him, to have him, to own him. On his hard, flat stomach he could feel the perfect buttocks as they ground him down, could love the divine moisture that was the undeniable evidence of Lisa's longing, and it seemed that his heart stood still as he contemplated the worship in his soul. Lisa. His Lisa. The goddess who in short minutes would journey with him to the gates of paradise in the shuddering truth of the orgasm. How many times like this? How many more times?

Above him Lisa was lost in ecstasy. But the beauty of passion was not all that she sought and found. Here, now, she was free of the disturbing longings that shaped and molded her existence. It was a moment of sublime forgetfulness, an oasis of heart-rending pleasure amid the desert of exile, the shifting sands of pain and anguish in which she remembered the world and the tiny helpless child she had left behind. As if to blot out the disturbing visions of Palm Beach and little Scott she quickened the pace, a furious horsewoman punishing the saddle of the mount she so effortlessly rode.

Lisa could feel the beginnings. Inside her the alien being was speaking its need, its earnest intention. Growing, pulsating, it called out to her for mercy, crying for release from the wonderful torment.

As it started Lisa stopped. This was the way she had learned to like it: soft, still, no motion distracting the awesome force as life flowed. There was no going back. The orgasm already had an existence of its own. It had had its beginnings. Nothing could prevent a middle and a sublime end. The wheels were turning, and the two lovers were now mere spectators, standing outside themselves, suspended in nothingness as they watched the chariot of happiness career toward the cliffs of abandonment.

She threw back her head and gasped as the familiar yet always unexpected feeling took her. It was only just inside her, quiet, yet ominous, its gentle whisperings muttering rumors of the storm to come. So fragile was the union. The chaste kiss of unpracticed lovers, the touch vulnerable, dangerous in its capricious wantonness. One careless move and contact would be lost and the precious moment destroyed in a travesty of wasted emotion and unconsummated love. But Lisa held her precarious position and was repaid by the sensations of the delectable twitchings, the lightning flashes that warned of the thunder to come. At the gates of her sexuality she loved the promising vibrations, and her muscles quivered in rhythm to the bearer of the gift she was about to receive.

Michel's desperate call of warning was unnecessary—a meaningless sound borne on the winds of passion, telling her only what her body already knew so well. The first offering of love bathed her hot body as it entered her mind. It came from below, but it was experienced above. Wet and rich, warm and fertile, soothing yet arousing, the sweet feed of masculinity.

In the presence of the catalyst that rushed into her, Lisa abandoned the fight for control. It was her turn now. The gates were opened; the pent-up longing was free. Down, down she sank, letting the muscles go, falling headlong, pushing the roaring, rearing pleasure machine into the heartland of her body. The long, lonely cry of anguish echoed around the small room as she howled her happiness at the uncaring heavens, the thrashing limbs, the twitching fingers clasping at the crumpled sheets, her head moving from side to side, eloquent testimony to the dreadful joy that coursed through her.

In the jingle-jangle aftermath, for long minutes there was silence. Only their thoughts spoke as the two lovers contemplated their journey to the mountaintop, and their descent to the valley on the other side. Leaning back heavily on him, her shoulder across his chest, her legs still holding him hostage inside her, Lisa spoke first.

"I'm going to miss you, Michel."

"You're determined to go?"

"You know I am."

"But London is so cold and wet. The people are all cold and wet. You'll hate it there away from me."

As she turned to look at him the Frenchman tried a watery smile. He only just made it.

It was true she was going to miss him. More true that he was going to miss her. Michel Dupré. Forty-two years of French charm, and a hard body that could distract her from the thoughts that plagued her. Lost and alone at Charles de Gaulle Airport, spat out from the mouth of the country that had borne her, she had needed somebody like Michel, and she had every cause to be grateful. Of course he had fallen in love with her, as he had stowed her Vuitton case in the back of his battered Citröen.

And later, over lunch at the Brasserie Lipp on the Boulevard St. Germain, he had already started to plan their future. Lisa had laughed at him then. At his charming self-confidence, at the occasional hints of the little boy inside the man, at his extravagant romanticism. For a few short weeks she had resisted him, but Paris had worked its magic and she had needed an antidote to the homesickness that gnawed away at her and the dull, aching desire for revenge that throbbed and burned within her. Now they were lovers, but she didn't love him—and she suspected that he knew that.

"But London is the place I have to be. From there I can see all the Blass operations."

"You're not happy with me and my art books?"

No, Lisa wasn't happy. A few minutes ago she had been, but reality had intruded itself into the dream, scattering the fabric of make-believe with its unforgiving winds. Paris was a marvelous, beautiful backwater. The French were proud of their decaying language and their artistic heritage and scorned the unashamed materialism of the Americans, and the self-centeredness of the British. The Blass books were indeed magnificent, their color rich, their paper fine, their cost exorbitant, their sales minimal.

She had used her Frenchman shamelessly. Used his body and used his mind. He had taught her to see with the eye of the French, to speak with the subtle accent of Aix, to understand about style —and above all he had told her everything he knew and all that he suspected about publishing. Michel had been a man of the world. He had dirtied his fingers in commercial publishing before seeking the safe haven of Blass, and now he had completed his retreat from a business for which temperamentally he had never been equipped. In the ivory towers of art-book publishing he was completely at home, cheerfully anachronistic, obsessed by quality and beauty, happily oblivious to the realities of the profit-and-loss statement. From time to time Lisa felt like Judas when she contemplated their mutual future, for it was obvious to her that Michel had dared to dream. To dream of a time when death would free Mrs. Vernon Blass from her extraordinary liaison. When she would turn to the man who had taught her, loved her, and pleased her.

Poor Michel. He couldn't know her, or understand the forces that had shaped her. He couldn't suspect that he was irrelevant, a pleasant interlude, nothing more nor less.

As if to emphasize this subterranean point Lisa withdrew from him, dangling her long legs over the side of the wrecked bed. She fought back the desire to say something cruel, something that would destroy the illusion she had allowed him to create.

She ran an impetuous hand through her sweat-soaked hair and tossed her head, shaking off the responsibility of love. In the shower later she would complete the process of dissociation.

What had he said? Was she happy with him and his art books?

She stood up. Dangerous, she knew, in her beauty. Love hurts. Love kills. Lost love needs so desperately to be avenged.

"I said I'd miss you, Michel," she said to his disappointed eyes.

But as she spoke the words Lisa was already walking in her mind on the wet damp streets, avoiding the blood-red buses and the odd-shaped taxis, picking her way slowly through the Blooms-bury squares, learning what she needed to know about the company she planned one day to own.

London

It was one of those London days when the cold dampness creeps into the brain and invades the muscles, propelling everybody into a deep well of pessimism and lethargy. Outside the rain drifted down, quietly relentless, determined to sink the gray world on which it fell in a slough of despond. In the Bedford Square offices of Blass Publishing, most had effortlessly succumbed to the all pervading sense of gloom, as they had every day for the last two weeks while the dreadful weather had called the psychological tune to which they danced. Lisa was no exception. She sat moodily at the big desk in the small room and doodled on the blotter with a black felt-tip pen, occasionally looking out through the dirty window at the red brick wall that was her only view.

About ten times a day in situations like this, she thought wistfully of the Florida sunshine and compared the anemic, miserable London rain with the Palm Beach variety. There, rain was a cleansing experience. A short sharp blast of warm energy, chasing the humidity from the atmosphere, setting the stage for the triumphant return of the sun. Here the rain was an end in itself, a scourge of the spirit, a character-forming impediment to happiness whose main achievement was the creation of the Englishman's traditionally jaundiced eye. Worse, far worse, the poisonous environment it so callously conjured up was a superb habitat for some of the nastiest viruses the world had known. It had been five long years since Lisa had left Palm Beach, and during that time she reckoned she had experienced them all. With clockwork regularity they descended at the most cunningly inconvenient times, laying her low, filling her mind with cotton wool, sandpapering the back of her throat, clogging up her lungs with the accumulated rubbish of the unhappy city. She could swear that at this very moment they were breeding once more within her. Beneath the navy-blue cashmere sweater and the matching pleated wool skirt, she was already blowing hot and cold in a rhythm that didn't seem to coincide with the vagaries of the firm's ancient ventilation system.

She looked down at her Hublot watch, the one she ought to be diving with in the warm waters of the Gulf Stream. Eleven o'clock. That meant tea, and Mavis. For a brief second Lisa's spirits made it off the bottom. Tea wasn't really tea. It was a brown, plastic-tasting liquid that came in a cup designed specifically for the burning of fingers. Still it was usually warm and possessed a limited amount of caffeine value. Mavis, however, was the real thing, a genuine Cockney tea-lady with a philosophy of gloom that made the day-to-day weather-induced depressions seem like the emotional highs of an ecstatic manic. On the principle that there is always someone worse off than yourself and that realizing it is the first step to contentedness, Mavis's effect on the workers at Blass was a tonic indeed—of infinitely greater value than the insipid liquid she dispensed.

Lisa smiled as she heard the knock on the door. Oozing concentrated gloom from every pore, Mavis trudged into the room.

"Good morning, Mavis," offered Lisa brightly, knowing exactly the response she'd get.

"Nothing good about it," came the predictable reply. "Three killed in that train crash, and my Len's tooth's gone septic."

Mavis had a way of pulling together different strands of tragedy and weaving them together into a tapestry of doom. Everything was taken personally, whether it was a small earthquake in Chile or her cocker spaniel's tendency to shed on the sofa.

"Oh dear," said Lisa supportively. "Hope the tooth's okay."

" 'Spect he'll get blood poisoning. Usually does. Of course, the doctor drinks. No bloody good at all."

Lisa sipped on the disgusting concoction. As usual Mavis's chapter of disasters was cheering her up.

"You know, Mavis, I'll have been away from home five years next month."

Mavis cocked her head to one side and looked at her suspiciously. "Seems more like ten," she said at last, her face as black as thunder. "Them's been a *terrible* five years. If the next five's like them five we might as well all give up. That's what I say."

She leaned phlegmatically on the tea trolley weighing up the advisability of a guided tour of the five years of tragedy. Where to start? So many dreadful things. Something made her decide against it. "Oh, well. Struggle on, that's what I say. Fight the good fight, though, Lord, sometimes I don't know why we bothers."

Lisa laughed, but after Mavis had gone the words wouldn't go away. Five terrible years. Five terrible years since that day when she had said good-bye to Maggie, to little Scott, and to Palm Beach.

She looked down morosely at her desk. The engagement book, lying open, caught her eye. Damn! She'd almost forgotten. She had a lunch date. Charles Villiers. Le Caprice at one. Lisa felt her spirits lift. Normally the thought of lunch with her boss would have had the opposite effect. But today it would be a distraction. Anyway, there was something she wanted from him. Very much indeed.

The trendy Le Caprice restaurant in St. James's was humming like the busiest bumblebee, but Lisa was oblivious to the glitterati and the bustle all around her. She was trying to sell something as if her life depended on it, and already she could sense she was on the verge of failure.

"Charles, have you read it? I don't mean speed-read it, I mean really *read* it. I'm telling you this book will be number one forever. I promise you. I *know* it."

Charles Villiers threw back his head and gave the whinnying laugh the secretaries liked to copy. It was a sort of a guffaw, but it was heavily involved with the nose and it always ended in a kind of a snort.

"Yes, I did read it actually. One *can* read, you know."

Three years in London publishing had taught Lisa the significance of the Old Etonian accent, the secret signals it could impart, its nationwide status as a badge of privilege and high class, but she never ceased to marvel at it. It was a phonetic work of art—no question—a cross between a high-pitched nasal whine and the sort of sounds you might expect from a person with lockjaw.

Charles Villiers's version of it was to Lisa the standard against which all others were judged. Having no chin to speak of seemed to be a help, but then so did the oily self-confidence, the aggressively Aryan face, the high forehead, and the crinkly short blond hair. In fact the bits of Charles Villiers were inseparable from each other. He was a job lot, the polka-dotted white and blue Turnbull and Asser tie at one with the cream Harvie and Hudson shirt, the wide-lapeled double-breasted gray flannel suit melding effortlessly with the shiny black lace-up walking shoes from Lobb, which had clearly made it through at least one generation. The inch of cuff; the thin, understated gold links bearing the faded family crest, worn away by the years; the blood red suspenders, the black woollen socks, all were potent statements about everything Charles Villiers stood for. From them one knew that he shot grouse, holidayed in the mountains of Scotland rather than on the beaches of Europe, "killed" salmon rather than caught them. One small mistake—ornate cuff links, a neatly folded breast-pocket handkerchief, Gucci shoes with buckles—would have revealed him instantly as an impostor, a posing parvenu, a minor public-school sham. But nothing spoiled the effortlessly patrician effect, no aftershave, no misplaced vowels, no warmth, no empathy.

He was a perfect specimen and Lisa disliked him with an intensity that bordered on paranoia.

Lisa leaned across the table and let the enthusiasm flow from her. She *had* to win this.

"Well, isn't it just terrific? I mean the hooks and the characterization. The girl's a genius. We've got to have her on the list."

"On a *Blass* list, Lisa? Remember the sort of company we're running here." Lisa didn't have to be reminded of that. Charles Villiers and Steven Cutting sang in unison, peas from the same disgusting pod.

"You're not going to go for it."

It was a statement. Charles Villiers never went for anything she suggested. It had been a forlorn hope. She slumped back in the chair. One more defeat. A brilliant author thrown away. Yet another golden opportunity missed. God, it was frustrating. Christ, she hated this apology for a man who understood so little. Since her arrival from the safe haven of Paris he had gone out of his way to make her life a misery.

He had started by attempting to patronize her, his natural chauvinism as much a part of his being as his Royal Yacht hair lotion and his membership of Whites and the Turf. Then, at an Eaton Square dinner party, his wife tucked away safely in the Lindo Wing of St. Mary's stoically producing their fourth child, and his high forehead glistening with the sweat induced by the consumption of too much after-dinner Kümmel on the rocks, he had propositioned her. Lisa hadn't minced her words. She had told him to his face that she found him both physically and morally disgusting, and she had not been forgiven. The physical bit he hadn't minded at all. An Old Etonian didn't rely much on things like that. But for Charles Villiers it was unforgivable to suggest that he had "behaved badly"—about as unacceptable as being called a "dangerous shot" or being accused of cheating at backgammon. Since that moment he had found it difficult to look her in the eye, and he had seen to it personally that her progress up through the ranks of Blass, London, had been along a path liberally coated with molasses.

Despite the obstacles so tenaciously placed in her way, Lisa had moved upward. In the early days she had done just about everything but make Mavis's tea. She had read proofs till she had thought her eyes would drop out, undergone months of numbing tedium in the accounts department, and put up with the blasé inefficiency of the Oxford undergraduates who pretended to be editors and the gushingly self-confident debs whose social training and "contacts" were thought to be of value in the P.R. department. In desperation she had volunteered to go out on the road as a sales rep, and had spent a soul-shattering three months among the dusty bookshops of the home counties attempting the all but insuperable task of selling the dreary Blass books to incompetent old men who had dreamed that bookselling would provide them with a "gentlemanly" way of making a living. So hard had she worked, so formidably efficient had she been, that even Charles Villiers had been unable to prevent her being given a job, first as an editor, and then as senior editor.

It had been as far as he was prepared to go. If she wanted to publish a book, then he didn't think it was suitable. It was as simple as that.

Lisa stared moodily around the restaurant. In three years a lot of things had changed, but a lot had remained the same. The David Bailey portraits were still on the wall—Mick Jagger, Roman Polanski, mythical heroes now, like the Harlows and Russells of old.

Charles Villiers was droning on, the platitudes dripping from his cotton-wool-filled mouth. "Really rather trite . . . can't write her way out of a paper bag . . . enough people about who want to publish trash . . ."

Lisa yawned rudely at him. She leaned back in the chair and looked down at her tits as they pushed out anxiously against the silk blouse.

"Now a *decent* writer . . . rely on sex . . . puerile ending . . ."

But Lisa wasn't listening. She had left him for the burning sand and the midday sun. And the unfortunate child she hadn't seen for so very long.

Mavis's knock on the door snapped Lisa out of her interconti-
nental reverie. Outside the rain beat against the window, drawing
crazy patterns on the grime, supremely oblivious to Lisa's magical
mystery tour of memory's lanes.

"Come in."

"Telegram, Lisa. Somebody's died, 'spect."

Lisa laughed. "Terminal pessimism, Mavis," she joked.

Terminal optimism, she should have said. The telegram was
brief and to the point. REGRET TO INFORM YOU VERNON BLASS
PASSED AWAY 7 P.M. LOCAL TIME, 14 DECEMBER. PLEASE CONTACT
OFFICES OF BROWN, BAKER, MCKENZIE 305-555-3535. DEEPEST
CONDOLENCES.

Things were supposed to swim before your eyes at moments like
this. They didn't. Lisa had never seen anything in her life so
clearly. She had bionic vision. It must be like this when you did
coke. The words sparkled up at her as their message burrowed
comfortably into her brain. It was over. The waiting was finished.
Her husband was dead. She could go home at last.

Mavis, peering expectantly across the desk, could see at once
that her worst suspicions were confirmed. Something of terrible
importance had happened. A close relation at the very least, perhaps even a child. She braced herself for the ghastly information
and prepared to etch the moment indelibly in her memory for later
regurgitation at the pub.

It was to make quite a good story.

Lisa Blass came out of her chair like a punch-drunk fighter reacting reflexively to the ringing of a bell. She made it around the
desk at light's speed and in a second Mavis was surrounded.
Strong arms gripped her, and as her feet left the ground, the war
whoop assaulted her ears.

The breath was crushed out of her by the exuberant bear hug,
but she managed to get out the words, "Somebody died then."

"Yes, yes," came the joyous response. "My husband. He's
dead. He's dead. Oh, Mavis, the filthy old bugger is dead at last."

The time difference was just right for the opening of the Brown, Baker law offices. How convenient, she thought as she waited for the overseas telephone connection. How accommodating of old Vernon to do his dying at the right time.

Lisa cut right through the traditional responses.

". . . how very sorry we all are . . ."

"Did he leave me the Blass Publishing shares?" she barked into the grubby receiver.

"Why, yes, of course. Didn't you know? They were in joint names—yours and his. It means we don't have to wait for probate to arrange the transfer. As surviving co-owner you get immediate title."

"I can vote the stock now? This minute?"

"Technically from the legal pronouncement of death. That was last night."

"And the house?"

"You are the sole heir. About the funeral. Will you be returning . . ."

But Lisa had heard more than enough. "I'll call you back later," she said, and she put down the telephone. Oh, God, this was going to be good. So very, very good.

She didn't knock at Charles Villiers's door. She just walked straight in. It was pleasing to see that he looked suitably irritated by the infraction.

He was having some sort of a meeting. One of the ones that Lisa tended not to get told about. One thing was quite obvious. He had not heard about Blass's death.

"Hi, you guys," said Lisa as brightly as she felt.

The young woman from St. Mary's, Wantage, and the editor from Northfallen Lodge exchanged supercilious looks. The earl's daughter who headed up publicity smiled patronizingly.

Lisa hovered over them, languid hand on a jutting hip. In this life there were moments of rare beauty. This would be one of them.

"We were just going through the spring list," said Charles Villiers by way of explanation for what was clearly a clandestine meeting.

"Gee, how depressing," said Lisa with feeling.

"What on earth do you mean, 'depressing'?"

Lisa stared back at him. She hoped this would be like being shot in the stomach. A slow, lingering, painful death. "I mean how depressing to be even thinking about that miserable collection of pretentious junk that rejoices in the name of the 'spring list'— that's what I mean."

Around the conference table the mouths were beginning to drop open. A lid was clearly being flipped. Did Lisa Blass drink? Was she on some stuff?

Lisa toured the faces. Then, her eyes roamed the room. It was too good to be true. Behind the Villiers desk was the big empty red leather Villiers chair. He was sitting with the minions at the long mahogany table.

She sauntered slowly toward it, aware of the piercing eyes on her broad shoulders, her slender back, her prize-winning ass. As she moved she turned back to look at them over her shoulder, the glorious smile playing over her radiant face. "Yes," she mused as if to herself. "I don't think very many people are going to miss the spring list—outside this room, that is."

"Lisa, for goodness' sake, stop talking nonsense. Are you feeling all right?" The exasperation was palpable. Charles Villiers was thoroughly irritated.

" 'All right'?" said Lisa, her voice incredulous. "I can truthfully tell you I haven't felt this good in years." She reached the desk, and her destination. As she sat down heavily in the managing director's chair she added maliciously, "I think widowhood must suit me."

It seemed like an age as the bomb dropped. One by one her audience came to grips with the news. To give him his due, Charles Villiers was there first. His face was still whitening and his thoughts were racing ahead of the words when he said, "You mean . . . Vernon is . . ."

"Dead," said Lisa cheerfully. She swept both feet up onto the immaculate leather of the desktop, the one that Charles Villiers kept clear of all sharp objects to preserve the surface. "Yes," she repeated reflectively. "Dead as mutton. And the lawyers tell me I'm your new boss. Just like that."

Everyone was there now. Lined up in the sights of the firing squad. The spring list would not be the only casualty.

"And it gives me the very greatest pleasure to tell you kind people that you're all fired. Every damn one of you."

And with that, Lisa let out a sigh of the deepest contentment as she ran the sharp heel of her shoe in a ripping path of destruction along the previously immaculate red-leather surface of Charles Villiers's desk.

For what seemed like an age the telephone rang unanswered. Please God, let her be there. Please God she hadn't signed with anyone else. Anne Liebermann. She thought of her disappointed eyes when Lisa had told her that Blass wouldn't be offering for *Big Apple,* her disbelieving eyes when Lisa had tried to tell her that the book was really a winner but that the head of Blass had overridden her, her great big brown eyes which would have mesmerized the coast-to-coast talk-show audiences and looked a dream on the cover of *People* magazine. Anne Liebermann with the potential to sell more books than the world had bricks.

The soft voice answered at last. "Anne Liebermann speaking."

"This is Lisa Blass of Blass Publishing."

"Hello."

The response was neutral.

"Listen, I'll get right to the point. There have been management changes here at Blass and I'm in a position now to make you an offer on your book. Is it still available?"

There was a long pause and what sounded like a sigh. "I am afraid it's sort of promised to Macmillan. They haven't actually *made* an offer, but they have promised to make one."

"Whatever it is, I'll double it and you can have a signed contract in the time it takes me to get to your flat in a taxi."

Anne Liebermann, whose characters were nothing if not decisive, showed that she prospected for source material within herself. "I accept," she said, almost before Lisa had stopped speaking.

"Would you be interested in a three-book deal—world rights—structured through Blass, New York?"

"Am I hearing this right?" laughed Anne Liebermann. "I've only had one gin and tonic."

"Don't move. I'm on my way with the contracts and the Moët," said Lisa as she slammed down the phone.

How was it the strings of your heart were supposed to go? *Zing*. That was it. They had just gone *zing*. God only knew what would happen to them when Anne Liebermann and Blass made it to the top of the *New York Times* best-sellers list.

Lisa reached into her drawer for a draft contract and some Blass letterheads. The lawyers could look it over later, but she just wanted something in writing.

For a second or two Lisa stood still trying to get a grip on her still surging thoughts. From the next room she heard what might easily have been the sound of tears, and of raised male voices. Boy, the hornets were stirred up in there. Any minute now they'd all come buzzing after her, threatening, cajoling, pleading, appealing to "better" instincts. Yes, any second and the whole motley crew would be creeping and crawling around as they tried to get a lick at her butt, feverishly trying to save their flats, and their mortgages, their mistresses, boyfriends, and wives, their pride and their prejudices. They would try collectively, and they would try singly. All but a very few would try in vain. She would play God with their futures and she would enjoy every minute of it in revenge for the slights and insults, for all the years of forced subjugation to terminal arrogance and amateur inefficiency, to glutinous hypocrisy and transcendental crassness. But right now there was another telephone call to make. She dialed 142 for information. "Pan American, please. Reservations," she said quickly. Lisa Blass could go home at last.

Lisa came out of what the English called the "lift" like a human cannonball in the circuses of old. The momentum carried her effortlessly through the swinging doors into the Madison Avenue Blass offices, and the receptionist jumped up as if she had been shot.

Lisa wore skin-tight soft blue jeans, a T-shirt bearing the legend

POVERTY SUCKS, and a full-length brown sable with big patch pockets. White ankle socks peeped out at the bottom of the jeans and disappeared into dark brown crocodile loafers. Her hair was swept back from her face and her whole ensemble screamed the self-confident style of Europe. Lisa Blass was home at last, and she was a girl no more. She had grown up.

The receptionist didn't recognize her at first. The energy of her arrival and her remarkable appearance had been the reason she had leaped to her feet.

Now, the truth dawned. The receptionist gushed nervously. "Oh, Mrs. Blass. I didn't recognize you. We were expecting you. How marvelous to see you again. Mr. Cutting has canceled all his morning appointments so that he could be available when you arrived."

Lisa was all fired up, running on the highest octane, and relishing the job that was about to be done.

"Do me a favor," said Lisa nastily, "and cancel all his afternoon appointments as well. In fact, while you're at it, you might like to toss the appointment book in the trash." She didn't wait to savor the confused and horrified expression on the old retainer's face. She knew the way. She'd been there before.

Steven Cutting stood up as Lisa crashed into his office. No condemned man due for lunchtime execution had had a worse morning than had the president of Blass Publishing. In his desperate attempt to produce order in his suddenly threatened world he had arranged and rearranged the pencils until they defined a right-angle triangle more accurately than any protractor. The look on Lisa's face did nothing to calm his shattered nerves.

"Lisa . . . after all these years . . . poor Vernon . . ." His hands tried to conduct the little mutterings.

"Bullshit," said Lisa loudly. She flung herself down in an armchair and cocked one long leg over its arm, letting a crocodile shoe dangle from her foot.

"Oh," said Steven Cutting.

Lisa felt a bit like the gunfighter in a saloon showdown. A girl could get hooked on this. It was better by far than sex.

Steven Cutting had a speech prepared. A bit like the last-minute application of the condemned man for a stay of execution. It even possessed a vaguely legalistic flavor. "Mrs. Blass, I would be foolish if I didn't admit that I made a mistake in underestimating your contribution to Blass. I have cause to regret that. Regret it very much. I hope you will give me an opportunity of rectifying that . . . of putting it right . . . I know we can work well together . . ."

"Hah," said Lisa, cutting him short.

She sent the other leg up onto the arm of the chair to join its fellow. "Do you have a contract with Blass?" she asked ominously.

"A contract? A contract with Blass." Cutting looked as if he were about to pass out, as if the word "contract" was entirely foreign to him—a verb, perhaps, in Swahili. "No. No contract. At Blass we never believed in contracts. A gentleman's word . . ."

"Is about as much use as a mixed metaphor," said Lisa, finishing off the Cutting sentence, and noting that he had used the past tense when referring to Blass. The worm was getting there, halfway up one side of the razor blade now. Lisa breathed in deeply. Was that the aroma of power mixed in with her Paloma Picasso? "Yup," she said reflectively, "gentlemen's agreements don't cut so much ice when the "gentleman" in question is measuring his length on the slab in the West Palm mortuary."

Steven Cutting drew himself up very straight, the way you did before the firing squad. "Am I to take it that you have decided to dispense with my services?" he asked unnecessarily. "If so, then I'm sure you'd agree that there should be some compensation. After all these years."

It was time for the *coup de grace*.

"Mr. Cutting, I want you out on the street in fifteen minutes flat, and you go with nothing. And let me tell you this. If you take one thing out of here, *including* those anal pencils, I will personally drag you through every court in the land, so help me God."

16

ittle Scott Blass knew it was supposed to be an important day, but he wasn't at all sure why. Some frightening person called "mummy" was coming to disrupt his cozy world, and he wasn't very keen on the idea. He pressed his nose up tight against the wire fence that surrounded the airport, and he shivered involuntarily, part anticipation, part reaction to the chill morning air. His small hand burrowed into Mrs. McTaggart's big one. "Nanny, is mummy nice?" he said uncertainly.

"Of course mummy is nice." The reply lacked conviction, and Scott picked up on that. Mummy was nice like rice pudding was nice, like "greens" were nice, like hair-washing was "nice."

Feeling that perhaps she was failing to carry her audience with her, Mrs. McTaggart compounded her error. "All mummies are nice," she added half-heartedly.

"I wish I could have gone to school today." The Wee Wisdom Montessori school on Flagler and the tender ministrations of the divine Miss Heidi appeared infinitely preferable to this little expedition into the unknown. Still the airplanes were always fun.

"Is mummy in that one?"

"No, dear. That's a little one. Mummy is coming in a great big one."

That gelled with his expectations. Mummy was clearly a great big person who arrived in great big things and made a great big fuss. Otherwise what was he doing in his best gray flannel trousers and black walking shoes and the super-clean white shirt? He sighed and said what he thought. "I don't think I'm going to like mummy."

"Nonsense, dear. Everybody likes mummy." Except me, thought Mrs. McTaggart, adjusting the wide belt of her immaculate uniform. It was way beyond the ken of the kindly Scotswoman that anyone could treat a child the way Lisa had treated poor little Scott. To walk out on a husband after a week of marriage and to leave a child in someone else's care with no direct contact for five years seemed like a cruel, unusual, and totally unwarranted punishment. During that time she had herself learned a few things about daddy that had made even her phlegmatic blood curdle. Perhaps that excused the parting, but it certainly didn't explain the callous indifference to the innocent baby. Luckily she had been there to fill the gap, and now the child was hers in love as if she had borne him herself. Daddy had kept out of their way, and on the occasions he had attempted to exert an influence, he had felt the sharp edge of her Celtic tongue, an experience for which, unlike Oliver Twist, he had tended not to return for more.

So Scott had reached the age by which the Jesuits believed that the character had been formed without knowing his father or his mother, and despite her valiant efforts as a surrogate, the scars showed. Scott's was a brittle self-confidence, outwardly impressive but a whitewash job. He seemed to be a leader, appeared to be ready for any adventure, but inside he was a fragile little soul, vulnerable and alone, nursing the great void in his heart where his mother and father should have been. For that, Nellie McTaggart could not and would not forgive Lisa Blass. For that, and for her sudden and unwanted return. If she walked in now and attempted to reclaim what she had so wickedly and capriciously abandoned then it was entirely possible that Scottie would be destroyed in the turmoil, chaos, and confusion.

Nanny's mouth hardened perceptibly at the dreadful thought, and the blood of her combative race began to warm at the thought of the coming conflict as she went out to fight for the little mite whose hand was so small in hers. She might technically be a servant, but she was a proud standard bearer of an ancient profession whose status was enshrined in the mists of mythology. Not merely an English nanny, but a Scots nanny. Belted earls and strutting dukes, posing politicians and High Court judges had all been reduced to nice, polite, clean little boys when confronted by the iron ruler of the nursery, the one who had potty trained them and taught them their p's and q's.

"Come on, darling. Let's go and stand at the bottom of the escalator. We can watch mummy coming down."

Lisa Blass's homecoming was very different from her departure. First there was the retinue. Two secretaries, neat and efficient, carried their Canon electronic portables as well as Lisa's Vuitton hand luggage. On the escalator they stood behind and on either side of her, like some latter-day Praetorian guard, framing the main event.

Then there were the visuals. Lisa was not the great big person of Scott's childlike imagination, but, her long hair swept back from her face, her wide-shouldered Kenzo tweed coat and skirt accentuating the sweeping contours of her body, she was clearly a formidable force to be reckoned with. She appeared, thought Mrs. McTaggart, absolutely astounded to see them.

Lisa was astounded all right, but not by the fact of their presence. As she glided down the short escalator a pint-size, perfectly formed Bobby Stansfield clone was staring up at her, his eyes unquestioningly following his nanny's pointed finger.

Lisa had been ready for anything except that. Scott Starr? Scott Blass? Oh, no. Her son was Scott Stansfield.

As the escalator deposited her in front of him, and he took a first awkward step toward her, his nanny's fingers pushing in the small of his back, Lisa found it difficult to catch her breath. Those piercing blue eyes, the identical sandy hair, the set of the mouth, the shape of the ears. God, how could she live with this while hating the man who had produced it?

"Welcome home, mummy," said Nellie McTaggart's accusing voice. "Kiss your mummy," she stage-whispered to Scott.

The Stansfield mouth went into a determined line. "I don't want to," he said.

"Of course you do, dear."

"I don't."

"It doesn't matter, nanny. There'll be time for that later," said Lisa, wondering as she spoke whether there ever would be.

What did she feel? Did the emotion fit with what she *should* feel? Not really. She was shocked by the extraordinary resemblance but that was just unsettling. It stirred her up, but it didn't turn her on to him. He was a little person. Pretty, beautiful even, but not hers, not part of her—even he seemed to know that. In a way it was the lack of feeling that worried her most, the void, the vacuum where the love should be. Somehow that brought home to her the damage the world had inflicted on her. Outwardly she had survived intact, but inside the wounds were horrendous, her personality scarred and twisted. To abolish the pain she had had to surrender her power of tender feeling, leaving only revenge in emotion's cupboard. Intellectually she knew what damage must have been done to the innocent who looked at her so accusingly, but emotionally she was hardly able to care.

"We've got to get to know each other right from the beginning, haven't we?" she said as much to herself as to anyone else, but even as the chauffeur moved forward to organize the baggage, she was thinking of something else—of the huge mortgage loan she had arranged against the freehold of the Madison Avenue offices, and of the four million she had borrowed from Citibank on the security of her Blass stock. Already the money was at work, and over a few short days the slickest editors and the hot-shot authors had received offers they were finding it difficult to refuse.

Geared up to the hilt, it was a dangerous, high-risk game that Lisa was playing, but the long years in the wilderness had made her hungry for success, and she wanted it now. As she had dreamed of the power she would one day inherit, Lisa had targeted the men and women she wanted. The plan had been there, needing only Vernon Blass's death and the keeping of his word for it to be put immediately into action.

As she stalked toward the Rolls, a curious son in tow, she was already talking over her shoulder to one of the secretaries.

"Get a memo off to Ken Farlow in Rights to auction the Liebermann book to the paperback houses the moment it's copy edited. And tell him I'm looking for a big price. I don't want chicken shit. Okay?"

"What should we do about the mini-series inquiry from HBO?"

"Screw the mini-series, let's sell the book big first. Sorry, nanny."

"Screw," said Scott and giggled.

"Nice little boys don't say naughty words like that," said nanny as much to Lisa as to Scott.

But Lisa had missed the putdown.

She was back, heading the right way this time, up the coast road from the Southern Boulevard bridge. Nannies and the activities of small children were already expunged from her mind. What she

282

needed to do was to make a killing on the Liebermann book to provide cash flow for the new-look Blass. And then . . . and then. There would be time for the eating of that cold dish on which she had set her heart so long ago.

Christie Stansfield had eaten rather too much of granny's chocolate cake and now she was feeling slightly sick. But she wasn't going to let on, because that might spoil the event she looked forward to all week. So she sat there looking exactly like the little angel she was, all blond curls and blue eyes, and hoped that the funny feeling in her tummy would go away.

Bobby Stansfield stared fondly at her across the immaculate white linen of his mother's tea table. Some things could never be explained, and in his view his daughter was one of them. Whatever substances ran in his wife's blood, the milk of human kindness was conspicuous by its absence, and Bobby was enough of a realist to admit that neither parent qualified wholeheartedly for the adjective "good." By some extraordinary quirk of fate, however, they had produced Christie—the dearest, kindest child it was possible to imagine.

From the very earliest days Christie had been quite unlike other children. Placid and calm, she had hardly cried at all as a baby, and the terrible twos, that period of controlled horror that seemed to afflict most parents, had been a dreamy interlude of sweet reason and gentle learning. Christie had never had to be told to share her toys. Instead the problem was to stop her from giving them away. All she seemed to want was for the people around her to be happy, and she worked toward that end with the single-minded determination of the genuine child of God. Insofar as she had a vice at all, it was the one for which she now secretly suffered. She was very fond of her food and was totally addicted to anything covered in chocolate. So although her face would have made Botticelli drool, it was beginning to be clear that, in adolescence at least, baby fat might well be a problem. Bobby, who had desperately wanted a boy for traditional Stansfield reasons, was, with regard to his daughter, a born-again convert and he loved her with an intensity he had not dreamed possible. Loved her and was not a little in awe of her.

"Are you all right, darling?" he said unnecessarily across the table.

"Yes, thank you, daddy. I'm having a lovely tea," she lied. She felt a little guilty about the fib, but then she didn't want to upset the traditional calm of her father's and her grandmother's weekly tea. She knew how much they both looked forward to it.

"Another piece of cake, dear?" Caroline Stansfield had lost none of her uncanny ability to hover instinctively around the burning issues of the moment. The enormously rich cake from the hot Poinciana delicatessen, Toojays, was affectionately known throughout Palm Beach as the "killer" cake.

"No thanks, gran, but I'd love another cup of tea."

Caroline Stansfield manipulated the Limoges china with the practiced ease of one to the manor born: cold milk first, tea through the Georgian strainer, a little hot water from the fine George III silver jug, the sugar bowl passed to her granddaughter with the cup and saucer. Her ancient hands worked smoothly, eloquent testimony to the continued high quality of the mind that age had not withered.

"I think we could do with some more hot water, Brown."

The creaky butler slunk awkwardly from the shadows of the terrace to do his mistress's bidding. The tea taken care of, it was time for politics. It usually was.

"How did your support look in Dallas?"

"What there is of it is dedicated. All the work over the years with the fundamentalists has paid off. Trouble is, their support is a double-edged weapon."

"For now that may be true," said Caroline reflectively. She fingered the double row of pearls on the wrinkled neck. "But I sense a new mood in America. Hungry for purpose, for spiritual rebirth. I think cars and washing machines have had their day. Politicians will ignore that need at their peril. Ten years down the road we may not recognize this country."

She paused, seemingly uncertain as to whether she wanted to be able to recognize it or not. She made her decision. Anything would be all right as long as a Stansfield was at the helm. "I think you should stick with the zealots, Bobby. They may sound a bit fanatical today, but the way things are going, yesterday's conservatives seem like closet socialists now.''

"I'm inclined to agree, mother.''

Whoops. Christie's stomach was on the move. The tea didn't seem to have helped. What had been an outside possibility was beginning to look distinctly probable. "Granny, please may I get down? I need to go to the bathroom.'' She prayed nobody would notice how white she was.

"Of course, dear.''

Caroline Stansfield took the opportunity of Christie's absence to raise a delicate subject. In a way it was about politics, too. "Such a dear, sweet child, Bobby. How's her mother?'' Caroline tended not to use Jo-Anne's actual name. She was always "your wife,'' "Christie's mother,'' or, occasionally, things less flattering.

Bobby laughed dismissively. "Oh, you know Jo-Anne. Busy playing the social game as if her life depended on it. Ever since Marjorie Donahue died she seems to have been right in the thick of it. If she spent an ounce as much energy on my political thing as she does on her charities and parties I'd be home and dry, no question.''

Caroline's face had acquired a rather sly expression. She watched her son carefully. So very good looking. Presidential material definitely. A good chance. Better than poor old Fred's. There had been a time not so long ago when she had been far from sure whether or not he wanted it enough.

"I gather that Lisa Blass is back in town. Old Vernon left her everything, apparently. Not bad for five years' work.''

The shadow passed briefly over Bobby's face. Lisa Starr. His Lisa. Married to a geriatric. Bearing him a son. Aborting Bobby's own child.

In his mind he saw the stricken face as his cruel words exploded into it, and he remembered her bitterness, the hatred eating up the beauty, the poison spilling from the eyes. He no longer knew what he felt about her, but he had never forgotten her, and his political training told him that in some subterranean way he had reason to fear her. Especially now that she was at last a woman of substance.

In the downstairs lavatory Christie Stansfield wasn't feeling well at all. Nobody must know. She would get this done, clean up, and go back as if nothing had happened. Chocolate cake. It was always her downfall. Chocolate cake. Oooooh. She placed her small head firmly over the bowl and waited for the inevitable, and while her father mused over the girl he had treated so badly, the woman who would now be a power in Palm Beach, she puked out her tiny heart into the sparkling waters of the immaculate toilet.

17

Scott Blass lounged moodily on the slubbed silk sofa, as he watched his mother. His expression of sulky indifference was common to rich teenagers all over the globe, but it hid feelings that were far from usual. The emotions were conflicting, and extraordinarily tangled, a mass of barbed wire and roses, of sharpness and sweetness, of adoration and rage.

Oblivious to the effect she was having on her seventeen-year-old son, Lisa Blass talked into the telephone with the single-mindedness of the born dealer. Into it she poured her charm, her energy, and her desire, and Scott would have gladly settled for any of these. It had always been like that from the moment he remembered seeing her first, smelling like a sweet dream and looking like a startled goddess as she descended from the escalator at West Palm International. From that moment to this he had been in love with her, and from this moment to that his love had been unrequited. It was by far and away the most frustrating aspect of his life so far. Wasn't a mother supposed to *love* her son? Endlessly he had sought the reason for her indifference, and being unable to find one, he had concluded it must be some inadequacy on his part that had led to this unhappy state of affairs, some dreadful character deficiency that had in some mysterious way made him uniquely unlovable and unworthy of maternal affection. In the years of dreadful yearning, one thing had remained constant. He had never given up hope, never stopped trying. In bed at night, riding the waves by day, he schemed and planned to make her care, to force her to really love him.

"You ought to get a surfboard, darling. Such good exercise," she had said to him. He had been six at the time. Now he was Florida State Champion.

"I do so admire men who know about car engines." He had

begged Charlie Stark to take him on as an unpaid mechanic the very next day and had worked all summer at Mustang Paradise until he could rebuild a '77 from scratch in the pitch dark with one hand tied behind his back.

"A boy brought up on the streets of West Palm is worth half a dozen of the pathetic specimens you see around here." For two straight years he had refused to talk to anyone with the right accent or clothes, and had mixed exclusively with the rough, tough kids from neighborhood bars like Roxy's and from the country-music dives on the other side of the coastal railroad.

But it had all been for nothing. His mother's glacial indifference, like the laws of the Medes and Persians, altered not. It wasn't that she was aggressive to him, or even that she ignored him. She was always ready with advice and encouragement. It was just that she didn't seem to *care,* and it drove him into a frenzy of frustration.

His mother was doing a lot of smiling at the mouthpiece, but Scott could tell she didn't like what she was hearing. "Well, Mort, you could knock me down with a feather. I had no *idea* Anne was unhappy with the contract. I mean, she's staying here this week-end. She's out by the pool right now. She never mentioned it to me. Not a hint."

Somebody at the other end did a lot of talking.

"No, no, of course not. We're all friends. Annie and I go back to the very beginnings. Together we put Blass on the map. The contract isn't the point. I wouldn't want to force anything on Annie if she's unhappy."

Lisa paused. She had made the point obliquely. The contract *could* be enforced if it came to that. But it would be the baddest of bad scenes, and Anne Liebermann was enough of a prima donna to ladle tons of it into the fan. Damn! Why did everybody have to get greedy? Five consecutive number-one best sellers all under the Blass imprint had made Anne Liebermann a multimillionairess, but she was apparently happy to blow the relationship to smithereens for that little bit more. Except that a million dollars wasn't such a little bit.

She looked up at the ceiling for inspiration as the New York agent made his pitch. Boy, he was good. Worth every dime of his fifteen percent commission. He'd taken the trouble to line up the other houses, and Lisa knew he wasn't bullshitting. By Monday morning Anne Liebermann could be a Random House author. So far Blass had never lost one and had successfully poached a score from the other publishers. If it was to lose the jewel in its crown, then maybe other authors would get ideas. It could be the beginning of a slippery slope, as others jumped on the bandwagon, and Lisa's heart went cold at the dreadful thought. No, Anne Liebermann would have to be bought off, but hopefully for far less than a million bucks.

"Look, Mort, darling. Give me the weekend to think about it. Can I call you on Monday morning—first thing? I'll see what I can do to soften Anne up. Break open my best claret. Ha, ha. Yup. Okay, Mort. Talk to you then. Bye, darling."

She slammed the telephone down hard. "Damn it to hell. That thieving, greedy *bitch!* Where is the fat, money-grubbing cow?"

Scott's ears pricked up. As always his mother made him disturbingly ambivalent. He was pleased somebody had irritated her, and yet agonized by it all at the same time. "What's up, mom?"

Lisa cast her eyes over her superb-looking son as if he were the third banana in the fruit scene. "That goddamn Anne Liebermann is trying to wangle out of her contract and score a whole lot more money."

"Can't you make her stick to the contract?" It seemed a reasonable question. That's what contracts were for.

"In this game, if you haven't got a happy author, you've had it, no matter what the contract says. Trying to chain her to a typewriter against her will would be bad news for everyone. No, I'll just have to pay her what she wants. Try and soften her up over the weekend, I guess."

In his mother's eyes there was suddenly a faraway, speculative look. "Perhaps you could be a help, darling. You know, flatter her a little. You're so good at that sort of thing. I thought at lunch she seemed rather taken with you."

Scott felt the warm glow explode through him. That was not a million miles from a compliment. His mother had just told him he was charming, and indirectly she had even asked for his *help*. God! That was *really* something.

He stood up, trying desperately to look as cool as he didn't feel. "Okay, mom. No sweat. I'll see what I can do. Did you say she was out by the pool?"

Anne Liebermann's body was singing like a souped-up soprano on speed, and she didn't want the sublime feeling to stop. What a night! Two in a row, and she had hardly dreamed it could be possible. It was far from unusual in her books for the heroine to be pleasured by a blond-haired blue-eyed surfer Joe equivalent, but she had hardly been prepared for the reality of the experience. Next time she would set the typewriter on fire. It would be faction, not fiction. There was only one interesting question, and that was "why?" She was rich, she was famous, but she was under few illusions about where she came in in the beauty stakes, and Scott Blass was just about young enough to be her son. For the moment, however, that was of academic interest. The problem right now was how to get him back into bed for an action replay before breakfast.

She stared up at the intricate carved wood ceiling searching for inspiration in its colored patterns. But the ghost of Addison Mizner wasn't interested in her predicament. In fact the whole room, with its heavy furniture, somber paintings, and Andalusian "feel" seemed sexually sterile, globally unconcerned with such trivial pursuits.

Through the open window of the bedroom, Scott could see the white-topped rollers drifting in gently toward the beach. Great! The surf was up. Later he'd meet with the boys at the East Inlet and do some tube riding on the new Impact board. *If* he was allowed to tear himself away from the world's best-selling authoress.

"Penny for your thoughts, Scott." Anne Liebermann's voice and her sparkling brown eyes were by far her most appealing physical attributes. The rest of her was a federal disaster area, but it was mercifully hidden beneath the silk sheets that she had drawn up to her neck. She had a chance.

"Oh, nothing. I was just looking at the surf. Should be a good day out there later."

Anne said nothing. The fish wasn't biting. Damn! He wasn't really into her. There was no getting away from that. And after two nights of ecstasy she was well on the way to becoming addicted. Suddenly, getting him out of his blue jeans and back under the sheets was one of the more important things in her life. Like pushing the mini-series rights to ABC, or copping the *Cosmopolitan* serialization.

"Did you enjoy last night, Scott?"she heard herself say coquettishly. Damn it to hell. How come people still believed in free will? That was the last thing she'd intended to say.

Scott turned to look at her. Enjoyed it? He had endured it. Endured it for the mother he worshiped, to save her the money that she wanted saved. He had survived it somehow, but both his back and his mind bore the scars of the ultimate sacrifice. He had closed his mind off and thought of his mother, not his country. She had wanted him to be "nice" to Anne Liebermann, and boy, had he been "nice." He just hoped to God the results would filter down to the Blass bottom line. Maybe, just maybe, Anne would stay with Blass and drop her asking price from a million to five hundred thousand. If so, every single penny of the money saved would have been hard earned.

He fought back the irritation. "Oh. Yeah. Sure. I mean, of course I did." The lie didn't sound very convincing. What the *hell* did she want? A vote of thanks? A quote for the dust jacket of her next novel? In between the one from *People* and the one from *Newsweek:* "Anne Liebermann screws as well as she writes."— Scott Blass, surfer.

Anne Liebermann tried to believe him, but she had not written five consecutive number-one best sellers for nothing. For some reason Scott Blass was humoring her, and she was not a million miles from suspecting just what that reason was. She sat up in bed, taking care that the bedclothes covered her ample bosom. "Scott. Did your mother mention that there's a chance I might be leaving Blass?" Anne had never been spoiled as a child, but her phenomenal success over the last twelve years had enabled her to make up for lost time. She was direct, worldly-wise, and quite ruthless. She peered at him intently to see how he would react to her fast ball.

His face told her everything. Scott took it right on the point of his chin. That was the last thing he had expected. In the clinches, Anne Liebermann had abandoned herself to passion. Now it seemed her critical faculties had been placed only temporarily on ice. He felt the color rush up into the sunburned cheeks, and he prepared his fervent denial of what Anne Liebermann now knew to be true. "Oh no. She never mentioned that. How awful. Why would you want to do that?"

Anne Liebermann missed none of the confusion. Okay, so that was it. Lisa Blass had detailed her son off to sweeten her up with some sexual candy. Wow. That was pretty heavy. Mothers usually drew the line at that sort of thing. Or maybe young Scott had gone into private enterprise, and Lisa had been an unwitting co-conspirator. Whatever. One thing was for sure. Two nights of bliss had been offered to induce her to stay with Blass. She almost laughed out loud as she thought of the words. Bliss and Blass. Blass for Bliss. It sounded like a good slogan.

"Oh, I might not leave, Scott. I might just stay right where I am," she said cunningly. She rolled her eyes. The initial disappointment that she might not be loved for herself alone was fast fading. In this life precious few people were, and she was enough of a realist to realize that. No, on this earth you had to be prepared to use what you had to get what you wanted. It appeared she had something. It was certain that she wanted something. It would be a straight trade.

"I hope so."

"Do you really, Scott? I wonder how much you hope that."

"Well, of course I hope that, Anne. C'mon. I would, wouldn't I?" Scott wasn't at all sure he'd gotten away with it. It seemed to him that his plan had been uncovered. There was still hope, but it looked as if his investment were going to have to be increased.

"Why don't you come over here and prove it, Scott."

Scott's stomach headed downward. Oh no. Not before breakfast. There had to be a way out, and a polite one, too.

"Not now, Anne. We'd miss breakfast. And that really irritates mother. Later, maybe."

Mother. Even now, he couldn't get away from her. He had screwed for her, and now he was using her as his excuse. And all, almost certainly, for nothing. If he delivered the goods his contribution would be ignored. As always he would be discounted, overlooked, patronized, treated like some beautiful, but ultimately pointless Ming vase. A thing to be admired, valued even, but ultimately forgotten. If only there was a way to gain the spotlight, to hijack the dead center of the stage, so that his life could be played out before his mother, a captive audience of one in the front row. It was all he asked for. It was all he had never been given.

Suddenly Scott was tired of the whole business. Tired and hungry. In the dining room there would be hash browns and French toast, bacon and scrambled eggs. This thing needed to be wrapped up. He had done the best he could.

He threw what he hoped was a warm smile at Anne as he headed determinedly toward the door. "I'll make sure they save some breakfast for you. See you later," he managed as he fled the scene.

"How dare you sit there like some chubby cherub and tell me how I ought to behave! Christ, Christie, that's a dangerous world out there. Believe me, I know. If you don't shoot first you end up in the shit."

Bobby Stansfield came off the sun bed in a shower of crumpled newspaper. Already his sunburned face was turning a dangerous cherry red.

"Don't you *dare* talk to my daughter like that," he screamed at the top of his voice, advancing menacingly on Jo-Anne. "Don't you dare. Do you hear? Do you *hear* me?"

In a second Christie was between them. Referee. Peacemaker. Conscientious objector to violence, disharmony, anger. Her long golden-blond hair ran free to her shoulders, bangs framed the round, appealing face. Freckled cheeks, blue eyes, a retroussé nose, full, generous lips. The effect was as fresh as new-mown hay, cuddly puppy dogs, the first taste of summer strawberries.

"Please don't fight. It was my fault. I didn't mean to sound pompous, mom, but I realize I must have. I'm sorry. Forgive me."

An apoplectic Bobby could hardly get the words out. "Don't apologize. There's no need to apologize. I heard what you said. You were absolutely right. There's more to life than social climbing. She's got no right to speak to you like that."

"She does because she's my mom, and because I love her very much." Big tears appeared in Christie's eyes.

Bobby deflated like a pricked balloon. Christie always did that.

The talent for turning the other cheek. Where had she gotten it from? There had never been a Stansfield remotely like her, and from the precious little he knew about his wife's family it didn't appear they had been overburdened with people like Christie, either.

"Oh, that's a very sweet thing to say, darling." Jo-Anne felt the alien emotion of tenderness flow through her. In the presence of transcendent goodness she usually felt acutely uncomfortable, which was one of the reasons she found her daughter almost impossible to live with, but occasionally it struck a chord within her.

"I'm sorry I overreacted, dear," said Bobby at last, swirling in the currents of forgiveness that seemed so suddenly to have engulfed the trio.

Somehow the atmosphere seemed ripe for the confessional. "You're quite right, Christie, it is un-Christian of me to hate Lisa Blass so much. I should be able to rise above it, but she's so damn full of herself since that company of hers hit the headlines, and she's made so much goddamned *money* it's just indecent. She sits there in that huge house and stuffs it with everyone one's ever wanted to meet, and lords it over the rest of us. People in this town will shed blood to get to one of her dinner parties. Apparently last week she even had Michael Jackson there, and this weekend she's got that guy who discovered the AIDS cure and Anne Liebermann." Jo-Anne mused gloomily over the unfairness of it all. Palm Beach wasn't *supposed* to be impressed by meritocrats. It was the only place in America where it was considered poor form to ask a person what he did. When the only truthful answer was "not very much," the question was thought to demonstrate insensitivity in the questioner. In fact Jo-Anne's voice had taken on such tones of utter dejection that all three of them had to laugh.

"Oh, mom, you are incorrigible. What does it matter? So what, she's a social gadfly. If it makes her happy there's no harm."

Bobby couldn't resist a contribution. "Lisa makes Palm Beach nervous. It can't control her, and yet it can't ignore her because she has the commodity it worships above all other things. Money."

Jo-Anne felt the juices begin to flow once more. "Well, all I can say is that she's an ungrateful bitch. She was my friend once and she sided with that ludicrous old bag of bones Marjorie Donahue

against me. It's all your father's fault. He introduced her to everyone, and now she won't even talk to him.''

Christie was determined to keep the flame of good humor alive,
as Jo-Anne's venomous breath threatened to extinguish it. ''Ah,
now I get the picture. She had a fling with dad and you're jealous
after all these years. Isn't that cute? For sure there must have been
something good about her if she was a girlfriend of dad's.'' Christie
was trying desperately to keep it light.

''Don't be ridiculous, Christie. How could I be jealous of a nobody like Lisa Blass? She hooked that myopic old fart Vernon and
then left town a week after the wedding. I tell you, if you love me
I don't want you mixing with that bitch or anyone who'll even
speak to her.''

''I wouldn't be disloyal to you, mom.''

''Don't be,'' said Jo-Anne nastily.

''Frankly,'' said Bobby, disengaging himself from the family
group and retreating to the sun bed to retrieve his drink, ''I admire
what Lisa Blass has done. She turned Blass into the money spinner
it is today entirely on her own. She invented Anne Liebermann,
whose books you seem to read so avidly, and she restored that
magnificent house to its former glory—by all accounts.''

He took a long, self-satisfied sip on his dark Dewar's and water,
confident that his remarks would have hit the spot.

In many ways time had been kind to Bobby. The presidency had
so far eluded him, although, like Ted Kennedy, he was constantly
mentioned as a possible future contender, but in the Senate he was
a formidable figure indeed, his seniority landing him the chairmanship of the Foreign Relations Committee. In that august institution
he was a potent force, a leading light in the inner circle. He was
the best of the good ol' boys, the man whose nod and wink could
smooth the path of the most controversial bills, and as a result he
walked the corridors of power with a measured, self-confident
tread, the president's ear never more than a telephone call away,
the mightiest media men hanging on his every word, fascinated by
his cocktail-party asides. He wasn't the king but he was the maker
of kings and it was almost . . . almost . . . enough.

There was nowhere on earth he wasn't welcome. No corner of
the globe where the arms wouldn't have opened for him. With one
glaring exception. The Villa Gloria on South Ocean Boulevard.

Lisa Starr, Lisa Blass, had not forgiven him, and it rankled. It was easy to blame Jo-Anne for the bad feeling, but he knew in his heart that it was unfair. It was he who had insulted her and thrown her out cruelly when she had honored and loved him. It was he who had called her a lesbian on his wife's word and told her in effect that Stansfields didn't marry street trash. For some people, the years would have smoothed the jagged memory, but for someone of Lisa's spirit and self-respect the wounds would live on, still sore, never healing in the damp atmosphere of hatred. Lisa had lain in his arms in the moonlight and learned the language of passion, an eager student, a brilliant pupil who had surpassed the teacher in the creative innovation of her lovemaking. Even now after all these years the perfect body lived on in his mind: its curves, its secret places opened up to him, its wonderful aromas, its tantalizing textures. Never before or since had he had such a lover, and he never would again.

He was vaguely aware of Jo-Anne's bad-tempered withdrawal, the too loud slamming of a couple of doors. To hell with her. The bitch. All her cunning manipulations had failed to bring her happiness and satisfaction. Nobody could win the social-climbing game. There was always someone just a little bit higher than you.

But there was one thing Jo-Anne *had* done for him, and it had changed his life. Christie. Kind, wonderful, beautiful Christie. About her he could not be objective. She was the Mona Lisa, more beautiful than the most highly paid model or the most successful film star. To him she had it all. Miss Peaches and Cream. Miss Young America. The sort of girl the Marines would die for in some foreign field. The living embodiment of everything that was wholesome and wonderful about his country. Christie didn't drink. She didn't take drugs. She was an active member of her church. She honored and loved her parents. She worked hard at school. Christie didn't sleep around.

He smiled ruefully to himself as he thought about that one. Fathers always had that problem sooner or later. He hoped fervently he would avoid the possessive-father role, but he was far from sure he would be able to. Just thinking about Christie's future boyfriends made him anxious as hell. Please God it would be somebody who was kind to her. She surely deserved that, but in this life you didn't always get what you deserved. He blotted it all out.

It hadn't happened. Yet. "Come on Chris, let's shoot a few Frisbees on the beach. My spinning wrist is itching like hell."

"You're on, dad."

The two looked more like brother and sister than father and daughter as they scampered out over the lush lawns toward the cooling sands of the early evening seashore.

None of them, except Anne Liebermann, had really wanted to go, but she had been adamant. So they had gone, and now they were there.

It was Palm Beach in flagrante delicto.

The huge El Bravo Way house was throbbing like the tight skin of a big bass drum, throbbing, shining, and shaking with the mighty, roaring party that it harbored in its bowels. Lisa had promised that the Von Preussen party would be over the top, and she had been proved magnificently right. The valet parkers had set the scene. Usually they wore neat little uniforms, red waistcoats, clean open-necked shirts, black trousers, black shoes. Not tonight. Tonight they were stripped to the waist, their torsos glistening with oil, shining and shimmering in the light of the storm torches that each carried. They wore what looked like short, pleated white skirts ending just above the knee, and nothing else at all except for ankle-length boots laced up with leather thongs. There were two to each limo. One to hold the light, the other to park—and everyone was forced to remember that the great gold-embossed invitations, extravagantly engraved with the Von Preussen baronial crest, had mentioned that the theme of the party was to be "Ancient Rome."

Anne Liebermann roared her appreciation. "I told you all it would be marvelous. I met Heine Von Preussen in Venice once at the Biennale. He's completely mad. Deliciously, wonderfully mad. Really Lisa, you oughtn't to be so stuffy. It's just what this town needs—a bit of eccentricity."

Lisa laughed politely. Anne Liebermann was happy, then so was she. If a few descendants of German war manufacturers wanted to part with some of their ill-gotten gains and in the process entertain her star author, then she would try to get through the evening with her insides still inside.

Scott's thoughts were running along parallel lines. He knew some of these guys. The ones that rich guy had gotten to dress like this. A couple of them were pals, fellow surfers, and as far as he was concerned the whole thing so far was a sick joke. The skirts were bad enough, but the oiled skin was Technicolor yawn time. Of course it was supposed to be *haute* camp, a lovely jaded joke, but the bottom line had to do with bottoms. Von Preussen was a queer, and that was why the valet parkers looked like they did. It was the final straw that Anne Liebermann found the whole disgusting fantasy "wonderfully mad." He tried to control his temper. After all, he had lost points by opting out of the prebreakfast coupling. It would be a shame to have wasted two nasty nights.

The girl who sold the subsidiary rights for Blass was hovering in emotional uncertainty. Her genes told her that there was something sinister, something deeply disreputable about what she was about to experience. But she was young enough not to be immune to the sight of rippling young flesh and the conspicuous if possibly decadent consumption that she was about to be asked to enjoy. Also there was the Liebermann factor. It might be a house party, but for Blass employees life was work, and so it was also an office party. Liebermann was flirting with another publisher; she must be humored.

"I agree, Anne. I think it's going to be fun."

The house party—a hot plastic surgeon from Brazil and his starlet wife who doubled as an advertisement for his ability to hold back the tide of time; the Nobel Prize winner who'd discovered the AIDS vaccine and his incredulous, middle-American wife; a fashionable, "straight" novelist who Lisa had just poached from Knopf; the guy who bought the mini-series rights for ABC, and his fast-talking, faster-looking "friend"—were gathering in front of the wide-open iron-studded oak door beneath the towering white marble columns of the vast portico.

"I have a feeling," Lisa said to Anne, "that you ain't seen nuthin' yet."

Just inside the door were four very beautiful young boys. In the Von Preussen establishment there was nothing remarkable about that. The surprise value was that they made the parking boys look seriously overdressed. They wore absolutely nothing at all except for an apology for a G string and a thin coat of the finest white talcum powder that extended all over their fine "Roman" features. Each stood still, striking a sculptor's pose, and each held a short leash that attached them to four sleek, sharp-toothed cheetahs. Guests were thus channeled through a perverse tunnel of danger before being deposited in front of their host.

Heine Von Preussen was not outshone by his surroundings. Tall and thin, he seemed to hover over the proceedings like some wizard from a land of childish dreams. He was about thirty, maybe fifty, possibly in his early twenties. His face was feminine, with big, liquid eyes and a fine full mouth in which small white teeth flashed prettily. It was perfectly clear that he had made it a life's preoccupation to avoid the sun, and his alabaster skin, soft and delicate, mimicked the porcelain of a Meissen figure. Although he was six feet tall, all his gestures hinted at those of a tiny, delicate person, as did the width of his shoulders and the rather obscene bulge of his little stomach that protruded crossly beneath the tight white toga. His dainty feet, their toenails painted blood red, peeped from beneath the Egyptian cotton; his fluttering fingers danced and plucked at the air as his reedy voice warbled its welcome.

Lisa led the way, shepherding her flock toward their host.

"I thought this was supposed to be Roman," said Anne Liebermann loudly. "Why am I picking up Greek vibrations?"

"Catch the Caravaggio on the right," said Scott to the virologist.

"Good evening, baron," said Lisa Blass.

Heine Von Preussen's eyes mocked her hostility. He had been in Palm Beach long enough to know the score. The locals didn't understand parties like this. Or if they did, then they didn't approve of them. Okay, so a few young people like the Loy Andersons, who every year gave the wild, Bruce Sutka-designed Young Friends of the Red Cross Ball at the Henry Morrison Flagler Museum, knew how to let their hair down and have some real fun, but the Europeans did this sort of thing better, and gay Europeans did it best of all.

"Lisa Blass. How very kind of you all to come to my party."

He bowed gracefully from the waist and held Lisa's hand the correct centimeter and a half from the deep red lips that matched the color of his pedicured toenails.

Lisa made the introductions, her tone formal. None of her party, despite the demands of Anne Liebermann, had made the effort to dress according to the theme. In the milling throng behind the baron, she could see that they would be in the minority, as she had hoped.

"If there is anything you want that you don't see, then promise me you will ask for it." The baron waved an all-encompassing hand, his eyes knowing. The coded message was not far from the surface. Substances were available. And possibly people, too. "First you must drink from the fountain of life." His words hung in the jasmine-impregnated air as he stood back to let them pass.

The "fountain of life" stood six feet tall. It was a real fountain in which stone cherubs endlessly urinated into a large marble cachment area on the surface of which floated the finest and most delicate pink hibiscus flowers. Every now and again the recycled liquid was replaced by a powdered, pomaded, white-wigged flunkey wearing white gloves and beauty spots in the Versailles style. The liquid, it could be seen from the labels on the jereboam bottles was Pol Roger's 1975 Vintage Pink Champagne. The servant's job was endlessly to fill frosted Lalique champagne glasses from the "waters" of the fountain.

Scott fought back the desire to ask for a Bud. Lisa gasped at the vulgarity of the ostentation. Anne Liebermann howled her delight. The Nobel winner began to see how he might enjoy himself and vowed to tell no one how he had won his award. He might get mobbed in a place like this.

Apparently there was one more receiving line.

The two people who stood waiting for them now were an unlikely couple. One, tall and regal, looked like royalty, albeit minor royalty. She was straight as a die, wearing a tiara with stones the size of crown jewels, long white gloves, a classic full empire-line white dress, and a look of long-suffering dignity on her pleasant but far from beautiful face. Beside her, and half her size, stood a smiling, be-togaed Vietnamese.

The old ballroom had been extended by a giant white-and-gold marquee, and it was difficult to tell where the house ended and the grounds began, the more so because all doors and window frames had been removed to amplify the feeling of the party's theme.

Right now they appeared to be in the middle of a thriving and extremely active slave market. Around the walls were hay carts, with wooden spoked wheels, each guarded by a couple of stern centurions in period costume. Spread about on their surface were the most extraordinary cross section of humanity, many of them in heavy chains, that Lisa had ever seen. There were cheerful dwarfs, buxom old ladies, scantily clad maidens of decidedly specific charms, and cheeky black urchins, who looked like, and almost certainly were, the back street hustlers of the poorer areas of West Palm. From time to time a garrulous old man would stand on a stool and conduct a make-believe auction in which the Von Preussen guests would "pretend" to buy the slaves on offer. It was perfectly clear to Lisa that the enthusiasm with which the "sales" were being conducted was quite definitely in excess of that demanded by fantasy.

The one in progress was a case in point. The small black boy, a chain around each skinny leg, was standing center stage in the protective crook of the auctioneer's arms, smiling broadly at the descriptive extravagances that were being applied to him.

"A charming little chap to have around the house . . . instantly available to satisfy your every whim, and I mean *every* whim, fellow citizens. Now I am only asking ten pieces of gold. That's because he's so young. But the young can be trained, can't they? They can learn to do exactly what you like, can't they? Now who'll buy this polite little boy . . ."

Apparently several people. Lisa recognized one of the better connected Palm Beach realtors among the active bidders, locked in combat with a big, greasy German industrialist whose fortune apparently came from soap.

"Would you like to feel him, fellow citizens? Feel what he's made of?" To shrieks of delight the contestants leaped forward to experience their pound of flesh, and for one second Lisa allowed herself to wonder if it had really been like this in those far-off days before the empire, its strength sapped by hedonism, fell prey to the marauding hordes from the north. If so, was there a lesson to be learned from history? Was this party trying to tell the world something about latter-day Western civilization? It was almost worth thinking about.

The dancing seemed to be a sideshow to the main attraction of the slave auction, but here, too, both money and creativity had been spent. The dance floor was the swimming pool. In itself that was far from the most original thing in the world; at lots of Palm Beach parties they boarded over the pool for dancing. It was standard procedure, especially for a town in which space was at a premium. The Von Preussen establishment, however, was not short of space, and the pool had been selected for more unusual reasons. The dance floor was not of wood but of transparent Perspex, and raised a few feet over the surface of the hundred-foot-long pool, it left plenty of room for people to swim beneath it while looking up at the dancers above. Huge water lilies floated beneath the dancing feet, and sylphlike water nymphs, both male and female, their diaphanous robes failing completely to hide their strategically revealed nakedness, cavorted in the ninety-degree water. Several of the braver guests had already joined them, and now, their faces pressed rudely to the underside of the dance floor, their features squashed against the Perspex, they shouted ribald remarks up the togas of the cheerful dancers, as they swung and swayed to the reassuring rhythms of the Mike Carney band.

Lisa, firm in her desire to avoid either buying a slave or providing a peep show for the hoi polloi, managed to get everyone to a table where both spectacles could be seen without being indulged in.

"Well, Anne—you wanted to see the soft underbelly of Palm Beach. Here it is."

Anne flung out an arm to embrace the scene. "Darling, it's wonderful. Just wonderful. *Forget* Fellini."

Lisa raised a casual eyebrow. Anne Liebermann was being uncharacteristically girlish, and it was not a pretty sight. Usually she liked to affect a hard-bitten, tough-as-nails personality, her conversation peppered with fruity swear words and references to bizarre and unusual sexual practices. Now, however, she was simpering and giggling like a teenager on her first date.

Lisa had already identified its cause. Scott. Anne Liebermann was all over her son like a hot rash. The worst part was that Lisa had a suspicion she herself just might be the cause. She had asked

Scott to be nice to Anne Liebermann, and it appeared that he had taken her at her word. What was the name of the king who had asked his knights to rid him of a troublesome priest? He hadn't expected them to take him literally. Or had he? After all, he'd demanded to be punished for it afterward. Should she accept responsibility too? The boy worshiped her. That was his tragedy. And for some reason that she had never quite understood she appeared to be congenitally incapable of returning his affection. That was *her* tragedy. Time and time again she had tried to love him. The raw material was all there. He looked almost too good to be true. A Stansfield clone and a dream to behold. He was sophisticated and vulnerable, charming yet insecure—everything that a mother should be drawn to.

In vain, however, had she sought for the spark of maternal instinct. But where love should be there was only blackness, coldness where there should be warmth. As far as she was concerned, her indifference to her own son was more than a weakness; it hovered on the borders of illness. She knew, too, that there was no cure for the disease and no therapy that could make something of the nothingness in her soul. Maybe if he hadn't looked quite so much like Bobby . . . every day those steel-blue eyes reminding her of the one-time love and of the ever pressing necessity for revenge on the man who had fathered him, and on his dreadful wife.

She forced herself out of the uncomfortable reverie. Perhaps she had asked her son to do too much, but at least Anne Liebermann was having the weekend of a lifetime.

In the glittering candlelight Lisa watched with interest as Anne Liebermann's short fingers plucked at her son, her square chin hovering at the shoulders of his immaculate tuxedo. Doubtless beneath the table her ample thigh would be rubbing insistently against his.

"Lisa, I think your son is the most delicious thing I've ever seen. Do you know I saw him *surf* today? He's the best thing in the world. I sat on the beach transfixed. Literally transfixed."

Everyone laughed except Scott. He had just been referred to as a "thing." God, she was awful.

For the novelist who'd been with Knopf it was too much. Most of the things Anne said were too much for him. "Really, you should have more respect for language, Anne," he said. " '*Literally* transfixed' means you were impaled through and through."

"I choose my words *extremely* carefully," shrieked Anne Liebermann, rolling her eyes in a charade of lewdness, as she dropped a huge dollop of beluga and melba toast into her mouth.

Everyone was expected to get the message. Everyone did. There was embarrassed general laughter that Scott and Lisa did not join in. Anne gushed on, capitalizing on the spotlight's descent on her glistening face. "In fact, Lisa, I've had a wonderful idea for a new book. Surfing. Just like that. Surfing and surfers. What do you think?"

"I think we should know if it's going to be a Blass book," said Lisa slyly.

"Darling, of course it's going to be a Blass book, and Scott can help me with the research. I think this book is going to need an *awful* lot of research."

Her hand massaged Scott's on the white damask in full view of the assembled company. With a superhuman effort he managed to keep it on the table. The triumph in his mother's face was reward enough. There was nothing he wouldn't do to see that.

Lisa wanted the *t*'s crossed and the *i*'s dotted. "I'm sure we have a deal, Anne. Scott's your researcher and Blass is your publisher. You'd better let that high-powered agent of yours know the score."

She turned to her son. It was time for a sugar lump. He'd just made Blass a million dollars. "We ought to give you a commission, darling. For helping our authors dream up their ideas."

But a twinge of guilt shot through her like a knife as she beheld the slavelike devotion in Scott's eyes.

18

In the Norton Gallery, funded almost exclusively by Palm Beach money and yet situated unhappily on the wrong side of Lake Worth, East and West met in anxious union. Both inside and out it showed the class of its parentage, and its Neoclassical exterior enclosed one of the finest collections of modern art outside the major centers such as New York, Malibu, and Houston. The faded houses that surrounded it provided a complete contrast. West Palm Beach's bustling, thrusting expansion had, for some reason, been almost entirely toward the north, and the seedy, run-down apartment buildings and factory warehouses still clustered greedily around the Norton like some rusty scaffolding about a soon-to-be-renovated architectural gem. In the entrance foyer the names of its benefactors were advertised prominently on polished wooden panels on a list that could have been lifted almost unchanged from the shiny social pages of the *Palm Beach Daily News*. It was one of the very few places on earth where the Blass and Stansfield names attempted an uneasy coexistence, their closeness in dramatic contrast to the unbridgeable gulf that in reality separated them.

Even though he preferred the gaudy self-confidence of the gallery's famed Gilbert and George collection, Scott had to agree with his mother that the Picasso was rather magnificent.

"Some people still sneer at Picasso and say he was a rip-off merchant, but look at the date on this: 1924. That's three years *before* the Braque next to it, and yet the subject matter and the treatment of it is almost identical in both paintings. Amazing texture. Wonderfully rich colors."

Lisa spoke with the authority of an expert. In Europe it was not the publishing business alone that she had mastered. It had all started in Paris under the adoring and penetratingly perceptive

305

guidance of Michel Dupré. In London she had been her own tutor, but after Paris, the foundation had been there. She had attacked the museums of Europe like a hungry lioness, devouring voraciously the contents of the Prado, the Hermitage in Leningrad, and the Florentine galleries. The Norton could not hope to compete with these, but it contained paintings that would not have been out of place in even the greatest museum. This Picasso was one of them.

Lisa waved her elegant fingers to demonstrate her point, and Scott watched her reverently. No painting could compare with his mother. No artist would have dared attempt a likeness. Even if one had managed to capture the outside, he would have missed the restless energy that beamed from within, the steely purpose that hung around her like an ice-cold aura. It was the motivation that was the mystery. What provided the force for her dynamism, the thrust to mighty endeavor that flattened obstacles in her path and banished all opposition to her purpose? He had never learned the answer to the fascinating question, although he had spent his life trying. Somehow, though, he knew that in the answering he would find the key to his own ambition. Once he knew the secret of his mother's needs, then his own desires would be hovering on the brink of actualization. Once he knew how, he would become her champion, make her dreams his dreams, and in turning her fantasies into reality he, Scott, would be able to bask forever in the warm rays of her gratitude. In that dawn of new light he would be born again, the loved and wanted son, a mother-and-child reunion promising an eternity of bliss.

His mother had moved on ahead to admire a fine Matisse and he had lingered over the unusual Picasso sculpted head. A female voice, icepick sharp, cut into his thoughts.

"Over on this side of the bridge again, Lisa? Can't drag yourself away from the back streets?" said the sneering voice. "Amazing what marriage to a geriatric can achieve, but you know what they say. Money doesn't bring happiness. And it never changes a tramp into a lady."

From his vantage point twenty feet away Scott felt the shock waves break over him. He couldn't believe his ears. Was this some bantering joke, the hilarious jibing of an old and trusted friend? The tone of the voice—cruel and supercilious—said "no-way," and the persona of the speaker backed that up. It was Jo-Anne Stansfield, wife of Senator Stansfield, patroness of the arts, looking good enough to eat, and spitting poison through clenched lips.

Scott's initial response was to walk forward and smash her instantly to the ground, but instead he stood rooted to the spot, a force far stronger than emotion freezing him, like Lot's wife, to the place where he stood. Deep in his guts the howling cats of curiosity had been let loose. He knew instinctively that he would learn something now which would be of vital importance to him. It was a strange feeling, of itching intuition, of the dawning of an awareness that he hovered on the brink of fundamental knowledge. Jo-Anne Stansfield and her husband Bobby. His mother disliked them both intensely, but he hadn't a clue as to why. She always avoided parties at which she knew they would be present, and she had never had them to her house even when the entertaining was some arm's-length charity affair, and the guest list anything but hand picked. He had sometimes wondered about it, but had concluded it was unimportant. Some people you liked, and some you didn't. It was as simple as that. Until now.

Like a small child glued to the keyhole, Scott watched in horror as the scene unfolded before his eyes.

Reeling from the initial surprise of the verbal ambush, Lisa had initially gone white, but she recovered quickly and already the color was returning to her cheeks. She turned to face her foe, a tiger at bay, the hunted about to become the hunter. "You yourself are a marvelous example of the truth of what you say, Jo-Anne. Unlike you, however, I have absolutely no inclination at all to forget my origins. I'm proud of them."

Lisa stood perfectly straight, her head thrown back in defiance, as she moved into the counterattack. Proud and undaunted, she was not, however, unbloodied, and Scott could see that the attack had left its mark. Never before had he seen his mother at war like this. It was a weird and awesome sight, but one that had to be endured. Still, he didn't go to her, secure in the subconscious understanding that what he witnessed was a necessary prelude to a mighty and more effective intervention later. For the very first time his mother's ghosts were visible. He had to get to know them.

Looking Jo-Anne evenly in the eyes, Lisa gave her the second barrel. "The only thing that's changed about you, Jo-Anne, is that over the years your fee's gone up. The service hasn't changed one bit.''

''What? *What?*'' Jo-Anne screamed in disbelief. ''You're calling me a hooker? You're daring to call *me* a hooker?''

On some astral plane of detachment Scott watched and waited.

''Listen, Jo-Anne, everybody knows the panties fit. You've been wearing them for years.''

Lisa smiled a triumphant smile. The skirmish she hadn't sought was over, and she was its victor. It was time to withdraw, not to retreat. In front of her, Jo-Anne looked as if she were on the verge of some dreadful explosion that threatened to cover the entire Norton art collection with her bodily tissues.

Lisa turned and walked toward her son, her gait even, her step measured, as Jo-Anne's infuriated howl wafted after her. ''You're nobody from nowhere, Lisa Starr. Nobody from nowhere.''

Over her shoulder Scott took in the amazing visual. Jo-Anne Stansfield, her beautiful face twisted with her terrible rage, had sunk gently to her knees as if in prayer for the thunderbolt that would strike down her enemy. There in the middle of the empty gallery she was closed off to everything but hatred, the emotion pure and undiluted, beamed at his mother's back. Its strength was incapable of description.

As Lisa put out her hand for his, Scott could feel that it was shaking. Nobody could be unmoved by such phenomenal and naked aggression.

''Come on, darling, we're leaving.'' The voice was almost conversational. But as he was swept along in her wake its character changed. Small and still, its power equaled the passion of Jo-Anne Stansfield's anger. ''I pray to my God that one day He will rid me of that dreadful woman,'' she said.

It seemed to Scott that it was the very first time his mother had ever spoken to him.

In Palm Beach, the beating heart of any house was divided not into four but into two. The dining room, of course. And the swimming pool. The Blass mansion, like many others on South Ocean

Boulevard, boasted a couple of pools. One, salt water, nestling next to the beach cabana on the south side of the road above the sea, was considered the "casual" pool, for children and horse play, rubber rings and boats. But at the freshwater pool behind the house, protected from the sea breeze and hidden away among the pink grapefruit, banana, and lemon trees, formal elegance was the game's name, and nothing was allowed to interfere with the tranquil serenity and the formidable neatness of the ordered setting.

The pool was one hundred feet long and the clear blue water, disturbed by the powerful skimming system, was clean enough to drink. Intricate mosaic tiles of a Moorish design lined the edge of the uncompromising rectangular surface, and the eye was effortlessly drawn along the pool to the Doric-columned terrace that graced one end of it. Here, in the shade, four Tropitone sun beds were spaced in military line on the white Carrara marble floor. On the end one, flicking half-heartedly through the pages of *Surfer Magazine,* lay Scott Blass. From time to time he looked up, an expression of worried concentration on his face, unseeing eyes scanning the serried ranks of manicured citrus trees that fronted the formal gardens along the pool's west side, ranging without purpose over the gashes of red of the stone-potted geraniums, the strategically placed statues of cherubs and seraphs, the tiny white scented flowers of the sticky sweet jasmine bushes.

How could it be done? Since the day in the Norton when he had learned the secret of his mother's hatred the problem had gone around and around in his mind. A window of opportunity had opened for him, but try as he might he hadn't been able to figure a way of getting through it. Somehow, he must damage the Stansfields. Hurt them, and hurt them badly. They had been revealed as his mother's enemies, and it followed as the night the day that they were his, too. He had assumed the mantle of revenge effortlessly. It would be the way to his mother's heart, the combination to the lock on the gates of paradise, and he had schemed and searched for a way to touch them. But the Stansfields were inaccessible. They were rich and powerful, protected physically by guards and electronic devices, by armies of lawyers, by ingratiating friends and acquaintances, by a complex web of patronage, influence, and political and social prestige. He had sought the Achilles heel in vain, spending long hours in the library with back copies of the weekly news magazines as he hunted for signs of weakness, for skeletons whose existence he might exploit. He had come up with nothing. There was a daughter, who would be about his age, and it seemed that the Stansfields were a perfect caricature of Mr. and Mrs. America. She had been a Duke and he was a Stansfield, a family of fixers whose fingers had never been far from the wheels that controlled the direction of the country's political and social machines. Money and power. Power and money. The wall that surrounded them appeared to be impregnable.

The cheerful voice broke into his thoughts. "So this is how the idle rich live. Sure is fine for them as has it."

Scott sat up. "Hi, Dave baby. You made it just in time. Department of Sanitation was about to order this pool *closed,* it's so dirty."

The jokes were fine, but actually Scott felt a bit guilty when Dave came to do the pool. It wasn't just that they were the same age and were good friends—fellow surfers who shared the same waves on the North End beach even when the water temperature dipped down into the fifties during the December cold spells. It was more than that. It was the guilt the rich felt when their money was flaunted in the face of the poor. The pool at the Villa Gloria was the ultimate symbol of wealth. It looked as if it might have well belonged to some fabulously rich ancient Roman, possibly the emperor himself.

And Dave was undoubtedly a card-carrying member of the poor fraternity. No question. The truth of the matter was that Dave's three weekly visits were largely unnecessary. The chemicals these days were fed into the pool automatically and there was a continual automatic monitoring of water pH. That combined with the awesomely efficient filter meant that Dave had very little to do. However, in Palm Beach you had C and P do your pool, Boynton to maintain the gardens, and Cassidy to service the air conditioning. Everybody had them, and so you did, too. After all, it was a *very* traditional town.

"Shove it, and break me out a Bud."

Dave, a.k.a. Dave the Rave, was a marginally more rugged, slightly down-market version of Scott himself. That is, his hair looked as if it had spent a year or two pickled in bleach, some of which had dripped unevenly over the sawed-off once-blue denim shorts. There were fine blond hairs on his craggy legs and scuffed Dexter ankle boots on his feet, worn with no socks. The clean white T-shirt read C AND P POOL MAINTENANCE.

Scott leaned down into the cavernous interior of the poolside cabana's refrigerator. He spoke over his shoulder. "Okay, Rave, how's business? And I don't mean chlorine an' filters an' all that crap."

It was a convention that Dave's friends half believed that the job of pool attendant came with "perks" in the shape of bored house-wives and their college-kid daughters. It was a fantasy that from time to time had a happy knack of turning into reality—especially in Palm Beach.

Dave sniggered. Scott might be a rich mother, might *have* a rich mother, but he was a regular guy. He reached out to take the bottle of ice cold Beck's, noting phlegmatically that the Blass household clearly didn't deal in anything as mundane as Bud.

He flipped through the inventory of half-true pseudoseductions, of come-ons imagined, of flirtations dreamed about. Okay. Right. There was one juicy one, and it was real as a shark in the shallows on a rough day in summer. "Hey, Scott. You ready for this? I got a story for you."

"The two sisters on El Vedado? The ones with the teeth braces? Dave, you're really *gross,* you know. Did they come across? *Both* of them?"

"Naw, better'n that. Not something I done, something I saw."

He bent down, scooped up a sample of the immaculate water in his testing kit, and splashed in a few drops of hydrochloric acid.

Scott smiled his anticipation. This sounded good. Dave was a character. Poor as a church mouse, but hot shit on the aerials and a real stayer on a Saturday night. He usually helped him vacuum the pool—one of the few things he did that annoyed his mother.

"Yeah, Scottie boy. You heard of the Stansfields?"

Scott's mind stopped. Then it started again. "Sure. Everyone knows them. Up on North Ocean by the Kennedy house."

"Well, I do their pool, don't I?"

"I didn't know that." Scott's tone was sharp and inappropriate. There was an implication that Dave should have mentioned that before. He caught hold of himself. Careful. This conversation had started out light. If he wanted to milk it of all possibilities he should keep it that way.

"I'm so sorry I didn't mention it before." Dave laughed at the rebuke and Scott joined in.

"No, go on, Dave. Sure, I know the Stansfields."

"Well, I only just started there, but let me tell you, that wife is really something. I mean *real* neat. Like she's built, and stacked, and she sort of smells of it. You know. Just amazing."

"You mean you *made* it? With the senator's wife? I don't *believe* it!" Scott ladled on the enthusiasm. That was the way to get Dave to open right up.

"Listen, baby. Nobody gets to make it with Jo-Anne Stansfield. I mean, no fella, anyway."

Dave had assumed the inscrutability of a politician laying out his budget-cutting proposals. "What do you mean, Dave? C'mon. Lay it on the line."

"I mean, like she's into chicks. But *heavily* into chicks. There's a different one up there every day. Terrific-looking girls and they don't even 'see' me. Me. Can you believe that?"

"She's a dyke? How on earth do you *know?*"

"I saw her kiss one of them in the cabana." The look on Dave's face was pure triumph.

"You didn't."

"I swear it."

"Christ!" Scott could hardly believe his ears.

Already his thoughts were winging away. His mother's enemy was a lesbian. She was married to a right-wing senator with enormous political ambitions. It was dynamite. He could explode their lives with this. The *National Enquirer* in Lake Worth? One of the big nationally syndicated columns? No, that wasn't the way. Where was the proof? A poolman's testimony. And Dave would clam up tighter than a Jesuit's mind at the threat of losing his job. The Duke money and the Stansfield influence would make it a kamikaze trip for any journalist brave enough or stupid enough to print the rumor. No, there was only one thing to do. One intriguing possibility. He had to get inside the Stansfield house. Once inside the ramparts of the Stansfield world he would figure out a way of blowing it apart. Already it began to look as if he had discovered a Trojan horse.

How to handle this?

"Dave. You're a betting man, aren't you?" Dave would respond to a challenge like that.

"I'm listening."

"A thousand bucks says I can make it with her."

"What!" Dave was incredulous and amused all at the same time.

"You heard."

"Thousand 'gainst what."

"Your hundred says I can't."

"Ten to one. You gotta be joking. It's money in the bank. You're crazy. Anyway, how'd you get to her?"

"I take your place for a few weeks. You come by here first and loan me the van. Nobody would know. I can clean a pool as well as you. I've had enough practice cleaning this one."

"Ralph would blow me away if he found out." Dave looked doubtful. He really needed the work.

"C'mon, he's not going to find out. You know you guys are always changing around. Like that asshole of a geriatric who comes here when you're on vacation. I'll just say you're sick or something."

"What are you trying to prove, Scott?" Dave's expression was quizzical. It wasn't like Scott to be throwing his money around. Or to be playing superstud either. He got more than his fair share as it was. Still, a thousand bucks would get the bike all straightened out with enough left over for a trip to the islands with Karen. One thing was for sure: if Scott lost he would pay. And it looked certain he would do just that. It was tempting. Tempting enough not to get too involved with motives.

"I got my reasons," Scott answered the question enigmatically.

"Babe, you got yourself a deal." Dave put out his hand to cement it.

Scott took it. "Which are your days next week?"

"Monday, Wednesday, Friday. I usually get there in the early afternoon."

"Meet me here anytime after one, okay?" Scott picked up the pole and basket. "C'mon, Dave, I'll help you clean this mother. God knows though, I don't know why anyone bothers."

In his nostrils he could already smell the scent of victory.

313

Scott attacked the wave as if it had just insulted him. He swooped down it, the edge of his board carving mercilessly at the smooth water, chopping it to pieces like a surgeon on angel dust. With the spray in his hair, the roar of the surf in his ears, and the exultation in his soul, it was a good day on the North End beach. The rollers were coming in smooth and strong, breaking to order, and the water between the frothy white heads of the waves was pancake flat. The board was doing everything right, too. Perfect balance, sharp and light, tight as a drum on the turns. All morning long he'd been riding the tubes, and now he wanted a few aerials to rap up the session before lunch. He gritted his teeth and braced his powerful legs against the rough surface of the Impact board as he rode up the wave toward the lip. The mechanics of the movement were old hat, but he needed to perfect the style. At Daytona a few weeks before he'd lost points there.

This wave was perfect. Four to five feet, a lot of power on a clean face and buckets of hollow. Scott pushed for speed. That was the secret of a good aerial. The lip rushed up toward him, and he extended the vertical takeoff by unweighting. Wow! That was it. Suddenly it was an upside-down world. Keep tucked. Keep tucked down. Don't let the hands go up. Don't reach for the rails. That was for the rookies. The world was righting itself. The position looked good for wave reentry. Except . . . Damn! The stupid bitch! The girl was right on his line. Slap bang in the middle of his own wave. The one he had just dominated, owned, created. The fierce possession of surfers for their own water didn't have a chance to express itself further. To avoid catastrophe Scott pushed down as hard as he could and jumped sideways into the cauldron of crashing white water. As he went down into the blackness his mind's eye replayed the perfect, screwed-up aerial. He'd been there. It had been *right*. Until some bitch . . .

In the dark anonymity beneath the waves Scott planned his revenge. The girl was about to get a tongue thrashing she would never be able to forget. His golden head burst through the surface into the sunlight, and he flicked it angrily from side to side, sending off a cascade of shining diamonds into the sticky air. There she was. Standing in the shallows and looking a bit like a doomed aristocrat awaiting the sharp kiss of the guillotine blade. His powerful arms devoured the few yards to the shore line, as his tongue rehearsed the syllables of abuse.

He waded straight toward her, and they both spoke at once:

"Look, I'm terribly sorry. It was all my fault. I didn't . . ."

"You goddamned amateur. You were riding my frigging . . ."

They both stopped for the same reason, but neither of them knew what it was.

To Scott it seemed as if he had walked into a mirror. The girl was him. It was almost as simple as that. Useless to insult yourself. And totally unsatisfying. He heard the words dying in his throat. The girl stood there, the water dripping from the lush brown body, her wet hair plastered down flat over the gorgeous face. She had stolen his hair color, his nose, the baby blue of his eyes, the fullness of his mouth. What was it called? Döppelganger? When you saw your double. His eyes wandered on down. The tits of a seventeen-year-old, the bra an irrelevance. Small but perfect. Stomach, just a little too full—hips just a little too wide with the baby fat of adolescence. But everything hard and firm. The body of a cheerleader, a baton twirler, the sort that drove the boys on the football team into a lather of sexual frustration. Ridiculous. She was incredibly pretty. Anytime she liked she could wreck his wave. Be my guest, amateur surfer. You can even try my board.

"Sorry," Scott heard himself mumble. "I guess I overreacted." He waved a hand in a gesture of apology.

Christie Stansfield had always believed in angels but hadn't expected to bump into one on the North End beach. The boy was insanely good looking. The tousled hair was matted by the sand and surf, curled and basted by the endless ultraviolet, crying out for the touch of fingers, of caring hands. And the face—open, wide open to emotion, to anger, to sudden and inexplicable embarrassment, hinting already of a desperate desire for the warmth of intimacy. Wide shoulders tapering to the cliché of a finely muscled and thin waist. Long, long legs, and the undeniable excitement of the bit in between, hidden from view by the torn and tattered white cutoffs.

"No. No. What I did was unforgivable. You're absolutely right to be angry.'' Somehow this boy's anger would be a wonderful thing. Paradoxically Christie wanted it and its intensity more than the mumbled small talk that threatened to replace it.

Scott bent down to escape the girl's intent gaze and pulled the board in toward him by the ankle cord. ''You find some good waves this morning?'' He tried to sound casual.

''I'm just a beginner. They're all good to me. All good, but totally impossible!''

The laugh was really neat. Open in the beginning then closing up tight at the end, as if she felt she hadn't really the right to laugh about a subject so serious. Scott smiled back at her reassuringly. She was a nice kid. A sweet turn-on. Far, far away from the West Palm girls with their dirty talk and wise bodies. Light years, too, from the Palm Beach variety with their whining self-confidence and their preciously guarded, milk-white complexions.

''Wanna beer?'' Scott subconsciously stayed in surfer mode. From the flush on the beautiful rounded cheeks he reckoned he wasn't doing so badly.

''If you have one to spare. Thanks.''

Together they walked across the sand to the Polystyrene freezer box, trailing their boards by the fins.

''My name's Scott.''

''Hi, I'm Christie.''

''That's a nice name.''

''Thanks.''

Scott turned to look at her. As intended, the twin specks of red were expanding nicely. The eyes were gratifyingly downcast.

He threw himself down on the hot sand, languid and abandoned, letting out a sigh of satisfaction, of ostentatious relaxation. Leaning on one elbow he reached inside the cooler for a cold beer, watching the girl carefully as he did so.

Christie squatted beside him, vaguely self-conscious, uncommitted yet already hopelessly compromised. It was a pickup pure and simple. Christie Stansfield picked up by a surfer in her own back yard, about to down a Budweiser with a Greek god whose ancestry would be anything but divine. She suppressed the uncharitable thought. Who cared about things like that? She was always trying to reeducate her parents in precisely that area. Not that she'd ever had much success.

She felt the unsettling eyes boring through the bikini top, sensed them creep all over the warm flesh around her nipples. It was a delicious feeling, but extraordinarily illicit, the heady scent of forbidden fruit wafting tantalizingly through her mind as she felt the hardening in her breasts. Suddenly her throat was dry, and she wanted to swallow badly. But he was looking straight into her eyes again now, temporarily abandoning her swelling breasts. He would know all about the hormones that were jumping around inside her. And then what would he do? Would he laugh at her and touch her leg as he did so? Would he pull her down on top of him there and then and taste her tongue, uninvited, needing no invitation?

Scott watched the parted lips and saw the breath coming faster, as the erotic moment built its power. Two beads of sweat lingered charmingly between her nose and upper lip, moisture he could wipe away with his finger, with his tongue. He'd never known it to happen so fast. Was it narcissism? Was he drawn to the face that looked so like his? Whatever. In his stomach the familiar flutterings began as the caged butterflies were released, and the first hesitant movements heralded arousal's dawn.

"Christie," he said reflectively. "Christie. I like that name a lot." On purpose he made the soft syllables sound like a caress. He reached out his hand, and for a second he let it rest on the soft skin of her knee.

"What's your second name?"

"Stansfield," came the murmured reply.

19

There was definitely something alluring about him from behind. Something very feminine, a strong resemblance to somebody. Who on *earth* was it?

Jo-Anne hitched herself up on both elbows to improve her view. Her full breasts jutted down, almost exposing the dark nipples. She had been sunbathing with the straps of her bikini top undone. Yes, from the back he could almost have been a girl, and an incredibly pretty one at that. Blond hair, all long and curly at the back, almost ringlets really. A slim frame, and a tight upturned ass like the aerobics girls had. She tried to remember the face. It had been sort of familiar, but at the same time she knew she hadn't seen him before. Well, it was definitely intriguing and a dramatic improvement on the faceless oaf who usually came to do the pool —all soulful gazes and macho poses. A right little turn-off.

It was the way he held himself she liked best: delicately, as if he were aware of his body and its perfect proportions, but at the same time was a little embarrassed by it. Almost as if he didn't want it to cause any harm, to inflame any passions—although he was more than conscious that that was what it tended to do. Mmmmmmmmmmmm. Very graceful, but naturally so. No poses. Just shapes that looked good for the task at hand, which right now was reaching out to flick a few hibiscus leaves from the center of the pool. Jo-Anne took in the ropelike muscles of his extended forearms, and the wide shoulders.

He was working down the side of the pool toward where she was lying. Jo-Anne was interested enough to try some conversation. For sure he would blow that. Pretty boys always did. "What happened to the regular guy?" she said to the suntanned back. As if she cared.

"Oh, he got sick, ma'am."

Scott turned to look at her. It was working like a dream, and it was far too good to be true. A little while ago he had about as much chance of getting to the Stansfields as being selected for the space shuttle, but now he was almost an insider. Two incredible coincidences had come right on top of each other: Dave was their poolman and Christie Stansfield liked to watch the surfers on the beach. Neither in itself was that remarkable. After all, Palm Beach was a small town. But in terms of his plan those two events could well have been conceived in heaven . . . or rather in hell. Mother and daughter. Both were accessible to him now, and Christie had already shown the early signs of being a plum ripe for the picking. Right at this very minute and every weekday she was safely tucked away, hawking Polo sweaters to the yuppies in the Esplanade. It was mummy's turn.

At a glance one thing was obvious: Christie Stansfield's mom sure had it all. Had it, and clearly worked like hell to keep it. The tits were bigger by far than her daughter's, and from the way the nipples brushed the material of the undone bra, it was plain that in the normal way they would need a bit of support. But the legs looked powerful, the thighs muscular and the butt tight, from the generous portion of it that was visible for appreciation around the minimal thong-type bikini briefs. Face? Time had left its wrinkles around the steel-cold eyes, and the rather cruel mouth was wickedly determined, but it was still beautiful—if a million miles from Christie's angelic countenance, all wide-eyed innocence and pre-Raphaelite purity.

How should he play it? The softest of soft sells to be sure. This one was a huntress. She wouldn't want to be hunted. He turned away from her. Deferential. Humble. The lowly poolboy, who knew how to behave in the presence of his betters.

Jo-Anne eyed him speculatively. Okay, so far you haven't hanged yourself. How about some more rope?

"You look like you do some surfing. Are you one of those pests always disobeying the parking signs in the North End?"

Jo-Anne made it sound taunting, the hint of flirtation softening the abrasive content of the question. The relationship between the surfers, nearly all of whom came from across the lake, and the town of Palm Beach had been a disastrous one for years. The Palm Beachers, who themselves rarely visited the beach, nonetheless thought of it—when they bothered to think about it at all—as their own private property. Despite the fact that every beach in America to the high-water line was supposed to be open to the public, the inhabitants of the North End spent much of their time discouraging the presence of outsiders. This they achieved in two basic ways. One was to disallow parking on any of the town's roads within three miles of the North End breakers. The other was to enforce rigorously the trespass laws while failing to provide public beach access. Undaunted, the surfers would either walk for miles from the one public beach in the center of the town, or cheerfully disregard both private property and the town's no-parking signs, which a large portion of West Palm Beachers thought unconstitutional anyway.

Once again Scott turned toward her. He put a casual hand on a cocked hip and smiled what he hoped was his boyish smile. "Yes, ma'am. I mean I do some surfin', but mostly down at Deerfield, or up Jupiter way. You ever tried it?" he added daringly.

"Do I *look* as if I have?"

Jo-Anne smiled at the cheek of the question. This one had charm. A *lot* of it. He was really rather sweet. Almost coquettish. Who the hell *did* he remind her of?

"Well, you look in pretty good shape, ma'am. If you don't mind me saying so." He ran a hand nervously through his hair. He'd washed it the night before.

Jo-Anne peered up at him, lifting a hand to shield her eyes from the early afternoon sun. Scott loomed over her, silhouetted against the clear blue sky. Then, on an impulse which she didn't herself really understand, she hitched herself up farther on the Grossfillex sun bed, allowing both her breasts to fall free in front of her, totally exposed to the gaze of the young boy.

Whatever the effect the gesture had on him—difficult to judge against the bright sun—the effect on herself was dramatic.

The thought of his eyes roaming free all over her suddenly naked torso was for some extraordinary reason thoroughly erotic. Jo-Anne could hardly believe what was happening. It seemed literally light years ago that she had last been turned on by a member of the opposite sex. She couldn't even remember the occasion. Had there ever *been* one? Women were different—soft, and sweet smelling, gentle and giving, pretty and clean. Infinitely attractive. A man? It was ridiculous. But it was also undeniably real.

Hovering over her, Scott swallowed hard. He'd been quite wrong about the tits. Strong pectorals had scooped them up, winning effortlessly the battle against gravity. Now the twin orbs, glistening with a thin film of what smelled like the all-but-unobtainable Charles of the Ritz Bain de Soleil suntan gel, imprisoned his gaze and dried out his mouth. The ball had been returned to the baseline of his court and it had buckets and buckets of topspin.

Things were moving along faster than he had dared to hope, but strangely, as the goal got closer the stakes got higher and higher. One wrong move, one uncool gesture, and the moment would be vaporized. It was the oldest problem in the world, and even at his tender age Scott had experienced it: how to cross the border into intimacy. Would there be more talk? Should there be? So, not knowing what to do, Scott did nothing. He just stood there watching the things he was clearly supposed to watch.

The reality of the situation was enough for Jo-Anne. Her whole life she had been nothing if not a sexual adventurer, a pleasure voyager who grabbed at the moment the second it came within reach. Some were like that in business; they only had to see a cheap stock or an expensive currency and they moved like lightning. Well, bodies were Jo-Anne's equivalent of pork bellies, precious metals, and interest-rate futures. And when the time was right she *traded*. Right now it appeared she was confronted by an excellent buying opportunity. So, at the very time when Scott felt that he was a mere spectator to events, Jo-Anne Duke Stansfield moved impatiently into the driver's seat. This boy was young enough to be her son. Good! Great!

With all the time in the world she stood up, moving slowly, languidly. If she wanted this thing to pleasure her she shouldn't frighten it away. The trick was to get just the right mix of firmness and femininity. From Big Apple days she remembered that there was a thin line between ball breaking and passivity. You had to lead them, not force-feed them.

Scott, playing the unaccustomed role of hypnotized rabbit, let it happen. The body was now standing up straight, and it fulfilled all the promise of the one that had been lying down. Jo-Anne made Dave's description sound like the incoherent ramblings of a neutered blindman. Before his eyes he could actually *see* her tits hardening, the moisture appearing as if by magic as her tongue traced the contours of her upper lip. In reaction the band inside him had already started to tune up. There were the dancing insects in the pit of his stomach, the squirting of the stuff that sent the heart into overdrive. His plan was on the back burner now, crudely displaced from the front of his mind by the total intrusiveness of desire. This woman was going to use him. Later she would spit him out, throw him away, until it suited her to act the replay. He was about to be pulled like the cork on a bottle of indifferent Algerian burgundy—crudely, roughly, and with no ceremony at all.

Jo-Anne stepped right up to him, putting her face close to his. During her brief walk she had already seen the hardness move in the tight jeans and the pupils widen in the deep blue eyes that reminded her of someone. For what seemed like an age she stood stock still, breathing in the unaccustomed masculine scent and allowing it to go to work on her hormones and to make free with her mind. So *very* different. Variety's spice. With all the time in the world she reached downward and laid the flat of her hand on the no longer flat denim, enjoying the heat beneath her palm and the impatient movements of the young boy's need. It was all so deliciously unusual. Perhaps she had missed out on this for too long. The smile that mocked her own lips was saying it all.

"Lend me your body, toy-boy. I need it for a while. You can have it back later."

Christie Stansfield had taken the plunge and worried about it all morning, but now she didn't care anymore. She was out there—dancing, feeling, being. There was a cotton-wool cloud under her feet. In her nostrils was animal heat, in her soul the steep banked fires of love. This workout suit was state-of-the-art, but state-of-the-art London rather than West Palm. As usual, the English had gone overboard to produce today's shocker but tomorrow's norm, and the sheer hot-pink creation looked more like bondage gear than the leotards of old.

During the five minutes of easy social intercourse that always preceded the workout the other girls had showed their envy by thinly veiled jokes and the occasional flashes of pure malice in their envious eyes. "Christie, sweetheart, you look like something out of an X-rated movie. You are 'brave.' " "My, my, Christie, I wish I had the nerve to turn up in that . . . whatever it is."

But Christie didn't care what they thought. She was dressed for one person only: the beautiful boy with the worried eyes who had come out of the sea. Scott Blass. He was meeting her here. In a few minutes *he* would be the judge. And he was a *man*.

Now the adrenaline was making her feel as good as a young girl in love and with a resting pulse of fifty could possibly feel. Christie flung her head to one side and caught her reflection in the mirrored wall, and with the narcissism of the very young she enjoyed what she saw.

It was all there to see, brown and firm, the sun-baked skin basted by the thin film of sweat, framed by the daring pink thongs of the workout suit. There were muscles in the strong back, upper arms and thighs, but they were rounded out with youth's young flesh— intensely feminine, universally alluring. Her breasts were not big but they hardly moved as her body powered through the routine, and the sweat-soaked low-cut bodice gave away the secret that the conical nipples were the salmon pink of late adolescence. Her abdomen was revealed from just about every angle—the top part of the suit being joined to the bottom by four single strands of material that left open panels at front and back, and at both sides. If there was a criticism, Christie guessed it was around the hips. Just a little bit too generous, but kind of voluptuous, sort of neat really, and as part of the total picture far more than passable. Anyway, it was all getting better every day. Especially her bottom. Now it was real firm, and hard. It would be her gift to Scott. A toy for him to play with, factory fresh, unsullied by the touch of a male hand. He could have it, and when he arrived to pick her up he would be able to see it first—heaving and straining beneath the skimpy material, her wild buttocks bisected by the thin strip of pink material lodged deep in their cleavage, barely covering her most secret places. Even if he was late, the class would still be in

323

progress when he arrived. Christie had thought of that. Maybe after all there was a *tiny* part of her mother in her.

Maggie's voice cut into the voyeuristic reverie.

"Make it smooth. Stroke the rhythm out. Concentrate on the *timing*. Lose yourself in it. Let the body take over the mind. That's it. That's it."

Christie tried to do as she was told and to still the raging thoughts. "I am my body. My body is all I am," she tried to tell herself. That was the philosophy. That was the way you were supposed to go. She pumped out her long leg to the side and tried to lose herself in the delicious feeling of stretch and exertion, of squeeze and relaxation as her powerful gluteal muscles orchestrated the doggie lifts. Spine straight, head down. Pump easy, pump slow. Would Scott see this from behind? She imagined his eyes upon her. The night before in the country-and-western bar he had looked at her like that and so now she could imagine the dangerous eyes. Mmmmmmmmmmmmmm. It was so very nice. What had the world done before they had invented exercise? And had anybody *ever* been as much in love as this?

The beat of the rhythm was unashamedly repetitive now. For ten minutes it had pretended to possess melody, but its purpose was at last exposed. It was a metronome, no more a tune than the ticking of a clock, and its aim was to conduct the movement of bodies. No more, and no less. The bass was turned up high and from ten or twenty speakers around the vast penthouse studio of the pink Phillips Point building the drumming beat etched its message into those parts of the brain that lived below consciousness, below wisdom, below feeling. The fundamental message could not be disobeyed. To hear it was to obey it as it merged the class into one single entity, beyond pain, beyond individual existence. Then, there it was. Tiptoeing around the edges of the insistent beat and gaining in strength second by second were the clarion notes of the national anthem. That was another vital ingredient. They were all one now, one nation, one body, one bundle of purpose. Joy through strength. Power through beauty. Happiness through the physical in the dawn's early light.

Alone in the throbbing room Maggie remained inoculated against the fever of the wild, abandoned music. Twenty years of exercise had given her that freedom, and sometimes, like today, she wished for the slavery that bound her class. She could see the ecstasy on the sweat-stained faces, could imagine the purity of the pleasure they were experiencing from the peak exertion. But for her it was over. She was so far ahead of them all she had come out the other side, and the body that encased her spirit was the evidence of her journey. It would have been untrue to say that she looked good. "Looking good" had always escaped Maggie. What *was* true was that she looked extraordinary—her body constructed like a suspension bridge, a complex system of levers and struts, of steel hawsers and massive concrete supports. It looked as if it could perform any task that the most inventive of masters could dream up. It had endured, and it would endure. When she and Lisa had started the old gym on Clematis she had never dreamed it would develop into this. Lisa had left, but Maggie had not lost the faith, and in the exercise explosion of the following years she had followed the developing trends and started a few of her own, and now the gym had a nationwide reputation to match its height. And so did she. Now, there was young Christie Stansfield in her class. Bobby's girl. The one who should have had Lisa for her mother.

Lisa Starr. Lisa Blass. Her Lisa. A superstar now, shining brightly in the firmament of the highest society as Maggie had always known she would. They had grown apart, but Maggie still loved her. Her memory. Her brave spirit. Her seemingly endless zest for life. They saw each other occasionally, at the bigger parties, and they would both try to pretend that nothing had changed, while each knew that everything had. It was a different Lisa now, and probably a different Maggie too, but mainly a different Lisa. The charm was there, the incredible beauty—but the warmth was gone—all snuffed out by the bitter frost of too much heartache. The ice had touched poor Lisa's soul, and it had killed the part of her that Maggie had loved the most.

Maggie forced herself back to the here and now. In front of her the class members were hurting, losing themselves in the delicious pain, their wet faces and steaming bodies crying out for the relief that another part of them didn't want. She should commune with them as they indulged in the sacrament of physicality. She should be with them as they suffered in the name of beauty.

"Come with me, you guys. Come with me all the way. Lose your minds. *Become* your bodies."

325

Exercise was getting metaphysical these days.

Suddenly in the midst of the frenetic activity Christie experienced the quietness of the hurricane's eye. Scott was leaning in the doorway, his eyes lazily flicking over the seething mass of prime feminine flesh, his mouth parted in a half smile—of patronization? of shyness? It was difficult to tell. He looked as if he had come straight from the beach. The salt was still all over him, and the dirty gray T-shirt and baggy white canvas trousers had quite obviously spent long weeks in the back of the vintage Le Baron ragtop he always drove. That was all part of him. The "to-hell-with everybody" attitude that raised the temperature of Christie's teenage dreams. As she watched him his eyes found her, and the flush on her already hot cheeks deepened as she felt the reality of what had been a few minutes before only imagination. She tried a smile. It was not returned, but he nodded to her.

"Finish your business," his look seemed to say. "You're doing something important. Don't let me distract you. I wouldn't give you a second thought if I was riding a wave."

Christie dropped her head in acknowledgment of the silent rebuke. Of course he was right. She tried to concentrate on the job at hand.

"Okay, you guys. On your backs now. Let's work away those buns."

Christie groaned inwardly. Oh God. Why did *this* exercise have to come now? She arched her back and thrust her pelvis into the air, the pink thong plastered tight against her wide-open vagina, the outermost blond hairs hardly hidden by the skimpy material.

"Come on now, squeeze it out, and in double time now, and one and two and one and two . . ."

She closed her eyes to hide her embarrassment, and tried to forget where she was, and who was there. But the movement kept reminding her. She was making love to the air. There was no other interpretation of the action. The only thing lacking was Scott on top of her, and try as she might she couldn't get that awesome thought out of her mind.

Inside her the funny feeling grew and grew. The more she rejected it, the stronger it became. She should stop, but she couldn't do that. So desperately uncool.

"Push upward, you guys. Go for it. Make it work for you."

Christie did as she was told, and as her buttocks alternately contracted and relaxed the strange tingling sensation ran up and down the inside of her long brown thighs. Oh no. Not now. Not here. That would be just totally impossible.

She opened her eyes. Could the reality stop it happening?

Scott had moved. He was no longer in the doorway. He was at the side of the gym, close to her, and there was an odd faraway look in his eyes as he peered intently at the all but naked body that thrust and reared at him.

She flicked her tongue nervously over her lips and tried a half smile that didn't quite work.

Which was the exact moment she saw it.

There, framed in the gunsight of her thighs, sitting at the bottom of the deep V of her crotch and barely ten feet away, was the sight that put her way over the top. Inside the crumpled white trousers Scott Blass was rock hard.

Christie let out a little gasp of surprise at the thing that was happening to her. She had time to close her eyes, and then she lost the coordination altogether. Her legs froze, her back locked, and her mind stopped.

"Ohhhhhhhhhhhhhhh, dear," she heard somebody, who might easily have been herself, exclaim.

She sat down hard, allowing her bottom to whack into the boards in a forlorn attempt to camouflage the obvious, but the event inside her was undeterred. It had a life of its own now. It wouldn't answer to anybody. In the velvet underground it held sway, living its terrible moment to the full, singing its beautiful, crazy song. Gripped by the shuddering madness she could not control, Christie sunbathed on the bean-bag cloud of awkward ecstasy, as she played host to the transient visitor. Invisible, secret, it lived out its brief moment of cosmic time, selfish, unrepentant, unashamed. And then, at last it was gone, leaving nothing behind but the trace of memory . . . and, more pressing, the growing legacy of wet desire on the pink material that shielded her pulsating core from the outside world.

When she opened her eyes Scott was staring directly at it. It was the first secret they had shared. It would not be the last.

For three quarters of a century the Paramount had been a Palm Beach landmark. First a theater, and then for years the only cinema in town, it had fallen into disrepair in the sixties and seventies. But now it was back. Restored to its former glory, and by the light of its flickering screen it was impossible to miss the doe-eyed devotion beaming out from Christie Stansfield's face. Like a billion girls before her she snaked her hand out across the lush seat and wormed it gently into Scott's. Three short whirlwind weeks hovering on the brink of ecstasy had all but destroyed her resolve, and she knew that she was about to fall. Maybe tonight. Maybe tomorrow. She wasn't in love, she was obsessed. It was a grand passion, the headlong romantic involvement of adolescence, quivering, magnificent, awesome in its force and power. One by one, the guiding lights of her life were being flooded out by the intensity of the gleaming vision—the meeting of body and soul in the longed-for flesh dance that she had so far resisted. Perhaps later it would happen. On the floodlit beach where he had promised to take her after the movie. Whatever. Already the cloak of her firm personal morality, worn as always on her sleeve for the world to see, was wearing thin. Soon the threadbare garment would protect her from herself no more, and she would be free, free to feel, to enjoy, to want and to need.

She looked up at the beautiful face and refused to see the cruelty there, preferring to construe it as the capricious strength of the young at heart. Scott would look after her in her moment of weakness. He would know what to do. He would not let her down. God, she worshiped him. Never before had she seen such a specimen, never in her polite and correct world where everything was predictable, all was safe. Scott, like some wonderful creature from lost Atlantis, had come to her out of the sea with his easy laughter and his daring. Every emotion was alive, vibrant, a reaction to stimulus never its effect. First of course there was the surfing and the single-minded addiction to excellence that went with it. Christie, surrounded always by friends who worked hard at their affectation of boredom, found that enthusiasm the biggest turn-on of all. That, and the body that went with it, the godlike outer shell that was the instrument of his power over the sea.

But there was so much more. The rough friends from the mainland, and the even rougher places he would take her in the early hours when sedate Palm Beach slept. In the tough bars of Old Okeechobee, and in the hookers' haunts of Riviera Beach, Christie had her eyes opened for the first time to the throbbing reality of the other half's life-style. She had been plunged into the midst of Dante's inferno, but with Scott at her side she had felt as safe as in the smooth shiny pews of Bethesda-by-the-Sea. He knew them all, and not as some rich, barely tolerated outsider. He was one of them, at ease with their jokes, happy with their gestures, sharing effortlessly their accents and their prejudices. And when in the dark of the night tempers frayed and minds bent and unwise hands reached for her, his fists would clench and his jaw would set as the creatures of the twilight zone saw the error of their ways. She had felt like a medieval princess on the arm of her champion, deliciously safe in the midst of danger, like watching the snow fall against the windowpane while sitting snugly by a big log fire.

It had been several days before she had found out who he was, and by that stage she had bitten deep on his hook. Scott Blass. Lisa Blass's son. The son of her mother's enemy. Briefly there had been a moral dilemma. Was it disloyal to go out with him? Should she indulge herself in her mother's vendetta against her father's old flame? The baby-blue eyes that looked so like her own had made up her mind. The sins of the fathers and mothers *shouldn't* be visited on the children. Anyway, Scott didn't seem to have inherited the hatred. He knew she was a Stansfield, and was neither impressed nor put off. She had, however, made one concession to pragmatism. She had avoided telling her mother the identity of her persistent date. Jo-Anne, steadfastly self-centered and globally uninterested in the doings of others, hadn't bothered to ask anyway.

On the sidewalk outside the Paramount Scott took her hand again. He didn't speak. He didn't have to. In the warm still of the scented night they walked down Seminole Avenue to the beach. They slipped off their shoes when they reached the sand and looked up at the three-quarter moon. Christie's firm chin obeyed the command of Scott's forefinger, her eyes locked onto his in the moonlight, and her warm, uncertain breath bathed his face with its fresh fragrance. She felt her lips part, dry like the rustling fronds of the palms above. Soon he would kiss her and transfuse his wetness into her, bringing dampness and fertility to the desert of her longing. What was there in the eyes of this boy she had learned to love so completely? Was it sadness, a melancholy loneliness all mixed up with the hunger of desire? If so, she wanted to satisfy all his yearnings. She wanted to make him whole and to fill the void in his soul of which his eyes so eloquently spoke, to banish the loneliness, to slake the physical appetite with the generous gift of her own young body.

Christie reached around the thin waist and she pulled him in toward her, feeling the startling hardness of him, pushing shamelessly against it. Still he didn't kiss her. He watched her, strange emotions surging like wild surf behind the twin curtains of his eyes. Why did he hesitate?

Then he moved down toward her, tenderly, slowly, irresistibly. Christie closed her eyes and heard herself moan as she readied to receive him. With all her might she focused on her lips. That would be the first touch, the first feel of him.

His lips arrived on hers as uncertain strangers, curious, polite, attentive, tentative. They seemed at first to hover in space, like a humming bird at the mouth of a wide-open flower. Then, dry and warm, they nuzzled in. Up and down Christie's skin the feeling played over her, plucking at her, caressing her with its glorious subtlety and power. She could feel it in the throbbing tautness of her nipples, feel it crawling over the tight skin of her full buttocks, feel it soft, warm, and liquid deep between her legs. And then Scott's tongue made her mouth his. Wise and willful, it took her with its confident, infinitely knowledgeable touch, and the long shuddering sigh it pulled from her was eloquent testimony to its skill. Christie opened her eyes and the stars rushed in, as Scott, gentle no more, moved with the impatience of adolescent lust, his mouth darting at hers, devouring it, savoring it, as it tried to draw her lips, her tongue, her teeth into the heart of passion's hurricane.

Christie fought back with him. He wanted her mouth. She wanted him so desperately to have it. He wanted her taste. Her taste was his.

Scott's hands moved urgently behind her back until they found the skin they sought. He eased the plain white T-shirt away from the waist of the blue jeans and ran his fingers softly up the warm skin of Christie's back, searching for the strap of the bra that wasn't there.

Slowly he sank down to the sand, kneeling, as if in church, in front of her. Then, firmly he drew her down, too. With reverence, his hands lifted the soft cotton, unveiling her, exposing her, thrusting her into the no-man's land of nakedness, the place from which there was no turning back.

Scott looked down at his gift. Proud, almost defiant, Christie stared back at him as she tried to tell him with her eyes that she belonged to him, that she would not fight him, that her will was intertwined with his as their lips had been short seconds before. The strength of her emotion was already too great for fear, but uncertainty hovered uneasily in the still night air. Her breasts were small. Perfect, firm, but very far from large. Would Scott mind? God Almighty, could he see them *throb?*

In answer to the unspoken question Scott leaned forward. He took each hot, tense breast into the palms of his hands and for what seemed like an age he communed with their urgent fullness as if the desire that coursed in them was a palpable thing, stiff and alive with the energy of passion.

Then he moved into them, his tongue anxious for each pink nipple, for its soft innocence, and Christie's heart stopped as his mouth enclosed it. Her fingers found the back of his neck, and she held him close like a suckling child as she fed him the nourishment of her young body, matching his desire with the feverish intensity of her own. She ran her fingers through the blond hair, star of her dreams and crowning glory of her lover, and below, inside her, the waterfall of need roared and foamed. Christie heard her body's voice, shrill and wonderful, as it told her what was about to happen. She wasn't ready for it. She could hardly believe it. But it was a fact. Along the inside of her thighs the express train screamed its approach, and in her lower stomach the avalanche rumbled its advance warning. Her mind was a mere spectator to the glorious accident that was about to happen as the irresistible force and the immovable object prepared for their earth-shattering union. There was no time to warn Scott. Hardly time to ready herself. Just time to shout out to the stars and to the sky and to the sand of the deserted beach the mystical intensity of her experience.

Scott heard the messages of her body as inside his mouth the once-small nipple bucked and reared like some frightened colt, filling his mouth with its suddenly compromised sweet innocence. He knew what would happen and he wanted it. Through the tropical storm of her orgasm he held on to her, his arms around her as she shuddered her satisfaction. Wet and violent, vibrating with its raw energy, Christie's climax rocked on and on, and through the torrential chaos of feeling she knew but one thing. She was empty and she wanted to be filled.

In the aftermath of orgasm Christie felt the first impossible flutterings of panic. Had she frightened him away? Had her inexperienced lack of control undone his desire? She had to know. Had to save the moment that every atom of her body so feverishly wanted. With bold hands she reached for him, an innocent no more. Her fumbling fingers found the hardness, found the way to expose it, found the vision of which she had dreamed. In wonder she felt it, and as she willed it to take her, her fingers communicated their rampant longing.

She lay back on the sand and undid the belt of her tight blue jeans, pushing them down over the full hips, her panties peeled away by the hard denim to reveal the blond secret, glistening in the moon's pale light. In her moment of total abandonment came the flash of self-knowledge. Little Christie Stansfield. Round and sweet. Pretty and pure. Everybody's American dream. Lying on the sand wracked by lust. Demanding, screaming to be entered, to be filled up with a young boy's desire.

Above her Scott's body blotted out the sky. And then, quite suddenly, Christie saw the thing that should not be there. In the eyes, around the mouth, was the outline trace of the inappropriate emotion. For one single second she saw it—triumph? cruel victory? the flickering flame of hate?—and then it was gone. Inside her mind the warning bells clanged their alarm, and intellect's forces mobilized to explain the intuition. Then there it was. The knowledge. This was wrong. Deeply and fundamentally wrong. Something she and he would regret forever. A crime against the ocean, the fragrant air, against the star-spangled sky.

But it was far too late. Already there was the searing pain, the feel of the warm red blood on her thigh, and already there was the siren cry of physical desire blotting out all thought, all sense, all prudence. And at the very moment she knew she had sinned against God in His heaven, Christie Stansfield reached out to her lover and pushed her hips off the sand, forcing him deep into her body, and deeper into her mind.

Jo-Anne stretched herself like some sleepy but contented cat on the white wicker chaise longue. Three times a week for the last three weeks she had experienced a beautiful dream and today she would dream again. This young boy had it all. He was not too proud to learn; he was obedient; he had stamina. For two blissful hours—Mondays, Wednesdays, and Fridays—he had made clock-work love to her in the early afternoon. He had been clean as a whistle, hadn't tried to hustle her for bread, and hadn't even both-ered to ask her name. That, and a gravity-defying prick on the body of an Adonis, made him very special indeed. Now, for some reason, there was to be a change in the established pattern. He was coming over to "do the pool" on a Saturday, and at three thirty rather than the usual two o'clock. He had made a point of telling her, and Jo-Anne had made a point of listening. Who knew, maybe he had an earlier appointment farther down the beach. Well, as long as he was all tanked up and ready to go, who cared?

Jo-Anne flicked moodily through *House and Garden* and sipped petulantly on a spritzer. Twelve o'clock. Three and a half hours to go. Patience had never been her strongest suit. She looked around for somebody to irritate. Christie, looking pensive in the shallow end, would do. Damn! She'd almost forgotten. She'd have to get rid of Christie somehow. Usually she was safely tucked away on Worth Avenue, but on the weekend if the weather was good she tended to hang out poolside.

"What on earth is the matter with you these days, Christie? You're either manic or in the depths of despair. Don't say you're in love or something boring like that."

Christie's laugh was totally devoid of humor. Scott hadn't called for twenty-four hours, and it had been a very bad day indeed. Her mother's remark hadn't helped. But then her mother's remarks seldom did. It wasn't Jo-Anne's fault, and Christie was sure she didn't mean to be unkind. It was just that she had the unhappy knack of sowing little seeds of unpleasantness every time she opened her mouth.

She dunked her shoulders beneath the still surface of the pool as she planned her reply. "Maybe I am," she said mysteriously. Christ! How had she managed a lie like that. If love was an illness then she was ringing the doorbell at the Pearly Gates. She'd never known anything like this roller-coaster ride. Scott Blass was a nuclear explosion of pure wonder who had atomized her former world and left her oscillating frantically between the sumptuous delights of heaven and burning daggers of the most dreadful hell.

"Well, if you are, then I suggest you enjoy it and don't forget to take the pill. Can't think why you have to look so damn miserable."

The surfer stud hadn't made *her* miserable. Just a bit irritated that he couldn't have made it a little bit earlier than three thirty.

Christie groaned inwardly. Great! A mother's concern for a much-loved daughter. But she had more important things on her mind than her mother's lack of maternal affection. There was only one person on this earth whose affection at this moment she craved, and he hadn't picked up the telephone to tell her he loved her. A shuddering communion on the sand, followed by the silence of the grave. It was driving her quietly mad.

The butler's voice, coldly formal, came to her rescue. "Miss Christie. There's a telephone call for you. A gentleman who wouldn't leave his name. Would you like to take the call?"

Christie was out of the pool.

The butler passed over the cordless telephone as if it were the baton in a relay race.

"Hello." Christie panted the word. Her heart prayed it wasn't a junk call—a time share in Boynton Beach, the man from the Pru.

"Christie, this is Scott. Can you talk?"

"Sort of. Oh, I'm so glad you called."

"Listen, I need to see you."

"I need to see *you*."

"What about this afternoon?"

"Wonderful. Where? When?"

"Can you meet me at your cabana? Just after four o'clock. Not before."

"I guess so. What a funny place. Yes, sure, that's fine. I want to see you so much."

"Okay. Look, I've got to rush, but see you then. After four. Remember."

Christie flicked the switch on the telephone as her heart took flight.

Her mother's voice failed completely to dampen her soaring spirits. "I *suppose* that was Captain Fantastic," she said with all the sarcasm she could muster.

"You'd better believe it," bubbled Christie.

And then there was a silence, as mother and daughter retreated to their own private worlds. So much anticipation to be enjoyed. Waiting for three thirty. Waiting for four.

Christie wasn't sure if she really wanted to die, but life had failed her and death couldn't be worse. She looked down at the big blown-up photograph of Scott on his surfboard, riding the North End rollers. She'd loved him then—so very, very much. And now despite the horror she had witnessed, despite the incredible, premeditated cruelty of what he had done, she loved him still. She reached out for the bottle and popped another of the yellow-and-black pills into her mouth. How many was that. Ten? Fifteen? She'd lost count, the bottle blurred through the tears. The celluloid of the photograph already wet with her grief.

In her mind once again the dreadful movie played. The open door. Calling out his name. Hearing something. Seeing it. He'd said just after four. He'd wanted her there. Wanted her to be his audience of one as he had broken her heart and expelled her from his life. Never before had she contemplated such wickedness. It seemed as if the naked force of evil had been unleashed, that it was washing over her, polluting her with its terrible stench. For a second she had stood there unable to believe her eyes. Her mother's back had been toward her, Scott's hands on her naked buttocks. Over Jo-Anne's shoulders, his eyes burning with the awesome mixture of hatred and cruel triumph, Scott's face had stared haughtily into hers. For long seconds she had endured the horrendous vision as she tried to understand it. But Scott's expression said it all, and it was more, far more, than she could stand.

Letting out her cry of anguish she had rushed from that terrible place. She had run through the house as the tears came and her wild mind tried ineffectually to handle the horror. The bottle of pills from her mother's cabinet. A can of soda from the fridge. The photograph from her room. The car keys from the hall table. Did one need anything else for a trip to eternity?

Through blurred eyes she had driven through the gates and made the right turn toward the North Inlet. The sparkling sea was calm that day, mocking her sorrow with its blue tranquillity, hinting at the peace which now she would attempt to find. She would need a quiet street.

Here, outside a storm-shuttered house on Arabian, she had found the spot that would be her springboard to a kinder world. They would find Christie Stansfield asleep forever, and nobody would know what had made her want to die. That much she would give them, for even now she wanted no harm for the mother she loved and the boy she idolized. No note. No last testament to turn their lives upside down at the hands of her avenging father.

"Oh, dad," she said aloud in the emptiness. "I love you so much. Don't be sad for me."

The bottle was empty now, but still the sleepiness wouldn't come. Had she taken enough? There was no way of knowing. It was a giant gamble, and one which she didn't care if she won or lost. She didn't even know what winning would be, or what it would be to lose. She just knew that things would change after this.

And then the still small voice spoke to her. Firm, insistent, it sent out its messages to her hands and feet. In response, the ignition key was turned and the engine fired. In response, her feet pushed down on the accelerator and her fingers found the gear stick. She had to do it. She had to save him from the evil in his soul. She had to protect him from the guilt that would surely follow from his deed. It was something atavistic. She was dying but it was

Scott who needed help. He had been possessed, his wonderful mind and body hijacked by an alien invader. He needed desperately to be saved from himself. And there was nobody else on earth but her to do it.

Paradoxically as she found her resolve the dust storm of sleep blew toward her, and she felt the numbness as its grains touched her. It called to her at the moment she had stopped up her ears to its previously desired voice, and now she had to fight against it. She opened the windows of the car, flicked the air fan onto full blast, and turned on the radio for stimulus to her suddenly sluggish mind. How many times had she driven this coast road? She thanked God for that now, for it looked as if literally she might have to negotiate it in her sleep. Would Scott be there? Thrown out by her mother in the anger of her shame. If not she would wait. Wait outside the door of the cottage in the grounds of the Blass house where he lived. Perhaps he would find her. Asleep on the grass. Gone from his world. Her death the shock that would exorcise his demons and allow the kindness that she loved to own him once more.

She hardly made the left on Barton and narrowly missed the gatepost of the Blass home, but the adrenaline surge counterattacked sleep's vanguard when she saw his much-loved Le Baron in the drive.

Scott slumped into the big armchair and tried to get a hold on his emotions. He'd done it. His dreadful plan had worked. He'd struck a blow against the Stansfields from which their family was unlikely to recover. Mother and daughter had shared his body, the one casually, the other with the shuddering intensity of first love. Christie would never forgive Jo-Anne. Neither, when she told him, would her father. At the very least there would be divorce. Almost certainly violence. Yes, he had confounded his mother's enemies and cast them down into the pit. For that she would have to be grateful. For that she would have to take notice of him. For that she would have to love him.

He drank deep on the dark beaker of Scotch. This was the mo-

ment of triumph. But it didn't feel like it. Again and again the
stricken face swam before his eyes, haunting in the beauty of its
sadness. Christie had been so very good. She had given herself to
him—trusting, believing in him deeply, throbbingly in love.
Shamelessly he had built her passion and kindled the fires of her
devotion. He had laughed with her and chided her. He had taught
her and flattered her. And then, on the moonlit beach he had taken
her virginity and locked up her soul. To do what? To gain the love
of a mother who was a stranger. For revenge against an innocent
for some ancient and unknown wrong. The whiskey circulated in
his mind but it didn't drown the whispering voices of guilt. He had
exploded into her quiet, well-ordered world like a psychopathic
killer, and he had wreaked havoc upon her and those she loved.
There was no good in it. No good in him.

Outside the window the dusk was gathering and the lights of the
main house were coming on one by one. Soon it would be time for
the bars and the rock clubs. Lauderdale? Boca? But the bars without Christie. Without the fresh-faced angel to show around. To
show off. Even when setting her up, he hadn't been able to dislike
her. There had been something about her, something vulnerable
and yet so strong, reassuring, and strangely familiar.

The doorbell rang and didn't stop ringing.

She was the very last person he had expected to see.

Her tear-stained face was deathly pale, and the beads of sweat
stood out like dewdrops on the once-proud forehead. The usually
wide-open eyes were hooded with lids made heavy by the forces
of sleep, and as he opened the door to her she stumbled in the
entrance. Christie's voice was slurred when she spoke and Scott
could barely make out the words. "Scott. Help me . . . I took
some pills." They were her last words to him.

Taking one step forward she collapsed unconscious into his
arms.

In the white-walled emergency room of the Good Sam, the atmosphere was thick with the emotion of controlled panic. It was
all action and no words. The white-uniformed nurses and fraught

doctors were alone in their own world of dripping IV bags and life-support systems, priests of their own scientific religion muttering the jargon of their trade, oblivious to the desperation in Scott's heart and the wild tears in his eyes. Normal saline, Ryle's tubes, forced alkaline diuresis—that was what they cared about, not Christie, all alone in the darkness of her coma. Scott hovered on the brink of the life-and-death struggle—supremely ineffectual, desperately affected. Nobody seemed to mind that he was there on the periphery of the action. They were too busy for that. And so he watched the battle helplessly as the experts fought to save Christie's life.

Earlier, as he had rushed through the swinging doors with Christie in his arms, he had, briefly, a role to play. They had sat him down and tried to draw from him a coherent story of what had happened. In their cold eyes he could see that they had done all this before. Teenage suicide. The American epidemic. This would be the boyfriend. The unconscious girl would be his lover. His would-be lover. His ex-lover. The permutations were infinite, but they had been interested in only three things. What type and quantity of tablets had she taken? When had she swallowed them? For how long had she been unconscious? As Scott had tried to tell them they had hung on his every word, but the second they discovered that he did not know the answer to the first vital question they had discarded him like yesterday's newspaper.

The young doctor, harassed and unkempt, was thinking aloud. "We have arrhythmias on the EKG now. Could this be tricyclics?" Nobody answered. "Was she on antidepressants? For God's sake, somebody ask the boyfriend. Did she have access to antidepressants?"

The note of exasperation communicated itself to the team. "Stomach contents are on the way to the lab now. We should have an answer in ten minutes."

"Ten minutes and it'll be blowing in the wind. I'm getting ventricular tachycardia here. Get some lidocaine into the drip site, Sue, fifty-milligram bolus, and get another syringe with the same dose ready in case we need it. We've got sodium bicarb ready. Okay? What did the boyfriend say about the antidepressants?"

The boyfriend in his agony of ignorance had nothing to say.

Christie hadn't been depressed until he'd crumpled her up like a blank sheet of paper. Maybe Jo-Anne had been on that sort of medication. It was more than unlikely that Senator Stansfield had.

"I just don't know. God. I don't know," he managed in despair as the accusing and questioning eyes fixed on him.

"How is she? Is she going to be all right?" he pleaded to the now deaf ears. But he was once again the invisible man. For now he could bleat out his remorse all by himself.

"Hit her with the lido again. This isn't working. Give me a BP."

"I'm getting seventy over fifty."

"Shit, I think this one's going. Hook her up to the ventilator. Come on, *shift* it. Is the DC converter ready? Hand me that electrode jelly, Sue. Tom, watch that EKG readout like a hawk. The moment we get ventricular fib we give her a squirt of juice. Okay?"

"I can't hear diastolic now. BP's going down out of sight."

Scott's heart felt like it was in worse shape than Christie's. He didn't understand most of what was being said, but there was no mistaking the urgency of the action. Someone was pushing a tube down Christie's throat, another hand was fiddling frantically with the knob controlling the IV inflow, and a nurse was winding at the lever that raised the end of the bed.

"Don't go, baby. Hang on in there. You can make it." The doctor was murmuring to himself again, willing the lidocaine to bite, to calm the wriggling, uncoordinated heart. Unless it could regain its smooth pumping action, the pressure of the blood in the arteries would fall away and the vital heart muscle would be starved of oxygen.

"She's so young," said somebody.

"Are we all plugged in?"

"Damn, I'm getting VF now. The trace is all over the place."

"BP unrecordable."

"Okay, folks, let's go for it. DC countershock. Four hundred watt-seconds."

In dumb horror Scott watched as Christie flirted with death. She was dying. All but dead, and he'd killed her. And that made him the world's most repulsive creature. Please, God, let her live. And now as the tears rolled down his cheeks he sank to his knees in prayer as around him the doctors hustled and the nurses ran.

"Please, God. Please, God," he heard himself say out loud to the uncomprehending white walls as the doctor leaned over Christie's proud pale breast with the electrodes.

"Ready everyone. Stand back."

Scott was hardly aware of Christie's body as it bucked and reared under the current from the defibrillator. He was talking to God. Pleading, promising, bargaining.

"What are you getting, Tom? Still VF?"

"Yes."

"We'll go again."

Again he leaned forward to administer the crude antidote. Again Christie's small body reeled under the shock.

"That's better. I'm seeing sinus rhythm. She's flipped back into sinus. Brilliant. *Brilliant!*"

"Are you getting pressure?"

"There's a few millimeters of mercury now. Yup, pressure's coming back."

"Goddamn. She nearly went there. That was *close.*"

"All the vital signs are stabilizing now. BP's coming up nicely. Rhythm looks rock solid. Bradycardia of fifty."

Shakily Scott stood up. The atmosphere had changed. The room was lighter. The cloven hoofs of the Horseman had clattered away. For the moment his prayers had been answered, but it was going to be a long night.

They had thrown him out at midnight with the consolation prize that Christie would make it, but mouths had gone all hard when he had pleaded to be able to see her. They hadn't wanted his desperate need for forgiveness to be satisfied, and already all sorts of pictures were beginning to emerge. This was a *Stansfield* daughter, while the boy looked like some cheap beach bum. The mother was on her way. Somebody was trying to contact the senator in Ohio. It was far better that this bit player be swept out into the wings before the principal actors arrived. In the rush nobody had even bothered to ask his name.

341

On the fetid West Palm streets Scott had been left alone with his relief, alone with his guilt, alone with his self-hatred. He had walked along the shores of the lake and tried to understand the things that had happened to him, the thing he had allowed himself to become. There had been no answers to the fevered questions. He had slipped into the role of monster with the ease of a quick-change artist. The motivation had been enough. To please his mother. To gain her love. But now in the cold reality of the warm night the force to action looked a sad, pathetic thing. He had always believed that he was unworthy of love, but Christie had loved him. Loved him enough to die if she couldn't have him.

Perhaps all along there had been another explanation, even now scarcely perceived, hardly perceivable. Maybe, just maybe, the fault was with his mother. Was it the void in *her* heart that had caused so much hatred, so much insecurity, and so much pain? Even now the thought was almost too hot to handle.

Scott wanted desperately to escape the war that raged within him and to hide from the unhappy emotions that chased him. There was a time-honored method of doing just that.

Roxy's Bar. In the brash new world of hustling West Palm Beach, where the buildings now fought each other for a patch of the sky to scrape, few things remained the same. Roxy's and its drink-sodden owner Willie Boy Willis were two that had. Willie, who had known his mother and her family in the days before she had married his father, monosyllabic Willie of the strange looks and the buttoned-up mouth. He would be a good enough partner for a few hours of oblivion.

In the dimly lit innards of Roxy's, Willie Boy's welcome was warm. As usual he inhabited the no-man's-land between drunkenness and sobriety that seemed to be the stamping ground of the genuine alcoholic. His lopsided grin and his filthy face, bemused and fuddled by the years of booze, tried to make sense of Scott's presence.

"Hi, Scottie boy. What brings you down here? Ain't seen you in months. You been neglectin' ol' friends?"

It was a friendly greeting. On the whole, Willie Boy was a friendly soul. Though sometimes, toward closing time, he could turn mean. Tonight, however, Scott was in no mood for charity.

Already a dreadful anger, directed at himself, was beginning to form within him. There was more than enough to spill over.

"I haven't been neglecting anyone," he said shortly. "Hit me with a big Jack Daniel's, and, Willie, I mean *big*."

Willie Boy let it go. Scott wasn't usually so touchy. Pretty easy-going in the main. Still, everyone was entitled to a bad mood from time to time.

He reached for the bottle of bourbon and poured a generous measure into a far from clean glass.

"I said *big*, Willie." Scott's voice was tense. He'd had about as much as he could take. The pain needed anesthetic. Now.

Willie Boy felt the burst of irritation within him. Scott was pushing it. Usually he came in Roxy's with some surfers. He talked rough and joked rough like a regular guy. But today he seemed all Palm Beach. All tight-assed. Like some stuck-up rich kid. He kept pouring, but he couldn't resist the dig. "Big drink for a big man. Eh, Scottie?"

"What's that supposed to mean?" Anything to avoid thinking about himself. Any distraction. The drink. An argument. Anything.

"Means what you want it to mean."

Willie leered across the polished bar. Lines like these he'd exchanged a million times before. A few times a week there were fights in Roxy's. Some you won. Some you didn't. With Jack Kent and with Tommy Starr the trick had always been to apologize. There wouldn't be any need for that tonight.

"Means you talk a lot of shit, man," said Scott nastily, taking a long pull at the bourbon.

Willie Boy's narrow eyes narrowed further. The punk. The little stuck-up punk. He ought to slam him all around the room. But he looked pretty fit, and he was obviously pretty mean. And then, quite suddenly, the final straw descended on Willie Boy Willis's long suffering back. He'd always been a loser, a drunk. A prisoner in the cellar of life, condemned to scratch out his existence amid the sawdust, the sweat, and the beer. People came in through the door and pissed on him in his misery. Men like Jack Kent who'd treated him like the scum he knew he was. Men like Tommy Starr, who'd been too gentle to tell him what he was but who'd allowed the truth to shine out of his eyes. Women like Lisa Starr who'd pretended he was her friend until she'd passed across the bridge into glory. And now this. This wet-behind-the-ears preppy—coming on like a great big man and trying to push poor old Willie Boy around as his grandfather had in days gone by. Well, he shouldn't have done that. There were reasons why he'd regret it. Two mighty big reasons. And they weren't called fists.

The smile split Willie Boy's face from ear to ear. Most of his mind was gone now, all shot to pieces by the drink. But there were a couple of things he knew. A couple of little time bombs ticking away in the remains of his brain. They wouldn't last forever. Maybe he'd forget them. Maybe they'd melt when the liver went. He'd always thought of the bartender's role as being like the priest's. You heard everything, spoke nothing. But that was foolish, wasn't it? Nobody thanked you for keeping their confidence. They despised you for it and treated you like shit. Like young Scott was now.

He leaned across the bar. "How's that flashy father of yours?"

Scott waved his hand dismissively. Willie Boy was clearly out of it. His brains were a jar of pickles. It wouldn't even be diverting to fight with him. "Oh, forget it, Willie Boy. My old man's been dead for years. Leave it alone."

"He ain't."

Scott looked up. There had been something about the triumphant tone of Willie Boy's voice. It was matched by the triumphant smile that he now saw on Willie Boy's face. "Come on, Willie. Drink up and shut up. I don't feel like all this bad-vibe rap."

When Scott spoke there was uncertainty in his voice. Vernon Blass was just a name to him. He was vaguely proud of being a Blass and had often wondered about his father, but somehow it had been no big deal not having one around. It was his mother who had bestrode his world like a colossus. From the pictures and the stories, he had been able to piece together a portrait of a blemished Palm Beacher who, as a man, had been worse than some but better than others. In one area, however, his father had showed himself to be a total winner, and it was the only one that mattered. He had married Lisa Starr.

Willie's smile was cunning now. Sly and evil. He was going to go for it. He could feel it inside. He was going to right the wrongs. Wrong the rights.

Lisa Starr, who'd been his friend until she'd walked across the water. Lisa Blass, queen of the most successful publishing company in the land. Lisa loaded, loaded Lisa. She never came down to Roxy's. Old friends abandoned, old memories conveniently forgotten. No handouts. Nothing. But he knew her secret, and he knew the secret she didn't know. All his miserable life he had kept a secret, and for what? So that they would be boxed with him? Yeah, that would suit them all. The whole frigging lot of them. He had been loyal. He had kept his promise to Tommy Starr. And for what? So that he could die without a pot to piss in or the window to throw it out of? Now this rich kid could come in here and patronize him. Willie, who knew it all. Who knew the whole stinking rotten truth.

"I ain't rubbishing you, Scott, boy. I just wondered if you was strong 'nough for a bit of truth to go with that bourbon. Truth 'bout your old man, an' your mom."

"What 'truth'?" Suddenly the warm fire in his stomach wasn't from the alcohol alone.

Across the polished bar there was wickedness in the drink-sodden eyes. "Well, for one thing, you ain't no right to call yourself Blass."

Willie paused briefly before plowing on. He leaned both gnarled hands on the shining wood, to catch the effect of his words. Through the swirling mists, Scott's face seemed to come and go. One thing was clear as it clicked in and out of focus. It had gone white.

Through his bent mind Willie tried to work out the advisability of what he was about to do. It could still be a joke. Just. The alcohol talking. But his tongue was already out of control. The hell with it. Screw 'em all. Everyone had always screwed *him*. They'd never reckoned poor ol' Willie Boy. But late at night when the Bud had loosened them all up there wasn't much they'd been able to keep to themselves. Like that night with Tommy. The one he'd got all liquored up and tried to talk in riddles, with the tears streaming down his great big dirty face. Then there was Lisa. All those times in her little apartment when she liked him to tell the tales of the golden days. He'd known she was pregnant, known that she was carrying the Stansfield child who now stood before him across the glistening bar. He'd been sober when she'd talked of her love for

Bobby Stansfield. Sober enough to keep his mouth buttoned up tight on Tommy Starr's secret. Okay, so he had discouraged her. The likes of them never marry the likes of you. That sort of thing. But he hadn't expected their relationship to work, and it hadn't. When Stansfield threw her out she'd gone for Blass on the re-bound—and from that moment to this, West Palm, Willie Boy, and Roxy's Bar had been painted out of her life as if they had never existed.

"Yeah, Scott boy. Your last name's Stansfield. You're the sen-ator's son. Ha ha. Ain't that great? You're a rich bastard. Your mom had the hots for him, and when he didn't want to know, she gone and married ol' man Blass. Told me so herself. Never let you in on the secret, eh?''

Scott felt the room creeping all around him. Like an Indian around a cowboy's campfire, it seemed to come and go, circling, crawling about on the edge of vision, on the periphery of hearing. What was Willie Boy saying? He was drunk. But he had been his mother's friend. So often she had talked of him, and of her one-time friendship with this living link with the past, with those she had loved and lost. It wasn't the sort of thing you made up, drunk or sober, mad or sane. And it explained all sorts of things that were otherwise scarcely explicable. His beautiful mother in the arms of a man old enough to be her grandfather. The hatred for the Stans-fields and particularly for Jo-Anne. That could have stemmed from the jealousy of the jilted. His own looks. Blond and blue eyed like the Senator Stansfield of the glossy magazines. Like the baby blue of Christie's . . .

He took a step back from the bar as the world began to roar inside his head. Christie Stansfield. On the sand. Christie Stans-field, bucking and rearing under the current as they tried to start the heart he had stopped. Christie Stansfield, who looked so very much like him, and who loved him in such a strange, compelling way. His hand flew to his mouth, as the blood drained from his cheeks and his mouth sought the words that would express the dreadful feelings he felt. He had met her in anger, but immediately he had liked her. Only his terrible mission had blinded him to a truth that was trying to be told.

He took another step back from the messenger who was grinding to powder the remainder of his universe.

But, unbelievably, Willie Boy had not finished. His face was flushed with the enormity of what he was doing, the adrenaline wiping out temporarily the dulling effects of the alcohol. His voice was almost clear and soft as silk as he embarked on the second half of his roller-coaster ride into horror.

"Strangest thing is something even your mom didn't know. Mary-Ellen kept it from everyone 'cep poor Tommy. When she married him, she was carrying Lisa then. An' you know who was the real father? Ol' man Stansfield. Mary-Ellen worked in the house, an' he got her in the worst kind of trouble. Best thing Tommy ever did taking her on. Sure as hell I never would. But he told me that night, and he couldn't hold back the tears when he did. Never seen him cry before. He wanted her so bad he'd have had her under any circumstances, loved her that much."

Uncomprehending at first, then with the dawning of awareness, stark in their terror and hurt, Scott's eyes stared back at the bringer of the dreadful tidings.

He walked backward, stumbling over the leg of a chair, the feet of a customer. His hands reached behind him for the door to the street, and still his stricken eyes stayed locked on Willie's. Brothers and sisters. Happy families.

And as Willie Boy watched, sobered by the enormity of his act, the West Palm night swallowed Scott up.

20

All her life Jo-Anne had dreamed of getting there, but now that she had arrived she couldn't help wondering whether the arduous journey had been worth it. The view from the throne had certainly been better in fantasy than it was in reality, and the Jupiter Island Garden Club Bazaar, perhaps the most chic garage sale in the world, was the example that proved it all. Hobe Sound. The grandest place in America, bar none. Grander by far than Newport, effortlessly superior to Scottsdale, the social mecca that relegated such down-market towns as Beverly Hills and Palm Springs to the status of sniveling also-rans. Hobe Sound, nestling against the white sand of the arrogant Atlantic, was the most secret bastion of the oldest money, where privacy ruled, and where the American aristocracy hid from the world of television and newspapers, which the lesser mortals they despised so desperately sought.

It was a place of contradictions. Called Hobe Sound, it wasn't really that at all. It was the town of Jupiter Island, or rather the residential portion of it. The real Hobe Sound was across the electrically monitored bridge, a run-down place where the rest of Florida lived, and where the mighty went to pick up their mail: the inconvenience was minor compared to having those dreadful mail vans buzzing about to remind them of the real world from which "the Island" was their escape. Sand, sea, and seclusion for the two hundred Old Guard families who wintered here from New Year's Eve to March, hidden away in the four hundred mansions they preferred to call "places." Mellons, Adamses, Roosevelts nestled snugly in the refined and reverent silence of the scented Australian pines; Scrantons, Searles, and Olins cavorted with decorum around the side-by-side rectangular and kidney-shaped swimming pools of the Jupiter Island Club, a place so formidably upper class that it could dare such brave experimentation with good taste; Pierreponts, Fieldses, and Weyerhaeusers peered serenely over snipped lawns at their sour-faced gardeners as they dusted dustless pathways and tended immaculate orchids; Paysons, Lamonts, and Coleses sipped Scotch as they grumbled about servants and groused over the unsatisfactory behavior of grandsons and Democratic politicians.

"Can I get you something to drink, Jo-Anne? Some lemonade, perhaps?"

Laura Hornblower was suitably solicitous. After all, she was in charge of entertaining visiting royalty. The kingdom of Palm Beach had sent its reigning monarch on a state visit to the smaller but enormously prestigious one of Hobe Sound, and as aide-de-camp to the autocratic but enlightened despot who ruled it, Laura was working hard.

Jo-Anne looked unenthusiastic. Eleven o'clock in the morning and what she really needed was a shot of something much stronger. There in a nutshell was the difference between the two towns. Hobe Sound: tea, early risers, spartan ascetics, and wall-to-wall environmentalists. Palm Beach: booze, late nights—by Hobe Sound standards at least—hedonists, and achievers.

"Yes, wonderful. Thanks." Jo-Anne groaned inwardly. Power brought responsibility, at least, like now, when the visibility was high. God, how the hell was she going to get through this without a real drink?

The sun beat down with an unseasonal intensity over the sparse crowd, as they picked their way suspiciously through the stalls. There was more money here than in a medium-size South American nation, but they were still on the lookout for a bargain: some Percale sheets at fifty cents, an old wicker chair at two bucks, a wrought-iron table cheap at fifteen dollars. They didn't haggle, but they fingered and felt, relishing the pretense that they were shopping for a bargain. Making believe they were ordinary people. Later in the afternoon they would put the receipts for the things they had bought into a long-playing record sleeve or a shirt box, and in due course the grubby scraps of paper would make it to New York to the offices of Price, Waterhouse where, spread out on polished mahogany desks, they would be turned into tax deductions. Deduct five hundred thousand dollars for the donation to the

University of Virginia Law Library. Fifty cents for the used sheets. It was all an affectation, of course, but it meant everything.

The parsimony, the horror of ostentation were all part of the secret language by which these special people communicated. *National Enquirer* readers, brought up on a staple diet of trash people —actors and celebrities—thought that the point of being rich was to spend money extravagantly. But they had no conception of how the really rich behaved. Any one of these Hobe Sound plutocrats could have bought Elizabeth Taylor with the income on the income on the income, and yet they would carefully write each other a check for $1.50 if that was what they had won or lost at bridge and canasta. And they saved silver paper, and Christmas wrapping, and drove around in clean but old Ford "Woodies," leaving the navy-blue Rolls-Royces and the black vintage Bentleys in their commodious garages. Nobody "designed" their houses, their yachts were ancient, their food was plain, and their self-confidence was boundless.

Jo-Anne stared moodily at the nearest stall. She knew she should buy something. Nothing too expensive. That wouldn't do at all. Up here, Palm Beachers had a reputation for unacceptable extravagance. But something. After all, there were gimlet eyes guarding the cash box, the all-seeing eyes of the most powerful person in Hobe Sound—its undisputed ruler and social arbiter— Permelia Pryor Reed herself. Permelia Reed owned the Jupiter Island Club and decided exactly who was allowed through its hallowed portals. She ruled the small community with an iron hand, keeping it small, select, and upper class, and nobody who aspired to be anything but a hermit could afford to ignore her. Once, it was rumored, an unwise girl had worn a too-brief bikini at the club, and the beady eyes of the queen had descended upon her. A waiter had been dispatched with a pink cashmere sweater to cover her unseemly nakedness. Ever after, the story went, bad behavior in Hobe Sound was rewarded by the gift of a similar garment, a potent symbol of social death, as the white feather had been of cowardice. Nobody who received the feared cardigan had remained in Hobe Sound to live the life of the social "undead."

Jo-Anne wondered briefly about a set of beautifully molded brown wood coat hangers, bearing the carved initials G.D.H. That would just about do. But a bit bulky.

"Aren't they wonderful, Mrs. Stansfield? I can't stand the modern ones, can you?"

The Jupiter Island Garden Club member who manned the stall went through the motions. Wasn't it fun being a saleswoman—or salesperson as she supposed they were called nowadays. The largest single block holding in Smithkline was pretending to sell things. For charity, of course. The Hobe Sound Nature Center this year.

Jo-Anne murmured her acquiescence as the blue-blood carefully calculated the change from the five-dollar bill. Jo-Anne took it religiously. God, even in Big Apple days she'd have said "keep the change." Now, for appearances' sake she wondered if she ought to count it.

Laura was back with the warm lemonade. "Would you like something to nibble on? I can recommend the spinach balls. I made them myself."

"No, thanks, Laura," said Jo-Anne shortly. This whole thing was turning into a nightmare. Thank the Lord, the Sothebys of garage sales only happened once every two years. In all those years of clawing her way to the top, Jo-Anne hadn't realized it would come to this—picking her way through the attic treasures of the wealthy to fund some charity that could have been as easily enriched by one meaty check. How many long hot nights had she lain awake longing to be asked to join the Palm Beach chapter of the Garden Club of America, that ultimate symbol of social "arrival"? Now she was its ruler and had discovered the numbing tedium of its functions. Here she was, sweating beneath the canopy of the Christ Memorial Parish House tent, playing charades with fuddy-duddy moldy oldies whose bank balances were only equalled by the length of their pedigrees.

"Oh, Jo-Anne, I'm so glad you're here. Lovely to see a Palm Beach face." The unctuous tones, heavy with flattery and groveling friendliness, belonged to none other than Eleanor Peacock.

Jo-Anne turned to look at her former enemy. She bit deep into the ice-cold cake of revenge. "Eleanor, dear. What on earth are you doing up here? Shopping for a few bargains? I suppose the quality of the rubbish is a bit better than the West Palm thrifts."

As she had done a thousand times before, Eleanor Peacock swallowed the insult with a good grace. She had never been forgiven for her attempt at social murder on the eve of the Planned Parenthood party, and she never expected to be. Marjorie Donahue had effectively written her off the face of the earth. Later, during her all too brief rehabilitation at the time of the Jo-Anne/Marjorie wars, she had been born again, only to be cast down once more by the Donahue death. As Jo-Anne had moved to fill the power vacuum, Eleanor's social stock had completed its roller-coaster ride to rock bottom. Then, when she had least expected it, and when she had been on the verge of persuading poor Arch to give up his job and move to Connecticut, the new queen had offered her an unspoken deal. It hadn't been a very good one, but it had been a sort of salvation. Jo-Anne was apparently prepared to allow her to survive. In exchange she must suffer all the insults and indignities that a cruel and clever mind could dream up. And she must never, *never* answer back.

"Oh, Jo-Anne, you *are* unkind," laughed Eleanor, the false smile plastered uncomfortably all over her face. She stood her ground, preparing to accept a few more verbal blows before the cat tired of playing with the mouse. She was almost used to it now, but not quite. Trading her pride for Palm Beach social survival. There was scarcely an hour of the day, of course, when she didn't bombard the Almighty with prayers for a thunderbolt to descend on her hated superior, but she had more or less given up hope of divine intervention.

"Well, I suppose it's nice to have a Palm Beach ally up here even if it's only you, Eleanor. These golden oldies give me the creeps. This place is Costa Geriatrica. I wonder how soon I can decently get away."

Get away. Yes, that was it. Escape. Escape from the half-dead crinkly-wrinklies. Escape from responsibility, from genteel conversation, from hypocrisy, from Hobe Sound. Jo-Anne was sick of it all. Sick of being the queen, of all the snobs, of all the money. Of everything. She experienced all at once the overwhelming desire to blot it all out, and to travel to the farthest corner of the earth where people did things differently, thought different things. But where? How? The answer, born of claustrophobia's panic, came through with the clarity of a still, small voice. There was another world. A dangerous, exciting, alluring world.

She would drive south on Dixie to the place where Riviera Beach met the outskirts of West Palm. It was a dirty run-down area of flyblown bars and broken-down shops. It was the place the black hookers hung out.

The West Palm suburb was a steaming cauldron, and the air was like hot fudge, sweet, thick, and sticky as hell itself. It blanketed Jo-Anne's body, wrapping her up in a wet towel of humid heat as it bathed her in its dampness and drew the abundant moisture from her own pores. At the wheel of the convertible she gave herself up to the delicious tackiness of the experience. It wasn't that she didn't have an alternative. One flick of a switch and the convertible top would have covered her. The touch of another and the icy cold of the air conditioner would have brought everything back to normal. But Jo-Anne was luxuriating in the sensuality of her own body heat. The long white pleated skirt, unbuttoned now to midthigh, was already awash with sweat, and the Turnbull and Asser cream silk shirt clung to her chest, providing a delicious friction to her hardening nipples. She ran her tongue over her top lip, clearing away the salty dewdrops of moisture. Hey, this was great. Turkish-bath time. She must be losing pounds. That was it. That was what she was doing. Cruising and losing. What a way to go. The Hobe Sound Garden Club Bazaar seemed already a million miles away.

Now she was about to blot it out in the most dangerous and exciting way possible. Jo-Anne laughed out loud. She should never have deviated from the straight and narrow, never attempted the disastrous transition from pussy to prick: the scene with Christie and the blue-eyed blondie with the intense eyes had been the baddest of bad trips. She'd never understood her daughter; but to attempt to do yourself in because you caught your mother on the job with someone just a little younger was surely carrying straightness too far. Still, there was one hell of a lot to be grateful for. First, she had survived, apparently as good as new. Second, she had failed to tell the tale. That much at least had been predictable. Christie made Goldilocks look like a two-bit Times Square hustler. Anyway, it was a relief. Bobby Stansfield wouldn't have understood about a woman's needs and the necessity of satisfying them, and it was just as well that the ignorance of his bliss would not be replaced by the folly of needless wisdom.

Again and again Jo-Anne had tried to understand her daughter's weird motivation, despite the fact that speculating about the thoughts of others was not her specialty. Christie had been tight mouthed both in the hospital and, later, at home. She had tried to pass off the suicide attempt as a "terrible mistake," an overreaction to the shock of her experience, and she had been completely forgiving, and even understanding of Jo-Anne's predicament.

"Don't worry, mom. I won't tell dad. But please, please promise me you'll never be unfaithful to him again."

Words being cheap, Jo-Anne had promised. "I swear it, darling. On my life I promise you."

Did this little expedition count as marital infidelity?

The wild side demanded its own precautions. Jo-Anne had hidden in the trunk anything that could identify her. Platinum American Express card, Chase Manhattan "Thousand Club" card, checkbooks, driver's license. Blackmail was something she for sure didn't need right now. She had also tucked away the jewelry—the Van Cleef diamond-encrusted bracelet, the ruby-and-diamond lucky horseshoe brooch, and the pear-drop diamond earrings.

She checked herself in the rearview mirror. Damn. She'd almost forgotten. The twin ebony diamond-lined hair combs from Cartier. They would have signaled "retirement" to most of the inhabitants of this part of South Dixie. Impatiently she swept them off and jammed them without ceremony into the glove compartment, letting her hair fall free over her shoulders—a symbolic loosening of restraints, an embracing of abandonment.

Jo-Anne wasn't at all sure how or where she would get it, but she knew exactly what she wanted. She wanted the lowest of the low. Some dirty, back-street black girl. Somebody whose edges were all rough, with no manners, no graces, nothing, except a willing body.

Mmmmmmmmmmmmmm. The thought was turning her on. Memory lane was all but impassable now, overgrown with undergrowth, but the idea had the power to shift juices. Jo-Anne, who had sold it, was about to become a buyer for the very first time. Yeah, it was a real nice idea. Haggling in some shady parking lot over the price of a girl's body. Then, once she'd handed over the bucks, the delicious thrill of knowing that for a brief time she would own it, that it would be hers to do with as she wished.

She had a vague idea where she was heading. The Port o' Call Bar looked like the sort of place she wanted. Several times as the Rolls had purred up North Dixie to Hobe Sound dinner parties she had noticed the gaggle of taut-assed black hookers hanging around on the pavement trolling for passing trade in the damp heat of the early evening. It was a bit early, but then early birds were supposed to be the ones that scored, weren't they?

The paint on the bar's sign had seen better days, but then so, presumably, had the bar itself. Jo-Anne drove straight past it, noting the open door, the silhouette of a pin-ball machine, the green light shining inside. She took a deep breath. God, how would she have the nerve to walk into a place like that, let alone make a deal in there?

To the honking of a couple of outraged motorists she made a U-turn and headed back, drawn to the danger like an insect to the flame. To the danger and the promise of alien delight.

She twirled the wheel and sent the big Mercedes roadster winging into the seedy parking lot. She caught sight of them immediately. Three of them, talking and hanging out against the peeling paint of the wall. Their clothes said nearly all of it; their lazy, wandering eyes said the rest. The two on the right were way past anything, flyblown, clapped-out junkies, blowsy and battered by the "good-time" life.

Slack minds, slack bottoms, faded dreams, faded jeans.

But the third girl was *really* something. As she pulled up Jo-Anne took it all in. She was very young. Fifteen. Possibly a little older. Probably a bit younger. Everything was on show and it was all tingling tight. The tall ass sat at the top of long gangling legs, and the tits, mocking gravity, made the sharpest of angles with the thin torso, a living indictment of the toneless mounds that belonged to her two older colleagues. Her face was alert—cheeky and alive, the big brown eyes very far from jaded—ready for all the adventures that life around the Port o' Call Bar promised. Her hair had been ruthlessly straightened and back-combed to give the appearance of late teens, which the rest of her body and demeanor de-

nied. She wore a skirt so short it looked like a wide belt, no
stockings to hide the cool chocolate-brown skin of her legs, ankle-
length white boots, and a long shoulder bag of black plastic. Across
the front of her T-shirt, the large letters A and Y hovering uncertainly on the pointed nipples, was the word ANY. And as she turned
casually to see who had arrived in the sharp convertible, Jo-Anne
could see that across the shirt's back was written in bold capitals
the word THING. Jo-Anne laughed out loud.

The spark of interest in the expensive car was not completely
extinguished when it took in the sex of the owner. In the dead eyes
of the other two girls, however, Jo-Anne clearly rated about as
much importance as a body in the Hudson to a New York cop.

Jo-Anne was five feet away from the three girls. She didn't even
have to get out of the car. "Hello," she said.

The old pros didn't blink . . . or answer. Taking her cue from
her "elders," the fox didn't speak either. But she looked a lot.

"I was wondering if you could help me."

Jo-Anne wasn't daunted. She knew this scene. And it was promising as hell.

"An how we gonna help a rich whitey mother like you, honey?
You lost or somethin'?"

The bewigged hulk on the left showed bad teeth and hinted at
worse breath as she spoke. The fox kept looking, a marginally
puzzled expression on the full mouth, a casual thumb stuck jaun-
tily into the rim of the belt/skirt.

"Well, I hoped you might be able to help me spend some
money." Jo-Anne made her voice go provocative. It wasn't hard.
The palms of her hands were already moist. The rest of her was
getting there fast.

In four of the eyes dawned the beginnings of comprehension. In
the youngest pair there was surprise.

The sound of the original speaker laughing was not nice. Apparently it wasn't meant to be. "You tryin' to score chicks, honey,
you in the wrong place. You even in the wrong *state*. You better
hit New York or L.A. or one of them *dirty* places where they do
all that *jazz*."

Jo-Anne looked long and hard at the one she wanted, ignoring
the discouraging words from the shit bag. She'd gotten there at

last, and the amusement was pushing the surprise right off her beautiful young face.

"I have three hundred dollars to spend," said Jo-Anne quickly, before positions became too entrenched.

She had center stage now, all right. As intended, three big ones was way, way over the top for this market, and money was the loudest language there was.

The spokesperson for the trio wavered visibly, and when at last she spoke there was an angry disappointment in her voice. In this neck of the woods you just didn't *do* dyke scenes if you wanted to stay healthy. The men that looked after you didn't understand about things like that. It was a tooth-losing trip. But three hundred bucks? Christ, the chick must want it bad.

"Get drivin', honey. We don' want your stinkin' bucks," she managed at last. "Hey, wait a minute." Like clockwork, thought Jo-Anne. The target had spoken. "What you wanna do for three hundred bucks?"

The young girl wanted an answer to the question. She understood folding money, but she had no idea what was expected from her in return. A kiss? Something else? "We could make it up as we went along. You'd get the money up front."

"Now don' you mess with it, Mona. You don' know nothing, sweetheart. This is bad news, man. Clive, he don' like this kind of thing. You'll go an' get yourself all sorts of trouble. Ain' that right, Suzie?"

Suzie, unaccustomed to the role of arbitrator and clearly not long on words, nodded her agreement vigorously.

The two beaten-down dogs were united. Selling yourself to chicks just wasn't done. A little like converting to Catholicism on the island maybe, or wearing rough-soled shoes to drinks on board a yacht. And Clive, whoever he was, shared the view that such behavior was a definite *faux-pas*. Jo-Anne laughed to herself. It was a topsy-turvy world and rules were different, but still, whatever they were they were meant to be obeyed.

Jo-Anne now addressed herself directly to the gorgeous little girl. She was halfway there. Halfway to paradise. "Listen. Why don't you hop in and we can discuss this, you and me. You get fifty for just hearing me out. No harm in that."

The girl let out a laugh of delight, all warm and funny from the back of her throat. Life was still fun for her. She was young enough for that. And enough of a child to take the risk and to scorn the nameless threat because it was a future thing.

She didn't hesitate, and without even looking at the colleagues who had been so free with their advice, she signed the unwritten contract by crossing the space to the now open door of Jo-Anne's car.

As her pert bottom hit the soft white leather, the skirt/belt ceased its hypocrisy. There were acres of long, black thigh and shocking-pink panties, and there was the smell too of the cheap scent and, beneath it, subtle, heady, a much more potent aroma, the mind-bending perfume of hot little girl.

Jo-Anne didn't waste any time. The engines were already running inside her. She did the same for the car and was out of the lot before anybody was in the business of changing minds.

On the highway she turned to look at her catch, and as she did so her right hand was drawn to the magnetic skin of its exposed leg. She ran a tongue over her dessicated lips and tried to swallow as she felt the eager heat beneath her hand. Her voice when it came was positively quivering with anticipation. "Where to?"

The big full lips pouted back at her. "I ain' done this before."

Jo-Anne tried to make her smile reassuring. She'd heard the line before. The tones had been more patrician, but the sentiment was not new. Neither was the response. "Trust me. It's a whole new world."

The black girl liked the sound of new worlds, but of other things more. "You got the bucks?"

Jo-Anne smiled ruefully. She'd almost forgotten. This was a different trip. Business sex. Did the girl feel like Jo-Anne herself had felt in all those endless hotel rooms? Had the johns felt as she felt now? The tinge of disappointment that this whole thing wasn't being done just for the love of it. Then she laughed. No, the reality was the turn-on. She'd rented a body. For an hour or so she'd own it. There was no need for the seduction routine. The bucks cut right through all that shit.

"Take three hundred out of the bag, and let's have the directions.'' There was a new sharpness in her voice. "I want this show on the road,'' her tone seemed to say.

"How old are you, anyway? Tell me the truth. It makes no difference.''

The liquid brown eyes went careful, but the three hundred in the long chocolate fingers blew away caution. "Fourteen,'' she said, as she moved around a bit beneath Jo-Anne's hovering hand. "That too young?'' The question was provocative, even a dare.

"No, it's not too young.'' But it would be the youngest ever. By about three years. That was a nice touch. Fourteen, black, and, as far as women were concerned, a virgin. Why the hell hadn't she thought of this before?

"Hang a right at the next light and pull into the lot on the left. I got the use of a room at the Sea Grass motel.''

Jo-Anne did as she was told, relinquishing her position on the young girl's leg with regret as she made the turn.

They didn't speak as they walked up the stairs of the run-down motel. Already Jo-Anne could picture the room. It would be a facsimile of a million such rooms all across America: plastic, cigarette burns, Dacron, rayon, or whatever other synthetic they made fabric out of these days. Somebody would have cleaned his shoes on the drapes; there would be a ring around the bathtub, and a monster TV with a crackling four-channel-only selection, a mean, foam-filled pillow, a lopsided standard lamp. But in front of her walked the tight, high bottom that she had hired. That was more than enough to send the heart into overdrive and to set the stomach whispering.

The room lived up to its promise. There had been no concessions to aesthetic susceptibilities. None at all—from the dented tin wastebasket with its white plastic liner to the pink-plastic-framed mirror that would catch the action over the single bed.

But the prettiest thing was emphasized by the seediness of the surroundings. The little-girl hooker slung the cheap bag onto the bed and tried to look as if she were in control. Turning to face her client, she attempted to sound businesslike. "Okay, how do you want it?'' The truth was she really didn't know at all.

"Every way in the book,'' said Jo-Anne simply. "But we'll start right here. Standing up.''

She crossed the three steps into the younger girl's space. "Stand quite still. Don't do a thing."

The girl watched her. The eyes were unsure, but there was interest, almost a sense of fascination in their depths. She looked as if she had been hypnotized—her will all gone as she prepared to surrender herself to Jo-Anne's superior power.

Not taking her eyes off the black girl's face, Jo-Anne reached down and gently lifted the skirt. Only when the panties were completely exposed did she look down to enjoy what she had unveiled.

The sigh rushed through her parted lips at the sight. The almost fluorescent pink briefs were a good size too small. They looked like they had been spray painted on, and the tense mound of the teenager's sex thrust anxiously against the skimpy material. Twin thongs raced away to the back, plastered tight over the delicious brown buttocks, while the third dived down deep into the infinitely alluring mystery that lurked between the firm flesh of the thighs.

Jo-Anne's fingers found the rim of the tight elastic and slowly, centimeter by centimeter, she eased them away.

Now Jo-Anne knelt down, her face level with the place she wanted. Radiating against her cheeks, the heat rushed toward her. This young girl was too new to the game to be in control of it. Her switch had been turned. Her motor was on. Jo-Anne could feel and smell it.

"Just relax, honey," she murmured more to herself than to the girl to whom she was about to make love.

The pants were away now. Slung across the curved thighs, they were a lewd hammock brushing against the skin of Jo-Anne's chin as her eyes devoured the vision they had revealed. Pink lips close to her lips, the demanding scent next to her nostrils, the warm soul of the young girl asking to be taken, quivering in anticipation in front of her eager mouth.

Jo-Anne heard the moan from above, as her lover gave her the permission to proceed. For one beautiful second she hesitated as she milked the moment for every ounce of its pleasure-giving potential. Then she moved forward.

Jo-Anne didn't hear the door open. But as her lips tenderly brushed against the lips before her she felt the rush of panic immediately. The slippery wetness against her mouth coincided with the explosion of rage.

"You *evil* girl! What you doin'? What you doin', you *evil* girl?"

The stinging blow caught Jo-Anne full across the left side of her face, sending the stars billowing through her head as her ear echoed with its force. She toppled sideways, crashing into the end of the bed.

Her almost lover, the pink pants pinioning her legs accusingly, stood stock still, a look of visceral fear contorting her formerly beautiful face. In the doorway stood a hundred and ninety pounds of muscled black hatred, disgust beaming from his eyes and murder humming in his heart.

"Clive, I didn' mean no harm. Clive. . ."

Somehow both girl and woman knew everything would be all right if this dreadful man could now be made to speak. But Clive was past speaking. He had seen his own private horror, and in his drugged, psychopathic eyes the emptiness said his girl had betrayed him. Not with the johns. They didn't count. They were income. His income. But with a white chick! With some white trash. Some cheap whitey whore. Some no-account pervert girl.

The switchblade knife was already gleaming in his palm.

Dear God. This was the pimp. The one called Clive. Clive, who didn't approve of the thing she had been trying to do. And in the mad, staring eyes, Jo-Anne could see what was going to happen. He was going to hurt her. She was going to be punished. After all the long, long years, retribution had finally arrived. All she could foresee was pain, pain and its roaring, gnawing aftermath. Disfigurement. By the foot of the bed she watched the actors in the drama. Three of them, herself included, strutting their brief moment on the boards.

She was literally outside herself, riding the frantic tide of adrenaline, suspended in time and space by pure panic. How could she stop what must be? Some clever word, some subtle gesture would stop the mad play in its tracks. She would lie back laughing and the horror would go away as everyone relaxed into the joke. All quite funny really. Scary but funny. But even as she allowed the hope to build, Jo-Anne knew that it had no substance. Born of the thirst for life, it would die in a desert of destruction.

Clive walked toward her and the knife was against her stomach, rucking up the material of the flimsy silk shirt as his anger beamed at her.

Her leathery tongue, shorn of moisture, tried to form a word of protest. ''No,'' she murmured.

''Yes,'' he replied.

She dared to look down at the tightening fingers as she saw the ripple of muscle along the strong forearm, felt the cold splash of nausea in the pit of her stomach. And, as panic's fingers death-danced up and down her spine, Jo-Anne froze—as if through still-ness she could be safe.

Like a sacrificial lamb she looked up into the eyes of the man who held the knife, but they were cold as the snows of winter, dead as the forest's dark. In that cosmic second they communed, sharing the intimacy of the damned as their souls touched at the edge of terror.

In vain Jo-Anne tried to make contact with the vacant eyes, but they did not respond. There was nobody there.

In her disjointed mind the frantic thoughts piled over themselves as they tumbled before the searchlight of consciousness. Present-ing themselves in bits and pieces they were the jigsaw puzzle of her life. The New York streets, the strife and the struggle, the riches of the world dropped into her lap. Poor Peter's head and its red-vapor cloud, the senator's wife so cool and elegant at the ros-trum. Fast food, slow food, cheap tricks, expensive ones—and always, ever present, the silky strains of the sexual background music, the ones that had been playing such a very short time be-fore.

She should be thankful for the confusion of her thoughts. In the merciful haze of unreality there would be no pain. That was a relief. The pain would be for later. But for the sake of appearances really she ought to scream. In a situation like this any respectable person would certainly do that.

And so with a languid lack of enthusiasm, Jo-Anne Duke Stans-field began to scream as the knife turned into the fin of a shark. Northward it swam. Lazily, effortlessly across the tranquil sea of her lower stomach. Behind it there was the neat red line, at first thin and clean, then growing blurred and furry in an increasingly messy wake. It would swim right up to her face, between the twin breast mountains, along her beautiful neck, and across the promontory of her chin. Then at least she would have a little peace from the awful noise that somebody was making. But the peace was coming sooner than she thought. Wonderful sleepy peace. Just what a girl needed at the end of too long a life. And so with the sensation of amused surprise at the ease of it all, Jo-Anne let go, as she nosedived gracefully into nothingness.

21

It was one of those Florida dog days when the irritable sky threatened all kinds of unpleasantness, and Bobby Stansfield felt totally in tune with the elements. It had been a disastrous six months. Christie's suicide attempt, followed closely by Jo-Anne's brutal murder. The first had affected him emotionally even more than the second, but it was Jo-Anne's death that threatened to change his life. Even now the media wouldn't leave him alone. They were still clustered in the driveway, with their cameras and their note pads. Always a celebrity, he had been precipitated by his wife's messy ending into the ranks of the notorious—a position which, for a Stansfield, was about as welcome as a spell on a Florida chain gang. His ever-brightening political prospects seemed totally ruined, and Jo-Anne had been the culprit. For that, more than for the almost casual and totally bizarre infidelity, he would never forgive her.

He stared out moodily at the angry sea and the acrobatic pelicans as they soared on the rushing air. Was there any way to salvage it? Time and time again he had gone over the options. After all, Teddy had recovered from Chappaquiddick, and Nixon had made more comebacks than Frank Sinatra. There had to be a way.

He turned around and his heart lit up like a shaft of sunlight piercing the slate-gray sky. He hadn't lost Christie. There she was —curled up tightly on the sofa—a good deed in a naughty world. From the moment she had recovered from her own ordeal she had been a tower of strength in his. The loss of her mother, on top of the mysterious sequence of events that had caused her own sorrow, would have sunk lesser mortals, but Christie had weathered the storm. Now there were just the two of them. Alone against the world. Bobby knew he would never understand her. She was so desperately unlike him, and light years removed from anything remotely resembling her mother. Whatever had propelled her into the emotional depths had never been revealed, despite the hectoring questioning of a far from stupid politician. Bobby only knew that she had loved someone, and that he had let her down. Nothing more than that. Occasionally, from the wistful, faraway look in her eyes, it was obvious that whoever he was he was not forgotten.

"You know, dad, you mustn't give up. I know I've said that before, but it's true. Stansfields don't give up, do they? I think I've got that engraved on my heart."

Bobby laughed. It was supposed to be true. Certainly he'd always believed it. And his mother was still saying it. It was only the other day that she had made what she thought was an encouraging little speech. "Things change, dear. The time requires the man. Look at De Gaulle. Look at Churchill. When the world is running smoothly, they pick the man without Mafia connections who has the best teeth. But that's a luxury, dear. When the going gets tough they pick the man with the biggest balls. The dreadful business with Jo-Anne would be overlooked if times ever turned really hard. That would be your moment. It's not over yet."

Again Bobby laughed out loud as he thought of his mother's uncharacteristic crudeness. In a lifetime he had never heard her say anything like that, but it had had its intended effect. The message had been clear. There is a time for gentility and breeding, but when it's hitting the fan, a man must learn to shovel shit.

"It's true, Christie. I won't give up." The smile lit up the handsome face, backlighting the beautifully broken nose. In front of his audience of one he felt the familiar old confidence creeping back. He walked over to the sofa and threw himself down next to his daughter. "But if you were my campaign manager, what the hell would you advise me to *do?*"

"I know exactly what you should do."

"Tell me."

"You should remarry."

"My darling daughter . . . and who do you think I should marry?"

"You should marry Lisa Blass."

Like a red-hot needle the thought seared through Bobby Stansfield's brain. Lisa Blass. Lisa, who he'd never been able to forget. Lisa, who all through the years had never forgiven him for the ambition that had forced him away from her. Lisa of the hard body and the soft skin. Of the gentle sweetness and the cold revenge. Lisa Starr. She'd carried his child and thrown it away, as he had discarded her. A back-street girl who had risen to a prominence few women ever achieved. How many times had he remembered her, longed for her patience and understanding and for the mind-capturing excitement of her touch? Instead he had taken Jo-Anne Duke. Married a hooker for her millions to further his own ambitions. It was a choice he had never ceased to regret and one for which he had never imagined he could be forgiven.

"Christie, do you know what you're saying? Lisa Blass hates my guts. You didn't know that, but then how could you? I wasn't very good to her, I'm afraid. I treated her badly. I didn't want to, but I did, and for years she's hated both me and your mother. I was very fond of her . . ."

Bobby saw the cloud pass over Christie's face. Sadness? The sort of look you had when you began to understand something that had long troubled you.

"Has she ever tried to harm you? I mean, I guess with that business of hers she could have maybe done that. Do you remember that dreadful book they wrote about us? The one they sent you a few years ago? Nobody would publish it, but she could have done so if she'd wanted to hurt us that much."

Bobby looked thoughtful. "Well, that's true. Certainly. But she's always avoided us like the plague, and in this town you know how difficult that is."

"Did you love her?"

"What is this? The third degree?" Again the laugh. The one that turned the crowds on. Then, more reflectively, "Yes. Yes, I did love her. Very much. She's a wonderful person. She was a wonderful person."

"Mom was more difficult to love." Christie's statement was matter-of-fact.

"Yes. I think we all found that."

Bobby turned to his daughter. The tears were there again. Jo-Anne was difficult to love, but Christie had achieved it. Christie, who was so full of love there was enough for everyone. Christie, who had blown her love on some no-good creature of the wasteland who had never even showed up at the house to be introduced to her parents. Whoever he was, he deserved the fate of the freaked-out maniac who'd murdered Jo-Anne. He, Bobby, would have volunteered personally to administer the poison—and he would have taken all day about it, reveling in the boy's facial expressions as he fought off the sleep that would kill.

"She has a son now. I never see him around, but he must be your age. Blass, he'd be called. Can't remember his first name."

"Scott. Scott Blass."

Bobby stood up. "You know what I think we both need? A *fantastic* margarita. Come on, Christie, I'll make it myself. I used to be famous for them. Let's see if I still am."

Christie smiled through the mask of tears. Her father could be like that, with the infectious enthusiasm of the youngest child in the body of the famous politician. But she wasn't going to let him off the hook. Not totally.

"I think you still love her, dad. You should meet up with her. See what happens. I wouldn't mind. Remember, I suggested it. There's been so much sadness, so much bitterness."

Her reward was the look on her father's face.

Lisa flicked morosely through the *New York Times* best-sellers lists. This should be best part of the week. They were all there. All the Blass books. The ones she had nurtured, the ones she had invented, the ones she had bought. But there was no joy in it. No excitement. No enthusiasm. No nothing. Just the emptiness all around. It had been six long months since Scott had left. He had gone like a thief in the night, stealing away for no apparent reason, and since his departure there had been only the sound of his silence. The earth had devoured him. He had vanished without trace.

How many times had she tried to understand the reason for his bitter departure? It was as if he wanted to hurt her for some terrible wrong. But what had she done? Nothing had changed. The note had been little help.

She could remember it by heart, but still she couldn't understand it: "I am going away, mother, and I am not coming back. Please don't try to find me. All my life I have tried to make you love me, but now I understand why you never could. It's nearly destroyed me, and others, too—so if I can't be part of your love I don't want to have anything to do with your hatred. I trusted you so much, but you lied to me. And everything you pretended to be you weren't. So I'm going away to learn to live with myself and to try to learn that what's happened was not my fault, but yours. You sent me away a long, long time ago."

Love? Hatred? It meant nothing. Nothing anyway that *he* could know or care about. Yes, she had been hatred's friend. It had sustained her through the years of struggle and been the mother of the phenomenal success that screamed itself from the black-and-white pages of the *New York Times*. But now, like some spent bullet, the emotion was all tired and worn out, and with Jo-Anne's dreadful death, it had plummeted thankfully to earth.

"How's Anne Liebermann's surfing book coming along?" asked Maggie brightly. Cheering up Lisa was getting to be a full-time occupation these days.

"Terrific," said Lisa without enthusiasm. "The synopsis and chapter breakdown are just wonderful. Has to be another number one. No problem. Oh yes," she added wearily. "Still raking it in. Blass is still on top." She paused as the bittersweet thought crossed her mind. "I wonder what poor Scottie would have thought of it." The voice had a catch in it.

"It was his idea, wasn't it?"

"It was Anne Liebermann's screwy idea. Or I should say it was Anne Liebermann's idea of screwing. Scott was sleeping with her, you know."

"Good God! Was he really? What an extraordinary thing to want to do."

"He didn't want to, Maggie. He did it for me. Liebermann was cutting up rough on her contract. He sweet-talked her into staying with Blass. He paid in kind."

"Oh, Lisa, don't be so ridiculous."

"I'm *not* being ridiculous, Maggie." Lisa stood up abruptly, throwing the paper onto the floor with an impatient gesture. After all these years Maggie still treated her like she was an innocent teenager. People seemed to think she was the same old Lisa, but she wasn't. Things had changed. It was irritating that people didn't recognize that. Especially old friends.

For a second or two there was silence. It was the sort that gave birth to things. "He wanted so desperately for me to take notice of him. I never could. I tried but I couldn't. There wasn't anything there before. But there is now."

She turned to face her old friend, her beautiful face suddenly drawn, the tears glistening in her eyes. "I want him back, Maggs. So . . . much." She threw out her hands in a gesture of impotence and shook her head from side to side. "He was so much like Bobby. It was ridiculous. Every time I looked at him, all the hurt and the anger just bubbled up inside. Poor Scott. He never had any idea. I couldn't tell him. Even now he doesn't know."

"Perhaps if he knew . . ."

"He's gone, Maggs. He's just gone. And it's my fault."

Lisa was talking to herself now. "So very much hatred. It was everywhere. I took it with me. I smelled of it. I reeked of it, and it made me so *strong*. So *damned* strong. It was like a pact with the devil, wasn't it? I could have everything, even revenge, if I gave up my soul."

"You can get it back, Lisa. You can get everything back. Everyone back."

"No. It's too late, Maggie. They've all gone. All gone. And there's nothing left except me. And all this . . ."

Lisa flung out her hand in despair to the high-ceilinged room with its exquisite Old Masters, its superb jade collection, the miraculous Rodin sculpture poached at auction from the underbidding Louvre. But she meant more than just that. She was the survivor. She had inherited it all. Palm Beach. The most desired thing of all was hers now, to bend to her will, to humiliate if she wished, to have and to hold, from this day forth . . . Her only rival was not only dead, but desperately discredited by the manner of her dying. The field was clear to the social priestess who ran the most successful publishing empire in America and yet still had the time and the skill to play the Palm Beach game. So she had won the Pyrrhic victory, and the taste of the ashes in her mouth was turning her stomach. What would Marjorie have said? Dear, wise Marjorie who had hidden her kindness and her compassion beneath the mask of her social ambition?

"Contact Bobby, Lisa. He must be so alone. Just like you. It's all so long ago. So very far away. Tell him it's over. Understand him. Understand yourself."

Maggie's voice echoed her thoughts.

As she heard the words, Lisa knew she would do it.

It was like a revelation. So obvious, and yet an idea not entertained by consciousness. In the depths of her psyche, however, the need was there. Without Bobby there could be no new beginning.

And suddenly, and with the desperation of the soul-sick, Lisa began to long for a new dawn.

Christie stood stock still as the words buzzed around and around her head like an angry swarm of bees. Occasionally some of them peeled off from the milling horde and flew right into her ear: on a one-way trip into consciousness: "Half sister." "Brother." "Forgive." "That night on the beach."

In disbelief she shook her head from side to side, sending little droplets of Madison Avenue rain all around the tiny third-floor apartment. But even as Christie reeled with the shock of the revelation, her mad refusal to accept the truth of Scott's words was already starting to weaken.

"You mean we're brother and sister. That dad is your dad, too," said her disembodied voice.

Scott, his head still buried deep in his hands, nodded bleakly. All crumpled up on the dirty sofa, he looked as if he had given up the fight. It wasn't just the stubble of the beard, the filthy fingernails, the tangled, tousled hair. They were just the clichés of defeat. His whole body spoke the language of despair. Scott looked like a cardboard man who had been left out in the rain.

Even as she tried to digest the fact that the man she had loved so completely, who had hurt her so deeply, was her own brother,

Christie's great big heart was opening up all over again. Into it flooded both relief and compassion. "I'm glad, Scott. Do you hear? I'm glad you're my brother."

And as she said it she felt it. She had lost a lover, but now she was no longer alone. Suddenly there was so much understanding of emotions, which, previously, had been inexplicable. She had a brother, a dear, wonderful, crazy, sad brother to walk through life with. A brother who would join her in turning up a nose at a ludicrous world.

Through parted fingers Scott looked up at her in disbelief. "Christie, what on earth do you mean?"

The warm smile was all over her face as she tried to explain. "I mean it's all fine, Scott. I forgive you, and we can love each other again. When I was a little girl, I used to pray to God to give me a brother. He's just been a tiny bit late in answering my prayers."

"Then you don't hate me . . . even after what I did?" He needed more reassurance. It had never occurred to him that Christie would react like this. He had focused solely on the tragedy, and as a result he had not been able to hope. For the last dreadful six months he had hardly left the apartment that had been his hideaway. Endlessly he had examined his conscience as he had tried to scourge the evil from his soul, but there had been no solution. Always the conclusion had been the same. He was a warped, misshapen thing—a genetic accident who had expressed his twisted inheritance in the most diabolical of ways. He, the son of an incestuous relationship, had maimed and mutilated the happiness of his own flesh and blood. He had seen his own sister's heart stop as the direct result of his wicked love plot. He had taken her on the sand. He had hated she whom nature demanded he should love, and he had defiled her with his polluted genes. And at the end, when confronted with the enormity of his act, he hadn't even had the courage to kill himself. Whichever way he had looked at it, there was no health in him.

Christie melted down toward him. Sitting next to him she reached out to him, and there, on the threadbare sofa, he fell gratefully into her arms as she cradled his head comfortingly.

"Oh, Scott. Poor Scott. Poor baby. You've had such a terrible time. Poor baby. My poor baby." As his tears came she rocked him gently, allowing the grief to break through the log jam that had blocked up all his sorrow. For long minutes brother and sister did not speak.

Scott broke the silence. "Oh, Christie. I didn't know how you'd react. I felt so guilty. I had to tell someone. I had to tell you. When I wrote, I thought maybe you wouldn't answer. Or perhaps you'd not even open the letter. I was so ashamed."

Christie pulled him in toward her, holding him tightly, feeling the wet splash of her brother's tears on her brown forearm. "It's all over now, Scottie. It's gone. You did it because something had hurt you very much. I know that. I forgive you. Listen to me. I forgive you."

And she lifted up his face toward her and made him smile the uncertain smile, encouraging it with her own. There was more to say. She must say it all. Clear it all away—the debris, the baggage of the past. Only if directly confronted would the ghosts be laid to rest.

"I guess I sort of knew right from the start. When we met on that beach. It was so immediate. So incredibly natural. All the emotions were so mixed up, but so close. Mainly they were just *strong,* I guess. Okay, so now we know what it was all about, but there was a kind of a way I knew then. When you made love to me. Just before . . . it suddenly felt terribly wrong. Wonderful, but wrong at the same time. There was a part of me that didn't want to . . . but it just didn't have the votes. Do you know what? I don't even regret it. I remember it, and it was the best moment of my life so far. I loved making love to you because I loved you, Scott. And I still love you now. Right now. Do you hear?"

She turned the stricken tear-stained face toward her and wiped away the wetness with her fingers, watching the softening of the hurt as her words eased away the pain.

"But I was so cruel . . . so evil to you, Christie. How can you forgive that?"

"It was you who was the victim, Scott, not me. I was just the passer-by who got drawn in by Fate. All that hatred. Somebody had to get caught in the flame. It's amazing about your mother, and mom and dad. Why did she want to hurt them so very much? And why didn't she love you? I can't understand that. It seems so incredible."

"It *is* incredible, Christie. I'm afraid you've only heard half the story." Scott sat up and took his sister's hand in his. "I still don't know whether or not to believe it, but Willie Willis says that my mother and your father are half brother and sister, too."

"What?" Christie's face managed to mix incredulity and humor in equal proportions. If Scott could joke at a time like this, then that was progress of a sort, but he seemed to have a rather macabre sense of what was funny.

"I know, it's crazy, isn't it? Absolutely mad. Anyway, he told me that my grandma used to work in your grandfather's house. They had an affair, and mom was their child. That was what he said. Even mom didn't know. Nobody knew. If it's true, it means my mom and your dad are mirror images of us. History repeated itself."

"Could he have made it up? To hurt you for some reason?"

"I guess it's possible. It seems anything is possible. I just know he was right about us. I mean, we look like we've been photo-copied."

Like the sun shining through the clouds of a gloomy sky, the mutual laughter filled the room. They were partners at last. Co-conspirators against life, the dealer of dirty cards.

It was true. They not only looked like brother and sister, but could have been taken for twins.

"But how can we find out? We ought to know for certain, I guess. About them I mean . . . not us. I want us to be brother and sister, even if we're not."

"God knows how we find out. But does it matter? Maybe we should spare them that. After all, both their lives are sort of ruined anyway. Maybe it's better they shouldn't know."

"You're right, Scott. It's far better buried . . . if there's any-thing to bury. God, it's amazing. All that venom when the blood was screaming for love and not war. What an incredible waste."

"What will we do now?" Scott looked wiped out, sponged clean of emotion. If there were feelings left to feel, he scarcely knew what they were.

"That's easy," said Christie brightly. "We're going home."

Lisa Blass was a child again. Uncertain, excited, peering up once more at an outsize world. For the hundredth time she stared impatiently at the seemingly sticky hands of the Piaget watch. Today, time was moving at a snail's pace.

What to wear had been a problem. What to think had been a problem. In a few minutes' time, how to behave would be a problem.

Fate had excelled itself in the role of conjuror. Egged on by Maggie in her quest for a new beginning, Lisa had actually been reaching for the telephone when it had rung. Bobby Stansfield's voice had been tentative, unsure, devoid of confidence, but it had been his voice. He had stumbled several times as he had attempted to give her the message she was on the verge of giving him, and her heart had flown back to the time when life had been alive, way before the laughter had died.

It had seemed too simple as the staccato words had dug hatred's grave. "So many years . . . so much sorrow. It would mean a lot . . . see you again . . ."

Precipitously she had rushed headlong across the bridge of souls, her flying feet devouring the years that had separated them. "Yes," her voice had said. "Yes, I would like to see you again, Bobby."

Now Lisa was nervous as hell. Try as she might, she didn't know whether she wanted the meeting with Bobby or not. Yesterday it had seemed like the most wonderful idea in the world. But today it was different. In some ways it seemed that everything had changed, in others that nothing had. She and Bobby were the same people. Could Scott's disappearance and Jo-Anne's extraordinary murder turn the world upside down? It was impossible to decide, and impossible to entangle the mess of rushing emotions that raged like a tornado through her heart. Was it possible that she was still bent on Bobby's destruction and that this decision to meet him was the prelude to yet another battle in an ongoing war? As the clock ticked away the minutes to the time when she would see him once more, her level of anxiety rose toward the heavens. If she didn't know what she wanted, how could she know how to behave? If she didn't know how to feel, how could she know how to think?

To cover her confusion she had telephoned to change the time

of the meeting. Tea was so neutral. So English. So safe. At four
o'clock the butler would show him in.

"Senator Stansfield, ma'am."

And she would put out a cool hand and say, "Bobby, it's been
a long time," or some such appropriate remark. Sophisticated.
Formidably self-controlled. Suitably distant.

The butler's knock on the door was deferential.

"Come in."

"Senator Stansfield, ma'am."

For a moment Bobby stood framed in the open doorway.
Around his mouth played the easy, open smile, its creases well
worn now with constant repetition. Bobby Stansfield, strong and
reassuring, promising the world, demanding attention, beaming his
charisma. So much for mental rehearsals. As her insides turned to
water and her soul began to crack in the packed ice that had surrounded it for so long, Lisa managed a breathless, "Oh, Bobby."

Somehow she hadn't been quite prepared for this, and the shock
was as real as if it had been a total surprise. It was as if she were
standing outside herself, a separate person altogether, watching
with interest how she would behave. The physical feelings could
easily be understood—the chemical rush of fear, excitement, almost anger, the strange feeling that something of enormous importance was happening, something that would change you forever,
the sensation that nothing would ever be quite the same after this
moment. Perhaps a car accident was like this. No pain. Just the
knowledge that you were at the turning point, that things could go
either way, and that they were out of your hands. Unable to control events, the body lapsed automatically into spectator mode, as
it passed over the reins to an infinitely more powerful destiny. The
intellect was a sad, helpless thing at a time like this, and yet as
always, it continued its feeble, doomed attempts to explain and to
predict. Was the real Bobby causing all this confusion? Or was she
reacting to a memory? If so, could mere memory possess such
strength? Must it not then be reality in its own right?

They were together now. Close to each other, and for a long
moment they held on tightly—to the past, to the present, to the
might-have-been. There were tears in her eyes, and deep within
her essence Lisa felt herself begin to melt. Had it all been for
nothing? The struggle. The passion. The yearning for revenge. Had

the tiger she had ridden for all these long years been another creature in disguise? In the forests of the night, had it all the time been
love, not hatred, that had burned so brightly? It seemed so impossible. It was so very obvious.

They stood back to look at each other.

Bobby saw the glistening eyes, the perfect curve of the well-
remembered chin. How many dreams? So many visions, but nothing compared to the raw beauty of the reality: the softness of the
skin on the rounded neck, the sculpted lines of the strong shoulders, the mouth that no woman had the right to possess. The magic
wafted out from her and billowed around him, bewitching the mind
that had always been wide open to Lisa's spell. With God's help
he would keep her now, and to emphasize his determination he
took her in his arms once again, nuzzled his head down in her
warm hair as he whispered gently, "Lisa, my Lisa."

But there was a part of her that was still fighting him. Habit. The
unforgotten memory of his cruelty. Gently but firmly she pushed
him away from her, looking up into the blue eyes. Time had been
kind to him, but there was a legacy of sadness painted into the
corners of the handsome face. He had suffered, too.

"I wanted to contact you when Jo-Anne . . . ." Lisa spread her
hands to signify the impossibility of it all. There were so many
things to be said. But no place to begin.

"I know. I know."

"I hated her so much. Now it seems so very pointless."

"And you never forgave me, either."

"No, I never did. Now I'm not sure that there was anything to
forgive."

"The son we could have had together?"

Lisa smiled back at him. It seemed to be the right moment. Scott
was gone, but he was there. For too long his reality had been
denied. Its denial had sent him away. Perhaps its affirmation would
bring him back. "We have a son, Bobby."

She watched the incredulity creep into the well-known eyes.
"My son, Scott, is your son too. I didn't want you to know. Ever.
Even he doesn't know."

"But you said you'd . . . Vernon Blass . . . You mean that time
in the hospital, when Christie was born . . ."

"Yes. Yes. Of course the child was yours. I couldn't kill it. God,

I wanted to. To kill it because I couldn't kill you. But I never wanted to give you the satisfaction of knowing you had a child by me. A son.''

Bobby put out his hand to touch her, to douse the flames of bitterness that crept around her words. "Oh, Lisa. I'm so sorry. I just didn't know.''

"What do you feel now?''

Bobby looked down at her, at the beautiful, deeply wounded woman who had loved him too much, and he knew exactly what he felt. "I love you, Lisa,'' he said simply.

"Then kiss me,'' she said. And she smiled.

Their mouths were dry at first, tense and nervous, like the lips of first-time lovers, as they hovered fearfully, frightened that the moment would pass before the flower of passion could grow. But the escalation of desire, so long denied, so long dormant, had a momentum of its own. Effortlessly it rushed and roared as it sought expression, carrying all in its path as it consumed consciousness and devoured caution. Side by side it ran with tenderness in a wild conspiracy of souls, Bobby and Lisa, joined together, their hearts beating against each other as their strong arms cemented their commitment. For long moments they luxuriated in the well-remembered tastes of each other, crushing themselves together so that no one nor anything could drive them apart. Lisa could feel his hardness, and she loved him for it. Loved it, as she had loved it so many years before. They had reached beyond words now, to the land where emotion lived. There was no need to analyze, no need to explain. They needed only to feel, and to be felt. Once again they were lovers.

The strident sounds of the busy airport forced Scott to shout into the receiver. Crammed into the telephone booth beside him, Christie tried to keep track of the dialogue by watching his face.

"It's me, Scott. Can you hear me? It's noisy as hell here.'' He crushed his hand over his other ear in a vain attempt to shut out the background.

Christie could imagine the response. From someone like Lisa

Blass it would be as likely to be anger as anything else. Anger that she had been deserted. Anger that she had been worried. Anger that she had failed as a mother.

"I'm fine, mother. I'm calling to say that I'm coming home.

"We can discuss all that when I get there, mother. It's impossible now. I can barely hear what you're saying."

Christie squeezed his arm in support. She knew all about powerful parents. It wasn't all easy being a child.

"What. *What?* Oh, my God."

Christie saw Scott stiffen, saw the color fade from his face, saw the tentacles of shock crawl all over his body.

"What is it, Scott? What is it?"

Scott put his hand over the receiver. When he spoke his voice was shaking.

"They're going to get married, Christie. God Almighty, they're going to get married."

"Who? What do you mean?"

"My mom, and your old man."

"Oh, no. Oh, no. They can't do that."

And in the crowded airport brother and sister stared at each other in horror as they contemplated the impossible union.

22

Christie and Scott sat side by side on the sand, staring out morosely at the velvet smooth sea. Sometimes it was like this on the North End beach, the waves gone, the water the aquamarine blue of the Caribbean—a surfer's nightmare, a beach person's dream.

Scott scooped up a handful of sand and allowed it to fall slowly through his fingers. It was a symbolic gesture; the sands of time were running out.

"If Willie Boy was telling the truth, we can't let them get married. It's as simple as that. They'd have more children like me— all screwed up, inbred. God knows what the problems would be. We just can't let them do it."

"But, Scottie, we don't know for certain. The old drunk could be lying. Or he could have gotten it wrong. Or maybe your grandma's husband, that Tom Starr, was paranoid. Maybe he was just jealous. You know how much drinking they're all supposed to have done, and you said yourself that Willie is zoned from dawn till dusk."

"Yup, I guess all that's possible," said Scott doubtfully. "And I guess it's *possible* that grandma herself wanted to believe she was pregnant by one of the mighty Stansfields. Mom said she was always going on about how wonderful your family was, and how Palm Beach was the best and most beautiful place in the world. Maybe she talked herself into believing that mom was a Stansfield because it was grander than being a Starr." He paused. "But that's the whole problem. We just don't know for *sure,* and we can't know. I don't think we can take the risk."

Christie's face reflected the heavy atmosphere of gloom. "But, Scott, surely we can't blow their happiness out of the window. They've both suffered so much pain. Most of their lives so far have been ruined one way or another. It's their last chance to make everything okay. In the last analysis, does it matter if they're sort of related? I mean if they didn't *know* . . . and if they had children then they'd be like you, and for sure that's no big disaster.''

Scott smiled back at her. His own little sister, and as far as he was concerned the best and wisest person on earth. That was one thing that Willie Boy had gotten right. They were in this together up to the hilt. Whatever was decided, it would be a family decision.

"We couldn't let them do it, Christie. It'd just be too irresponsible.''

"Oh, God—and the wedding's tomorrow. Everybody's been invited. Imagine the chaos if it had to be canceled. I honestly think dad would die. He cares so much about what people think. It's the politician in him. And your mom—after all the hatred. Now at last she can rationalize it, exorcise it, and have a chance at living again —and we pull the plug on the whole thing.''

"Is there any way at all that we can find out more?''

"It's all so long ago. Everybody's dead. I've been trying to remember all the things people told me, but it doesn't amount to much. I mean, if it took me this long to find out that Vernon Blass wasn't my dad, how many other things have I been kept in the dark about?''

Christie said nothing. It was true. How little the children knew of the sins of the fathers.

"Tommy Starr, Jack Kent, and Mary-Ellen were all dead before I was born. The only thing I have to go on is what mom has told me, which isn't much—and it seems that a lot of that was bullshit.''

"I remember grandma saying once that grandpa was too friendly with the servants. I thought she meant not distant enough. I suppose it could have meant a little more.''

"Hmm, hardly cast-iron proof, is it? What we need is something like a birth certificate.''

"Yeah, but that's bound to say 'Starr,' isn't it? In those days you didn't advertise things like that. The only absolutely certain evidence would be a blood test. From what I remember from biology you can sometimes prove that people *aren't* related, but you can't prove for certain that they are.''

Scott laughed. "Oh, Christie, that's great. I can just hear the conversation. Mom, can I borrow a bit of blood? Senator, could you let me have a bit of yours? I'd like to run a few tests. Just general interest. They'd probably arrange to have me admitted to the funny farm.''

They turned to each other and their eyes locked. "Blood test," they both blurted out.

It was a federal law, wasn't it? Nobody could get married without a blood test. The idea was to stamp out syphilis, but the bottom line was that somewhere probably at this precise moment in time samples of Lisa's and Bobby's blood were sitting innocently in a test tube on the Formica counter of some West Palm laboratory.

"If I could find out where they sent it, I could telephone the lab, pretend to be the senator, and ask for them to run a blood-group test on each sample. People are always interested in their blood groups. It'd be a pretty reasonable request. It is blood groups you need, isn't it?''

Christie could hardly contain her excitement. "Yes, that's right. It's like when you're trying to prove fatherhood in a paternity case. It could be that my dad and your mom have blood groups that are incompatible with their having the same father. God knows what the odds are, but it's worth a try. If it's okay, we let everything go ahead, and if it's still doubtful then we stop everything."

Scott was on his feet.

"Great! That's what we'll do," Scott agreed.

"How will you find out the name of the lab?" asked Christie.

"I'll just ask mom. She wouldn't be remotely curious as to why I want to know. She's always much too preoccupied to worry about things like that."

"Oh, Scott—good luck. Pray like mad."

Christie rose up on tiptoe to kiss him good-bye. As she did so she felt the warm sand of the North End beach run through her toes—a potent reminder of the raw emotions that had raged and blown over two shattered families. Could the shipwrecked lives make it to the safe haven? It was up to them.

Epilogue

It was time, and both Lisa and Bobby knew it. The confirmation was in the face of Father Bradley. He took a deep breath. "Well now, senator, Lisa. I think we should get things under way. Then we can get to all that champagne!" He laughed nervously, not a hundred percent sure that he had hit quite the right note.

Bobby and Lisa, however, weren't listening to his small talk. He was there as a symbol alone. As God's agent. He was there to do the job that both so fervently desired.

Lisa could almost hear the words she was about to say. They rolled around in her mind like sparkling marbles sending off starbursts of happiness as they jostled her soul.

"Do you, Elizabeth Starr Blass, take Robert Edward Stansfield to be your lawful wedded husband?"

"I do," sounded ridiculously inappropriate but wonderful all the same. There should be more. A few more sonorous sentences, filling in the details of the bare bones of the commitment:

"I have always wanted this marvelous man. Nothing on this earth would give me so much pleasure as to become his wife . . ." Something like that, and then Bobby would reply in similar fashion. It would be like a creative act at the beginning of their life together. The exchange of poetry as they made known the full extent of their love before the army of their friends.

Side by side they walked up the steps behind Father Bradley and took their places on the raised dais in full view of the assembled company. The rector turned to face them, with what he hoped was a reassuring smile on his lips. In his experience there was nobody in the world who was not a little nervous at this minute. He opened his prayerbook, without taking his eyes off Lisa and Bobby.

Inside the old ballroom the excitement was almost a visible thing. It crackled in the air, darting hither and thither with capricious abandon, infecting the players and the spectators with its heady drama.

Maggie, formidably neat in her subdued coat and skirt, was swept along in its current. Her instinct must have been wrong. It was going to be all right after all. You could see it in Lisa's face. It wasn't just her look, it was her "feel." It was as if the most majestic sailing ship had turned the Cape at last. Battered and threatened by the storm, she had survived the elements and, tried and tested in the threshing sea, had emerged, stronger and more serene, into the calm waters on the other side. There was a radiance about Lisa, a glorious self-confidence, a deep peace that Maggie had not seen before, and her heart went out to her friend.

And yet, and yet . . . there was the sense that the menace had not passed. Try as she might, Maggie could not see the direction of the danger, could not know its nature or its cause, but around the edges of intuition the feeling was undeniable. It wafted gently, a sickly aroma of decay unsettling those who smelled it, subtle yet insistent, present yet invisible.

But nothing could go wrong. There was Bobby beaming good humor, eager and willing to make the commitment he should have made so many years ago. No impediment to bliss would come from his direction. Caroline Stansfield, too, looked worried but controlled. Any mother could expect to feel anxious at the wedding of her eldest son. Once before she had been Lisa's enemy, but she was one no longer. Old and bent, her mind was still robust, and in the short conversation Maggie had had with her earlier there had been no signs at all of opposition to the marriage.

Once again she turned to look at Scott, and immediately she realized that it was from him that the unsettling vibrations were beaming. From Scott, and from Christie. It wasn't just that they appeared nervous—everyone's nerves were on edge. It was something more. It was their pallor and the total absence of Scott's normal languid air of laid-back cool. All his gestures seemed abnormally jerky and forced, almost as if somebody had replaced the red blood in his veins with a strong solution of caffeine. He looked uncomfortable as hell in the formal clothes, but it was much, much more than that. And why did his furtive eyes keep darting toward the telephone that sat on the table by his side?

Christie could actually hear the hammering of her heart. She had never dreamed it would end like this. One dreadful problem had replaced another. At first the blood samples had been lost, and all through the long night she had lain awake in her bed, knowing that Scott would be tossing and turning on his. They had bombarded the Almighty with their prayers, that the samples be found, that they would be discovered in a refrigerator and not in some warm corner of a humid laboratory, the temperature having rendered them useless for blood grouping. At ten o'clock that morning the test tubes had been located, only two hours away from the ceremony that might prove a disaster. Even then fate had intervened. A multiple traffic accident had strained the resources of the Good Sam lab, where, as a special favor, the Stansfield/Blass samples were being processed. The surgeons were calling out for transfusable blood, and the technician had had to put the Stansfield request on the back burner. There was nothing left to do but to wait . . . to watch . . . and to listen.

"Dearly beloved . . . friends. We are gathered here today on this *very* happy occasion to witness the joining together in holy matrimony of Robert and Lisa . . ."

Scott's mind was numb. Although he heard the words that signified the beginning of the ceremony, there was nothing in his world but the telephone. It had taken over the room, a living, throbbing thing, far more alive than the players in the human drama. Soon it would speak to him. Across the room he saw Christie's worried, questioning eyes. Somebody, who might or might not have been him, smiled unhappily at her.

Father Bradley had allowed himself a few sentences before the main event as a warmup to his fifteen minutes of fame. "It is indeed a wonderful thing when the Lord seeks to bless two of His most worthy servants with the gift of eternal happiness . . ."

The congregation was quiet now. Sitting back, they could enjoy the platitudes as a tasty hors d'oeuvre to the ceremony itself.

Lisa thought of tonight when she and Bobby would make love, as they had done so long ago. The pages of time, dripping still with the blood of her emotional wounds, were to be wiped clean at last.

Bobby's heart filled with pride. It was true. The Lord had

blessed him and would continue to do so. With Lisa at his side he could resume the march toward greatness. Higher and higher in the firmament of America.

The soft warbling of the telephone sounded to everybody in the room like the blast of a nuclear explosion.

Christie's hammering heart seemed to stop altogether.

"Oh, dear," said Father Bradley in mid-cliché. Surely somebody should have thought to disconnect the telephone?

Bobby, thinking exactly the same thing, fought back the irritation. "Wrong number!" he said loudly to general laughter.

Lisa was not to be outdone. "More like my office. One of the authors has writer's block and needs to be talked through it."

Scott's hand darted out with the power and precision of a striking rattlesnake, as, all around the crowded room, annoyance at the unwanted interruption wore the mask of humor.

Eight hundred eyes turned to watch him, eight hundred ears swiveled to listen to him.

"Yes," said Scott. "Yes, it is. Ah. I see. What precisely does that mean? Ah. You're sure? No possibility of a mistake? None at all? No. I see. Thank you. Thank you."

"Who on earth is it?" asked Caroline Stansfield querulously. Why did Scott look as if he had seen a ghost?

The sound of the receiver making it back to the telephone jangled in four hundred minds.

Christie's voice, quite loud, just said, "Scott."

For one single second of omnipotence Scott held his secret.

At last he spoke. "Do you know what I think?" he said. "I think we should get the hell on with this wedding."